SIGNS OF THE TIMES

"What's that sign at the bottom of the gangplank?" Irving asked. "It looks like Earth writing, but I can't read it."

"It's Latin!" Marge exclaimed. "It's a quote from Dante, I think. The fancy big letters say 'Abandon Hope All Who Enter Here.' The standard for Hell, I suppose."

"Yeah? Then what's that phrase in small letters below?"

"It says to have a nice day."

By Jack L. Chalker
Published by Ballantine Books:

HORRORS OF THE DANCING GODS

Jack L. Chalker

A Del Rey® Book
BALLANTINE BOOKS • NEW YORK

A Del Rey® Book
Published by Ballantine Books

Copyright © 1995 by Jack L. Chalker

All rights reserved under International and Pan-American Copyright Conventions. Published in the United States by Ballantine Books, a division of Random House Inc., New York, and simultaneously in Canada by Random House of Canada Limited, Toronto.

Map by Shelly Shapiro

Library of Congress Catalog Card Number: 95-92333

ISBN 0-345-37692-7

Manufactured in the United States of America

First Edition: December 1995

10 9 8 7 6 5 4 3 2 1

To Steven Lloyd Chalker,
in spite of whose best efforts
this book got finished anyway.

CONTENTS

INTRODUCTION

I WRITE VERY FEW SERIES IN SPITE OF MY REPUTATION. OH, I write a lot of very long books, which publishers like to chop up into thirds and fourths and sell as "the latest series" but they're really not, and those who read them *know* it for the most part. The *Dancing Gods* books, however, are very much a series and so open-ended that even I have no idea when I start one if it's going to be my last.

For those who don't remember and those who came in late, the *Dancing Gods* is set in an alternate universe separated from ours in which the realities of our myths, legends, fantasies, and phantasms exist along with humankind. Connected by an ethereal realm known as the Sea of Dreams, we are influenced in our thoughts, fantasies, and imaginations by reflections of this alternate reality. The framework is Judeo-Christian in terms of good and evil, right and wrong, and so on, and while Heaven continues to stay out of things directly—so far—Hell, as usual, cheats.

This alternate Earth in fact was created as a reflection and in the backwash of the Genesis creation of *our* Earth, our universe, and God spent all His time, along with the time of the top angels, in setting ours up. Being merciful, He didn't destroy the other one, just assigned all minor angels and such to straighten it up. Being minor, of course, they weren't really up to the job and were prone to shortcuts. Magic, for example; it was more convenient than inventing a lot of physical laws. And how much easier to let the wood nymphs protect and keep the trees healthy, and

1

the water sprites the seas, instead of actually having to deal with the complex sciences involved.

In fact, all the natural laws and shortcuts were basic enough to fit into a fairly stock volume, the Book of Rules. The few details the book missed were left to the powerful magicians and sorcerers to tidy up, and they've been doing it ever since. In fact, they've been overdoing it ever since, acting just like a massive bureaucracy. Nothing is too minor for their notice; no cliché remains untouched or unmandated. My theory is that this is why it often seems that everybody's sword and sorcery epics are variations of the same book—after all, we know they are better writers than that, right?

Under the Rule that mandates that all great adventures be at least trilogies, the *Dancing Gods* series was always intended to be at least three. This is, I believe, the fifth. In the fourth, *Songs of the Dancing Gods,* we resolved a ton of questions and polished off a lot more enemies, but we left one in the wrong state and another in the lurch. I'm here to get him out.

I hesitated to take on the horror boom at its height, even though it probably produced the most hackwork since cyberpunk. Movements always tend to do that. Some folks who are really good do something new and original and creative, and then it's piling on the bandwagon and going to the Sea of Dreams to see what clichés and stock situations drift through. Still, I figured they'd have their day— everybody deserves one now and again—and I pretty much waited until the cycle crested and fell.

This book is an excellent example of kicking people when they are down. I've limited my easily recognizable targets to the dead and the superstars (and been fairly nice to the latter lest their lawyer birds and Del Rey's lawyer birds have sky battles). The knowledgeable can pick out all the little items here and there that twit those who really deserve it. Have fun finding them.

As with *Songs,* this volume departs from the first three in being a lot more serious for a long segment, possibly the first third of the book, then goes through occasional gags, broad throwaways, gratuitous slaps and kicks, and the like, until at the end we just throw everything down the tubes and go completely bananas. In here is both serious writing and the sword and sorcery equivalent of the Marx Brothers doing *Hamlet*; while I managed to talk myself out of introducing a character (for now) named Fungie, as in Fungie from Yuggoth, I have committed some puns so horrible that I feared I was getting cross-linked with Piers Anthony. The idea is to eventually have a lot of fun, get a little serious stuff in between the nonsense, and in general build to a point where the reader has a really wild ride. Since this is also the first book I have written since quitting smoking, anyone who thinks maybe it isn't up to the others should examine his or her conscience for the logic of that.

Enjoy.

—JACK L. CHALKER
April 1994

ENCOUNTER ON A LONELY ROAD

The immortal hero/heroine doomed to wander the world until judgment shall always be placed in proximity to important damsels in distress.

—Rules, XXVI, p. 234(k)

A RELIGIOUS PERSON EXPECTED TO GO TO ETERNAL RE-ward or punishment at death, but to be suspended indefinitely in limbo made even Hell seem attractive.

It wasn't just the wood nymph part, although that was bad enough; it was all of it. She'd never even fully accepted becoming a she; the rest was just dung on the cow pie. That wasn't a matter of good and bad, either; it was just that a person was more than a collection of cells. A person was the sum of all the experiences from birth, too, and had an ego, an identity, a sense of self that defined that person, made that individual unique. No matter what anybody said, a body's sex was one hell of a determiner in that whole sense of who a person was, and to have it wrenched out made you culturally nothing at all.

So if you hadn't started out as female, you were never going to get comfortable as a female. And everybody of course treated you as if that was the first defining thing you were—they couldn't help it. You didn't grow up that way, think that way, see the world that way, act and react that way. So you didn't really fit in comfortably with the ones who did, but you hardly fit in with the boys, either. Not when you looked and sounded like she did.

She'd accepted her lot grudgingly for the sake of the boy and seeing the boy grow into manhood, but even that was not the stuff of dreams. You couldn't have a father-son relationship when Dad had been changed into a wood nymph. Somehow it just couldn't be the same. And since he had been separated from the boy for so long while the kid was growing up, there wasn't anything in the past to hang a really strong relationship on. Worse, having any kind of close relationship with a wood nymph when you were an adolescent boy was likely to create a situation more embarrassing and downright distasteful than anything else.

Because of that, she'd never gotten close to him—Irv—and had left his upbringing to other hands. As far as Irv was concerned, Dad was dead and gone in a hero's fight to the finish against the epitome of evil, the Dark Baron; both had been destroyed, consumed, in a fiery volcanic ooze, thus saving Husaquahr and the world beyond it from being overrun.

Most times she felt as if it would have been better if it had really happened that way. Certainly it would have been better had she been able to die like the Baron rather than emerge as the wood nymph bound to the Tree of Life itself. Even the deities of High Faerie had at least one vulnerable spot—their powers were dependent on the number of believers. Remove the believers and you removed their powers. They wouldn't *die* exactly, but they would cease to exist for all practical purposes.

Not her. She required no believers, no supplicants at all. Even if something unthinkable should happen to the Tree of Life, its juices flowed within her and made her totally, irrevocably immortal. She was the only wood nymph who didn't even need a tree, although there was this instinctual affinity with them. Wood nymphs had no need to eat; they made their energy from sunlight or could absorb it indirectly from plants. She didn't even need to drink like the others of her kind; the fluids of the Tree never evaporated and never wore out. Lack of carbon dioxide to breathe or prolonged cold might make her go dormant, but that was the extent of it, and that wasn't a very pleasant experience, as she'd discovered. It kind of felt, well, like death in slow motion, not quite asleep or awake but very definitely aware—and the nausea after coming out of it lasted what seemed forever.

Sister wood nymphs weren't much company, either. They

had rather boring and basic lives, had no major life experiences, and, unlike her, couldn't travel far enough not to get back to their trees by dusk. Even if they had great mental potential, which they didn't, this didn't exactly give them much of a chance to broaden their points of view. In fact, they weren't quite as smart as the bimbos they looked like, and emotionally they were something like thirteen. And frankly, that was all they needed to be in either area. Their entire function in life was to create a psychic group that could maintain their woods.

That and one other thing. The wood nymphs had a symbiotic relationship with plants but not much with animals of any sort. Animal control and management, from the pest to the squirrel and bird and beyond level, was entirely under their male counterparts, the satyrs. Those lecherous half goats weren't much brighter then the nymphs, but they played their songs on their flutes, did their dances, ate leaves and grasses, and, of course, made it with the nymphs. If there was a need for any reason, that was the way you got new satyrs. Nymphs didn't reproduce that way—they budded. That's why they all looked and sounded and thought so much alike.

Avoiding satyrs was one of her daily goals. The romance of faerie was more than overstated; rather, it was an existence suspended halfway between animal and human, with a mind that could think, could reason, could even learn, stuck inside a body even more constraining than the ones humans had, in which instinct and certain behaviors were beyond thought or resistance. She still didn't enjoy the process, but those flutes were hypnotizing and irresistible.

It was scary to be in a situation that was totally irresistible, to be completely helpless and enslaved to the will of another. As much as ego and self-identity, that fear drove her to try to beat the system that had snared her in this nasty trap.

There had been an Aladdin's lamp once, one that really could grant any and all wishes. Although *it* was gone, far out of reach—in effect wished out of existence—the mere fact that it had existed gave her hope. Given a nearly infinite amount of time, which she had, there *had* to be something else here, something beyond that one lone lamp, that would restore her true form. She had the time; the real question in her mind was whether she'd lose her sanity and her memories before she found the key that she was convinced, against all statements by the magical hierarchy of this world, existed.

She had been wandering some of the world of Husaquahr; it was too painful to remain back at the castle, watching a son grow up without parents but unable to get the nerve to tell the boy the truth. You just couldn't be much of a father when you looked like a teenage boy's bimbo dream.

She'd been away quite a while, searching—or so she told herself—for that magic way back to "normalcy" once again. So far: lots of rumors, lots of legends, nothing real. Not that some of those legendary pieces of magic didn't exist; it was just, well, they weren't exactly on the scale of great devices their press had built them up as being or in any way the equal of the Lamp.

The Stalk of Stavros, for example. Now, *there* had been one with real promise, a magical staff, they said, that could turn anything into anything. It had taken some effort to find it and get to it, only to discover it was useful mostly for giving long-distance hotfoots. And as for the Pincushion of Ptolemy—no, that was just too painful to think about, dud though it was from her standpoint. The Owl of Ozymandius had at least known something, but it had been the answer to the question all owls asked.

The Owl of Ozymandius *knew* who was who.

That hadn't done her much good, either.

She had no idea how long she'd been out in the land seeking and not finding; she had long ago lost any sense of time beyond day and night. But the worst part was what some sages termed the Curse of the Gods.

It was getting pretty damned boring.

Oh, originally there'd been some excitement, but after a

few adventures and risks and losing some life-or-death gambles only to discover that she couldn't really lose, the thrill had vanished. She couldn't die, she wouldn't get hurt, she didn't grow old. The hoariest monsters of the land were in the end helpless to do her harm. When you combined that with a total lack of need for anything—food, clothing, housing, whatever—there really wasn't much left. She'd never been much on school-type learning, and lately it just didn't interest her, anyway. She'd never been much of a collector, either, owning things for their own sake. Besides, where would she keep things if she had them? She could have the scents of any of the plants of nature, so why use artificial things? Even any jewelry would have to be organic so that it would not obstruct her if she chose to merge with tree or bush.

And when you neither wanted nor needed anything at all and there was no risk, no sense of family or attachment, nothing—what was there?

This sense of nothingness in her life, of a gray lack of meaning and purpose, along with the failure of her quest for a way out, was now bringing her back toward Terindell, back toward the only people who meant anything at all to her, now or ever.

But there was also something more, something much harder to pin down, a kind of grayness seemed to be settling in, permeating Husaquahr, almost as if it were some strange sort of vampiric fog, draining the energy from the land. It really wasn't anything you could see or put your finger on; rather, it was something you sensed, felt, lurking there, all around, omnipresent yet just out of sight in the corner of your eye.

It wasn't just faerie sense, or imagination, either. They all felt it, or so it seemed, mortal and faerie alike, although they could no more put it into words than she could. It was as if something ancient were stirring, something none of them had ever known before. Something impossibly old, unimaginably powerful, and of a nature that might be called evil but was something far worse.

It was the kind of gray that made the whole world seem tired, made ambition seem not worth the effort and inhibition a sucker's play. People tended to be surly; violence was up, tolerance was down, and nobody really knew why he or she was feeling and acting this way.

It gave whispered voice to thoughts she didn't want, too. *If Joe survived the lava, no matter how transformed, then why not Boquillas as well?*

What about it? What did the damnable Rules have to say about *that*?

She shook the dark thoughts from her mind and looked around. It was late; dusk was about to give way to total darkness—not a good time at all to be walking the trails and roads of Husaquahr alone even if life was not threatened. As a wood nymph, the only power she had was with the trees, so she made her way quickly toward a thick stand of massive tropical monarchs that probably was home to quite a colony of her kind. She never felt all that social toward her more limited sisters, but the forest certainly had room for one more, and she could use some rest.

Suddenly, not far ahead, there came the sound of shouts and a woman's terrified scream and then the clang of metal against metal.

It startled her more than alarmed her; she'd been walking half a day on that road and had barely met anyone who didn't live in and around the area of the road. Now she approached the sounds cautiously, carefully, straining to see if this was something she might avoid. With her greenish coloration and in her natural element, she could move with amazing quietness and near invisibility, at least to mortal eyes.

It had been three against two: three big, swarthy bearded men with the look of brigands or worse against a well-dressed and handsome middle-aged man and a chubby-looking young girl horrendously overdressed in a long brown cloak and full dress. It must have looked like easy pickings to the men, but the older fellow had put up quite a fight. One of the attackers lay, possibly dead, along the trail, and another had a torn jerkin and a spreading blood-stain on the right side of his chest, although it was clearly a superficial wound.

There were, however, too many of them; the one with the wound had grabbed the girl, who might well have gotten him with a dagger of some sort; he held her firmly while she futilely struggled to break free of him. The man who'd been untouched had beaten the old man to the ground with his heavy sword and now brought the blade down hard on the defender's neck.

The girl screamed again, then seemed to lose all will to resist further as blood spurted from the certainly fatal wound to her companion.

Joe looked around, trying to think of some way to help. Physically no longer a match for the pair, although her old self ached to pick up a sword and have at them, she was not without power and resources here.

"Put her down!" Joe shouted as menacingly as she could. "Let the girl go!"

Both of the surviving attackers froze in the deepening darkness; the one with the small wound frowned but kept his grip on the girl.

The other one looked around, trying to get a make on the newcomer, grinning as he thought things through. "Come on out yourself, darlin'! We got enough for two of you!"

"Take what you want but leave the girl here and go," Joe responded, moving around the periphery of the trees and bushes. This would be tricky, but it was makable.

"Well, now, I don't think we kin do that," the grinning man said. "See, we think we want her, too. We got real plans for her, y' see. What's she to you, anyways? You got to be a nymph from the sounds. Hell, this is what you's *built* for! Plenty of room for more!"

The girl, too, was suddenly paying attention. She looked desperate and her eyes were more than a little wild, but clearly she was looking for some kind of opening. Touching the great trees just in back of the man holding her, Joe decided that this wasn't something she couldn't provide.

Vines suddenly shot out from the tops of the trees and grabbed the man who held the terrified woman, wrapping themselves around his neck. While not thick or strong enough actually to do him in, they were enough to cut off his wind and give him a sudden and direct choice between letting his captive go and letting the vines keep wrapping around his neck. There wasn't even a contest; reflex made him let go of the girl and grab for his neck.

The girl dropped to the ground, spied the dagger she'd dropped after stabbing her captor, picked it up, and rushed toward her assailant, who was just pulling the last vines free, his head leaning back so he had room to grab them and break them loose. It was almost as if he were offering his throat, and with a desperate reach and a slashing motion the girl shoved the dagger right into his Adam's apple.

He went down with a gurgling sound, pulling out the dagger as he fell to his knees, but by then the blood was filling up his air passages, strangling him. He knew it and could do absolutely nothing to stop it.

"You bitch!" the remaining attacker screamed, grin now gone, and he ran to where the girl was just turning away as if to flee. As she turned, he struck her hard on her back and shoulder with the flat of his sword. She cried out once more and fell, crumpling from the force of the blow.

The man stepped back, not wanting to get trapped by vines as his companion had been but also unwilling to abandon either his prize or the possibility of revenge from the still not clearly seen attacker.

He stepped over the girl's still body and put his sword down on her. "All right," he growled menacingly. "Show yourself! Show yourself or I start on the girl here. She's not much, but it can be a little hard to watch, especially if'n she comes to! First a foot, maybe? Then the other'n? So's she won't walk away on us? Then the hands, arms, legs, that sort of thing. What do you think? What should I start with? Maybe this here leg? You got five seconds to try'n stop me!"

The bastard was good; Joe had to give him that. This

was no common robber or cutthroat; he knew his business too well. He also had picked a stance and a position where it would be next to impossible to get him with vines, and there wasn't much else around, either, except maybe throwing rocks and sticks—and Joe knew just how little arm strength she had for that sort of thing.

"What would it get you?" Joe tried, hoping to stall while she thought of something.

"Satisfaction," the man responded. "In fact, I don't think I like stalling. You've used up your time, girlie." The sword arm came up a bit, the muscles tensed, and Joe, familiar with the stance and the move, had no doubt what was coming next.

"All right," Joe said, stepping into the clearing but away from the swordsman, out of easy reach. "So now what?"

The man obviously had some faerie sight; he didn't seem at all bothered by the nearly pitch darkness around them, and he stared carefully at the wood nymph. The kind of bravado and guts she was showing, as well as quick thinking, was beyond most nymphs of any stripe, but aside from this one being a bit taller and having if anything an even more inhumanly exaggerated set of proportions than the usual, she didn't look all that different.

"I guess you didn't hear me," the man growled with a kind of confident, even smug tone. "I didn't ask you to come out. I said you had to stop me."

The sword hand moved, and Joe sprang at him without even thinking, leaping over the distance and hitting him in the chest. Since he stood maybe five-ten and weighed a hundred seventy pounds or so, he was a brick wall to her four-foot-eight, perhaps eighty-pound bulk, but it was enough to knock him back and break his sword motion.

To him it had been a solid punch; to Joe it was that whole brick wall and it hurt like hell, and she fell onto the ground, slightly dazed.

He was over her with the sword before she got back her bearings.

He put out the tip of the sword and touched her left

shoulder, and there was a hissing sound where metal met faerie flesh, as if the sword were not solid at all but some kind of horribly caustic acid, and an acrid smell of boiling flesh and a tiny whiff of white smoke came from the wound.

"You know, it's gonna be a shame to kill you," he said, almost sounding as if he meant it. "Never saw a nymph with this much guts. Can't have you doggin' me and threatenin' my back, though, or callin' in some damned army or the cops. Good-bye, girlie," he added, and plunged the iron sword deep into her, making a horrible gash along her entire breastplate, probably all the way down to her back.

The hissing and smoking and smell were terrible, and the nymph screamed in pain and then went still.

The man pulled the sword out, satisfied that he'd done the job, and returned to the fallen girl. She was coming to, but there would be some time to go, and he didn't like this particular forest, not at all.

He put down his lethal short sword, reached into a small knapsack he had brought with him, and removed two very delicate sets of bronze cuffs. No iron here. He rudely grabbed both of her wrists, brought them in back of her, and put on the smaller cuffs. Then he pulled off her boots and brought the ankles together, clearly with the intent of cuffing them as well.

Suddenly he felt a horrible, burning pain in his back, and he cried out and straightened up, dropping the cuffs on the ground. He stood, frantically trying to reach between his shoulder blades and remove the dagger that had been driven in between them, but he could not reach it.

He looked around, totally confused, wracked with pain, yet desperate to see who had gotten him, only to see the wood nymph standing there, looking at him in grim satisfaction, the ugly gaping scar on her chest blazing but already beginning to somehow heal and disappear.

"But—but—that was *iron*!" he managed. "How . . . ? It's not . . . *possible*!"

He then pitched forward, shuddered, and was still.

"This is Husaquahr, bub. They got a rule for *everything* here and an exception to every rule," Joe commented.

She was probably the only one in all faerie—save the dwarves—who could not be killed by iron. But it really did hurt like Hell.

The girl groaned, tried to get up, found she couldn't put a hand out to steady herself, and didn't quite make it.

"Try getting yourself into a sitting position," Joe told her. "I can check and see if he has a key to those cuffs on him."

"No, no," the girl managed, feeling the bruise of that blow. "These are held by spell. I can feel it." She managed a sitting position, and Joe went over and looked at them. There were tiny little bands of color, like spiderwebs of varicolored light, all over the things.

"You're right," the nymph said, sighing. "Unless you've got the knowledge to untangle that mess, I guess you're stuck until we can find somebody who does."

"I probably could, if I could see it, but I cannot," the girl responded. "It's all right, though. It is not as important as it seems." She paused a moment. "My father—he is dead?"

Joe was startled by the question; somehow the idea that this might be a father-daughter pairing just hadn't occurred to her. She went over to the well-dressed man and scanned him.

"I'm sorry. He's gone," the nymph told the girl. "I think it's just you and me right now. And an audience of stunned fairy folk of all sorts peering out from the bushes."

The girl sighed but resisted breaking into tears. "I—I suppose I knew that the moment I saw him fall. He—he was a good man."

"I'm sorry I wasn't here to help him when you first got attacked, but I didn't even know anybody was ahead of me until I heard the sounds of battle."

"It—it's all right. I owe you a great deal for what you *did* do. More than I can ever repay. My father—he'd been a knight and a soldier once, and I think this is the way he would have wanted to go, if it hadn't been for me, anyway." She stared at her savior in the darkness, so obviously using faerie sight. "My goodness! You really *are* a wood nymph!"

Joe smiled. "I, too, was a knight and a soldier once, and this is definitely *not* the way I wanted to go, but I'm stuck. Call me Joe. I use other names now and again, but that's the one I prefer."

The girl ignored or hadn't comprehended the oddity of a wood nymph stating that she'd once been a knight and a soldier and concentrated on the pragmatic. "All right—Joe. I am Alvi. Short for Alvida Zwickda of Morath Keep, which is too big a name for anybody, anyway, and never really did fit me, I guess."

"Morath Keep? That's not anywhere I've heard of before."

"It is a land beyond the Western Dark, as it's called here. A very long way away by land and sea." She sighed. "Not far enough away, though."

"Farther than I've yet been, and I thought I'd really seen this world. *Huh!* Who were they? The other two seem like common cutthroats, but that leader there, he was a pro. And they weren't out to ravish you like I thought at first. He was taking you somewhere and to somebody."

"Yes. We've been running, you might say, for a very long time."

Joe didn't press, not right then, but looked around to see if there was anything else of hers to be gathered up. She spotted the boots, carelessly tossed to one side by the chief attacker, went and got them, then brought them back. "At least we can put you back together," she began, then suddenly noticed the girl's feet. They weren't like any feet the nymph had seen before, not on anything or anybody. Long and somewhat broad, with downward-curving claws for nails; more like the feet of some animal than any human.

"You're *faerie!*" Joe exclaimed.

"No, I—oh, what's the difference now? I'm so sick of hiding and pretending anyway. The truth is, I'm *part* faerie."

Joe suddenly understood. That certainly explained the

long cloak and hood in this climate. "A halfling! Well, don't worry. You're among friends here."

Halflings were the offspring of humans and faerie, two groups not really intended to mate but in some cases close enough that it was possible to do so and have offspring. Such creatures were of both worlds and neither and tended to be what might charitably be called monsters. The laws of most lands said they were to be killed at birth, but it was very hard to kill your own kid, no matter how misshapen or distorted it might be. The vast majority were caught when very young, anyway, or died in infancy, unable to sustain themselves in a form not intended to be sustainable, but occasionally one was not only stable enough but also resourceful enough to stay hidden among society and grow to adulthood, where at least halflings were no longer subject to death.

Still, they had little status and few rights and tended to live lonely and often bitter lives.

Alvi sighed and nodded. "I have spent my whole life disguising my curse. As a child, my life would have been at stake; as an adult, I might have to forfeit any inheritance. Not that any of that matters now."

Joe arose and checked the dead. Her father had quite a purse on him, which Alvi perhaps would need; there was also a large signet ring on his right hand that she pried off. Something to remember him by, perhaps.

The highwaymen had less of interest. A few coins to be added to the small treasury, little else of value. She did retrieve the bronze dagger and a folded sheet of paper from the knapsack of the head man that contained mostly the chicken-scratch type of writing used there that Joe had never learned and almost certainly wouldn't, but that also contained a fairly decent sketch of both father and daughter.

It certainly was no official "wanted" poster; there were no official seals, symbols, or such on it. This was a private matter; someone had hired mercenaries to track them down.

"Can you get to your feet?" Joe asked her. "We'd be better off moving into the trees and away from here a bit, if only because of what these bodies will attract in short order."

Alvi managed to get to her feet rather handily, almost as if somebody had pushed her from behind. Joe was becoming curious at just what she *did* look like under all those clothes.

Still, this wasn't the place or time for details. It was best that they move well away from there, and Joe led Alvi off into the very dense, dark grove of woods.

When they were well enough in, protected and away from the likelihood of discovery, Joe found a soft area well protected by trees and broad leaves and, very much in her own most comfortable element, told the stranger to settle there.

"Thank you," Alvi said sincerely. "It has been a *very* hard day. Let me rest here for a little while. Then . . ."

Joe nodded and replied, "Rest all you need. I will be here when you wake up."

After all, there certainly wasn't anything better for her to do or any hurry to do much of anything at all. The day had proved to be dangerous and very painful but also very interesting.

It was the most fun she'd had since she'd wound up in this situation.

Alvi slept well into the morning, and Joe only tried to ensure that they were undisturbed. Someone had found the bodies and the remains of the fight; that much was certain from the commotion off toward the trail, but she didn't bother to investigate. It didn't sound like much that couldn't have been expected, and they wouldn't know about the girl, anyway.

It was enough to discuss the situation with the local faerie, who would do little or nothing to save or protect a halfling but had just as little to gain from doing it harm, either; also, they were willing to give a little to Joe. In fact, all the creatures, no matter what the race, seemed to hold the strange wood nymph in mixed fear and awe; a faerie immune to *iron* was not someone you wanted to cross.

Alvi looked quite ordinary in her dress and cloak and hood, with a pretty heart-shaped face that seemed very innocent and very sweet with just a tuft of straw-colored hair peeking out from the center. She seemed taller than Joe, perhaps five-one or -two to Joe's four-eight, more toward average for a mortal woman of the land, and there was certainly nothing in her face or hands that said "faerie" to any onlooker. But her face was too thin and too normal for that bulk.

The hands, though, did tell a few things about her. They were quite smooth, unblemished, the nails not so much shaped and polished as professionally manicured. Likewise, her facial complexion was perfect, without blemish and with little sign of weathering or stress. Whoever she'd been, she'd been brought up in a wealthy household and protected against all elements both natural and sentient.

Joe guessed her age as no more than the midteens— perhaps sixteen, certainly not much older than that—and certainly still a virgin. No faerie or one with faerie sight could fail to sense that right off. Virginity was in fact a handy condition in civilization but pretty dangerous out here, a red flag that would draw predators like flies to honey.

Alvi finally stirred, yawned, stretched out her body, and brought herself awake. Only when she tried to bring her arms out for a full stretch—to find them still cuffed behind her—did she suddenly become fully alert. She looked startled, perhaps a bit scared, and sat up. She spotted Joe sitting on an exposed tree root and sighed. "Then it wasn't a horrible dream."

"Afraid not," Joe told her. "Welcome back to reality, such as it is."

Alvi turned up her nose. "I smell like a horse, I need to freshen up and relieve myself, and I can't do anything at all with my arms like this."

"I think I might be able to do something about those, but

we'll have to wait a bit now. There's a Mossuk—that's a small race that lives inside the tunnels created by these old tree trunks—who knows some of the basic spells and thinks he can get you free. We didn't want to try it with you still asleep, and I think he's off doing whatever Mossuks do right now. In the meantime there's a fairly nice pool fed by a warm stream not much farther over, and it's not deep enough for you to drown, so it might be fine for freshening up."

Alvi looked around at the somewhat forbidding jungle. "There are . . . creatures . . . around here? All around here? Looking at us?"

"Sure. You get used to it. There's nobody here that's going to hurt you or cares much one way or the other. You leave them alone, they'll leave you alone, period."

"I—I have to take your word for it. I suppose I'm at your mercy, really. It's just that, well, you'll have to forgive me. I've—I've never been completely on my own before, and I've never addressed any of the faerie at all."

"*Never?* That's hard to believe."

"Not if you saw the ones that lived around *our* estates. Besides, my father believed that if my true nature were generally known among them, they'd be out to get me or something. Inside the walls was strictly human staff. Many of them knew of me, of course, but like most such staff, they had worked for my father's family for generations. Except for two handmaids, no one ever saw me except fully dressed, properly concealed. Then no one could tell. I don't give off a faerie aura or have much in the way of magical skills. I *do* have serious problems with iron, but I can sense its presence and be a bit careful around it."

"So you've been raised as, and passed as, a normal human girl," Joe said, nodding. "But surely your father and you knew you couldn't keep this up forever. There would be young men, family influences, pressures to marry, and so on."

She nodded. "True, but in another two years I would have come into proper inheritance on my own, and my father intended then to sign full rights, title, and birthright to me. After that, well—I should not like to be married to a man who found me repulsive or monstrous. If anyone stopped his pursuit of me because of this, it would be good riddance."

"Maybe." Joe personally had her doubts about this. Born a full-blooded Native American, she knew that the value of papers and legal documents when race was an issue wasn't anything sacred and inviolate. And she had seen more than one of the type of man who'd swallow hard, marry, get the money and the estates, then denounce his wife as a monster. In *this* world her testimony as a halfling against his as a full human wouldn't even bring a contest. Still, it was kind of a moot point now.

"So with all those plans, why were you over here in the middle of nowhere being hunted by these men?"

"I—I'm not sure. One night, months ago now—seems like years—my father woke me up, told me to pack everything I could, particularly clothes, and be ready to leave immediately. He said that some very evil forces were coming that he couldn't fight off or stand against in any way and that we had no choice but to flee. He hoped that we could find safety with old friends, powerful wizards apparently, until things blew over. When I asked him who could hate us this much, he only said that once he'd had to make a bargain with somebody who otherwise he would never even have acknowledged and that he had hoped to be able to fulfill the bargain without involving me or risking everything but that it had proved impossible. He never would say more. We have been on the run ever since, often only minutes ahead of them. When we left home, I saw them ride in."

"Who? Those guys?"

"No. Ugly, nasty things on shining demonic horses with blazing red eyes and nostrils spouting fire. Tall, scary horned riders in shiny black armor and great bat's wings folded against their backs. Since then I've seen them again, but only in ones and twos and in the dark. Most of the time it's been ones like those last night. Mercenaries and robbers going for some sort of reward. Well, perhaps my father's body is enough for them now!"

Joe doubted it. They hadn't shown any care in taking the old boy out, yet they had bound her and had been making ready to take her someplace. No matter what, it was Alvi who was the prize here.

This was getting interesting, and it had been a very long time since anything or anybody had interested Joe.

A small creature, perhaps no more than a foot high, emerged from under one of the big roots. At first glance it seemed like some gigantic bug, but two four-fingered white-gloved hands, big round eyes, a round bright red glowing nose, and a purple mustache over two enormous protruding buck teeth said otherwise.

"Hey, girl! Still want me to look at the halfling's bond spell?" the creature piped, whistling through its teeth.

"Yes! Over here, old-timer!" Joe called.

The Mossuk scurried over and looked at Alvi with a distasteful expression. "Well, don't just stand there! I can't climb up, y' know! Just set here and look the other way and I'll see what I can do about them cussed cuffs."

Alvi was startled. "Um—I'm sorry!" She sat and put out her wrists as much as she could for the little creature. She realized that *she* was the stranger and the freak there, but all these creatures were so *new* and so very odd . . .

There was a sudden click, and she felt the cuffs give way. The sudden pain in her shoulders as she brought her arms forward was more than compensated for by the relief of moving freely again and feeling blood course through her arms.

There was a motion deep within the baggy dress. Joe could almost swear . . . No, never mind.

"Thanks! Maybe I can do something for you sometime!" Joe told the little creature.

"Could be. Doubt it, though. No big problem here. Simple stuff. Cheap bonds, really. If you could see it clear, you could get it loose. Just a bunch of standard knots, that's all."

Joe went over to Alvi as the little creature vanished back underground, stood in back of her, and began massaging Alvi's neck and shoulders as she sat, trying to get her fully back to normal.

Alvi breathed an excited and heavenly sigh. "Oh, don't stop! That feels so *very* good!"

Eventually it was time to stop, though. "Where are the rest of your things?" Joe asked her. "I'm sure you had a lot more than what I saw."

"We did, but we had to leave it in a hurry. We had two pack mules, but when it was clear we were being followed, we had no choice but to leave them and hurry on."

"You had no horses?"

"We should have, but a wagon or surrey would have been too large and hard to manage on these kinds of roads, and I can't really handle much of a regular mount, I'm afraid."

They reached the pool of fresh water. "Well, you're going to have to take off what you have in any case," Joe noted. "For one thing, you'd sink with all that on. For another, it's not practical out here. Third, they're pretty filthy and we're a long way from a laundry."

"I—I'm sorry. I'm just not *used* to this! I mean—my whole life has been one of concealment! Now, suddenly, I'm here, with nobody I have known, and I'm—well, it is difficult. I never knew how much the monster I was until we were on this trip. There have been times—it could not be helped—when others have . . . seen. And I have endured their looks, their pity, their revulsion, and whatever. You are so perfect. You cannot know what it is to be like this! You can never know how I envy you!"

Joe was taken aback. *Perfect? Envy* me*? If only she knew!*

But the fact was, putting aside the couple of extra inches of perfectly proportioned height and dimensions, Joe *was* physically about as perfect as one could be—for a wood nymph. It was just that, well, Joe had been neither born nor raised a wood nymph, or a member of the faerie race, or even female and culturally was even more cut off from this existence. Somehow she'd been feeling so damned sorry for herself that it had never once occurred to her that to any stranger she really was perfection of her race and for *this* world, anyway, normal and acceptable.

And of course there were far worse things to be than a wood nymph, particularly in this world. Somehow, though, the idea that one who considered herself such would actually feel *envy* for Joe was unreal, unheard of, and hard to deal with.

"Well, I might as well see it," Joe told her. "I promise I won't turn away or treat you any differently. I wasn't born like this. I was born so different that this form and existence are to me so unhappy that I've been wandering the world trying to discover how to change it, to go back. I'm hardly the one to be turned off by the way anybody looks."

"But it is just a disguise and a pleasant one to look upon, at that," Alvi noted. "You don't have to hide half your body from the world, always fearful that someone will see, will start yelling and pointing out your shame."

By that point Joe's imagination had already conjured up far more horrible things than were likely to be hidden under that baggy dress of Alvi's. Still, she could understand the problem and sympathize. "Anyone who sees me sees only a simpleton, an oversexed, ignorant, dumb little faerie girl with only one reason to be looked at and one thing on her tiny little mind," Joe noted. "At least, with your dresses and cloaks, you could be treated more as a person."

"It was not the same," Alvi responded. "Not only was the fear too great, but the limits were much too restrictive and even dangerous. It wasn't equality from *my* point of view. It was *play* equality, that's all."

Play equality. . . . Hey, chief! You ain't no Injun, are you? We don't serve no Injuns in this here place . . . Who'd ya kill to get a job drivin' that truck, Geronimo? Yours? Get outta here! Ain't no Injun afford a truck like that . . . How many times, after all those fights and the hospital time that almost caused him to lose his truck, had Joe tried to "pass," to deny his own self-evident heritage? That was why he'd resettled in the East once he could. In the East "Indians" were exotic, fascinating creatures, like people from Mars; the Easterners had other targets.

"You don't have to playact with me," Joe said gently, and helped Alvi remove the rather elaborately fastened clothing.

The real problem with halflings was that they made up survivable combinations of creatures with no reason at all for being other than that the mixture, for some reason, worked. Mostly things that would be okay on the proper creature just didn't turn out right or weren't in the right proportions or places on the body or things like that. They were deformed—mutations, sort of—and nobody ever felt comfortable around that sort of unfortunate. Still, in a land where Joe had battled zombie armies, monster carnivorous rabbits, real fire-breathing dragons, and even nastier types and one that had countless thousands of faerie races, demons, and monsters all its own that were "normal," how bad could it be?

The answer was not so much *bad* as very, very bizarre.

Alvi didn't have to go far to lose all illusions of humanity. In fact, she looked decidedly less human and more alien than Joe had ever been as a creature of this land. And it was easy to see why she'd not been terribly put off by being handcuffed. In fact, had that fellow managed to take her prisoner, he might have been in for a very nasty shock.

The head of course was normal: the face of a pretty girl with a nice short hairstyle, thin brows, big brown eyes, the usual, set atop a fairly long neck, nice shoulders, and a pair of medium-sized and fairly firm breasts. *Then* the fun began.

Just below this was a second set of shoulders, mounted under the first but tapered in just a bit from the top, from which extended two additional arms ending in hands as well and between which were two slightly smaller but otherwise perfect medium-sized and fairly firm breasts.

Just below *this* was yet a *third* set of shoulders, again mounted under the first and in just a bit from the second set, with a third set of arms, hands, even breasts, in a threesome that cascaded down in such a way that each succeeding set was perhaps ten percent or so smaller than the set on top and, interestingly, was proportioned so that all three pairs of hands ended at the exact same point on the body. This, however, left room for only a small flat stomach area with no visible navel, and then the whole thing tapered into the hips so narrowly that it all appeared to be on a giant ball joint. The only girl with top measurements thirty-six–thirty-three–thirty and a waist of maybe twenty-two, Joe thought. But the hips really blew it.

Those hips were *very* wide, supporting two thickly thighed and very nonhuman legs that might have more properly been on a bipedal lizard or perhaps a small dinosaur. That is, the legs were attached to the hips slightly splayed rather than straight down, which was why the hip area looked so wide in the first place, and it was this that had given her clothed figure the appearance of being fat. Extending out from the tailbone and crotch area rearward was a thick, tapered tail in keeping with the lower body but rather stiff-looking for all that and relatively short. In fact, it appeared to be somewhat rigid, although her movement showed that the tail could be brought in against the legs, forming a sort of third appendage between and in the back that wasn't quite long enough to reach the ankles, let alone the ground. This tail was designed as a counterweight, for balance, not support, and to some extent its operation was automatic.

As startling was the patterning of the whole lower area starting just below the small third breast pair. It was as if a gang of mad tattoo artists had beset her, producing a riot of attractive but totally abstract designs and colors over her whole lower body. The skin was quite smooth and had a texture similar to that of her human part; the colors were not dull, either, but bright and vibrant, the design about as complex as could be imagined. Only the underside of the tail, revealed through the opening between the legs, was left au naturel, a somewhat segmented-looking off-white.

There was no hair anywhere except on the head or any obvious sign of female genitalia. If it was there, then it was lost in disguise in that riot of color and shape and form, although Joe reflected that anything fairly small might well be anything *but* obvious in that riotous yet attractive mass.

"You kept—*this*—a secret even from part of a household? And from anybody around?"

She nodded. "It's not as hard as you think, and I was used to it, raised to control it. Growing up, they used to tie my lower arms to my sides all the time so I wouldn't reflexively move them, and my tail got lashed to my leg for the same reason. *That* was tougher. I always had to walk *really* slowly and deliberately because I couldn't use it for balance. The hands, too, were a problem, mostly if I lost my balance or something. Your instinct is to use everything you have to break a fall. I spent a lot of time in my quarters, alone or with the two serving maids whose folks had been with the family for generations, just to be *free* of those despicable straps and my tent dresses. I *yearned* to be outside like this, free, able to run and stretch and not pretend. But it never happened."

The tremendous difference in Alvi would have made any sort of medical solution more grotesque than the social one her father had adopted. Still, if a big, ugly Injun truck driver could wind up a nymph, surely there was something that a rich guy like her father could summon up from the magical arts. Joe didn't really know all that those Books of Rules contained—except that it was far too much—but surely in them was one of those universal laws: the rich could buy themselves out of almost anything. She raised the point in more delicate terms.

"It was not even an issue," Alvi replied. "There were occasional sorcerers as guests, of course—I told you that my father was friends with many powerful ones. They knew of my condition; it could hardly be hidden from them. I am certain that I was examined, perhaps without my knowledge, on magical levels many times, but nothing was ever done. The few who so much as alluded to it—none of them ever came right out, at least in front of me—suggested that there was some kind of curse, that whatever might be done by magic for me would only make things much, much worse. I never understood it. Many times my father *started* to tell me—I knew he truly wanted to—but each time something held him back. I was never sure if it was part of the curse or some promise he made, like to my mother, or what, but he *couldn't*, not even in these last few months on the run."

"This is beginning to sound very much like a curse," Joe agreed, considering her story so far. "Come, though. Get into the pool and wash off the grime. You'll find the water's warm and clean, and the bottom's basically stones."

In the water Alvi leaned back and enjoyed the warmth and clean feel—and only her neck showed. Joe wasn't very worried; of all the people she'd ever met anywhere, Alvi seemed absolutely drownproof.

"You're not coming in?" Alvi called to her.

"Sorry. My race is very good for showers, even better for being out in the rain, but baths are risky. If I absorb too much water without any sort of drain, I can become heavier than gold. Take your time, though, and enjoy. I've got absolutely nothing else to do and nowhere else to go."

"That's all right. I just feel bad because this is so *nice.* I finally have a tub that fits me!"

Joe let her enjoy herself for a while, then asked casually, "Just out of curiosity, what race *was* your mother? Do you know?"

"A mortal human and very pretty," Alvi responded.

"*What?* Now, wait a minute! I saw your dad, and if your mother was human . . ."

"That's not exactly the way it seems," the girl told her. "I always knew that he wasn't my real father, but he was the only one I ever knew, and he was very good to me and

to my mother. They had been betrothed, lovers since they
were very young, but before they could marry, something
happened. I don't know what. Neither would really talk
about it, but my mother went away for a while. After she
came back, my father insisted that they marry anyway, and
she agreed. He really did love her, and he was her whole
life. They tried to have another child, one for both of them,
but it didn't work out. The child was born dead, and the
result . . ." It was the first time Joe had really heard any
sincere emotion from Alvi about her parents and background. "It—it killed her. Not right off, but she was sick
and never really got better. I was four or five years old, but
I remember it. I remember all of it."

An interesting picture was emerging in Joe's mind. It
might be completely off, but it fit the facts. Young, handsome nobleman is betrothed to the daughter of some
wealthy local monarch or one of the landed gentry, the
dowry most likely the estate itself. That was how things
worked there. Everything set, going normal, when suddenly
something happened, something that threatened the marriage, caused her to go away for a bit, and forced everything to be put on hold. What?

Alvi was what. Was it actually an illicit human-faerie
affair? Some adolescent caprice that caused her extreme
guilt ever after? Or was it perhaps some sort of a rape? Not
all the faerie were nymphs and fairies and elves and other
cute characters. Those bat-winged creatures who'd come
for Alvi and her father, for example. Forces of the real father come to claim his child? The fact that she had no char-
acteristics of such creatures meant little; in perhaps the
majority of cases among the faerie, the male and female
were so different, they might well be mistaken for different
races or species entirely. Nymphs were a good example and
by no means unique—satyrs for wood nymphs, those Boy-
friends from the Black Lagoon for the water nymphs, you
name it. The colorful lower body patterns would be the
key; it seemed too complex and too natural to be a one-shot

affair and was almost certainly some sort of racial characteristic. But which race?

The mother had refused to kill the daughter even though it was most certainly a monster and a creature of rape. The father had probably agonized, then agreed to take them in and protect the girl as well as his own child. Things would have been arranged so that Alvi would be presented as a child born of the father but before wedlock; married, there would be no stigma, yet that child would be a constant worry and a reminder of the initial problem. Six arms and the lower part of a lizard weren't exactly something you could overlook even if, incredibly, you really could hide it.

He must have loved the woman very much.

But there was more to it somehow, something still missing in the puzzle. Why did they want Alvi now? Who could want her? Of what possible value could she be to anyone: neither of human nor of faerie and considered monster by both? What was the bargain that had bound the old boy's lips from even his adopted daughter's ears, and with whom had it been made, and why?

Damn it! I never watched soap operas!

"Alvi, did those creatures in black armor come close to a birthday or anniversary?" Joe asked her. "That is, close enough to some event?"

She shook her head.

"When was your last birthday? And how old were you?"

"I must be almost seventeen now. I was sixteen before they came, but it wasn't anything close. I mean, it was maybe a couple of *months* earlier."

Joe suddenly realized that the question meant nothing. Even if there *was* some sort of bargain or curse having to do with Alvi's sixteenth birthday, they would probably not celebrate the real date, in any event. In fact, it might not even be known, and whoever came to claim his or her or its prize might not be on a clockwork calendar schedule, either. There was, however, something that had been nagging at Joe, particularly since Alvi had awakened, and when the halfling emerged at last from the pool and lay down to dry off, Joe felt she had to bring it up.

"Um, pardon me for saying this, but everything you've told me says that your stepfather must have been devoted to you. He seems to have chucked everything for you, even the estates, position, titles, who knows? I just can't help but notice ..."

"That I can't cry for him?" Alvi finished. "I know. I feel pretty rotten about that myself, but I just *can't*. I'm not sure why. I *did* love him. I mean, he was the only father I ever knew, and he spent his life trying to do what he thought was best for me. The thing is, well, I don't know ... It's kind of mixed. In one way I can't think of him as really dead. I see him back at the manor somehow, supervising, tending, building. Part of me just can't imagine that he's really gone. He's been *everything* for me. I mean, my whole life's been planned and executed by him. Maybe that's it, too. I never was able to make any choices for myself. I was always hiding, always pretending, always in those painful straps, walk slow, special boots so it won't look like I'm walking like a chicken or something, don't go out, wear all this stuff even if it's boiling hot, don't work in the garden or you'll have to bend over and your tail will stick out ... And on and on and on ... It got so I became mostly a night person, wandering around late at night with little or nothing on, through my quarters, at least, and sneaking stretches on the roof terrace when it was dark enough. I was so lonely, so miserable, so full of fear that I felt more like a prisoner than a protected daughter. Does that sound inhuman, monstrous, maybe?"

"No," Joe responded rather gently, pleased with the answer. "It sounds very human indeed. I don't blame your father, and I doubt if you do, either, deep down; he was a product of his world and times and did what he felt was right and best. I'm sure he often wished he didn't have to, wished that you could just be yourself, but he couldn't. Not without the threat of losing you."

Alvi looked up at her, and there was a slight smile on her lips. "You really think so?"

Joe nodded. "I do."

But was it right? Hadn't she herself been so afraid that Irving would learn that his dad wasn't a dead hero but a live green bimbo and that she'd totally abandoned the kid? Left supervising all that growing up to somebody else "for the sake of the child"? Had she really done what was best for the kid, or had she instead inflicted as much pain and emptiness on Irv as the Duke had on Alvi?

How to know?

Damn it, if God wanted everybody to do the right thing, then why hadn't He written a clear and concise instruction manual?

She looked over at the very strange and very adrift halfling. Somebody was trying to nab this kid, who in any case had had no preparation whatsoever for this very dangerous and cruel world.

Ruddygore had his Rules, faeries had instinct, but what manual did she look in to tell her what the hell to do next?

FAITH, HOPE, AND CHARTERY

Halflings shall be shunned by those of both families but always be beloved of the heroic.

—Rules, Vol. XIV, p. 102(a)

ALVI POKED THROUGH HER OLD HEAPED-UP CLOTHES BUT made no attempt to put anything back on. Joe understood and was sympathetic. The halfling was luxuriating in being free and being herself with a friend but had been raised and conditioned all those years to conceal everything most of the time.

That was going to have to change.

Joe retrieved the broadside she'd plucked from the chief highwayman's stuff, unfolded it, and took it over to Alvi. "Can you read this?" she asked.

Alvi frowned, took it, then stared at the drawings. "Wow. Somebody knew a lot about us!"

"You *can* read it, then?"

"Sure. Can't you?"

"You'll discover that readers are few and far between in this land," Joe told her. "And if there's a nymph—any kind, any variety—that knows how, I've never heard of her. Truth is, I *can* read a language of the place where I'm originally from, but it no more looks or sounds like anything here or on that paper than these trees look like horses. I've tried learning that now and again, but I just haven't got the patience."

"Oh, anybody can if they want to. But all right. 'Fifty thousand gold pieces in the national currency of choice to anyone bringing the above to the nearest Alganzian Consul.' "

"Never heard of this Alganzia. Have you?"

"Yes, it's along the coast not that far from my own

home. Not my country, though, or my father's nobility. I don't know that we ever had anything to do with them one way or the other. It has been said that their trade includes black magic and the like from even farther-off evil lands, but I know nothing more, not even the truth of that."

"Middlemen for Hell. Interesting. What else does it say?"

"Oh. Hmmm . . . 'Nearest Alganzian Consul. Man is Duke Mahlaus of Morath Keep in the Western Dark. He is dispensable, but proof of death in the form of something personal of his, such as his signet ring, required. Other is called Alvida Zwickda, answers to Alvi, a halfling who must be taken alive and brought unharmed to the Consul. Death of the Duke without the halfling is no pay. Halfling without Duke will be accepted. Nature of the creature is known only to the Consuls. Do not insult us with ringers if you value your life. Anyone having information on either or both may gain a reward up to ten pieces of gold for submitting that information to a Consul, upon verification of the information by us. Note: creature will probably be disguised as human girl, possibly as the Duke's daughter.' *Creature!* The *nerve* of them, whoever they are!"

Joe understood the poster a lot more clearly than did the girl, knowing the type of people it would be going to. In point of fact, Alvi really was more creature than human and probably one of a kind at that, but putting it that way kind of ensured that she'd be delivered intact. It was a pretty effective sexual "keep off the grass" statement for thugs. "That's all it says? There is nothing else?"

"No. Nothing more. Except this little thing down here that says 'Local 286, KBRSS.' "

"Kidnappers, Brigands, Rogues, Scoundrels, and Sappers Union, printing division," Joe explained offhandedly. "Never mind about them. The fact is, you are not described."

"Huh? That's my *face* there! As good a drawing as I've ever seen! In fact, if things were normal, I'd probably try and buy the original for my wall!"

"Doesn't matter. The point is, because they're dealing with such crooked wretches, they didn't want to give anything at all away about how you differ from human or faerie normal. If they did, every Consul on the planet would be deluged with fake Alvis rigged up with fake arms, fake breasts, fake tails, even enchanted ringers that looked legit for all the world. But so long as you're one of a kind, as I think you are, there's no way to find out just what makes you different, so they have to deliver the real thing."

"But what good does *that* do?"

"Faces are easy. It's overall form that's hard. It's not that rough to do a little safe makeover of you so that you won't look anything like this sketch, and they wouldn't be looking real closely at the face, anyway. Short of you bumping into somebody who knows a lot of details, like one of those Consuls, the odds are pretty good that we can disguise you so that you can move around safely. Then maybe we can start trying to figure this thing out."

"But why would the Alganzia want *me*?"

"Not the Alganzia. If what you've told me about them is true, they're just middlemen, probably hired to do this for somebody or other, some client. Some very rich, very powerful, very important client, I have to say, if they risk being directly named like that on a broadside. The fact that they deal in black magic and darkest sorcery says a lot, too." For the first time Joe wondered if this had anything to do with the rising pervasive feeling of evil and malaise that was spreading throughout the whole land. Something was rising, something at least as powerful and evil as Boquillas and the crazy mad sorcerers and rebel Prince of Hell she'd already faced. What was it? Every five or ten years or at least once every generation?

Why, she just might have accidentally stumbled into something as nasty and bizarre as anything in the history of this twisted world!

Of course, she didn't really believe she could have that kind of luck, but maybe. Who could say for sure?

She reached down, found the pouch with the gold, and

brought it over to Alvi. The halfling looked at it, gasped at the amount in there, then frowned, reached in, and pulled out her father's ring. Joe had stuck it in there for safekeeping.

"Sorry. Thought I told you about that," the nymph commented. "It was all I could really salvage."

"It's—it's more than enough." She took it, found the ring finger of her top right hand, and slipped it on. It was much too loose, of course, but . . .

Suddenly there was a bright flash from the ring, and her whole hand seemed bathed in an eerie, unearthly glow. Joe was as startled as Alvi, and both could see the intricate strands of a previously hidden spell there.

Alvi nervously pulled the ring off her finger, and the glow died. "Some kind of spell! A trap!"

"No, no!" Joe exclaimed, rushing to her. "I doubt that. I know how some of these suckers think. Remember? They asked for the signet ring in the broadside, almost as an afterthought. But they *did* specify it. They want both you and the ring. They just don't want anybody getting the idea that he can hold them up for even more than a king's ransom to get both. Or—or maybe they don't want anybody so curious about that ring that they'll play with it. I wonder what they don't want anybody to find out."

"Well, here! You're welcome to it! *I'm* not putting the thing on again!"

Joe thought a moment. "It didn't try and stop you from removing it, did it?"

"No, but—"

"Did it hurt?"

"No, just tickled a little, but—"

"So? Put it back on. Be ready to yank it off if need be, but I doubt if you will. I don't think it's trying to hurt you or do anything to you. I think it's a message."

"Huh? From who?"

"Your father, maybe, or your mother, or who knows? It didn't go off when your dad had it on, so the odds are that it was intended for you if he should die. Probably activated only when he died. It might activate only on your finger, although being a common spell, it would most likely be crackable by any thief with any ability at all. Go ahead. Try it. I'm right here."

Alvi thought it over for a moment, then sighed and cautiously replaced the ring almost as if afraid it would bite her finger off. Again there was the glow, which enveloped the hand, but there was nothing else apparent in the effect.

"Turn your hand over or try different positions," Joe suggested. "It's got to do *something* more than just glow."

It did. With the palm out and angled slightly down, there was a crackling sound, and then, quite clearly, there was a man's voice, not loud but actually rather calm and conversational.

"Alvi, if you are hearing this, then I must assume that I am dead and you are now alone," the voice noted. "I also must assume that you or we failed to contact any friendly power among the established Majin, so that you are *truly* alone. If this is not so, then you should go with them. You are ill equipped, I fear, for the only alternatives and should use them only as a last resort."

"That's my father's voice!" she exclaimed in wonder.

"However, if you *are* alone and all else is lost, then there is no choice. Under the stone of this ring, released by a small catch that you will find if you feel along it, is a tiny pellet of poison. If you are captured by dark forces and there is no hope of escape, you must use it. Not only for your own sake—for they will kill you or worse after they are done with you, anyway—but for the sake of the entire world. They must not be permitted to use you! And your only hope if all else has failed is to go straight into the den of your worst enemies. Your only hope for a future and to banish this evil is to travel to Carcosa and within it to locate the path to Far Yuggoth. There, eons ago, one of my great ancestors, at the risk of life and soul, hid the Grand McGuffin, that thing that all seek. The McGuffin's power is vast but personal; any who meet its criteria may be granted what they need and most desire. But to ensure that it could never be used by darkness, a curse was placed upon it by my family so that only one born of woman who carries also the seed of faerie may approach it and live."

"That's *me!*" Alvi breathed.

And also me, Joe thought excitedly. *Seek all this time, go through all that crap, and when you give up and head on home, it falls into your lap!*

"Many years ago I betrayed much of this in order to regain your mother's freedom and safety, but they do not know where and they do not know how. The location and map I entrust to you alone. Trust no one but seek help from the good races of faerie. Farewell."

The glow faded. "That's *it?*" Joe said, frowning. "Where's the map? What's the location?"

"Good heavens! You don't suppose it was elsewhere on him, do you?"

Joe shook her head. "I don't think so. At least I *hope* not. Anything we didn't take with us last night is gone now. Here—let me see that ring."

Alvi slipped it off once more and handed it over. Nothing was evident except that ... Hmmm ... "That's odd," Joe muttered. "There's still a heck of a spell on this ring. I'd swear it looks more complicated now than it did before."

"I—let me see. Wow! That *is* some sort of complicated weaving! At least now we know what some of the master sorcerers were doing visiting us. But—what good does this do me? 'Trust no one,' he says, then leaves me with a spell so intricate that it would take an expert magician even to come *close* to figuring it out and no other clues at all. What do I do now? If I take it to a sorcerer, how will I know I haven't just handed something of great value over to somebody who shouldn't have it? And if I don't, *then* what do I do?"

Joe thought things over. "Poor kid. I don't know if your dad was supposed to unlock more of this, or one spell was supposed to unlock the other, or what, but whatever else we need is probably still locked up in here. I know a sorcerer

who could unscramble this easily and is about as trustworthy as any here—he had the Lamp of Lakash in his possession, and rather than use it for himself, he destroyed it. But
he's still *weeks* away up north, and they're bound to be on
the lookout for you. Still, I can't see any other way. To get
through *that* spell would take a master sorcerer, or . . ."

Alvi sensed that her new friend was thinking of something. "Yes?" she prompted. "Or what?"

"Or a master thief," Joe finished. "Hmmm . . . Maybe
two days back south and a few wasted days west, but if he
hasn't cracked up on a desert island already, he could do
this. It would be child's play for him. He stole the Lamp
from Ruddygore's own vaults."

"A thief? But wouldn't a thief keep it for himself? Or
double-cross all of us?"

"No, there's honor among thieves, no matter what you've
heard. At least there is here. The Rules demand it. He's
formally retired and hardly needs the money, so he
wouldn't care about it all that much. And if he *did*, he'd be
willing to come in with us and share any outcome. I
haven't seen him in a *very* long time, either. Yes, he's certainly the answer."

"You know a thief?"

"I know the greatest living thief in all Husaquahr, the
one they still tell legends about in the guildhalls of the nations. He's a very old friend who more than once helped
save us all from the forces of evil. He retired a while ago,
and when last I knew of him, he was running charter tours
of the islands and coast of Leander just west of Yingling.
We may be able to cross the River of Dancing Gods just
below here, in Quoos, so we don't have to also cross the
Rombis and then go down by older back roads to the
coast."

"But we just came up from there! It's thickly populated.
Not much jungle or forest cover. And if everybody in creation's got one of those broadsides . . ."

"Your nerve and your self-control will be all that's
needed," Joe told her. "First remove anything from any

pockets or compartments in those clothes, and then we'll weight them with stones and sink them in the lake."

"Sink them! But what will I wear?"

"Nothing. As crazy as it sounds, naked is your best disguise. Put on clothing and you'll call attention to your face. Then let me survey the plants around here. Many secrete very effective dyes. Repeating that wonderful pattern on your face and torso would be great, but I don't think I have either the materials or the artistic skill to do it. Blocks of color, though—that should be easy."

"You—you really think my pattern is *wonderful*?"

"Oh, yeah. It's beautiful, honey. Trust me. That, the arms, the whole thing will be what people look at first and will remember, too. Trust me. Let me see what I can do."

By soaking various small cuttings and leaves in water, Joe had managed to come up with several interesting colors. She chose a dark green for the stomach area, applied it carefully with some grasses used as a brush so as not to overlap the natural coloration of the hips and the area below, then extended it around to the back and up so that two rounded areas on the back went up and met at a point right at the small of the back. Next a golden yellow for the lowermost breasts and arms, again layered to a point design on Alvi's back. The middle arms and breast area she made a pink color, the topmost a pale blue that extended to the upper shoulders, neck, and face. The hair, cut as short as possible with the knife and some stones, turned a much darker blue when touched with the same dye. Joe thought that bald would be better yet but knew that Alvi was already going to be as self-conscious as hell.

Then the wood nymph mixed several of the dyes together, added more water, poured the resulting dark mixture into a gourd, and said, "Now, the finishing touch. Take some of it, swish it around the inside of your mouth, all over your tongue, you name it, then spit it out."

Alvi looked uncertain but did as she was told. She made a face when she spit. "Tastes *awful*!"

"Yep. Now open wide. Uh huh . . . Very nice. The whole inside of your mouth, including your tongue, is purple except your teeth, which remain pretty much white." She stepped back. "I can guarantee you that you are now as colorful as I can paint you and that people will look at everything except the details of your face first."

"This stuff—it comes off, though?"

"Well, not right away, but eventually, yes." The truth was, Joe had no idea how long it would last, but she knew that the chemicals she'd used on normal human skin were as indelible as permanent ink. It would dull long before it washed off, which was just what Joe wanted. "The question is, do you have the guts to walk straight down a road like that?"

"Oh, my God! I don't know if I *can*!"

"Well, you've *got* to, that's all. You just *do* it. We'll take it easy, but you've got to get used to yourself as completely exposed, as you are, and to hell with the rest of the world. Now, people *are* going to look at you. They're going to *stare*, frankly. Some of 'em will make signs to ward off evil when they see you and rush their kids inside. Others will be mean, cruel, call you all sorts of names, tease and heckle you. It'll get you for a while, but sooner or later you just have to decide that this is who and what you are, and if others don't like it, they can just shut up and get out of your way. I'm going to be along the whole time, with you and right beside you. I went from being a man—tall, muscles, heroic type—to looking like *this*, and it was pretty damned hard. I never have fully come to grips with it, so in a way I've got nobody, either. I have nothing in common with my sister wood nymphs except my looks, and everybody else treats me like a brainless piece of elemental ass, so no matter what happens, there'll be at least me to regard you as a person and treat you like one. Clear?"

Alvi nodded, uncertain but also amazed. "You were really a *guy* once?"

"Uh huh. Born and raised a mortal man, father of a male child, teamster and barbarian hero at different points. A crazy bit of magic turned me into this, and since then I've been wandering this world alone, looking for a way out. You and me, we got the same damned problem, really."

"I think I'd rather have your problem," Alvi noted.

"Maybe. Maybe you just haven't discovered how little anybody thinks of wood nymphs—a reputation mostly deserved, by the way. It is true that you'll be an unwanted halfling, considered a monster by most, if a harmless one, but when they discover that you are a monster with money, some things will be possible. Right now we clean up and find you something to eat. I'm afraid it's going to be all fruits and veggies around here for now, but we may be able to do better on the road."

"That will be fine," she assured Joe. "I—I only hope that I can do it."

That, of course, worried Joe as well. Hell, it'd been *weeks* before she'd had the nerve to go out by herself, and that had been after a lot of unknowing preparation as a were in the time before the old body and its curse had been destroyed in the lava fires. Alvi could use a little were curse now, but it wasn't exactly something you picked up at the market.

Finding a good meal for Alvi, however, was even easier than going to the market—for a wood nymph. In fact, within a wood nymph's narrow range were some astonishing built-in abilities, including being able to communicate and in many cases use plants the way she'd used the clinging vines against the knife wielder and a kind of instinctive knowledge about plants and plant capabilities—even about plants she'd never seen before, in places she'd never been. She had known instantly which of the surrounding plant juices would make dyes and had been able to extract what was needed without harming the plants themselves. Similarly, there were drugs that could be extracted from others, drugs that healed, others that made you high or were anesthetics, all sorts of things like that. Once she identified them, she needed only merge with the plant to extract a safe amount, then hold it within her until she wanted to excrete it.

There were, of course, limits. Wood nymphs were hardly biologists, let alone biochemists; she had no idea how to mix anything if the raw stuff wasn't there. And it might be that Alvi's constitution wasn't nearly as human as she assumed. But the odds were that it was.

Now, was there anything possibly around here that might help the halfling over the initial jitters? Self-confidence would be important to her disguise; with a hue and cry out, they could hardly wait long or people would start looking more closely into things, and maybe those Consuls would start describing Alvi a bit more fully.

There seemed to be nothing around that was in the nature of a really strong hypnotic, although such plant substances did exist and always seemed to be handy when the bad guys needed them. The best she could find was a kind of mild substance that dulled the mind and made you a little euphoric but also uninhibited and open to a degree of suggestion. Risky in that it might cause Alvi to do something that might betray her, but it was better than nothing. It would be easy enough to remove from the leaves and place within the fruit, although finding the dose that was needed would take experimenting.

After Alvi ate, they got rid of the clothes as Joe had suggested—not without some regrets from Alvi—and, using some vines, Joe made her a kind of belt with loops that would allow the purse and the dagger to be attached and easily carried.

"What now?" Alvi asked the nymph.

"Overland, I think. If we can head west for a while, we should come to a secondary trail going pretty well south, which is where we want to go, and intersecting the great River Road. Come, my beautiful spider. Put your hand and hand and hand in mine and I'll lead you through the back country. No pain yet."

Alvi laughed. "Your *what*?"

"Beautiful spider. Eight limbs, all the colors of the world, a walking work of art!"

The halfling laughed again. "I like that! Why don't you call me that, then? It'll be a name between us."

"Huh? What?"

"Spider. You can't very well keep calling me Alvi, or what's the good of all this?"

"Hey! Why not? Joe and the spider lady off through the jungle! Sounds pretty good to me. Sounds like the start of another great adventure long after I'd decided that there'd be no more great adventures for the likes of me! Yes, indeed. This could very well be the start of a *be-you-tiful* friendship!"

The trail was just where Joe had said it would be and about the right distance. Alvi was impressed. "How do you know this area? Are you from here?"

"No, just a knack. You memorize all the main routes when you haul freight." But it was more than that, although the rest was beyond easy explanation. Somehow the trees always knew where they were in relation to every other growing thing on the planet, and if *they* knew, she could find out. Put *that* on top of the memorized routes, and she almost always knew where she was to a matter of a few yards.

Alvi was fine until they heard some traffic coming the other way. Then she suddenly froze, and Joe could see and feel the tension in her.

"Come on, let's break for a snack over there," she suggested, and Alvi put up no argument. It was, Joe thought, time to see if this stuff worked and test it out before they got into heavy traffic as they neared the great river.

There was no apparent effect, at least not in the few minutes after eating, and Joe wondered if she'd vastly underestimated the dose needed to do much of anything. However, when Alvi started to get up, she seemed suddenly dizzy and a little uncertain, then gave a silly laugh. "Must be tired, or my tummy's upset. Got a little dizzy."

"Come, Pretty Spider, let us be off. There's a fair amount of daylight yet today, and we want to get into a better area by nightfall."

"Pretty Schpider. I *love* it when you say that." More tittering, but they walked out side by side.

"You just tell yourself that's who and what you are, over and over," Joe prompted. "Just think like that and enjoy the walk."

And, interestingly, after some initial slight hesitancy, Alvi *did* manage actually to face and then pass a small party of humans heading north. It wasn't that hard to do; one look at her and they gave ground and just stared, and Alvi acted as if they were staring in admiration rather than being totally appalled.

Joe relaxed a bit. Maybe by the time something hypnotic was available, it wouldn't be needed.

Traffic was quite light most of the day on the trail, which was not one of the major routes in any event and basically serviced some feudal estates and small plantations in the region, linking them with the river. It was in fact what folks back in Joe's native world and land had once known as a "rolling road," designed to be fairly straight and basically downhill and just wide enough so that barrels or sledges could be transported from the places where they had been harvested to the river piers.

Alvi was a bit tipsy but somewhat emboldened; at least she didn't shrink when they met the occasional person or take offense at some of the muttered curses, exclamations, and religious exorcisms performed as she passed, either. She was basically oblivious, and there weren't enough people to really worry about.

Near the end of the day they emerged from the jungle and looked out over a vast floodplain and the monstrous meandering river that was the land's heart and soul as well, the River of Dancing Gods.

By that time Alvi's intoxication had pretty well worn off, and she gazed out at the tremendous display in front of her, set off in a combination of light and shadow from the low sun in the distance, and gasped. *"Wow!"* she breathed.

"You've seen the river before, surely," Joe commented.

"Not really. Not like *this*. I mean, we came in from the east and went through these big cities on the ocean and along this dirty flat region. Nothing like *this*."

"Well, that 'dirty flat region' and that plain out there are the reason so many creatures can live here," Joe pointed out. "All the good stuff that makes things grow and all the fresh water from countless rivers and streams far off to the north all come together here, washed down and deposited. You can look out from here and see all the river traffic, all the faerie colonies and such, and all the human towns, cities, and settlements as well. The really *big* cities are still to the south, but even from here we're probably looking at between a half million and a million souls as well as many times that in plants and animals. Thousands of kilometers north to here—that river *is* Husaquahr."

She was surprised at her own feeling at the scene and the sense of the great river as somehow hers and a part of her as well. Maybe she was getting more assimilated than she thought.

"It's so *wide*! How are we going to get across it?"

"Too wide to swim or bridge," the nymph agreed. "We'll have to be ferried across. We've got money, and there are many such boats along here, almost all run by some sort of faerie. We'll have to go down to the Great River Road, then walk south until we find someone who will take us. Not today, though. We've done enough for today. I suggest we camp out right around here somewhere and wait until dawn."

"I—I admit I could use it," Alvi told her. "I'm not used to this much walking, and I have been feeling a little sick for some reason."

Joe looked at the sky. "Looks like we might have some rain coming in tonight, so pick a sheltered spot and we'll relax. I should be able to find you enough to eat around here, and I'm afraid drink won't be a problem."

"What about you?" the halfling asked. "Don't *you* ever eat?"

"Not really," Joe told her. "Long ago I did, and enjoyed it, too. Now—well, all I need is sunlight and water and/or some healthy trees. I *can* drink and occasionally enjoy it, but that's about all. Just call me *very* low maintenance."

Somehow, for some reason, it seemed more like a boast than a liability even to Joe. That was definitely a change.

The storm held off, if it was coming at all, but the spot under some large trees that Alvi had picked out and Joe had approved was pretty damned dark. Off in the distance there were lights—thousands of lights, like fireflies congregating in swarms—representing many of the inhabitants of the lower valley, and beyond, a strong glow on the horizon betrayed the even grander City-States built along the river's massive delta. But right on the hill it was *dark*, and only faerie sight would do.

"You know," Alvi said softly, "all those years growing up, basically imprisoned, all I could do was dream about just this: being out here, free, looking over the whole of the world."

"And now that it's happened, you're seeing that the velvet-lined prison wasn't all that bad?"

"Nope. I'm seeing that I was *right*. I was never meant to live a lie. Besides, what good is all that if you can't enjoy it? No, the only thing was, I never was sure if I could really *make* it out here. I'm still not, but today got me through a lot of it."

"Meeting other people without concealing anything about yourself," Joe prompted.

She nodded. "Yeah. I've got to tell you, after the first one or two, I just sort of stopped being afraid. It was crazy. I started getting a *kick* out of it, out of the way they would make signs to ward off the evil eye or mutter incantations or in a few cases guys actually just kind of stared at all these tits. The thing is, nobody *did* anything. I mean, if anything, they were a lot scareder of me than I was of them. Scared of me just because I looked wrong to them. Well, who's to say they don't look wrong to me?"

"That's a good attitude if you can keep it," Joe told her. "People can be extremely cruel, and I'm afraid that's one area where the faerie aren't that much different."

"Well, it's not exactly something I can do anything about, is it? I think I decided long ago that this was me and I might as well accept it. It is other people who have trouble with it. I only wish I had the kind of freedom you have with your own form. It would be nice if I had the same."

Freedom ... Well, appearances were always for other people, Joe reflected, and no matter what they said, what you looked like defined an awful lot about you to other people, whether those definitions were true or not. Still, Alvi had a point, Joe hadn't been limited to anywhere in terms of going about the whole of the world; she hadn't been denied entry into any of the places of human or faerie where she'd really wanted to go, and she'd never had to worry about carrying supplies, even money or other mediums of exchange. The only thing she wanted, or so she thought, and didn't have was her old form back. Listening to Alvi, it didn't sound like a bright thing to wish for, and for the life of Joe, she wasn't at all sure why it would be such an advantage here, either. Had she been so depressed because she was no longer the mental and physical image of Joe's upbringing, or was it because her current form seemed so limiting? When it wasn't boring, when you were off to new places and on a new quest, it didn't seem all that much of a problem.

She cut that train of thought off almost as if it were dangerous. That way was the way of assimilation, the way to a sort of death, from her point of view. If she ever completely accepted this wood nymph incarnation and found it totally comfortable and natural, then she would truly *be* a wood nymph. She would cease to want to be what she was and have problems understanding why she'd once wanted anything else, and that would be that. Joe, the old, original Joe, would be dead, and she'd be somebody else.

"But you'd also grow old, and infirm, and eventually die," a voice inside her whispered. *"You already missed out on being a parent; you hardly know your son and wouldn't have much in common. Beyond that, you would lose your health, your skills, and your ability to pursue adventures. Why do you want to be a man again? You liked it enough at the time, but you haven't met many men you've liked since becoming like this, have you? You think of men now and you see aging, leering assholes. Face it—you really can't remember what you liked about it, can you?"*

Get out! Get out! Change the subject! Think of something else! Don't start arguing or thinking too deeply. Think of something else! Think about . . . Alvi.

The halfling's problems were quite different. She was trying against very tough odds finally and for the first time to be her real self. *I wouldn't want to be her,* Joe thought sincerely, not because of the grotesqueness of the form, which might be quite comfortable, but because it would be tough to be one of a kind and, worse, to be ostracized, cut off from much of this world. Getting Alvi an acceptable form was essential; otherwise she faced a life of quasi-exile in the lousy places of Husaquahr, along with a lot of other monsters, either eking out a subsistence living somehow or becoming practically enslaved to get the essentials. Right now, with Joe providing food and guidance and shepherding her through the region, she could see only the wonders.

Could this Great McGuffin, whatever it was, really change her into a real human woman? And Joe, perhaps, back to a youthful, muscular barbarian hero? Perhaps a restored Joe and a humanized Alvi together, barbarian warrior and consort, would go roaming the land in search of adventure.

That was a vision worth holding on to, if she could.

THE PATH OF THE McGUFFIN

*Mysterious all-knowing strangers with mystical powers may be
used only to ensure that heroic types remain in conformance to
other Rules in terms of behavioral choices.*
                                        —Rules, Vol. CXI, p. 67(c)

"DON'T GET TOO COCKY WITH THIS NEW FREEDOM STUFF,"
Joe warned Alvi as they made their way down to the Great
River Road. "Remember, a lot of people will hurt what
they don't like, even kill it, and we need some cooperation."

Alvi nodded, but she was really gaining confidence fast,
even to the point of altering her long-used straight-up pose,
letting the tail extend out stiffly, and bending forward while
walking, which appeared to increase her stability vastly and
give her not only a strong and confident forward gait but an
easy way to break into a run. Joe hoped she wouldn't,
though; wood nymphs weren't built for speed, and Joe had
not found any reason to rush.

On the River Road even Alvi's odd appearance was a
matter of culture and knowledge more than anything else,
considering the vast number of very strange faerie races
that were all around as well. There were ones with butterfly
wings, ones with gossamer wings, ones with little birdlike
wings, and a lot with no wings at all. Near the bank were
hippogryphs, mermaidlike Virgans, powder-blue water
nymphs with their transparent skin flaps like lace and the
somewhat unsettling illusion that if you stared at them hard
enough and close enough, you could see their insides, and
lots, lots more. More faerie folk, in fact, than humans, who
were there in good numbers as well, both on the river in
small sailboats and barges and along the shores.

The humans themselves were a variety of their own
races, with skins from near black through all the shades of

brown and tan and orange-yellow, very tall and extremely short, covered in every conceivable color and style of hair or with no hair at all. In and around them were various elves, their colors and tunics showing their origins and tribal natures. The more elemental the creature, the less the fashion; nymphs tended to be unclad, needing little, while many other fairies were even more costumed than the humans.

"Get outta the road, you halfling freak!" a gruff man's voice shouted, and Alvi turned and saw a big, bearded man on a horse-drawn cart right behind her. She stuck her tongue out at him and made a face, but when he moved his hand to the whip, she suddenly thought better of it and gave way.

Lesson one, Joe thought.

But she was undeterred generally, and one fellow, perhaps only partly in jest, shouted out a job offer—if she could handle three sets of oars at once. She smiled but declined.

Finding a ferry across the River of Dancing Gods at that point wasn't easy. There weren't that many, since the river here was so wide that only a free-sailing vessel could handle it and so meandering that there was little demand for crossings when you'd have to travel so far along the other side just to cover a relatively short straight-line distance. They had to go south anyway, though, so they kept on, hoping that they'd be able to do it by Yingling, where the river took a wide eastward bend that would take them not only in the wrong direction but toward the major City-States and their very dense and potentially hostile populations.

Alvi, in spite of the attitudes and looks, was having a ball out in the real world without playacting or being weighted down in a massive costume for the first time in her whole life.

"You said you knew the skills of war," the halfling noted to Joe as they went along.

Joe nodded. "Yes, although it's been a long time, and at

this weight and balance and with these muscles, I probably couldn't wrestle a two-year-old and win. Once, long ago, I fought one of the legendary battles of modern history on this floodplain, maybe twenty, thirty kilometers west of here. A war of armies, human and faerie, and demon princes, dragons—the whole works. Scared the wits out of me then, but it's great to look back now that it's so far in the past. I think that's the way with most great battles and the people who fight them. A time of killing, carnage, death, and terror with you crapping in your pants becomes more and more a glorious and wonderful heroic experience over time. I wonder if I was nearly as good as I think I was."

"You did pretty well against those guys."

"Yes, but that was improvising with what I had. Why do you ask, anyway?"

"I was just wondering if you'd train me."

"Huh?"

"My upper arms are pretty strong, really, 'cause they've done all the work. I often wondered what would happen with maybe a saber or sword in my top right hand, maybe a fencing foil or short sword for the middle, and even a rope or whip for the bottom."

Joe laughed. "Could you really handle all that at once if you had them? I mean, you're talking about doing three different things at once with your hands."

"No problem. It was one of my kid's games I used to practice in my room. I'd play a kind of catch, bouncing a ball and alternately catching and tossing or dropping it hand to hand to hand to hand and so on. Found that on my top and bottom set I'm right-handed and with the middle pair the left works best. You figure *that* out. I never did. I guess it's just the way it's wired. I always wondered if I'd be good in a duel, but I never had the chance, 'cause nobody was supposed to even *know* about the other sets, right? And training *me* with *those* kinds of weapons wasn't on Daddy's list of priorities. I *can* do pretty fair with a bow, though, and I wanted to learn the rest."

Joe considered it. "Well, I suppose I could teach you the basics, but it's years to get really good with any of them, you know."

"So? If I can get some decent training up front, I'll get better. How long did *you* have to train to get to be expert?"

Joe coughed, a bit embarrassed by the answer. "I didn't—much. A few months, really, with a good teacher. My edge was mostly the fact that I had a magic sword that knew more about the business than I did."

"Yeah? Where'd you get one of *those*? And what happened to it?"

"It was given to me by a powerful sorcerer, and where *he* got it from I have no idea. It—and me, too, I think— was to finish off the most evil sorcerer of our time, and it did. We did—but at the cost of me winding up as a wood nymph and the sword being consumed by volcanic fires. Since then I've been trying to get back to my old self somehow, and you can see the result. Heck, I often wonder if we were bound together, that sword and me, and if neither of us could live as we were without the other. It sure seemed like I lost something inside when it fell, impaling the body of the Dark Baron, Esmilio Boquillas, and consuming him as well."

"Lost something? Like what?"

"I don't know. I *thought* I knew, but I'm beginning to wonder if I haven't been wrong, that what I lost wasn't my big hero mode so much as my reason for being around at all. I mean, you're right, it's not all that bad being a wood nymph in Husaquahr *if* you were born one and raised one and that's all you ever were or were going to be. But it's pretty damned dull and limited if you've been other things and wind up one. I wasn't sure what I had of the old me left until that business in the woods back there. It stirred up something I thought was long dead."

"If it did, then you must have wasted a lot the past few years."

"Huh?"

"Well, if you found that feeling of fun, of accomplishment, again, then it was there all the time, right? So maybe if you'd been looking for some adventure and people who needed help and helped them instead of moping around and feeling sorry for yourself and trying to undo what was done, you'd have had a happy few years. Well? I mean, it sure *sounds* like it."

Joe thought it sounded like time to change the subject again. "Never mind about me. What makes you so bloodthirsty all of a sudden?"

"Freedom. This. All my life I've been told what kind of horrible existence I'd have if I ever got discovered and was forced out into the world. Well, maybe I don't know much yet, but I *do* know that most folks don't give a damn if you don't bother them, not around here, and that what you really need to get along is both a skill or skills and a way to defend your own self and whatever you own. The sword, the bow, the whip—these are the things that give people the feeling of power over others around here. If *I* have them and know how to use them, maybe that'll give the others pause about making comments or worse about me. I also have faerie sight and some small abilities with minor spells as well as a fair amount of book learning. Put them all together and maybe I stay free."

It was a real thought.

"All right," Joe agreed, "tell you what—if we can find an old, serviceable pair of fencing foils, we can start with that. I think even *I* can handle one of those, and rusty as I am on skills and totally unconditioned for any such use in this body, I still could probably hold my own for teaching. If you learn to fence reasonably, handle a rapier well, you're one up on a lot of people who only know brute strength defense with a saber or short sword. We'll see how long the money holds out and what we can afford here. Still, it's not a bad idea if you can handle it, and I've seen your nerve in action. I mean, if we go on any kind of adventure together, somebody is going to have to protect *me*!"

* * *

It wasn't that difficult to find a vendor in one of the towns along the Great River Road who had such a set; secondhand weapons were quite common in the region, particularly well-used ones pawned or lost in gambling by students at the civil and military institutions of the southern City-States. Finding them in any decent condition, well balanced and with the safety caps still present, was a bit harder. Joe also found that her very rusty and virtually never used knowledge of fencing foils wasn't really all that good, either. With the great sword, you just heaved and let it do the work. At Joe's best, as the person she'd once been, there wouldn't have been much of a contest with such weapons—Joe could put up a decent front and show but wasn't really all that good. Compared with someone who knew nothing and had never had *any* training, however, Joe was an expert.

They were able to make a decent deal on both an older set and a fair bow and quiver of arrows. It actually made Joe feel a little better that they had *something* to use, no matter how inadequate. This was still a fairly dangerous land and a primitive one, and in much of it life was very cheap. Just having weapons on display kept a bit of the threat away. It was sort of like putting a top burglar alarm on your house. The alarm wouldn't keep out a decent burglar, but an average one might look at the trouble of undoing yours versus the lack of trouble going into your alarmless neighbor's and decide to burgle next door instead.

After all, the only people who really knew how good you were with any weaponry were ones who'd seen you in action. Until then, you were always a potential threat.

Crossing the great river wasn't nearly as easy. Despairing of finding a decent ferry that far down, Joe finally decided that the only way would be to take a river tramp, a small ship that went from port to port along the river, up and down, carrying local supplies and commerce. Many were little more than filthy barges with single rectangular sails, occasionally in league with some river faerie or having a few muscular oarsmen aboard for the hard parts.

Such was the *Catarwahl*, apparently last cleaned sometime around the expulsion from Eden and smelling like it, too, manned by the somewhat questionable and unquestionably boozy Captain Letchu, along with his wife and son, who could be told apart less by age than by the mustache the wife had. They were going downriver now, which meant they could mostly follow the slow but dependable currents in a kind of diagonal pattern, crisscrossing the river in a series of triangles until they reached the end. Going back upriver, if they had no wind, was a matter of contracting with some hippogryphs or other river faerie to give them a decent tow.

"I'll takes yer as fer as Azkim," the captain told them. "No more for that pittance."

"You're a money-grubber of the first water," Joe retorted. "This is river robbery, and you know it. It just about cleans us out."

That was by no means the truth, but it was more than a bargaining ploy. Letchu was in fact charging them about ten times what any other ferry would, and it wasn't a good idea to give people like that the idea that you perhaps had even more money or valuables. This drooling, filthy trio was nonetheless bigger than bears and looked twice as mean.

Alvi seemed entranced by the prospect of crossing the big river and oblivious to most of the unspoken parts of the deal, but standing on the rail near the bow as they pulled away from the dock, she seemed excited and relieved.

"It's a good thing you *are* a halfling and me a wood nymph, considering *this*," Joe noted sourly. "I have a good idea that if we seemed to have any value ourselves, we'd wind up being tied up and sold down in Yingling."

"Really? They *do* that?"

"Sure. Back where I came from they called it 'Shanghaiing' somebody, after a city way off on the other side of the world where the ships would often be headed in ancient days. Unable to get sailors to go on those long and risky but very profitable voyages, they just hired men to find people in the bars, drug or knock them out, and they'd wake up well out at sea, where they either signed on as crew or got tossed overboard with lead weights. Most of 'em signed. The women, well, they were sold as domestics, field workers, prostitutes, you name it. Not much different here. There's still things like slavery here, too, handy if you have a need for planters and pickers and such back in those huge jungle plantations. That's why most of the good guys here travel in groups. The bad guys, too, come to think of it."

"Well, all I can say is that I don't see the world as quite as nasty as you," Alvi noted. "I'm sure that's all part of it, but there's so much more. It's kind of pretty here on the river, with all those creatures in the water, all the boats big and small, the colorful costumes—I am really getting to like it in *spite* of how mean some of 'em can be." She sniffed. "I have to admit, though, its smells leave something to be desired right now." She discovered that any exposed part of her that touched any part of the ship got covered in some thick, foul-smelling black stuff. Joe was not immune, either, but chuckled.

"It's peat, I think. They take it out of bogs up north, and it's burned for heat. It's cleaner than the dung, but it's no winner."

"They *cook* with it?" Alvi was appalled.

"No, they don't usually cook with it," Joe told her. "They use wood for that, if and when they can find it in condition to be properly burned. Sometimes oils. It's used to heat their houses. It gets extremely cold up north, I can tell you."

Alvi thought that over. "I—I *think* I know what you mean, but I don't remember ever being so cold that I had to heat the inside of a place. Is that where they make the snow?"

"Well, it's not made, it just falls. Temperature gets cold enough, it snows instead of rains. It's all water. They pack a lot of snow and ice in special boats now and use preserving spells to sustain them all the way downriver here so the rich folks can have chilled wines and store meat and fish for several days or even weeks."

"That's the only way I ever saw it," Alvi acknowledged. "Do you think we'll get to anyplace that's really cold on this trip?"

"Not for a while, I hope." Joe laughed. "We're in the tropics and heading south into more of them. Where from there, though—that's what we have to find out. *I* hope we stay warm. I can take the cold, but not for long periods, and it can slow me down. If I freeze, I can be stiff for years, centuries, maybe forever, until I'm thawed out. And if *you* freeze, you're dead. I had enough cold stuff the last time, in the place where I wound up like this. I think I'm owed the heat."

It took about ninety minutes to make the full downriver crossing to the very small town of Azkim, and by that point and with scrambling to get out of the boat, both of them were black as, well, pitch.

"Now what?" Alvi asked Joe.

"First, I think we find a shallow river access and wash this crap off us. Then we'll find a place for you to buy something to eat, and we'll camp somewhere close. Too late to do much more today. Tomorrow we'll continue south, on *this* side of the river. Down to the Coast Highway, then west to the Leander border. If we can keep going at this pace more or less, we should make it to the jumping-off place for the Marmalade Islands and their resorts in maybe ten days to two weeks. If we're lucky, my old friend will still be doing three-hour tours . . ."

It *was* slow going once they veered off the River of Dancing Gods and took older, rarely used trails to the south and southwest, but that suited them both just fine. It made it easy almost to forget that Husaquahr existed, that there was hatred and bigotry and violence all around, and instead made it almost seem to be an extended and entertaining picnic.

It had been a long time since Joe had allowed herself to

get friendly with, let alone close to, anybody else, and it was very strange: the longer they traveled together, the less odd Joe thought Alvi looked. In *this* world, where *everybody* seemed more than a little off, familiarity bred acceptance more than anything else.

Alvi, too, had the same reaction toward Joe, the first real *friend* and confidant outside of family members and close servants she'd ever known and somebody who seemed very wise and fascinating. The idea that Joe was a wood nymph hardly mattered; if Alvi had any prejudices toward the more elemental faerie, they surely didn't apply to Joe.

Several times they actually stepped behind cover when encountering parties of travelers, particularly humans; it was tough to know who was who and what was what in that unfamiliar region and whether anybody had yet caught on to who that six-armed halfling had been.

Joe did in fact try teaching Alvi a little of his fencing skills, but it wasn't anything serious. Alvi's body wasn't designed for finesse; clearly it would be better off with short swords, cutlasses, or possibly sabers, since a cut and slash would be most effective with all those arms. Joe wasn't that much better; the short reach, a lack of really fast reflexes, and easy tiring of the arm muscles just made swordplay ridiculous, and unlike mortals and perhaps halflings as well, all the exercising and workouts in the world wouldn't change a faerie body that was already predefined.

Shortly after reaching the coast, they came upon a small town sitting on a bluff above the wide ocean, and Joe was suddenly a bit wary. "You never know what's happened when you're out of circulation awhile," she commented. "Let me go in alone and snoop around and see if there's any kind of hue and cry for you. If there is, we'll bypass as much as we can. If not, we'll use the main road here and make a little time. I also want to get an idea of how far we still have to go."

Alvi didn't like it. "We been partners since we started; I hate to see you go in there alone. I mean, there's no trees, bushes, nothin' out there but grass and sand and this chalky dirt. You've got nothin' to defend yourself with if you need it, and wood nymphs don't travel much beyond where they live, do they? You're gonna stick out in your own way as much as I do."

"I'm used to that," Joe assured her. "Don't worry. Besides, I have nothing, so there's nothing for anybody to steal; I want nothing except some conversation, so they either talk to me or they don't. And I long ago swallowed my pride and decided to let the nymph part work if I have to. Just take it easy and use the fields here to get around to the other side, like that bluff with the gumdrop-shaped bush on it over there, and wait. I shouldn't be too long."

Alvi was strangely hesitant. "Okay, but—I dunno. I just get a really strange feeling when I look at that little place there. I don't think I ever felt anything really like it before. It's—weird?"

Joe knew that such feelings weren't to be taken lightly in Husaquahr. "What kind of feeling? Queasy? Shivers? Chills?"

"Nothin' like that exactly. I—I *said* I can't describe it. Like—like whoever's up there already knows we're coming. Like we're expected for dinner or something."

Joe frowned. "Well, if you're getting that kind of feeling, maybe concealing you isn't the best way, but I don't think we should give them both of us at once if it *is* something unfriendly. Trust me on this one. Easy, casual walk up the road and into town, but keep an eye out and play it by my signals. I've been in bad spots before."

It was Alvi's turn to doubt. "It *could* just be my imagination . . ."

"Probably not. Particularly when you start to doubt yourself. That's probably in the Rules someplace. Just be on guard and proceed slowly with me. No weapons. Unless we're attacked or you or I get a strong feeling of serious danger, we might just be spooking somebody unnecessarily."

It certainly didn't feel like an ambush. The tiny town of a half dozen ramshackle wooden structures looked to have

seen *much* better days and to have survived mostly because
the breeze off the land wasn't *quite* strong enough to blow
it over the cliff. Once it had clearly been a way station for
weary travelers on their way to and from the City-States
and the Leander ocean resorts, but commerce, for some reason, had passed it by. From the looks of a boarded-up well
and dry troughs, it appeared either that the well had run
dry—unlikely in that climate—or that it was contaminated
by something that had doomed this as a rest stop. Across
the road were the remains of stables, now little more than
boards on crude rock foundations.

As they drew close to the tiny town, Joe began to get the
distinct impression that this was no ordinary town in a
number of ways. The ramshackle buildings weren't close to
the sort you'd find anywhere in Husaquahr, for one thing;
for another, the signs were disturbingly out of place.

ALOJA PARA EL ALQUILER announced the faded sign on
one half-falling-down building. EL ALIMENTO BUENO said
another, weathered but clear enough for Joe to read. Inside
was an arrow painted on one of the buildings that pointed
to the wreckage across the road with the faded words LOS
ESTABLOS. Below it, in a graffitilike scrawl, were the words
"*Por un llamado bueno de tiempo Tina*, 555-3721."

"Sure looks weird," Alvi commented.

Joe nodded. All the weirder because it was so familiar in
many ways—but only to Joe.

A sudden wind came off the land as they actually
crossed into the tiny ruin, its whistling sounds almost but
not quite masking the sounds of the breakers on the cliff far
below.

On the creaking porch of the old hotel sat a figure in a
rocking chair, going slowly back and forth almost in time
to the wind. It was wrapped in a colorful serapelike garment that looked to be perhaps Navajo or Hopi; the figure's
head was down in its chest, masked by a huge sombrero.

As they cautiously approached, Alvi's hand went instinctively to the bow on her shoulder, easing it down in spite
of what Joe had said. Now, quite close, the enigmatic fig-

ure, still rocking slowly, raised its head. The big sombrero came up, and inside was nothing at all, nothing but two glowing red eyes.

"Faith and begorra!" the apparition swore in a thick Irish brogue. "Ya needn't be fearin' me much this trip! Put away yer weapons and be at ease!"

"You've got the wrong accent for the clothes and setting," Joe noted, still wary, eyes on the thing, whatever it was.

"Oh, one's as good as the other, really, isn't it, now?" the thing responded. "Spanish, English, Husaquahrian, or Navajo, what's the difference?"

"I'm an Apache," Joe pointed out. "Not much relation with the Navajos."

The thing shrugged. "Again, what's the difference? A priest's a shaman and a shaman's a priest, and ya talk yer talks in whatever's understood. Take this spit of a ghost town. Never was much to it in its heyday, and there's even less now. The Earth didn't even miss it when it got rotated out, now, did it? Now 'tis neither here nor there, y' see. The mortals, they be so blind, it don't even exist for 'em in *either* plane, except when they camp here or just glance back outa the corner of one eye and like that. Only them that's got faerie blood can truly see it."

"But not you," Joe noted.

The thing hesitated a moment. "That's me own dear choice, y' see. It kinda limits what I can do, but it's a good deal safer. Lets me see and hear them what's linked without bein' really there to be noticed. And as fer the Apache, I never did see a green Apache of your likes!"

"This isn't exactly—"

"Oh, I know, Joe de Oro. I knows just who you were, but ya ain't no more, are ye?"

Joe was startled. "So you know who I am! Then this isn't just an accidental encounter."

"Faith! Nothin' I do is accidental! Strictly within the Rules, though, I be. Yes, strictly within the Rules. Not like some."

"Everyone's bound by the Rules here!"

"Indeed, 'tis so, but perhaps not for much longer. They're coming, you see, and it's not likely they can be stopped."

"*Who* is coming? What's all this about?" Joe asked.

"Well, there's Heaven and there's Hell, and then there's the other place. The place of the pretenders, those gods and demigods who may or may not have held sway for a while in one place or another but who in the end did not make it, you see. Kind of a dustbin of the gods, you might say. They are some of the worst things ever to have come out of creation. Individually, each could be vanquished. Even as a class, perhaps. But together—ah, together they create a new power. They were tossed where they were because their egos were such that there was no conceivable way they could combine forces. But they are combining now. They have their own unique definitions of good and evil and grudges against both Heaven and Hell. Surely you have felt them, felt how close they are to becoming real once more."

Joe nodded. "So *that's* what it is. But surely both Heaven *and* Hell can handle them."

"They could," the apparition agreed, "but they won't. Heaven may be so disgusted with everything, it'll just take its remainin' folk out and leave the rest to these bastards. Hell—well, Hell only wants what Heaven desires, y' see. And besides, if such concentrated evil was to really overrun all this universe, then it'd pollute the very Sea of Dreams, bringin' nightmare to Earth and perhaps the battle Hell really wants. It's willin' to give up this place, then, to gain the bigger prize—but y' see, since most of the folks that'll be left if these creatures break through and rule are already in Hell's pocket, they're not too terribly pleased by the prospect. They're just too bloody evil to work together against the usurpers and treacherous enough to make separate deals and stab one another in the back."

Joe began to see, and he did not like it one bit. "And what happens if they *do* break through and take over here? To us, I mean."

"There's far worse than death. Surely ya knows *that* much. They'll apportion for a while and remake all in their own images, but eventually they'll start to devour one another. Who can say? They don't look or act or think like anything or anybody ya knows."

Joe sighed and shrugged. "Why tell *us* this? What can *we* do about it?"

"Not 'us,' just you," the apparition responded. Joe turned and saw that Alvi was just standing there, frozen, unblinking as a statue.

"What did you do to her?"

"Nothin'; don't worry. We're just on a kinda plane that she's not ready for. She'll not know any of this has passed, but she doesn't need to. In the end it will all come down to you. That's what ya were brought here for, wasn't it?"

"For the *last* battle. I've done my bit! I've paid my price! Too much, if you ask me! I shouldn't have to do anything more. I don't even know how I could."

"I don't, either," the creature admitted, "but it's still in your lap because it's not finished. You jumped into that lava knowin' what would happen, but you had little toime to think about it; you hated the Baron far more, and you had no idea of the long-term price ye'd pay. Now you know the price and you got vulnerabilities including your friend here and your own son, who you drug over, subjected to all this, and then abandoned. Now you got to think—would you do it again? Would you save the world if it meant you'd *always* be as you are now, period, and if it might cost the life of your son as well? Or would you go over to 'em and let billions perish and their souls become darker'n pitch, including your own and those you save?"

"I don't know. I hope I never would, at least on those terms," Joe answered honestly. "Why me, anyway? I'm small, slight, physically weak, unarmed: not suited for much of the kind of battle you set up. With all the sorcerers still around here, I'm not a sane choice even to do this."

"Three reasons for starters," the creature replied. "For one, it's what you were brought here to do. It's your job.

For two, you alone among the creatures of faerie and men in all this world are immortal. They cannot kill you or touch the Tree that gives you this great power—unless you let them. And most compelling of all, at the end of what *she* seeks is that which you will find most irresistible to fight. If you continue with her, you're in. If you do not go with her, then become the nymph in the tree and forget all else, for you'll never change until the end of toime and you'll never adventure again and you will sit and watch *him* win at last."

" 'Him'? *What* are you talking about?"

"Your destiny and those of others are intertwined. You have not yet completed your grand commission. Until you do, you can claim to win only battles, not a war. That evil which you feel growing and which threatens to pervade and engulf all of Husaquahr is partly of your doing. You must complete the task or, no matter how many victories you can claim, you will still lose it all."

Joe's mouth opened in shock and surprise. "Now, *wait* a minute! I had nothing to do with this—whatever it is. I know what my own task was, and that was accomplished when the Dark Baron fell into the lava and was consumed, and the great sword with him. If there is a new source of ultimate evil, that is for another. I know *that* much about the Rules!"

"And did not you, too, fall into the same lava? Did not you, too, find yourself consumed in fire? Yet, if this be true, *who* stands before me now?"

Joe had a sudden very sick feeling. "You're not telling me—"

"He had to get his powers back somehow. The way was through faerie. Unlike you, he really did die in that molten magma, but he was a bit better than that. He had long ago planned ahead. He went neither to Heaven nor to Hell but instead into the very Sea of Dreams, where the Beings of Power dwell forever, and what eons could not accomplish, he did in the blink of an eye. Now followers of things more evil than Hell itself have opened the way back for him, and he prepares the way for the others."

"So you're saying I have no choice."

"Sure. *Lotsa* choices and all bad. That's *if* ya gets there in the first place. It's a long journey, bein' faerie won't help you much, and the temptations, particularly for the likes of you, will be quite hard to resist. Make no mistake, Joe. Your life's not in real danger, but there's such ahead that may have ya prayin' for death. Forget the colors of the enemy, too, and keep checkin' your own. Either way, both the Baron and you are done with this trip. Both of ya. Ya wins or loses this toime, either o' ya. That's why ya gits this here warnin'. That and because it's not balanced if you don't know who and what's out ahead. Y' see, *he* is waiting for *you*."

"Who—and what—are you?" Joe demanded to know. "Are you with Heaven or with Hell, with *him* or with me?"

"That's not for now. Perhaps sometoime in the future. I'll be keepin' my eye on ya, and we'll see if perhaps I'll show up now and then, if I can do that much. I think ya got it in ya to do it, me boy. Just remember that until the Old Ones can come through fer real, the Rules still bind here. Use 'em. And don't spend no more time cryin' over what ya ain't got no more. Instead, learn to use what ya *do* have. That—and beware vampire gophers!"

And with that, the wind suddenly struck Joe's body and there was nothing on the porch except an empty old wooden rocking chair going back and forth in the wind.

"What is it?" Alvi asked nervously. "Somebody in there?"

Joe realized that the halfling in fact was unaware that there had been a conversation or that any real time had passed.

"No, nobody in there," the nymph responded. "Not anymore."

Deep down Joe wasn't sure if she'd have gone against such power, particularly now and on her own, no matter what the situation or even the potential rewards. Now, though, the two words that would drive her to go anywhere and risk just about anything had been spoken, and if they were true, there was no question that this was destiny.

Joe had defeated his enemy more than once and had killed him once in human form. Now it was in the realm of faerie, soul to soul, immortality or oblivion, that they must meet one more time.

But where? And how? Joe couldn't read those complex Books of Rules, but she knew one thing all too well: nowhere in any of them did it guarantee that the good guys would win.

Joe looked again at the halfling, who was still puzzled by what seemed an odd change of mood in her nymph companion. Something in those Rules, some kind of thread of destiny or fate or whatever, or possibly the workings of the Baron himself, had brought them together at this point. Somewhere on the girl was the location of the Grand McGuffin, whatever that was beyond being what Alvi needed to become whole in some way and what Joe needed not just to get out of her current circumstances but as the only weapon against a resurgent Boquillas, now almost certainly of dark faerie nature.

The first step was to unlock that map in Alvi's ring's spell, and that would mean Macore. She hoped it would be easy for the onetime self-styled greatest thief in Husaquahr; it would certainly be good to see him, just like old times.

One step at a time, she thought. *Like always.*

DÉJÀ VU ALL OVER AGAIN

Objectives may be achieved only after attempting to achieve them the hard way first.

—Rules, Vol. VII, p. 101(d)

TERINDELL NEVER REALLY CHANGED. ALTHOUGH A GREAT, imposing structure built by men, it had much of the quality of faerie about it both in its permanence and in its seeming impenetrability. The greatest wizards of Husaquahr never lived forever, but the best lived a very long time, and it was certain that the edifice built by and for the comfort and convenience of Throckmorton P. Ruddygore would last at least as long as he did.

A tall elfin creature with a pale face, pointed ears, and a permanent doleful expression answered the door, and when he saw who was there, he *almost* but not quite managed a very slight smile.

"Hello, Poquah," Marge said cheerfully. "You're looking much the same as usual."

"We seldom change on the outside, but my head says that I am growing much too old," responded the Imir—the Imir were a rare elfin tribe that could in some cases learn magic not a part of their own nature—tiredly. "And few of us can wash all our troubles away in supernatural fires."

The creature he was speaking to was also of faerie, and, save for the brilliant reds and oranges of her coloration and her large capelike wings, one might well classify her as one of the many varieties of nymph. She seemed, however, more exotic than a mere nymph, with clear intelligence and even some power inherent in her strong face, although she certainly was built at least partially for pleasure. She was in fact a Kauri, a kind of psychic vampire that could remove heavy psychological burdens in the act of making love to a

67

man in the guise of his ideal fantasy playmate, a positive succubus who literally fed on other people's problems.

This Kauri, however, was almost certainly the only one in Husaquahr who'd once been an English teacher in Midland, Texas, and still retained a hint of a Texas accent no matter what tongue she was speaking.

Poquah ushered her inside the outer castle area, and she immediately began to notice that some of the furnishings were quite different from what she remembered. While passing into the inner courtyard she noted that the layout and extensive flowers and exotic shrubs were totally different from what they had ever been before.

"That's new," she muttered to herself, frowning.

The Imir heard her. "No, madam, it was changed over the past few years. You have not been here in quite some time, you know."

The comment startled her because she *didn't* know, at least not really. Time had little meaning anymore, and clocks even less, and it hardly seemed any time at all since she'd last been here at the end of settling the final accounts with Boquillas and Sugasto. Now, suddenly, it bothered her. "How long *has* it been? Do you recall?"

"Yes, madam. Things run by clocks and calendars in this existence. It has been a good six years next month."

Marge was shocked. "Six *years*! My God! I had no idea! So little Irving—"

"Is not so little anymore," Poquah finished for her. "No, madam, I fear he's anything *but* that. And no end of trouble, too. After all this time you would think that he would have assimilated into the world here as one or another thing, but so far he's resisted. He's a good swordsman but not a great one, and more than capable with the basic weapons yet not of the warrior or mercenary class. No self-discipline. He's learned to read the Husaquahrian tongue to a remarkable degree yet has no feel for the language, nor a general interest in trade and commerce or in politics, which he holds in deep contempt. In some things he's quite brilliant—he applied himself for weeks to learning a specific set of spells, then, when he got so he could cast them, he did so and was done with more than mere 'puttering' around with occasional magic, all for mischief. He's also a passing fair pickpocket and thief, although I think he brought those talents with him when he came."

"Spells? What did he cast? And on whom?"

"On *what* is more like it. Turned the Master's entire collection of precious lawn jockeys white as snow."

Marge cracked up, and it was a couple of minutes before she could get complete control again. Ruddygore was wonderful and sophisticated in so many areas, but he had a bizarre fixation on the idea that cheap, tacky plaster statues, lawn jockeys, pink flamingos, and other total junk from the Earth of *her* origin were somehow great and unappreciated works of art.

"What did Ruddygore say about that when he found out?" she asked the Imir.

"He was initially not pleased, but then it occurred to him that the act was done not out of mischief but out of a sense of personal offense. Frankly, I do not believe that the Master ever considered that the objects might be considered offensive to or by anyone, and this brought home to him the fact that they offended very much indeed. It was the virulence of the spell as much as its nature that gave it away. I must say, once his anger cooled, he did not undo the spell, nor has he added to that particular collection since. I believe that in some strange way the Master feels he actually learned something new, and for one of his great age and experience *that* is more valuable than anything else."

"Maybe it is, Poquah." She nodded. "Maybe it is. What about Joe? What does *she* say about this?"

The Imir sighed. "I'm afraid that the question is without meaning. Joe remained here only a few days after returning from the north, then departed, stating that she had to learn to deal with the situation before she could be of any value. The Master has kept track of her travels but has never called her back."

"What about the kid, then? You mean Joe just hauled the

poor kid over, left him here, and bugged *out*?" She was appalled. "No *wonder* he's got no self-discipline! Who's been raising him, anyway?"

"We all have, to a degree. In a sense, he's the young prince of Terindell."

"But—what about him and his father? I mean, Irving at least *knows* what happened, doesn't he?"

Poquah shrugged. "I don't know. Sometimes I think he does; sometimes I think he does not. All the time I believe he thinks of it as irrelevant to him. It is not easy for anyone to fully understand another, but for an elf to understand humans to that degree—I fear not."

Marge shook her head sadly in wonder. "So what was I called here for, then? The old boy just wants to talk over old times or what?"

"I'm not certain, but I rather think it is more serious than that. You have certainly felt it."

"The dark chill, you mean. I think *everybody* can feel it, even the most nonmagical of humans. It's ugly and pervasive."

"And it is growing stronger," Poquah added.

"Yeah. But I hardly think it's anything *I* can do much about. Lord knows it's driving me to exhaustion, though. Everybody's so down, so depressed, I often have to cleanse myself every third or fourth person. There are times even now when I've felt fat, bloated, and too dense even to fly right. But hey, I *did* my bit. More than my bit. Besides, what could I do now against even the old enemies? Our company's long disbanded, and things aren't like they were. None of us are like we were."

"Less who we were than even we think," Poquah responded a bit cryptically. "Still, we are no more self-piloting than before, either. Our destinies run a strange race through the Law, the Rules, instinct, intellect, and destiny. Something is unfinished. I cannot explain it any better than that, but it has been constantly there. A sense that there is something among our own threads that remains undone.

Until we do it, we cannot pass the burden to the next generation. That's the Rules."

"I never did like the Rules all that much," she muttered.

"They *are* excessive," Poquah agreed, "but they are also necessary. Without the Rules, it is unlikely that any of us would be alive today or a stone of this castle standing. The Rules, like any good body of law, are good not because they are all necessary—indeed, most are quite silly—but because they are so mathematically evenhanded. Neither good nor evil can ever gain absolute victory so long as the Rules exist, and so long as they provide opportunity, the cleverest will come out on top. So long as the Rules exist, we tend to be guaranteed a tie, given an equal force on each side. With no Rules, with no margins built in, I, as a mathematician, wouldn't give a gold bar for good's chances."

They were now inside the inner castle and up the winding stairway to the Great Hall on the second floor above the arch. This one great room had changed the least; various suits of armor from countless periods—including some built for nothing remotely human—stood all around, great portraits of dour-looking nobles and sorcerers and the like stared down, and great fireplaces and wonderful great tables and chairs with arms and legs carved into fantastic shapes of gargoyles, wild animals, fairy folk, you name it, graced the hall.

Against the far wall was a massive bookcase running floor to ceiling and along the entire expanse without break, filled with huge heavy-looking tomes all bound in red buckram with gold-embossed spines. Hundreds of volumes, going off to both sides and up and down in a sea of blood red, the Books of Rules Existent under which the whole of this world, this *universe*, was governed.

"I will go and tell the Master you are here," Poquah said, bowing slightly. "He's been quite tired of late, what with this evil essence, so be prepared for a less than vital man. He is still quite strong, though."

"You didn't tell me he was ill!"

"It is not—exactly—illness. You will see. I'll fetch him."
And with that, he left her standing there.

She stared at the books with a mixture of awe and appre-
hension, as always, knowing that within those pages were
the very Kauri defined and limited, and also up there, in
some form or another, were the Rules for almost all that
had happened to them over the year since she and Joe had
first been brought here to battle the Dark Baron.

What a grand campaign it had been, too! For all the horrors and slipups and nasty surprises, it had been in many
ways a remarkable experience, the kind few people got a
crack at in their lifetimes.

She'd always promised herself that she'd learn the
Husaquahrian written tongue and read those Rules someday,
but she never had. Why not? She couldn't really say, but
somehow it just hadn't seemed *important* for her to do so.

It hadn't seemed important to do much of anything, in
fact.

That bothered her, although she was having trouble even
determining *why* it should bother her.

In fact, until Ruddygore's summons had brought it all
back, even those past exploits had faded into memories that
she barely considered anymore. For the first year or so after
the final showdown in the cold wastes she'd been pretty
faithful in keeping in touch here, checking on Irving, dropping in to talk over old times with the likes of Poquah and
Ruddygore, and even keeping in some sort of contact with
Macore.

Over time, though, things hadn't so much stopped as
faded out. The visits had become fewer and farther between; the conversations—when they did come—more basic, less substantial; and, finally, it had just stopped
altogether. She couldn't remember the last time she'd even
dreamed in English or thought much in that language. It
wasn't that the old Marge wasn't there anymore, it was just
that she had been, well, filed away somewhere under old
times and rarely was brought out except for infrequent re-
unions.

Was that bad? She didn't really know. She was a Kauri, pretty well indistinguishable from all her sister Kauris and doing what Kauris did. Not only was that not going to change, she enjoyed it. Was the price, the loss of individuality, too great? She wasn't sure. It didn't seem so, yet something in her old prechangeling Texas upbringing said it should be.

Throckmorton P. Ruddygore always made an impressive appearance even when he was feeling off. A huge man, well over six feet in height and impossible to guess in girth, he always reminded Marge of Santa Claus living the good life in the off-season. His thick but carefully managed flowing white beard and long, snow-white hair only added to the impression, and even in the worst of times his eyes seemed to twinkle with the suggestion that he was enjoying some cosmic joke at everyone else's expense.

"Marge! How good it is to see you again!" the sorcerer exclaimed, sounding both sincere and delighted. "I'm very glad that you could come." He went over, took her hand, and, bending down, kissed it softly. It was a very nice gesture, but it also served as a reminder of just how huge a man he was compared to her or, frankly, almost anybody else.

"I'm glad to be back for a bit," she responded, smiling. "But let's face it, when you're the one calling, it's not like I'm going to ignore it!"

He grinned and pulled over a huge, high-backed padded chair and then sank into it. The chair, made of the hardest woods and of ancient lineage that had borne the weight of sorcerers and kings, nonetheless sagged and almost seemed ready to scream in protest.

"You'll pardon my manners," he said more softly. "I'm sure that Poquah has already told you that I'm well off my feed of late."

"You *do* look and sound unusually tired," Marge admitted to him. "This new pall seems to sap the very energy out of folks."

"It's worse than that for sorcerers. The thing is, it is so

pervasive, we spend much of our energy just keeping things up to snuff. With no chance to renew or get away, it takes its toll."

"I assume it's why you called me here, or at least part of your reason."

He nodded. "More or less. It's not the pall itself so much as the cause and object of it. It is slowly, incrementally, almost particle by particle, draining the free magic out of Husaquahr."

"But that's impossible! I mean, the faerie, alone account for a great deal of it."

"True, but it is less of a drain on the faerie, for you are essentially defined as much by your powers as by your form. That is not free magic energy. You feel it, certainly, but not to the extent that someone like me feels it. I call upon the energy, I gather it, I weave it into the patterns we call spells. *That* is free magic, and *that* is what is slowly being sucked out. At this rate it's not going to be a terrible blow to us today or tomorrow, but sooner or later it will be. And since it puts pressure on all of us who use free magic, it drives us closer to exhaustion. When we can't fight it anymore, it will accelerate. I think that's the idea. Collapse those of us who can guard Husaquahr, and anybody can move in and take over. And whoever controls the free magic in the end controls the faerie as well, since you are subject to it as much as to your own predefined limitations."

She gave a low whistle. "Then this is serious."

"Indeed. Very much so."

"Do you know who's causing it?"

He nodded. "I think so. He took great pains to disguise himself, but the concerted efforts of the whole Council were brought to bear, and we've rooted him out. The thing is, we can't do much about him. The only member of the Council who could act refuses to acknowledge or recognize the problem. Whether it's because he's been bought off with promises of even greater power or has been deluded,

I can't say. Either way, under his protection, if only by his inaction, this continues."

"The rest of you can't stop it? I mean, you wrote all those Rules and you're stuck with something like *this*?"

Ruddygore sighed. "That really *is* part of the problem. We wrote those Rules and we're stuck with them. Oh, I suspect that the whole of the Council could combine in single unitary purpose to dislodge our recalcitrant brother and perhaps get to this evil source he protects, but that won't happen. We can't even change the damned Rules until every single sorcerer has a copy—that alone takes *years!*"

"Seems to me you dealt with Boquillas right off, at least in stripping him of his powers and exiling him to Earth," she noted.

"Indeed. Stripping powers. Exiling. With Boquillas right in front of us. But what if he hadn't been in our custody? We would have been helpless. We still needed the bunch of you to go off and pull him out to where he was vulnerable, and even then, he was only temporarily so. Finally Joe sent him to Hell, but the bastard still didn't go there—instead he sought out the enemies of all creation, consorted with them, and is mounting a rather effective takeover bid."

Marge was startled. "*Takeover?* Boquillas is alive—and he's actually trying to conquer *Hell*?"

"And other things. There seems to be no stopping that man."

Marge began to see where this was going. "You are telling me that the Dark Baron, last seen in the body of a pretty woman stabbed through the heart with a sword and falling headfirst into volcanic lava, is somehow behind all that's happening now. You really *are* saying that, aren't you?"

"I'm afraid so. Things are still unfinished with him."

She blew up. "How the hell can they *ever* be settled? Jeez! We've exiled him, stripped him of his powers, stabbed him, *dissolved him in molten rock* . . . ! If all *that* didn't work, then what the hell *can*?"

"I assure you that this is not exactly normal even for

such ones as Esmilio and myself. The Lamp of Lakash could have done it—its magic overrides natural law, the Rules, you name it. I—I thought he was gone, though, and that the Lamp had been shown to be more of a danger to us than a protection for us. I got rid of it. It was a very stupid thing for me to do. The whole reason why it was here, why it had been *allowed* to be here, was that it was the ultimate weapon against the ultimate attacks. Nothing could stand against it. *Nothing* save God and *perhaps* the Devil. That's why it was so dangerous. Like all ultimate weapons, defensive or not, it was always a two-edged sword."

"Great! You know what we went through to *get* you that thing? Can't you get it back?"

"Impossible. That route is gone."

"Then what are we talking about here? After all that stuff, all those adventures, all those fights and spells and wars and personal tragedies and sacrifices—after all that, *the bad guys win*?"

Ruddygore sighed. "What can I say to the first charges? That acquiring great knowledge and tremendous power makes one feel almost godlike? That you begin to forget that you are *not* truly a god and that the very last thing you are is infallible? Guilty. As to the second—not so long as the Rules prevail in Husaquahr."

"Huh?"

"Remember the one that got Joe in his fix but nonetheless saved both your tails more than once? That, no matter what, there has to be one out available? At least one? That nothing, not even certain doom, can be inevitable even if it *is* the most likely outcome?"

"Um, yeah. But—"

"That's why I've been studying here and racking my brains for so long. I am as much subject to the Rules as you are. It hit me after a fashion that the Rules would no more permit such an absolute action as I took with the Lamp than they would permit you to be executed without somehow providing a way of escape whether you discovered and took it or not. Like you, my first thoughts were on reversing the dismissal of the Lamp, and I wasted a lot of precious months trying to figure out a way around the action before I finally accepted that I had done too good a job. The Lamp is out, and there is no reversal of that—of this I am now certain. That meant, however, that under the Rules there had to be some sort of backup. Perhaps not as effective, but something had to exist beyond the Lamp, something here in this world and accessible, although perhaps not without great cost, that will at least do the job."

She thought it over but wasn't all that thrilled by the concept. "I remind you, sir, that many years ago now I was one of those who came to this world because of just such a problem. The Baron and his demon allies were beating up everybody and everything, and not even the great powers of this world could stop them, so off we went to find the Lamp and wrest it from its ten-foot-tall killer-bunny guardian. That deal brought Sugasto into the picture, and it was more than Hell to pay before we got rid of *him*, never mind the Baron. Okay, we got rid of them, and we got rid of the Lamp so it couldn't be stolen and do irreparable harm. Great. Now here it is, a few years later, there's some new evil spreading over the land, nobody can stop it or deal with it, and we have to find some kind of supermagic thingie nobody else knows about and steal it and round and round and round we go."

Ruddygore let her go on and get it out of her system, but he ignored her weary sarcasm. "Marge, there is no such thing as 'new' evil. There is only evil, eternal and vicious, and it is *never* new. Creative certainly, but it is very old indeed. It is the same evil that crept into the Garden, the same evil that sunk ancient Atlantis, that brought fear and war and horrors to *two* universes and more. It has many names. War, pestilence, genocide, hatred, intolerance, torture, fear—all those and more. But it's universal, it's been there almost since the beginning, and it will be there until the end. It varies mostly in degree and in its capacity to reinvent itself. Indeed, did you know that there is actually an entire *continent* devoted to evil right here in this world? Has no one ever told you of Far Yuggoth?"

The name had a familiarity and perhaps a slightly chilling tone to it. "I have heard it mentioned," she admitted, "but not often and never directly. I thought it was a myth, like the Boogeyman."

"Those who know of it don't *want* to think about it. Those who have ever known of it or been close to it never wish to think of its existence again. When you consider the amount of evil we have here even in quiet times, let alone when ones like our old friend the Baron was at large, and Sugasto, and the rest—well, a continent of concentrated evil is best left mythological. It is not, however. It is very real."

Marge frowned. "Yeah? Then why hasn't *it* spawned all the stuff that goes on elsewhere? And how come we aren't in a constant war with *it*?"

"We are," the sorcerer told her. "The Baron was once a good and noble sorcerer," he said, smiling slightly, "like myself, who got so caught up in the injustices he saw in *this* part of the world that he was led by demons to go down to Yuggoth and learn the parts of magic forbidden to any and all here. He did so, in contravention of our guild, and *that*, as much as or more than his breaking of the covenants and his war against us, was why he lost his powers and was exiled—but also why he was so difficult to beat. It was there he learned the gateway to Hell and made his alliances with the demon princes. Now you also know the source of Sugasto and his zombie trickery. We can keep it somewhat confined and controlled not only because of constant and heavy vigilance but also because, being evil, the denizens of Yuggoth are their own worst enemies, too. We also have a deal with the King of Horror, who reigns as temporal absolute ruler there, to safeguard his own throne and hide our support so long as he reins in as much as he can. Even so, you can readily see and experience just how much evil escapes to our regions!"

Marge nodded. This was all new and interesting . . . and not at all heading in any direction where she wanted to go.

Still, she couldn't help her curiosity. "The King of Horror? You mean Satan?"

"No, Satan's King of Hell, Prince of the Powers of the Air, ruler of a dimensional context you cannot imagine. The King is, well, a sorcerer, a great power like myself and my colleagues, with a decided bent for that sort of thing. He's propelled himself to the top there and remains, hated by all his subjects as you'd expect. You can imagine that his power is enormous—anything less and he'd have been knocked off long before now."

"And he *likes* that kind of existence?"

"Well, he's got more than he could ever want and is greater than he ever dreamed he could be. Why not? But staying on top—aye, that's always the trick, isn't it?"

"I've seen enough evil in this and the other world that I'm not too sure how good a job he does," she noted.

"But that's the point! He does a *superb* job. I seriously doubt if anyone can ever do it better. Certainly nobody has before. He's got both worlds to worry about, too. Just consider—we *have* always beaten what gets out here, and back on Earth, who would have wagered a fig that half a century after the atom bomb people wouldn't have already blown themselves to Hell without further intervention? Compared to *that*, wars, minigenocides, mass murders, demonic possessions, natural disasters, and the like seem rather trivial. No, he's definitely worth his weight in anything precious, that's for sure, but just as certain his eye is a bit too busy to be on sparrows."

"You almost make him somebody likable," she noted.

"In a sense he is. He can be a delightful chap. However, he rules an entire continent that mouths hatred of him and doesn't like itself very much, either."

Marge sighed. "I know you too well, Ruddygore. You're not bringing up this Yuggoth or this King of Horror just to be sociable and educational. You are heading someplace with the subtlety of a force-ten earthquake. Someplace I am absolutely, positively, under no circumstances going to go."

Ruddygore looked stricken. "Marge! How can you *doubt* my sincerity in this?"

"If it's so easy, *you* go this time. You've at least got the power."

He turned very serious. "It's not easy. It's *possible*, but I know *that* only because of my knowledge of the Rules and how things work. Just how possible and just how many mistakes, if any, are allowed, I cannot guess. Nor can I or any of my colleagues go. Not even at the very end this time, to solve the final problems. We, any of us, would be instant psychic magnets, drawing together all that is evil throughout all the planes and universes and unifying them as never before against us. Any of us either would become as corrupted as Boquillas was or would be utterly consumed."

She wasn't impressed. "Uh huh. And if it's too much for you, you still think that somebody like me can waltz in there and walk through it unscathed? Uh uh."

"Not alone, no. An army of faerie could not stand in that place for long. Only with an anchor—a mortal, corruptible individual of free will—could all hope to have any chance to survive, and that as much by protecting that anchor as by doing anything themselves."

She stared at him. "You are really serious, aren't you? And you're talking about the kid. Joe's kid. You're gonna take a teenage kid and throw him into *that* and count on me and maybe a few other experienced types to protect him? Ruddy, *that* is evil. That requires no King of Horror. You are sick."

Ruddygore sighed. "Marge—Joe is missing."

"Huh?"

"Joe went right into that region because the same thing that might save us would also quite obviously have no problems curing his situation. I received a message from Macore that Joe and a halfling girl—about whom I'm still trying to learn a lot of details—arrived many weeks ago, stayed a bit, pumped the port locals on Yuggoth and the like, tried without success to get Macore to join them, and ultimately went anyway. About forty days ago they were put off on a desolate shore on Yuggoth by a mercenary ship, and they vanished. I mean that almost literally. The King was aware of their landing yet can find no trace whatsoever of either of them."

That did concern her. "Jeez! Do you think—I mean, is Joe dead?"

"I believe I can unequivocally state that Joe is alive. Joe has a protection of life beyond any power here to alter, remember. The problem is, the protection is strictly limited to life. There are situations where life is the absolute worst thing to keep and where death would be longed for, and ninety-nine percent of those states were conceived on Yuggoth. Even being faerie doesn't lock you in; not only is great pain, misery, and whatnot as possible with your people as with ours, but the very purity of faerie existence is corruptible. The soul can always be turned and remade, and you are pure ectoplasm, as it were, and can pass to the astral planes without death intervening."

She thought it over but caught herself. "Uh uh. No go, Ruddygore! I did my bit! We *all* did. And you have to admit, even with all the help, it's a miracle any of us are still here at all. Every time something like this comes up, the odds against us are greater than before. Something inside me says that I've been too lucky for too long in this department. Send somebody else!"

The sorcerer sighed. "I shall, but they will lack your experience and your knowledge. The boy will go, you know. He'll go because it's his father, and because it's honor, and also because children that age believe they are immortal. He's the center of whatever power the new Company might have, just as Joe was of the original one. Poquah, too, although I admit that even I had reservations about him going on this trip. He is not powerful enough to withstand all the forces that may be represented just in the journey, but he is more than powerful enough to act as a magnet to draw such forces to him. He considers it a matter of honor. I have hopes that Macore might also join one last campaign."

"He didn't go in with Joe, I notice," Marge pointed out a bit acidly.

"No, of course not. There was nothing of cosmic significance, at least obviously so, that would have impelled him to do so, nothing to compel him to go, either, and frankly, he has just about everything he can want in his retirement and has no need for more."

"So what makes you think he'll go now?"

"For Joe, of course. Possibly even more for Joe's son. You see, Irving has spent some time with the old thief, and Macore has come to consider the lad as, well, not the son he never had, perhaps, but at least a favorite nephew. He's no longer in the peak condition he once was, nor is he as young as he used to be, but his skills and experience can substitute for quite a good deal."

"The next thing you'll be telling me is that Tiana is going, too."

"No. In fact, I have made it my business to keep Tiana ignorant of this affair. Tiana has adjusted *extremely* well to being not merely male but king. His experiences both on the highest and the lowest levels of society here have made him wise and capable in ways the old queen could never have been and wasn't. The country needs its king badly, and for the first time the monarch is perfect for the role. As I and my colleagues battle against darkness here on the magical level, Ti is essential to the holding together of the political and social fabric. To go now would mean renouncing his throne and all claims for all times. I cannot permit that."

"Well, I don't like it, anyway. It stinks, and I think you should be ashamed of yourself for even *thinking* of letting that boy go!"

"Transformed or not, blood is blood and relation is relation! I could not stop him if I tried! And if *he* decided not to go, he would be useless ever after both to others and to himself. He needs to define himself. If he goes and survives, he will be defined here both to his own ego and within the Rules. It will work out. If he goes and does not survive, then he would not have long survived life here, anyway. If he feared too much to go, he would be without courage, and if he refused to go, he would lack honor. No, it is unthinkable that he be stopped."

Marge gave a big sigh. "All right, all right. I don't agree with this, but I'll accept the point for now. The real question is whether this is just a hunt for a needle in a continent-sized haystack. Find Joe. Where? How? Even your King of Horror can't find Joe! What's the object here, Ruddygore? If it's to roam around until something there finally eats us or turns us or whatever, no thanks. There has to be an object to a quest. Even I know that much of the Rules."

"You're right. The object isn't to find Joe, but if you accomplish the object, then finding Joe will almost certainly follow." The big man reached into the folds of his robe, pulled out a small scrolled sheet, and handed it to the Kauri. She took it, unrolled it, and frowned.

"A big, mean-looking bird?"

"Not just *any* bird. That one's not alive, at least not in the sense that birds or you and I are alive. It won't fly; it won't even move. It's a sculpture, an idol if you will, carved out of black marble by some ancient faerie artisan in times long past, not here but on Earth. An island in the ancient Mediterranean, I believe. A good likeness of *Hammettus hitchcockius*, a very tough but majestic bird now nearing extinction everywhere. *This* one has an infinite number of names and has been fought over and had people die over its possession. Our own literature here simply calls it the Great or Grand McGuffin. It is on Yuggoth, having been switched for a fake one many years past and brought there by a man who tried to cheat the devil with it, and—as is standard for ninety-nine point nine percent of people throughout human history with such a goal—he didn't quite make it. It's been hidden, cared for, even worshiped on Yuggoth as a minor deity ever since."

She stared at it, suspecting that she knew the name of the

island where it had originated. "And this thing can actually grant wishes like the Lamp?"

"Not exactly, but yes, it has some of that sort of power. The Lamp, however, was a product of a totally alien universe, that of the djinn. *This* was brought into existence by other, darker, but more comprehensible forces and to do evil overall. It *is* somewhat neutral in most senses like the Lamp, but unlike it, the Great McGuffin, is designed to deliver less than its potential. No one has ever been able to use it without some sort of price being exacted, at least not that we know. You know the old saw about making a deal with the devil? He always gives you exactly what you ask for, but somehow you never think of everything. The McGuffin is like that and more. Wishes are granted instantaneously—even pausing for breath can cause horrible side effects. That's why not even the evil ones of Yuggoth have tried to use it. Too many bad examples. But it has the power, all the power anyone would ever require. Yes, indeed, it has that power. *That* is the object. Locate the McGuffin, steal it, and get out of there and bring it back here. Even trickier is to do this without using it, for to use it is to risk damnation."

"But *you* intend to use it," she pointed out.

"Perhaps. If I must. But I am better qualified to do so, because I know the limitations and I know the risks. Marge, I had no idea that this thing even existed until quite recently. Even less that it had this sort of power. Because it was fashioned in ancient times on Earth, it is not directly covered by the Rules; because it has been removed to here, there is not a whole heck of a lot left on Earth about it, either. I have confirmed, however, not only that it exists but that it can do the job. It can seal this rupture that is threatening to open between our world here and the bottommost layers of filth and decay that lie at the bottom of the Sea of Dreams. Irving, Poquah, and perhaps Macore will seek it with a *little* help from some denizens of Yuggoth who might prove more dangerous than the rest of the locals once the end is in sight but who are necessary for Irving to have any chance of moving within that realm."

"So you *do* have local help. Then what do you need *me* for in all this, other than because it's good symmetry?"

"Yuggoth is dangerous in the light of day, but it is truly nasty at night. You are a nocturnal with a great deal of immunity to the sorts of things that might threaten others at that time, and you can fly."

She shook her head sadly. "I think this is sick. Still, let me see the kid and I'll see if I can talk him out of this."

"The kid," Ruddygore repeated, smiling. "I think you might well be a bit disoriented on this as well. Come, let us go and find him by all means!"

The imp was about a foot tall and purple, with a perpetually nasty expression, rotten sharp teeth, and the personality of the gargoyle it resembled. It snarled and spat and its eyes flamed, and it was clearly a very dangerous creature restrained only by the candlelit barriers and the Tetragrammaton within.

And this was when it was trying to be helpful and nice. Irv couldn't imagine what the thing would be like if it didn't like him.

The human, wearing only a cotton loincloth, sat in a slightly modified lotus position facing the imp. In front of him were a series of small clay bowls with different-colored sands in each of them. Carefully and in the prescribed manner of the Rules on this aspect of shamanism—Volume 16 to be exact, which he had off to one side—he reached in and took a handful of several different sands at once, and with soft chanting and great care, he began to draw a design in front of him by letting the varicolored sands drip slowly from his fist. Although he had no control over the colors or the mixing, the result was an exotic design not unlike a varicolored mask of some strange, ancient creature on the dirt below.

The imp studied the design critically, craning its neck to follow the drawing at the correct angle as much as possible.

"Not too bad for an asshole," it commented. "Only thing is, this is a cross between a totem of the Benin City-States in the 1400s and Anastazi circa 1200. That kind of inconsistency weakens the totem. You get two different entities tryin' to answer, and they don't like each other much. Combine 'em and they just hate themselves."

"I can't deny my twin natures," the human responded.

"I keep tellin' you, it's *concentration*, you idiot!" the imp stormed. "You got to decide what in hell you're goin' for before you go, that's all! Isolate what you need from what you are. It's like you got a purse with coins of all sorts of shapes, sizes, and nationalities. You need coins that'll spend in *this* place, now, at this time. You don't reach into the purse and pick out all the coins and insist that they're all good! And you don't melt 'em down and give 'em a lump—which is about what you're tryin' here. You reach in and pick out the coins that spend where you are and put the rest away, right?"

"Yeah, well, that's a lot easier to do with coins than with your mind and soul."

"Of *course* it is! Otherwise *everybody'd* be doin' this and we'd never get *any* rest! That's the final knack of it. Most of the rest is all mechanical. Craft, that's all. The art's in how you can control yourself. What you got there is a plea for a hot fudge sundae from the god of turnips. The best you can hope to get is chocolate-covered turnips."

The young man shrugged. "Might make turnips edible, anyway."

The imp blew up almost literally in sheets of purplish flame. "Now, see! That's just what your problem is! You ain't got no discipline at all! They'll eat you alive when they get the chance! How you gonna ever best somebody who can call on the gods of war when you call up the gods of nosebleeds? Get with the program or say 'the hell with it!' and find something you *can* do well! You got all the talent, boy, but you ain't got the mind for this!"

And with that the imp vanished in a ball of flame.

Irving sighed and made a pass with his clenched fist over

the bowls, allowing a little sand from each to drop, and each color went back into its proper vessel. Once it was empty, he used his hand to completely rub out the weird face he'd drawn. What did they expect of him, anyway?

How could he make them see just how miserable he was? He'd been miserable since having been yanked here years before by his father, then abandoned while dear old Daddy went off to save the world—and did so at the cost of being turned into a green *Playboy* centerfold. The funny thing was, his father never even knew that *he* knew Dad hadn't died in the war. Nope, instead, brave old Daddy had run away in shame and hadn't been anywhere near his son, leaving said son to be raised by Santa Claus and his elves, all of whom lived in the castle of the Wicked Witch of the West.

He had the only father who'd flunked out both as a father *and* as a mother. Irving couldn't help but wish, as he had many times before, that Dad had at least tried *one* of those roles.

He heard someone coming and deliberately put the stuff away and got to his feet just as Ruddygore and Marge entered the chamber.

It was unclear which of them, Marge or Irving, was more shocked at the sight of the other. Irving at least had seen Marge and creatures like her, although not up close for a very long time. Ruddygore and the others here had spent a great deal of effort trying to ensure that he didn't have any private encounters with nymphs.

The last time Marge had seen the boy, he'd been literally that. Nothing so marked the dramatic passage of time in anyone's experience than seeing a child at one stage and then not seeing the same one again until long afterward.

Although young, the person who rose and stood facing her was hardly a child anymore. Irving was in fact pushing six feet tall with no absolute assurance that he'd stop growing. He was a handsome young man, too, with a finely honed muscular brown body that would have been the envy of almost any of his contemporaries and a finely featured angular face that seemed quite exotic-looking, blending the sharpest and most distinctive features of his Native American father and his African-American mother. Still, for all his lack of European ancestry, there was something of the Greco-Roman god in him, some kind of ancient ideal in deep, dark bronze, yet it was also clear by his looks that they had been attained by nature, not by any of Ruddygore's tricks.

Holy cow! Marge thought, a bit awed by the sight. He wasn't just a good-looking guy, he was *gorgeous*! She felt a little odd in a way she had nearly forgotten. She hadn't felt this way about the sight of a man since . . . since she'd been human.

"Irv, this is an old friend of your father's who was originally from your world. Marge, meet Irv," Ruddygore said.

"I don't remember seeing anyone who looked like you when I was growing up back on Earth," Irving noted, his voice already deep and rich yet with no trace of an accent at all.

"I've changed a bit since I got here," Marge assured him, sounding both nervous and a bit skittish. What was getting into her?

"It seems to happen pretty regularly," Irv commented a bit sourly. "After all, how many other people do you know whose fathers are wood nymphs?"

"I—well, nobody, of course." *Damn! What was wrong with her?* "It wasn't really his fault, though. It was that or die."

"We've been through this, Irving," Ruddygore commented patiently. "Until you are in a spot where you would have to make that choice for yourself or for someone else you care about—which I devoutly hope you won't have to ever do—you cannot sit in judgment on others. And by doing what he did instead of taking death or surrender, he also was able to dispatch one of the most dangerous and evil people I have known and make it possible to foil a plot to take over the whole world. I'd say it would have taken a lot more courage to do what he did than *not* to do it and let evil win."

"Yeah, well, I wasn't there," Irving responded petulantly.

Damn it, this is Joe's kid! Marge told herself, and got back some self-control. She was fascinated by his reaction in spite of the problems she was having. "I was," she managed, "and Ruddygore is right. I can promise you that."

"Yeah, well, it's what some of my tutors here have said. Dad won the war, but he blew the peace. Seems to me that if you have the guts to make that kind of decision, you should have the guts to learn to live with it, too."

"What . . . ?" Marge was totally confused at this attitude.

"Joe never told him," Ruddygore explained. "And didn't stay around very long afterward, either. Irving found out on his own. Somebody on my own staff slipped; still, we'd have to have told him sooner or later, anyway."

"Jeez! That's tough!" Marge said, genuinely sympathetic. "But your dad's one of the good guys—or was. Honest. Sometimes people do stupid things because they think they're better than what they *should* do. This sounds like one of those."

"I wouldn't know, now, would I?" Irving responded frostily.

Marge frowned. "Wait a second! You feel *that* way about your father and yet you're still willing to risk your neck and worse to find him? *Why?*"

Irving gave a wry smile. "It sure beats hanging around here."

Things wouldn't get any better, and Ruddygore, realizing it, excused them as quickly as he could.

"If I thought I was wrong for this expedition before, I'm doubly sure now," Marge told the sorcerer, relieved to be away. "It starts with his effect on me. I—I can't explain it, but it's not what a Kauri should feel."

Ruddygore nodded. "Yes, we've noticed it ourselves. It keeps growing stronger as he gets older, too. The odd thing is, he's essentially unaware of it and certainly has no knowledge of how to use it."

"You sure of that? That was a magic lab if I ever saw one back there."

"Oh, I'm sure. He has the talent of a major shaman but never a world-class magician. He's unaware of it primarily because I've had him under a fixed spell since puberty, one of many minor ones you might have noticed. We couldn't contend with all the temptations in a place like this."

"Oh, don't tell me he's gay! That would be too much!"

"No, he's not. At least I doubt it. He's nothing at all. He understands sex on an academic level, but absolutely nothing turns him on. Nothing. On a physical and emotional level it's still a mystery to him."

"You can't keep him that way," she noted. "Sooner or later that lid'll have to come off, and then the more repression you've caused, the worse the reaction. I'd really hate to see somebody like him, with that kind of power, let loose without learning control and responsibility."

"I agree, but there's little time for it. Besides, he'll be far too busy contending with other things to truly abuse it on *this* trip, and it may come in handy."

She stared at him. "*That's* what you want me for, isn't it? You want *me* to break him in, be both mother and play lover. I'm not sure I can do that, Ruddy. I'm not sure just which of us would be in control in that circumstance. I'm also not at all sure I like the big guy, no matter what his animal magnetism. That's one bitter and seething cauldron there. With that abnormal a background and his own resentment . . . I think he really blames his father for just about everything and wants revenge, not rescue. Frankly, he seems like one sick puppy to me."

"Perhaps. I've done what I could. The thing is, though, this is another of those matters where I have to be cold. *You*, even he, can go for Joe. That's fine, and I won't be judgmental. I suspect Joe's already fallen into much worse than even anything Irving can do to him, and if not, then no matter what either feels at the moment, I think finally bringing the two together in full knowledge of who the other is would be healthy for both of them. From my standpoint, though, I have to push all that to one side. The bottom line is that someone must bring me the Great McGuffin, period. I can solve the other problems if that occurs; if I do not get it, then everything else makes no difference. All that we know will cease to exist—Kauris, nymphs, and Irvings, too—and this world will be a pulsing cancer of pure evil."

Outside their ancient and sacred small homeland, the Kauris were few and were spread across the length and breadth of the world, so they seldom encountered one another in their wanderings until their mandated pilgrimage to cleanse themselves in the psychic and very real fires of their Holy Mother. Even so, they were never truly alone, though they usually were reminded of this only on the rare occasions when they needed some kind of correction.

"Marge?"

She was startled. *"Yes, Holy Mother?"*

"I didn't allow you to go over there to Terindell to beg off. I can smell the stink rising from fissures in Yuggoth even here. They cannot be permitted to widen and allow in that which must never take true physical form. Ruddygore's right in that regard: you let that happen and all our asses are grass."

"I came only because it was your command, as you know. I will go if that, too, is your command, but I would rather not."

"You bet your little wing tips you'll go if I command you!" The Holy Mother was not simply a leader but a supernatural force. If she commanded a Kauri, any Kauri, to stand on her head and spout poetry, then that Kauri would be absolutely powerless to refuse, and Marge knew it. The fact that they were having a dialogue at all was most unusual for the Holy Mother and definitely suggested that this was a high-stakes game.

"I do not lack the courage, Holy One. Surely you know that after all this time. It is the boy. He has a power over me that I am hard-pressed to resist and has it without even

knowing he does so. This kind of attraction is bad in most people, but it should not act at all upon faerie in general or Kauri in particular."

"But you controlled it."

"True," Marge admitted, *"but that was in an initial meeting, with Ruddygore present, and for a very short time. This would be day and night, constantly, and perhaps for months. It is not like the old Joe, even if he had also had this attraction. Joe was a genuinely interesting, likable man. This boy is cold and dark within; the attraction is un-merited, without reason, no more than a magical version of a love potion. Even as I feel the attraction, I find the man-boy behind it unlikable."*

She had once had a husband back on Earth who had been something like that. He was charming, sexy, hand-some, with tremendous animal attraction and a mean soul, a man who cheated anyone who loved him, whose promises were worth less than spit, and who took out his frustrations at the world by hurting others and feeling pleasure and re-lease by doing so. There was something in Irving de Oro's voice and something else in his eyes that had seemed very, very familiar.

"The boy was snatched from his mother and family and the world he knew, good or bad, and brought here, where he was subsequently abandoned," the Kauri goddess noted. *"He's been raised and educated in a household of strangers by people who do not understand families and the needs of growing boys and who think a kind word or a reward or a magic spell cures all. His father might—might—have saved him, by returning, by being honest, by raising the boy any-way and overseeing his development, and, most of all, by giving him the one thing he had little of back in his native world but expected more of here: love. His younger self came here because he sensed the loving and caring his fa-ther had for him in the mere act of coming for him. Then, at that tender age, he was abandoned and felt betrayed. He still feels betrayed. At heart he is still that little boy, looking for somebody to give him that kind of love."*

"Yeah, well, that might be true, but there's got to be some point at which you take responsibility for your own actions. My ex was beaten and abused growing up as well, but I knew men who also had been and who were determined that they would never be like that to others. Most poor people don't commit crimes, either. The majority of the people here are dirt-poor, but every time I hear poverty given as an excuse for evil, I have to laugh. I'm real sorry for Irving, but I didn't do it."

"Well, there's no getting around it, honey. That brat's gonna decide the fate of all our asses, so you got the job. I will give you some armor against his charisma, and Ruddygore can give you the keys to his fetters. Do I have to command you to go?"

Marge sighed. *"No. I'll go on my own, but for the sake of you and my sisters and to rescue Joe if I can. Not because Irving needs an education."*

"Start from down here near where Macore lives," Ruddygore instructed. "It's quite a long sea journey, and you will be dependent on ports in the region anyway for passage. As you might suspect, there isn't a whole lot of traffic, at least of the commercial sort, between Yuggoth and the rest of Husaquahr, and it's not the sort of spot folks go for holidays. Try to talk Macore into coming along—I think he'll be his usual great asset. In any event, he's the last person on *this* continent to have seen and spoken with Joe."

Marge, Poquah, and Irving all stood around, nodding at the instructions. Until then the boy hadn't evidenced much interest in getting to know Marge or the details of the trip, but now at least he seemed to realize that he couldn't just walk blindly off a cliff.

"I'd say it wouldn't be much on the usual shipping lanes," Marge noted. "Are you sure we can even *get* there in any reasonable time?"

"Oh, yes. That's the one thing about evil places. If you actually *want* to go there, there's always a way open to do so. The problem is never finding evil, it's getting away from it."

"All right, assuming we can get there in reasonable order, what then?" she pressed, feeling uncomfortably the leader of this mess. *Damn it! I was drafted—they don't draft generals!*

"Once you're off, I'll know where your first landfall will be and I will arrange for you to be met. Still, remember, once you're inside, you cannot trust *anyone* or *anything* on Yuggoth. The good people there are the ones who wouldn't stab you in the back for no reason at all, just if they had something to gain by it. Still, the agents we can use for this are primarily changelings like yourself, although of a darker nature. People whose absolute fanatic and uncompromisable lust for the McGuffin has taken them across the Sea of Dreams to Yuggoth but not completely to their goals. They will help you because you will facilitate them in attaining what they most desire. In general, you can trust them to get you there, but not once you get there or are clear to the goal. And if it looks like some other player can help them if they betray you, they'll have no hesitation in doing so."

"Sounds chummy," Marge noted glumly.

"You will be unable to find the McGuffin on your own; its concealed hiding place is known only to the King. He has agreed that if any of our representatives get to him, he will make that location known to them."

"Why not just tell us outright so that we may head straight for it?" Poquah asked, frowning.

"Well, for one thing, he doesn't want it known to others, and this decreases the chances of that happening," the sorcerer explained. "Second, if you can't make it to him, you can't make it there. And third, since you'll have native guides who also want the McGuffin—if they know, well, then, they won't need to be with you anymore, will they?"

Poquah was unconvinced. "But if we reach the King, assuming we do, and gain this information, won't the effect be the same?"

"Perhaps. Perhaps not. I'm sure he'll have something in

mind to guard against that. He always has the most arcane ideas for accomplishing things, but those things get done because nobody else can figure them out."

"How far will we have to go in this land before we reach His Majesty?" the Imir asked. "From the port city, that is."

"Yuggoth is roughly three thousand kilometers across by perhaps twenty-four hundred north-south. The King runs things from almost dead in the middle, atop some high mystical but natural formation called Castle Rock. That's where you must go."

"*How* big?" Marge was appalled. "Ruddy, that's something like fifteen hundred plus miles! That's longer than Texas is wide! And all filled with horrors and dark powers and creepy-crawlies, and all hands, tentacles, and whatnot against us! It can't be done!"

"Oh, I assure you that it can," the sorcerer told her. "Absolutely guaranteed. That is not to say that you *will* do it, but it is certainly possible with who and what you will have. What makes it more difficult than it is, is that this McGuffin must be in my hands—*in my hands*, not yours—in less than six months' time. If it is not, the fissures will be opened and the only option then will be a hasty escape for the powerful few. If the denizens of the muck beneath the Sea of Dreams actually make it through to reality, any reality, it is all over. If that happens, nothing, not even the McGuffin, will have the power to save us."

GETTING UP TO DATE

As a satisfactory motivator for actions of a Company, there must always be a McGuffin.

—Rules, Vol. VIII, p. 27(e)

"HE CERTAINLY HAS BEEN ONE FOR STUDY, THAT'S FOR certain," Poquah noted to Marge as they began their journey down the River of Dancing Gods to the sea and beyond in a private barge owned by Ruddygore. He was talking about young Irving, who seemed to be spending an inordinate amount of time sitting on deck studying a particularly fat book.

Marge nodded. "That's one of the Rules, isn't it? I wonder if Ruddygore knows it's missing."

"Oh, it's of no consequence," the Imir assured her. "We have several dozen sets around."

She had managed to control her less than rational reaction to Irving, but he still set off a peculiar mixture of emotions inside her ranging from animal attraction to severe distaste. It wasn't a good mix, but she felt she had to try to at least forge some kind of friendly business relationship with him if he'd allow her to do so.

She walked over to him and looked over his shoulder at the book, which appeared to have three parallel columns per page of markings resembling what would be left by a flock of wild birds in heat. This was not a language she related to any from back home.

"You can *read* that?" she asked, looking for an opening but also impressed in a very real sense. It was more than she could do after a lot longer there.

"It was tough at the start, but it's no big deal now," he responded. "There are a lot of words I still have trouble with, but you can usually figure them out by finding something inside that's familiar."

"Why so intent on this particular volume?" she asked him.

"It's the one on Yuggoth, of course," he said with a bit of impatience in his voice. "They got their own volume, believe it or not. I been trying to figure out what makes it so much worse than what anybody can meet here. I mean, we've got evil spirits, demons, zombies, vampires, and other kinds of things in the here and now, and ghosts are a dime a dozen. So what can be so special about *this* place?"

It was something she'd wondered about, too. "And do you know yet?"

"I think I'm getting the idea. Think of every horror movie, creepy story, you name it, that you ever heard. Put them all together. Now take out any *good* folks—that is, good races, good ghosts, good anything. That's Yuggoth. It's the place where bad dreams come from and where the bad guys go to learn how to be really bad."

"So how are we even supposed to survive this trip?" she asked him.

"Oh, I don't think they want to kill in Yuggoth. Too simple. They want to corrupt you, bring you over to their side. *That's* the real trick. Being good and honorable in Yuggoth? They can't even figure that out. They can't handle it. Giving in to temptation, to corruption—*that's* what they're after. *Then* it's payback time. That's gonna be a lot rougher than just fighting or sneaking around or something like that. No matter what, we've got to keep being the good guys."

She considered that. "I'm not so sure I like the sound of that. You can at least die and get out of it, but Poquah and me—we're already in as much of an afterlife as we get."

She also wondered if it was going to be as easy for the boy as he thought it might be. All that youthful, suppressed sexuality unleashed at once—who couldn't be corrupted, and fast?

And then there was Joe. Poor Joe. In that nymph's body,

tied to the trees to some extent and also to the flesh, how pure could he stay down there?

It took almost a week to get downriver, and it wasn't wasted time. In addition to getting to know the maps and layout of Yuggoth as much as possible, the three began to get to know each other a bit better. She got the impression that Irving was deliberately cool to her less because she was a woman than because she was a friend and defender of his father. Finally, one evening, she decided to press it a bit and see just how deep that went.

"Do you really hate your father, Irving?" she asked him, deciding that directness was the only approach that would work with the boy. "I mean it: is 'hate' the right word?"

"Maybe. I'm not sure," the boy admitted. "But I have no love at all for him. In fact, I think I'd rather have been left with Mom on the streets back home."

"From what I heard and from where you were living, you'd have been dead by your late teens, maybe addicted before that," she noted. "That's what he was scared of. It was partly drugs that split your parents up or at least kept them split, I think. He didn't want you going in that direction. He was really almost obsessed with saving you, Irving. He named his sword after you just so he'd always remember what he had left and what he was fighting for."

"But then he brought me here and left me! So now I got to go and maybe get killed or worse savin' his neck and hide to boot. And you're tellin' me it's better *here* than back home? That *I'm* better off? Mom had problems, sure, but she was gettin' clean. I know she was."

It was a point she couldn't press even though Poquah had pretty much clued her in that the boy's convictions were less that than they were the hopes and naivete of a young son who loved his mother far more than she loved him. In point of fact, Mom didn't have much use for her son at all; she just wanted him around because that denied the boy to Joe.

How did you tell a kid that, no matter what age he'd

grown to be? And how did you make him believe it when there was nothing else to fill that hole with?

"When a marriage splits, the two people who loved each other turn that old love to hate as often as not," she told him. "It was because your mom wouldn't let your dad even see you that a lot of this happened. Poor kid, you were just a football in a lot of this, I think, like a lot of kids get to be in these cases."

"You were human once. You ever have a kid?"

"No. I don't know if I couldn't or if it just didn't happen, but in the end it seems a good thing I didn't. If I had, I'd probably have stayed and taken it, and my husband would have gotten so drunk sooner or later, he'd have killed me or the kid and I'd have killed him." She sighed. "Kid, that's the one thing about this world. A select group of unhappy people from Earth get to try again here. Some make it, most don't, but they get the chance. You had no chance where you were. I'm not sure what chance you have now, but it's more up to you than it would have been had you stayed."

"Maybe. But my dad took a kid out of his own comfortable world—a world that might not have been real nice but was one I knew—and plopped him down here in the middle of Fairyland. Then he went off to fight a war and didn't come back. Only he *coulda* come back. *That's* what I hold against him. If he'd lost an arm or a leg or been scarred or burned or something, he'd still have come back, and you know it. Come back and been a dad. But oh, no! He got turned into a Greenie, a girl. Can't have *that*. The boy'll get screwed up if I'm not macho, right? Heap big Injun chief became a squaw. That was something *I* could have accepted—I didn't know him much, anyway. But it wasn't something *he* could accept or deal with. It was still Dad inside, though, in the mind, in the head. Like that, well, maybe if he really cared more about me than about himself and his big image, he coulda spent some time raisin' me and teachin' me and givin' me a little love and whatever else I needed in that big, lonely place. But uh uh. The kid might not *respect* him now as just a nothin', a *girl*. So he ran away and left me to grow up without *anybody*. I can forgive all the rest, but I can never forgive him for that. In the end he was more scared of bein' what he was than he cared about me."

"You're probably right on all that," she admitted, "but the fact is that being incredibly dumb in this area doesn't make him a bad guy, or girl, or whatever. He was raised in a very different way than either of us. I just don't think he could accept it. Maybe the *other* way, but the way it was, it was a kind of honor thing with him. I'm a little pissed off myself that he considered it a step down, but I wasn't raised his way. As dumb as it sounds or maybe is, I think he decided that you'd have no respect for him at all if he just showed up and told the truth. Somehow he really believed that if you could just be convinced he died a hero in that last battle, you'd somehow turn out better than if he showed up as a wood nymph. I don't know. Neither of your family ethnic cultures held women on a high plane. I think the real tragedy is that everybody just *assumes*. Nobody ever asks the kid what *he* thinks would be best."

Irving shrugged. "Well, I know one thing from reading this stuff. Either he's as brave as or braver than he ever was or he's even stupider than you say he is. I mean, Dad and one other girl went into Yuggoth cold turkey, without even the knowledge or powers *we* got, and that's not all that great."

She nodded. "Still, if you feel this way, why risk yourself to maybe try and save a perfect stranger, anyway?"

He gave a wan smile and said, "Because I'm not about to do to him what he did to me. If I don't at least make the *attempt* to save him, am I any better than he was by not coming back and being a parent to me? Besides, I got to know a little about myself. I want to know if I've got the guts I think he should have had or if cowardice and stupidity run in the family."

"I think you might be very surprised," she told him. She was. Deep down, if she could keep him in that kind of mood, there almost seemed somebody she could actually like down there.

"Um, Irv, are you also aware of the effect you have on women?"

He gave a dry chuckle. "Yeah. What a waste, huh?"

"You don't find them attractive? At all?"

"Oh, I guess, sort of. I don't understand women much. I've talked to you as an equal longer and more seriously than I think I've talked to any other woman since I left Earth. I understand on an academic level, I guess, but not personally. I know it's partly a spell—I have the knack for that myself, remember—but it's still not something I know firsthand. I'm not even sure I *want* to."

"Huh? Oh, I can tell you, there's a lot of fun in it."

"Fun? Yeah, maybe. Feel-good stuff, too. I know. But at what cost in self-control? You asked me if I hated my father. I'm trying very hard not to. I'm trying not to let any emotions overcome me other than maybe a sense of humor and a sense of tragedy. The spell itself isn't difficult, you know. It's a common spell used by adepts to keep themselves from being tempted during magical training. I see no profit in lifting it, particularly not now."

"Scared you couldn't control it?"

"Perhaps. Maybe I'm scared because I see how those girls react to me and how my mom and others reacted to their men. I don't think I want that. Not now. It's too much of a diversion. Better for now I stay where I am until I can control all of my mind and body."

Marge stared at him and sighed. "You're right, kid. What a waste."

Macore was still a few days away.

Quinom was an old and somewhat seedy but still very popular ocean resort on the southern coast of Leander. Although the town itself had obviously seen better days and the upkeep on a tropical tourist trap was a bit higher than the locals had been willing to pay, it still had a harbor crowded with small pleasure boats, fishing vessels, and all sorts of recreational craft.

Just beyond the pier was what Marge would accept as an obvious boardwalk area, a long line of shops, stalls, games, and whatnot that stretched in back of a wooden walkway that divided town from beach.

"The last I heard, Macore was talking about a nice, quiet, peaceful retirement," she noted. "This looks like a circus."

"It is suited to his temperament," Poquah responded dryly. "One suspects that the phrase 'quiet, peaceful retirement' means in Macore's world view a place where he is not wanted by the authorities."

"It's kind of a neat place," Irving put in. "I always loved it when the old man sent me down here for a while each year."

Marge looked at the crowded harbor and town area and shook her head in wonder. "Just where is he in all this? And what's he doing?"

"Up the boardwalk a bit, down at the end of that far pier there," Irving said, pointing well off to their left as they came in toward the dock. "This is the jumping-off point for the Mystic Islands, remember. Folks like to go out and see them and all the strange stuff without actually risking landing. With a good, fast vessel like Macore's you can get out there in about an hour, sail down the strip of islands for an hour and point out the main sights, then get on back. The tourists pay big money for that kind of thing."

"Three-hour tours of the islands," Marge muttered. "And I suppose his boat's called the *Minnow*?"

"Yeah, it *is*! How'd you know that?"

She sighed. "I'm afraid Macore's become too predictable. That's probably why he had to retire."

Making their way from the main dock over to the tourist boat pier wasn't very difficult, although Irving felt uncomfortable doing it. It wasn't as if he were actually doing anything, but watching all those female heads turn and follow him with their eyes and expressions as he walked self-consciously by, making him feel like a piece of meat or maybe an ice cream cone they all wanted to lick, was a bit unnerving. One thing about Irving—he was never going to be inconspicuous.

It was much easier to see where the boat had left from than to find it; clearly a tour was on, as the slip was empty. There was, however, a kiosk where you could buy tickets just in front of the slip, and as they approached, there came the sudden sounds of an unseen ghostly chorus.

> *"Just sit right back and you'll hear a tale,*
> *A tale of a fateful trip.*
> *That started from this tropic port*
> *Aboard this tiny ship . . ."*

"How's he *doing* that?" Marge asked, conscious that the last thing you would find in Husaquahr was electricity.

"Some sort of spell," Poquah responded with a weary sigh. "I believe the Master procured it for him, but he still had to pay a good deal for it. Not as much as he has to pay to ensure that his batteries keep being charged on those infernal Earth devices, but those at least are for him alone."

"I'm surprised the Council let him keep them," Marge commented, knowing that Poquah was referring to Macore's battery-powered television and videotape recorder, which he used so that he could view his complete collection of *Gilligan's Island* tapes. "They are a dangerous anachronism here."

"So long as they remain private, it is all right," Poquah assured her. "Also, Macore appears to have convinced a majority of the Council that maintaining them is the only certain defense against zombies."

"There is definitely a grain of truth in that," Marge acknowledged. "I always *did* wonder who the true audience for that show was until I saw its effect on the Army of the Dead."

"There's the boat coming now!" Irving shouted, and they looked where he was pointing.

The boat was a medium-sized sailing vessel, rather sleek

and trim and nicely kept up and in some ways a bit too elaborate for the kind of work it was being asked to do.

"Oh, Uncle Macore lives aboard," Irving told them. "The tourists pretty much stay above, and his own pretty nice place is below."

There were a half dozen or so tourist types aboard, clearly from wealthier merchant families in the City-States from their look and dress. The rest were crew members, with a greater number required for this boat than for the original television *Minnow*, and they were very, very different.

"Good grief! His whole crew is water nymphs!" Marge exclaimed.

At that moment a smaller boat crossed right in front of the *Minnow* and one exotic-looking crewwoman let out an unnaturally loud series of *whoop! whoop! whoop!* sounds that scared not only the small boat but half the harbor as well.

"Well, nymphs and sirens," Poquah noted dryly.

A few moments later gray shapes rose on one side of the boat and began bumping and nudging it toward its berth as all sails were taken in. That close in, all boats of any size allowed the pilot whales to bring them safely to a halt in the right spot.

Two buxom water nymphs threw out lines, and then one jumped to the dock and began tying off the boat. Water nymphs generally looked like all the other kinds of nymphs but tended to come in a variety of sizes and colors and seemed somewhat translucent. The nearest two were an azure blue nymph and a creamy white one, the first with green hair and the second with silver locks. The siren, another type of nymph, was a fiery red color and much larger than the average nymph, and it seemed as if there were at least one more somewhere in the back.

At the wheel aft of the mainsail was a small, wiry figure dressed only in a pair of shorts but wearing an oversized sailor's cap. His skin was tanned so dark that it seemed as if he were of some other, more tropical race, and his long,

unkempt hair and equally messy full beard were gray going
fast toward white.

Marge felt shock at the appearance of the captain. She
remembered Macore as an eternally young little man with
coal black hair and catlike movements. Somehow, sometime since she'd last seen him, the little retired master thief
had grown *old*.

The tourists were no sooner off the ship than Macore
spotted his visitors standing there on the dock and bounded
toward them with some semblance of his old energy. "Irv!
Poquah! Good to see you!" he called out cheerily, coming
down to greet them. He stopped, frowned, and looked at the
colorful winged faerie between them. "Marge? That you?"

"Hi, Macore. I hadn't realized it, but it seems to have
been a long time," she said with a smile.

He grinned. "Well, I'm fifty-seven now, and that's really
all right with me. I mean, ninety-five percent of all the people in my old profession would be either in jail or executed
by now!"

The idea of a fifty-seven-year-old Macore, let alone the
sight in front of her, brought home the different world in
which she now existed as even the sight of a grown-up
Irving couldn't have done. It was a graphic example of why
faerie were always taught that interacting with humans was
fine but they should never form attachments or get to know
them all that well. There was a phrase for it, universal
among the fairy folk of all sorts but one she'd never really
thought much about until this moment.

They pass . . . We endure.

She laughed at his still-flippant attitude, though, and his
apparent high spirits. "I'm glad you seem pleased to see us,
but you don't seem all that surprised," she noted.

His expression grew a bit more serious. "I kind of expected something of this sort. Not sure who all would be in
the Company, but it was kind of inevitable. Come on
aboard and I'll have the girls find us some nice, cool drinks
and comfortable seats."

"I see you have an all-female faerie crew," Marge noted.

He grinned in mock-evil fashion. "Hey, if I'm ever cracked up during one of these tours, I sure as hell don't want to be stuck on some deserted island for years with some dork professor who can invent anything except a way off, a mate too dumb to make fire, and a bunch of people who refuse to accept their fate. Uh uh. You pick who *you* want to crash with, and I'll pick who and what *I* want to crash with."

Marge was startled as they came aboard and all the faerie crew turned as one, sighed, and said, "Hi, Irving!"

"Hello, girls," he responded, a bit resigned but clearly impatient with the attitude they expressed.

Still, Macore was as good as his word, and soon they were all sitting on comfortable deck furniture or pads, relaxing, and the drinks were actually chilled. With a cold drink and a warm breeze near sunset, things were just about perfect.

"The cold drinks are a little secret shared by a few regulars here," he explained. "There's a cold current out there, and you can drag through it, and whatever bottles you have get cold and stay that way in the coolers here. Most folks here don't have a real taste for cold drinks, but I figured you still did."

"It's been a long time, but yeah," Marge agreed. As a Kauri she did not eat, at least in the way humans and animals did, but virtually all faerie still had to drink and had a real appreciation for flavored waters and good wines and beers.

"You said you were not surprised to see us," Poquah prodded after a while.

Macore nodded. "I figured it out when Joe and that weird halfling girl came through a few weeks back. Talk about somebody nearly impossible to recognize!"

"Who? The halfling girl? You knew her?"

"No, no! I mean *Joe*, of course. Frankly, unless you talk for a while, you'd be hard pressed to tell her—er, him—er, *whatever*—from any old garden variety wood nymph except maybe a lot spunkier. Um, sorry, Irv."

"No problem," Irving responded. "We aren't exactly close, remember, in the usual ways, and we aren't close by blood, either, at this point, considering that she runs tree sap in her veins."

"Yeah, well, anyway, we at least got to talkin' a little bit of old times," the ex-thief continued, "and suddenly it's questions about Yuggoth, of all places. I don't even like to say the *word*, let alone think about actually *going* there! And a wood nymph and a halfling girl by themselves? It was nuts. I wouldn't send the *old* Joe there with a legion of troops, let alone *those* two!"

"Have you been there yourself?" Marge asked him.

He shivered. "Once. Briefly. And I've been close to it now and again. I don't have any great ambitions to go farther, let alone get shipwrecked on or near the place. Unless you use one of the ships specially made for the passage, there's nothing around that whole damned continent except things to snare you and enchant or kill you: sirens, harpies, witches, sea hags, Circes, and all sorts of things, not to mention sea monsters and all the rest. It's nearly impossible to get there on your own safely except through blind luck. The place *breeds* those things!"

"But they went?"

He nodded. "I *guess* so. They had a little money, and it was probably enough for the hovecraft."

"You mean hovercraft?" Marge asked him.

He shrugged. "They all call it a hovecraft around here, that's all I know. Spooky ship, I'll tell you that. Takes folks in on occasions, but very few come back. They wanted me to go with 'em—at least Joe did. I got the impression that the halfling didn't want anybody else around. That and common sense was why I refused any offers of helping them out beyond what little I did here. I think, though, that they were between the rock and the hard place themselves. At least, not five days after the two of them left, the others showed up hunting them."

"Others?" Poquah was suddenly curious.

Macore nodded. "Real nasties, too. Couldn't tell much

about them. They came at night in shiny black armor, the interior of the visors jet black. I don't know why, but I had the idea of big, man-sized insects on horseback. They sure weren't human, but they weren't any faerie I'd ever seen before, either."

"And they were after Joe?"

"Actually, they were after the halfling, but I got the impression that Joe was on the short list of folks to get even with. I'll tell you this—you don't say no to guys like that. At least you don't do it twice. I could only hope that by being vague and not volunteering information I might buy 'em a little time."

"And did you?" Marge wanted to know.

"Hard to say. I think they already knew more than me, even about the two of them tryin' to make for Yuggoth. There was this magic ring from her late father that said to go there and get something."

"We know that part. But how could they possibly think they had a chance to do it? Even Ruddygore thinks that our chances are only so-so in alliance and cooperation with the King of Horror himself. These two wouldn't have nearly that, and what they're after is a secret from most everybody except the King," Marge told him, pretty well relating Ruddygore's take.

"Could be," the old man admitted. "Still, seems to me that you got at least as much chance if you have a map."

"A map! They've got a map to the McGuffin?" Marge was suddenly excited. "Where did they get it? How? Even Ruddygore doesn't have that information."

"They got it all right, because that's what I did for them. Broke the damnedest encryption spell I ever saw. Damned near got me, too. I was rusty, but I still got through it. There's never been a thief like me!"

"Stop patting yourself on the back so much and tell me about the halfling," Marge responded, shaking her head. "What's her story?"

Macore shrugged, then told them all pretty much what Alvi had told to Joe, plus Joe's account of her rescue. He also described the halfling in a way that made her seem far more of a monster than she really was. "Pretty face, though. Really pretty."

"You believe she was truthful?" Poquah probed.

"Leading Joe along, you mean? Naw. She wasn't that kind, and I can usually tell 'em. On the other hand, I'm pretty sure she's almost driven to try this crazy thing on Yuggoth."

"A curse, you mean?" Marge asked him. "You saw it?"

"Uh uh. With as much crap as most halflings have, you couldn't tell a curse from a beauty treatment, and you know it. Too much crazy magic on those one-of-a-kinds. No, what set my nose twitching was how determined she was in spite of the fact that I got the strong idea she wasn't at all unhappy just the way she was. Hell, *Joe* has more drive to find that thing and use it than she seemed to have. You spend your whole life hiding out, a virtual prisoner, denying what you are—and, like, she's never been anything *but* what she is, so she's got no comparisons—and then you come out like this, and the world doesn't end and the mobs don't grab torches and chase you. You even find a friend with tons of experience. See what I mean?"

Irving shifted. Until then he'd been taking no real part and showing very little apparent interest. Now, though, he said, "But somebody *is* chasing her, right? Those things in armor, the manlike insects? And somebody tried to capture her when her father was killed. I don't know, but if I had that kind of situation, I think maybe I'd want to change into something more comfortable myself."

"Good point," Marge agreed, a bit surprised at the boy's sophisticated reasoning. Maybe she *had* underestimated him. "But who *was* her father? And mother, for that matter? What are these creatures that seem so bold but nobody seems to be able to identify? Who wants her, and obviously alive? As a halfling, the laws of the human world here wouldn't allow her to inherit. She's classed as faerie whether any faerie will accept her or not. It doesn't make any sense." She sighed. "If only we knew her *real* father! But even she didn't know *that*."

"There is one possibility," Poquah commented. "An enchantment. An enchantment so comprehensive that it can be broken only by beating overwhelming odds and gaining what is most unlikely. A halfling could easily hide that."

"Huh? You mean she's really *not* a halfling? But what good would *that* do? I mean, if you can't break it without the McGuffin, then it's the same as real, and they obviously don't want her to get to that thing," Marge pointed out.

"True," the Imir agreed. "However, you overlook the obvious possibility of a truly perfect enchantment. Someone, perhaps only one person, knows. This one also is the only one who either knows how to break the enchantment or has the means, often a physical object, with which to do so. He, she, it, whatever, needs the girl at a certain age when the enchantment can be broken. Whoever, whatever, the enchantment hides may have great power, or great authority, or great wealth and knowledge, or be the key to gaining it. I wish we had her at Terindell. We might well be able to at least find out the meaning of it all. Now she's out there somewhere, with Joe her only friend, walking straight into the most dangerous place in the world, pursued by a legion. I would say that we have little time to lose on this."

Macore looked at them and shook his head in wonder. "So you three are going after them, after all?"

"Close enough," Poquah replied. "We will go after the McGuffin. They are headed toward the same goal, so it is one and the same thing. In my hands, the McGuffin may get safely to Ruddygore. In *his* hands, it will solve the problems and mysteries that vex us all."

"We kinda hoped you'd come with us for old time's sake," Marge told him. "Off one last time into the great adventure. Isn't it tempting?"

Macore looked around at his nymph crew and boat and tropical port and then fingered his gray-white whiskers. "No, it's not. It might have been once upon a time. Might even have been irresistible. The thing is, Marge, I'm not like you. I'm not like *any* of the rest of you, which should be pretty clear if you just think about it."

"Huh? What do you mean?"

"Marge—you, Joe, Poquah—you're faerie. You don't age. Time has only local meaning to you, as in morning, noon, night, or next week. Irv's a big, strong lad, and he's not faerie, that's true, but he's only in his teens and about primed to make a name for himself. Either that or he'll die, but I don't think you will, Irv. I think there's too much in the way of smarts in your blood and bone for that. So, what do we have? Faerie, a sorcerer who's beyond any of us, a kid out to carve a reputation for himself in the manner of Husaquahrian legends—and then you've got me. I'm old. I'm old and mortal, and I'm not getting any younger. I have aches in my joints whenever the weather's changing, my eyes don't see clearly the way they once did, and things that were once easy for me come hard. The *talent's* still there, and my brain almost always says, 'Macore, you're still twenty years old and the world's greatest thief,' but then my body interrupts and says, 'No, you ain't, either. You're an old fart, and your adventure days are past.' And that's the way it is. I'm lucky I can do it enjoyably and comfortably, but I'm falling apart. I can see the darkness at the end coming even though I can hardly believe it's me in this situation, and I can't figure for the life of me how it all went so fast. But the only thing I got left is my soul, if it's worth much these days and if it doesn't have too many second mortgages on it. I ain't sure what comes after the dark I can see, but I sure don't want to hurry it."

It was a strong, profound, and serious statement clearly coming from his heart, and it wasn't easy to dismiss what he was saying or talk him out of it because the truth of it was all too evident. For the first time since coming there Marge suddenly realized that there was a chance that one day she'd come for a visit and Macore wouldn't be there anymore, or anywhere else, either. Even Irving would age almost before her eyes and one day crumble to dust as well.

That was why you weren't supposed to get too close to humans, ever.

"Macore . . ." she began, but couldn't think of anything to say.

He smiled. "Don't worry about it. It's time. The younger generation replaces the old. In one sense I've got better odds than the rest of you, since there's *something* beyond that dark wall for me, but you're stuck where you are. In a sense, that's the other reason for not coming. Maybe I get killed, but that's looming anyway. But what if I got *you* killed, or Poquah, by being too slow or too sore or just not up to moving at the speed safety demanded? You're probably gonna get yourselves killed anyway, since you keep going out on these damn-fool quests, but if that happens, it should be on *your* head, not my conscience or my soul. You're immortals. You die and that's *it*. I won't be responsible for that."

"We'll miss not having a master thief of your experience, but I understand," Marge assured him. "Still, I wish we weren't going in so damned blind. This is tough enough as it is, but I think I'd give a lot for that map."

Macore grinned. "Oh, I don't think you need to give up *that* much," he said playfully, reaching into a folder and pulling out a large folded piece of parchment. He handed it to her, and she unfolded it.

"The *map*! But—you didn't let Joe go off without it, did you?"

Macore sounded hurt. "Of course not. They have exactly the same map you do right here. The thing was contained in a monstrously encrypted spell. You don't think I wouldn't make a *copy*, do you? It's almost second nature to steal anything that comes along, even this. I lifted some pretty nifty official secrets with this technique once upon a time, and several treasure maps."

It was quite dark, so they brought the lamps close to examine the map. It showed a continental mass that even *looked* ugly.

"Looks like a giant clutching hand with claws," Marge noted.

"If you take the hovecraft, which is the fastest way there, then you'll land here, at Red Bluffs," Macore told them, pointing to an area midway between the fingers of the "hand."

"Seems pretty much like an advertisement to land in a town," Irving noted worriedly.

"Well, it's not all that bad, and it's not like they won't know you're coming," the former thief replied. "The hovecraft is the only assurance that you'll get by all the evils that surround the place, and that means tickets, and that means everybody official will know, right? It's no big deal. You have to take Yuggoth on its own terms. Sure, it's the source of all evil, but in many ways it's just another place with a lot folks, a lot of races, a lot of threats, and maybe even some normal types. Even some good guys."

"Good guys? But you and everybody else said you couldn't trust anybody there!"

"You can't *trust* them, but that's because you never know who you *can* trust. Look, think it out. You can't have pure evil without victims. Otherwise it's just an intellectual exercise. So the vast majority of folks on Yuggoth are, like everywhere else, just ordinary folks. Hell, suppose there weren't any normal folks for vampires to bite. I mean, they'd all starve, right? And there have to be folks to dominate, to take over, to rule and oppress, like that. And now and again, from that kind of stock, rises somebody who can really battle the evil bastards. It's just a million times more likely that the scientists really are mad, that the nice boy next door really is an ax murderer, that the local meat market—well, you get the idea."

"Um, yeah. Sort of."

Irving held up the Rules volume. "I've been studying things about it. It's not a place where I'd like to live, but at least it's still got rules. Wolfsbane, garlic, crosses, those sorts of things still work. There's nothing over there that's any more absolute than here."

"Well, yeah. But there's a lot more of it, and it's a lot more concentrated and in a lot more varieties. And once you're there, you're committed to one of a limited series of options," Macore warned them.

"Yeah? Like what?" Marge asked.

"Well, get control of that McGuffin thing and you're made and home free. Otherwise, you'll wind up either being trapped there or corrupted, warped, and changed until you are more at home there than here. Nobody who gets on the hovecraft ever comes back and walks off it at this end."

"*You* said you'd been there—and you got back," Irving noted.

He nodded. "Yeah, but you don't know the deal I had to make or what I had to do. That's why I have such doubts about what's beyond that darkness I see ahead. You don't want to do anything close to that if you can help it, kid. I was stupid-ass lucky, nothing else. And these two—they are made of different stuff. Don't count on coming out of there whole. You plan to get that McGuffin and wish all of you out whole. You just don't want to deal with any alternatives."

CRUISING DESTINY'S THREAD

The Land of the Sources of Evil shall always be across the waters toward some bleak shore.

—Rules, Vol. XIII, p. 666(i)

THEY HAD DISCUSSED VARIOUS WAYS OF REACHING YUG-goth, but eventually the evidence both from Macore and from other old hands around the docks convinced them that the hovecraft was the only reasonable way in. Out was a different question entirely. Additionally, word came by messenger from Ruddygore that their passage had been taken care of, which kind of settled the question. The message also stated that as yet even the nearly all powerful wizard hadn't been able to put a background to the halfling or a true name to the slain stepfather. It seemed almost inconceivable that that much could be hidden from Ruddygore, and this indicated to them all that whoever was behind this was very powerful and very formidable, indeed, in all realms.

The boat sailed once a week from its own private dock about ten kilometers west of the resort. It was a lonely spot, forced on the operator by a tourist industry that didn't want anybody scared off.

In point of fact, it looked like *nobody* wanted much to do with them. The spot consisted of a large pier, a small closed terminal and ticketing kiosk, and nothing else or any sign that anyone had set up even temporarily to help the passengers either on or off. There wasn't even a large sign to indicate what docked or sailed from this remote place, but somehow, just looking at it, you *knew.* You could feel it, a kind of deep chill down to your very soul.

Of course, gargoyles on the ticket kiosk didn't help, either.

Large black birds circled above and occasionally came down and landed on the kiosk. The huge yellow-eyed creatures seemed to be the masters of the area; the gulls and others so prevalent elsewhere seemed to avoid the place.

"Ravens," Marge noted. "It figures."

Irving walked up to the kiosk, ignoring the birds, and read the very fancy sign in the window. "Arrives one hour after sundown every Monday, leaves one hour before sunrise every Tuesday. Nice. I wonder what happens if it's late and doesn't get off until sunrise. Does it turn to dust or explode or something?"

Marge yawned. "Well, being a night person myself, I can't complain about the scheduling, but I guess we ought to keep crucifixes and the like around anyway, huh?"

"No religious symbol, for good or evil, has any power without the holder's complete and absolute faith in what it represents," Poquah reminded her. "I'm afraid we are all much too jaded to depend on that."

"Um, yeah. It *does* sort of put us at a disadvantage," she admitted.

Irving wandered back over, frowning.

"What's the matter, Irv? Second thoughts?"

"No," he replied. "I was just wondering where everyone else is."

"Huh? What do you mean?"

He looked up at the sky for a moment. "I would say we're no more than an hour or so before sundown. It's Monday, so unless they're skipping a week, they should be here in about two hours, right?"

"Yeah, I guess so. So?"

"Well, where's the traffic? *Somebody* has to use this service. That's a pretty big dock from the looks of it, and the length of space between the knobs they use to tie things up shows a pretty fair-sized boat, too. You don't run a big boat empty. You either run a small boat or no boat, right? But here we are, maybe two hours ahead of the boat, and we're the only ones here."

Poquah looked around and shook his head. "I don't

know, but something tells me that we will find the answer to this shortly. I *feel* it. We will not be the only passengers."

And as the sun set and shadows began to shimmer and then blend into the landscape, he was proved correct.

You needed faerie sight to see them, but Irving's cultivation of some magical powers in his own right had given him that ability, which his two companions had as a matter of course. It was not, however, an unmixed blessing, particularly in this case.

It began with what seemed like the wind, although there was no wind, a great, deep roar of misery, a cosmic sigh of regret, coming, it seemed, from all places at once. Then, slowly, they began to arrive and resolve themselves in the total darkness.

People . . . long chains of people, male and female, all linked together by spell threads so deep and dense that they seemed jet black. All were nude, and in spite of a deathly pale cast to their skins and a hollow, hopeless series of expressions that were hard to look at, they seemed in the main no older than Irving and in excellent shape. It was easy to see, though, that they were not what they appeared; although they seemed to be regular humans of a number of human racial types, the bodies were actually entirely faerie.

"Human souls," Poquah explained, shaking his head.

Marge was aghast. In all the time she'd been on this world, she'd never seen anything like it. "But—they look so *healthy!*"

"In a sense they are. This is the true faerie component of humanity," the Imir told her. "Everyone comes out his ideal and ageless self, of course. However, these will soon change, as this material is both malleable and corruptible. It is raw material on its way to the foundry to be reshaped to their new masters' whims."

"Then they're on their way to Hell? Via *boat?*"

"Perhaps. Some will go there, some won't. Don't think of Hell as a place of eternal punishment. It is not, except in the sense that it is totally removed from all that is Heaven. These people are now at the eternal mercy of Hell and its rulers. In a sense, going the other way is the same thing, but it is generally felt that God and the angels are much better to work under than Satan and the demons. Just don't think of it as necessarily eternal punishment. These people are being sent where their souls' owners wish, to be used for those owners' purposes."

A mysterious tall, dark figure nearby overheard the explanation and came over toward them. It wore a dark robe and hood, and only the glow of two beady red eyes and a larger glow below showed any features at all.

"Hello, brothers and sister," the creature greeted them in a deep but convivial voice that sounded so silky smooth, it reminded Marge of a Texas politician. "Couldn't help overhearing your explanation, there, friend, and you're pretty much on the mark." A black arm went up and took something from the mouth, and as the glow swept down with it, they could see that the mysterious larger object was a very large, fat, and somewhat smelly cigar. "Nimrod's the name. Louie B. Nimrod. That's my string over there." He pointed to a long and typically unhappy lot, and they could now see the nearly absolute black of the spell against the night that linked them to the demon.

"You're taking them to Hell?" Marge asked uneasily. "I thought if you were supposed to go there, you just *went*."

"Oh, my, no! I'm taking them to Yuggoth, of course. I assume that's why you and everybody else are here. I mean, this boat don't go to Hell, little lady. You're right to some extent about not needing some of this in the more routine operations, but you *always* got to collect 'em. Even the enemy collects. They generally got an easier collection job than we do, of course. Damn fools actually *want* to go with them. They don't know the eternity of total boredom that awaits them up there."

"Your reputation for what happens to them after they go with you does not include boredom in general, I'll give you that," Marge commented dryly.

"Oh, it's not *nearly* that bad. I mean, we're not talking circles of punishment and fiery pits and all that rubbish.

Why would we? That would put us in the business of punishing the enemies of our enemy, wouldn't it? That lake of fire business is if we lose, and we've not lost by a long shot. We're at *war*. These are *soldiers*. They became soldiers the moment they enlisted in our cause when still alive, and they're even more useful now that they've gone through their enlistment incentives and bonuses."

"Enlistment incen— oh!" Marge suddenly realized that the demon was talking about whatever these people got from demons like Nimrod while still alive. It took a little mental gymnastics to switch points of view here. "So what do they do for you now?"

"Well, now that they're totally ours, they go to work. Privates all, of course. Pretty rare to get instant officer material from the living, although it *does* happen. These are mostly support troops in the making. We'll put 'em in and train 'em on Yuggoth in the basics. Sort of the ditchdiggers, heavy laborers, that kind of thing. We'll evaluate, test, observe, and the most promising ones will eventually get promoted, while the rest will stay down doing the crap work that always has to be done by somebody. And of course we'll be checking for special skills and aptitudes to develop."

"Is this normal, though?" Poquah asked him. "So many off to Yuggoth instead of to Hell?"

The demon took another puff and then replied, waving his cigar for emphasis like a prop. "See, we don't have to *enlist* most folks. They volunteer, whether here or on Earth. We don't even bother with them. *These*, though, are ones I had to enlist. Ones with a real possibility of going the enemy's way. *These* are the ones we really prize, since they're generally the most useful to us and have the most potential to harm the enemy. We always keep our bargains to the letter, so now they all get their chance before being sent down. It's not always easy, I don't mind telling you! I mean, we don't even bother with the usual types— murderers, rapists, torturers, politicians, lawyers, TV evangelists, that sort. *These*, now—revolutionaries, wide-eyed save-the-world types, bleeding hearts, guilt trippers—these people all had the best of intentions, the noblest and most self-sacrificing of motives. That's where *I* come in. My firm, Azaroth, Beelzebub, Zarnath, and Smith, P.A., is one of the top recruiting firms in Husaquahr. Why, in independent surveys by I. M. Power, four out of five of our *clients* rated us tops in delivering what we say, and our collection rate is among the best in the business. You won't catch ABZS clients haunting houses and stalking graveyards, no, indeed!"

"It is nice to see someone happy in his work," Marge whispered.

Another, larger demon noticed them and came over. "You been puffin' yourself up again, Louie? If you're that good, how come you're workin' the poor side of the street instead of Earth?"

"Seniority, that's all, and you know it!" Nimrod snapped back.

"Seniority, my ass!" the newcomer snapped. "You really want to know, folks? Because we're threatened with a two-front war, that's why! We need every soul in creation to build the dikes in Yuggoth or we're gonna get drowned, that's what!"

Nimrod sounded genuinely shocked. "Blasphemy! Can't *nobody* beat *Hell*!"

"Not one on one," the newcomer agreed. "But if we have to fight on two fronts, and if our ancient enemy is willing to turn its back on Husaquahr like usual, then we'll be stuck right in the middle. These souls aren't goin' to no backwater, folks! They're headed for the new front lines!"

"Pardon me," Poquah said with his usual quiet authority, "but do I understand that there is someone attacking your people on Yuggoth?"

"You heard me right, friend," the second demon said, nodding. "Somebody woke up the Ancient Ones from their long sleep and is preparing to let them through. The only common enemy we and you know who have is threatening to get loose. If they break out, half the dark forces will turn traitor just because they see the power, and since *we're* the ones who'll most get it in the neck over here, Old Sweetness and Light won't intervene until it's probably too late. He'd rather see this whole universe fall than help us. Makes you wonder how they can love a guy like that. And they wonder why we rebelled!"

Marge had a sudden eerie realization of just what the demons and the Imir were talking about. *God!* God from the opposing point of view . . .

"They didn't tell me anything about this," Nimrod sniffed. "This was supposed to be a milk run! They *promised*!"

"Yeah, well, you know what promises are worth," the other demon commented. "Buck up! You might have a chance to lead these miserable souls into battle against the greatest threat we can think of. Think of the *glory!*"

"Think of the hurt," Nimrod grumped.

The older demon turned from his companion in disgust and sniffed contemptuously. "How come *you* folks are heading toward Yuggoth?" he asked, apparently no more than curious. "Not too many faerie of your lineage go near the place, and that boy over there—he's red meat."

"Do not underestimate the boy," Poquah warned. "He is working out a destiny under the Rules. As for us, we have been asked to go down and see exactly what you were just speaking about. I am the chief adept and majordomo for Master Ruddygore, and the lady here is a long veteran of his service. The boy is under his general protection."

"Ruddygore, huh? I heard of him. Does he think he's gonna get a progress report from you or what? It's a lot tougher to get *out* of there than *in*."

"So we have heard, but do not underestimate our patron, either," the Imir responded smoothly. "We are under the seal and protection of His Majesty the King who sits upon the Throne of Horror. We should not be considered at risk in any event, I should think. Our job is to see how great the danger and its nature and to see if there is anything the powers of the Council might do to aid in keeping the Ancient Ones where they are. No return, no report."

"Yeah, well, good luck. Yuggoth ain't no place to fool around." He turned, and his eyes blazed. "Hey! I think the boat's comin' in!"

Sure enough, off in the distance there came a tremendous roar that canceled out the sound of wind and waves. It was a massive, powerful, pulsating sound, very regular and very controlled. It had been pulsing fairly fast, but now, as it approached them and the dock, the beat slowed appreciably, and all eyes, even those of the damned, turned in silent anticipation toward the pitch-dark sea. While not disturbing, the sound was certainly like nothing else any of them might ever have heard.

"Hove . . . Hove . . . Hove . . . Hove . . ."

"Well, it explains the name," Marge commented, trying to keep some semblance of humor and not think too much about what an idiotic thing she was doing even thinking of setting foot on that ship.

For a while there was nothing apparent, but then, out of the gloom, they spotted some lights approaching, lights that grew larger and brighter as they approached the dock.

There were shouts from out in the water, a sudden sense of huge black *things* suddenly letting go, and a settling of the boat into the water. What those things were they couldn't see; not even faerie sight helped with it except to show the nearly impossible massive shapes that were dark even against the pitch black of the night and that reflected not a thing, hovering up and over the boat, which was now and possibly for the first time floating in the water.

It was a large craft, a hundred meters or more in length, and shaped like an extended oval, with tapered black outer skin going from a thick base that sat in the water up at least three stories to a large enclosed bridge.

As it slid slowly up along one side of the dock and lines shot out from it and from shore to tie it off, Irving commented, "That's *some* ship!"

Marge nodded, gaping along with Irving. It was a *lot*

more than she had expected but also a lot more menacing for all that.

There was a loud, hollow sound like the noise a million lost souls might make in torment, and from this came an eerie-sounding male voice that sent shivers up their spines.

"The H.P. Lines hovercraft *Eibon* is now in port. Embarkation for Red Bluffs, Yuggoth, will be precisely one hour before dawn. All those needing passage must have checked in with the ticketing office prior to boarding and turn their documentation over to the purser. Boarding will be possible in one hour. We would reconsider if we were you."

"Cheery," Marge noted. "They don't seem to be anxious for new business, anyway."

"Considering the state of humankind, I suspect they get all the business they can handle as it is," Poquah responded with all seriousness. He turned to keep an eye on Irving, who, as a living, warm-blooded mortal was probably the one in most danger here. The boy was reading some pamphlet he had picked up at the ticket kiosk, which had just opened.

"What is that you are looking at, Irving?" Poquah asked, curious.

The boy showed him the face of the brochure, which contained a drawing of the bow of the ship flanked by a lot of dark shapes around which there was very prominent titling.

"*Hmmmm . . . Journey to Yuggoth by HP Hovecraft.* Rather standard-looking brochure. Any information of interest?"

"Not particularly. Not terribly encouraging, though, either. Sort of says that they wouldn't go if they were us and then describes a bunch of scary stuff." He looked up and toward the boat, which was in the process of off-loading goods and passengers. The odd thing was that although there were again hints of black against black movement, you couldn't see any of the crew or longshoremen at all.

The nature of the cargo also was impossible to determine, but for more conventional reasons: it was all more or

less in large boxes, crates, or containerlike rectangular
shapes that fitted into or onto the backs of waiting wagons
and wagon frames. While some of the smaller boxes did
seem to resemble coffins, overall there didn't seem to be
much unusual there.

The passengers, however, were something else again.
Since they had been warned that nobody who went into
Yuggoth tended to be able to leave it, it was something of
a surprise to see that traffic did indeed go both ways, after
all. These passengers, however, were probably not ones
who had gone in before or at least gone in looking like they
did now.

"Holy smoke!" Irving exclaimed. "What are *they*?"

"They" were several very distinctive-looking women of
supernatural endowments with exotic and erotic faces. They
were certainly faerie; their skins were deep crimsons and
purples and even had streaks of black, their hair was deep
purple and thick, tumbling sensuously over shoulders and
breasts, and they were wearing shiny form-fitting leather
pants and incredibly high heels. They were certainly fliers;
the wings on their backs, though, were sleek and stylized
batlike appendages.

Marge gasped at the sight of them and felt instant and
nearly uncontrollable anger and revulsion. Poquah was
ready and restrained her gently.

"Succubi," she spat, saying the word as if it were the vil-
est of poisons.

Irving seemed impervious to her tone and obvious loath-
ing. "Yeah? I've read about them but never seen them.
Funny, except for the colors and the wings and maybe a little more height, they don't look all that different from you."

She spun around angrily. "Don't say that! Don't *ever* say
that!"

In point of fact, though, the Succubi and the Kauri were
two sides of the same coin, the yin and yang of a single
species. The Kauri could purge or cleanse men of their guilt
and burdens through erotic sex and thus performed a service; the Succubi used precisely the same techniques to

suck out a man's soul and leave only corruption. Both indeed had precisely the same powers and worked them in much the same way; it was the purpose and limits on those uses that differentiated the good from the evil ones.

The Succubi got into waiting coaches with blinds drawn and roared off, but Marge wasn't off the hook yet. The next group off the boat was a small number of faerie males of much the same stripe. They had muscles on their muscles and the tightest of rear ends; their faces were totally masculine yet erotic, sensual, a male version of the Succubi, and the male organs showing through very tight pants almost as if they were naked were, um, *impossible*. They, too, were fliers, with wings that were far more pronounced as batlike but that when folded formed a kind of sexy and attractive cloak

"Incubi, the male version," Poquah told Irving. "Neither of the two sexes appears as you are seeing them to their victims, although they do much the same. Instead, they appear as the perfect dream combination, male or female, that the subject most desires or would desire if fantasies were reality. Even with faerie sight they are difficult to resist. *Without* it they are next to impossible to defend against, since they are the subject's sexual fantasy incarnate. Except for being too good to be true, most mortals would not even recognize them as faerie, let alone as a threat. They're not too common here, though, since any faerie race can see them for what they are and there is no power over us."

They were, however, the beginnings of a parade of very scary sorts, most of whom seemed somehow not quite so frightening in this context. There were vampires and ghouls and beasties and things that went bump in the night and all sorts of scary creatures, as well as a number of quite ordinary-looking people who seemed physically out of place but not the least bit uncomfortable.

"Those are the most dangerous of all," Marge noted quite seriously to Irving. "They look and act just like everybody else, and they're friendly and trustworthy types you'd never look twice at. The vampires and ghouls can go after one or two at a time, but *these* people can corrupt or destroy whole nations, races, and ways of life, often with no more than a word, or a gesture, or simply a refusal to act. I'd rather deal with a vampire or a ghoul any old day."

Had the Dark Baron once been a passenger like these? She wondered about that. Had he seen the misery and poverty around him here and found nobody but defenders of the system around his own people? He'd been a good man once; they all attested to that. In that sense he, more than anyone else, had been the epitome of the phrase "The road to Hell is paved with good intentions." That and the curse of the true intellectual searching for meaning and order in a universe that had little of them. Just one creeping thought, one blasphemous doubt, might well be enough for somebody like him. "If God permits such suffering and misery, perhaps the Devil *is* right."

In the end the Baron had betrayed both Heaven *and* Hell, and where his soul had gone was anybody's guess.

All of a sudden it was as if it were yesterday, but with that additional element of doubt. *If Joe could somehow survive, in some form, the fall into that lava, then why not the Baron as well?*

No, no! That way lay madness.

"You are suddenly disturbed," Poquah noted. "Second thoughts?"

"Tenth thoughts," she responded. "Never mind. Just seeing this dark bunch of villains and knowing where we're headed now kind of brings up all sorts of dark thoughts out of the dim corners of the mind—ones better left where they are, I think. Forget it."

Poquah nodded. "I know what you mean. Wait here and keep an eye on the boy. I'm going to see if the Master did indeed arrange for our passage. I almost hope that somehow he did not."

While Poquah made his way warily through the throngs of the damned toward the ticketing kiosk, Marge went over to Irving, who was simply sitting on the ground, half-reclined, looking at the assembled multitudes with a blank sort of expression.

"Worried?" she asked him.

He shook his head negatively. "Not yet. Maybe when we really get into it, but not now. Sort of neat to see all those white folks in chains. Kind of poetic justice. The rest? Well, I've seen their type before. Ruddygore deals with demons, you know, and I've had some contacts myself. You got to be careful and you can't trust 'em so far, but overall they're not nearly as scary for what they are as for what they can do to you if *you* let them."

"Yeah? Well, most kids your age tend to think they're both invulnerable and immortal. The ones who survive to grow up learn different. The rest learn right away."

"I don't think I'm invulnerable, but I don't underestimate myself, either. This is my trial. I don't have to go. I could hang back, and then I'd be just another human in Husaquahr, apprenticed to somebody for a regular job, pushing a pencil or a plow, living and dying a nobody just like most folks. One thing Ruddygore taught me that was important was that some folks—not all, but maybe most—come to some point in their lives, some time and place, where they have to decide. They either take a risk, maybe even a superrisk, or they don't. If they don't, they're meaningless to destiny. Most folks don't. They either don't have the guts, or they talk themselves out of it or whatever and spend the rest of their lives tellin' everybody else and themselves what they *coulda* been. Or they take the risk. A fair number of the ones that do take that risk lose, that's true, but at least they took the risk. They *went for it*. And a fair number don't lose. A fair number win, too. They're the ones that change history, run things, influence the world, make a difference. That time's come a little earlier here than it does for most folks, or maybe not. Maybe if I'd stayed back in Philly, I'd be on the streets now, either dodging gangs or in one, dealin' dope or bein' shot by cops or rival gangs or who knows? It wasn't a good place where I was. I remember that."

"Do you miss Earth, though?"

He nodded. "Sometimes. Maybe a lot. I also miss my mom. She wasn't all that much, but she was my mother. But that was a *bad* neighborhood. I wasn't even ten, and I'd lost two friends in shootings. One was coming home from school and just got in the wrong place. The other was sittin' on the front steps one hot night gettin' some air, and a bullet just came and blew him away. You saw the cokeheads and winos and all sorts, and you saw the gangs with their big man leader of the month—usually dead after that. I couldn't even blame 'em. They didn't see any future; they just grabbed whatever present they could. So maybe I'd already be dead or in jail or something. Well, okay. I'm sixteen, and I've had a lot of education here and a lot of training. I'm not the greatest swordsman or archer or knife fighter in the world, but I'm fair at 'em. I'm definitely not a world-class sorcerer, but I know more than most folks. I'm a big guy now, and I'm in pretty decent shape. Now's my time. Now I have to decide to go or stay."

"Well, you *are* going after your father, such as he or she now is," Marge noted.

"That's not it. Kinda hard to get choked up about somebody you barely knew and don't really remember and who hid from you all this time. The only thing I can say is that he made his own decision at a key time and changed history. He saved the world, and it cost him. But he couldn't follow through. He couldn't save himself, too. I don't know if I'd be any better, but I kind of hope I would. It isn't a question of living up to my dad. It's a question of proving to myself and the world that I'm *better* than him."

"Do you really hate him that much?"

He shook his head sadly. "No, no. I don't hate him. It's *impossible* to hate a stranger, the same as it's impossible to love one. To me this Joe is just another common wood nymph."

This was the area where she and Irving had always hit a wall, going round and round, and it was where she was determined to somehow break through. They would need total trust and confidence in the days and weeks ahead, and whatever barriers could be dissolved ahead of time, she knew, should be gotten rid of.

"Deep down inside that form is the same person who loved you, talked about nobody but you, and came for you when he could," she pointed out.

"Yeah? Are *you* really the same person you were back in the real world, or are you just kidding yourself? Would anybody really recognize the old you inside? Do you ever feel the same, act the same? Do you even really *remember* what it was like to be human?"

"Listen, *kid*," she responded, more than a little angry at his tone. "No, I'm *not* the same person, and neither will you be in another five or ten years if you live that long. But I remember who I was and where I came from, don't kid yourself. And your old man—well, he's a damn fool for what he did this last time, I admit that, but I can understand it, too. When you go from a cross between Geronimo and Conan the Barbarian to a tree nymph, you lose all sense of yourself. No matter what they say, guys like that don't have a sense of women as equals, and they see themselves as some kind of macho studs. It's pride, it's honor, it's everything. It's wrong, but it's their culture and they didn't ask to be born into it. You want to know what his problem is? He's *ashamed* to be seen. He'd rather be dead, but he can't die, not even like I can die. He considers himself the same as dead, though, and that's why he's hiding out from everybody he knows and loves. It doesn't matter what *we* think; he can't really see that part, can't accept it. It's the craziest kind of male logic, which I should pass on to you, but he ran away because he loves you so much, he didn't want you to see him this way. Get it?"

"Maybe. Maybe if I had known him better before, I could understand it better," Irving responded seriously. "Sure, I can figure out the line of thought, but it doesn't help me at all, and it can't be taken back. He can't even turn around and give me a father, not now. There's just no bond there on my part, anyway, even if he somehow got changed back and came up looking every bit the macho man on a white horse. The crazy thing is, he did everything right here for so long, then he lost it at the end. I'm not gonna let that happen to me. I'll die first."

"Huh? What in *hell* are you talking about?"

"See, I was going real good into this magic and sorcery business until a year or so ago. That's when I stopped reading all that crap they've piled on and paid attention not to the Rules so much as to the Laws."

"The what? They're mostly the basics of gravity, ballistics, the bare-bones sciences, aren't they?"

"Most are. But there's one tiny section, and one only, that makes the rest of little or no importance. That's why I stopped much work on it and just started preparing as best I could for the first test."

"What do you mean, Irving? There's something in the Laws about *people*?"

He smiled and nodded. "It's the system. Like I told you—everybody gets choices, and they either take a chance or forget it. On Earth that's maybe a small number of people to begin with. Here it's *everybody*. Every human, every mortal, that is. That includes you, too, even if you're a changeling and all faerie now. Same with Joe. It doesn't *stop* if going past mortal is part of the thing. See, everybody keeps being handed those risk and reward steps. Sometimes it's early, sometimes late, but *everybody* gets a crack. If you pass on the first one, you may get another, but probably not. You stop being important. You become a slave to the Rules and live out your life, and that's that. If you take it, you might win or lose. If you lose and live, you'll get another crack sometime. If you die, well, that's the breaks. But if you win, you know what happens? You get *another* monkey wrench thrown into your existence. And another. Finally, if you beat them all, you win the prize. Only if you give up do you lose for good unless you get killed."

"Yes? And what's the prize?"

"Power. Power is everything here. Power is everything

on Earth, too, but it's more spread around and not as clear-cut. Every time you get crapped on and fight your way out here, more knowledge and power come to you. Finally there's top status. Ruddygore. Demigod of the Kauris. You name it. Whatever you want that's at the top, you can have. But only if you keep fighting, keep battling back. If you give up, then you're a goner. Look at Dad. High school dropout, failed marriage, failed father, but once he got here, he kept at it and became a hero, a barbarian warrior, a king, and a confident and experienced power to be feared and respected. When he stood there with that lava, he *knew* what would happen, but he took the risk. He got a body he hated but also kept his mind and gained nearly absolute immortality. He came *that close* to godhood of a sort, and what did he do? Gave up and ran. That's not going to happen to me. I'm either gonna have Ruddygore's job or I'm gonna be killed getting there. I've spent the last year, year and a half testing myself. Facing demons, challenging myself, getting prepared. Now, here we go. Poquah is my wisdom; you are my experience. And you might well not be done, either. Macore's finished, that's for sure, but you came. There's some kind of thread. Something that binds you, and Poquah, and maybe my father, and even Macore if he'd decided to go one last time, and it leads out there. It leads somewhere. You can't see it, or Poquah, either, because nobody can see their own destiny, but I can, because even though mine is undoubtedly tangled up in yours at the moment, it's not the same."

"You can actually see this thread?"

"In you and Poquah, yes, and it's the same, so I know I'm right. It went from Macore as well, but it will break free of him when we leave without him. Most faerie don't have a thread of destiny; all is sameness. You reach the end of that thread, and who knows what's there waiting?"

"Hold it!" she said, considering the implications. "If you're right, and this thing exists, and that's the system, then what's out there, where this thread leads, is something bigger and nastier and more complex and threatening than any of the massive number of horrors and ancient enemies I've already faced. And Joe—he's had more than me by far."

Irving nodded. "I think so. I'm not sure about dear old Dad; I don't think he's got it in him anymore. But maybe I'm wrong. You got to figure, though, that if what you say is true, then this is the big one. You win, it's over, and *you* get the prize. Maybe not me, but you. Marge, you're either gonna win this one, or . . ."

"Or Poquah, your dad, and I are going to cease to exist," she finished, swallowing hard.

"*Hovecraft* Eibon *now ready for boarding at passenger convenience. Passengers only should board, please. Please ensure that you have your boarding pass before coming up the gangplank!*"

Poquah was coming back toward them, a fistful of papers in one hand, and Marge had a sudden urge to flee, to launch herself into the night sky and get away from all this.

At the same time, she knew she wouldn't do it. Damn his hide! Ruddygore left few options when he had a job to do, and she'd never be able to live contentedly if she watched Poquah and Irving sail away without her.

She sighed. "Once more into the breach, dear friends," she said softly to herself.

Irving got up and walked toward Poquah. "Here we go," he said simply.

Marge wished she were as ignorant of what this world could deliver as he was, to be able to almost look forward to this trip.

A MASSAGE FROM GARFIA

First, do no good.

—The Hypocritic Oath

FOR SUCH A DOOMED SHIP IT WAS IN MANY WAYS A MAGnificent vessel.

The whole thing was gleaming polished wood and brass; the lamps were bright and solid, burning only the most fragrant oils and putting out a light that almost seemed electric; and the windows and glass doorways had seemingly abstract patterns of stained glass that were impressive works of art in and of themselves. This was no cattle boat or common freighter; this was as high as luxury went in Husaquahrian ships.

Marge stared at the whole thing with a sense of nervous awe, both appreciating the quality and at the same time remembering that this was no ordinary ship and that it trafficked in no ordinary souls going to no ordinary place. This was a Hell ship, run for the convenience of the Prince of Darkness and his minions, and it was very clear that creature comforts were high on the demonic priority lists. There was, Marge thought, too much Judeo-Christian background in her; she was still surprised to see this sort of thing even though it was creature comforts and luxuries in the here and now that Hell always promised, wasn't it?

"What's that sign at the bottom of the gangplank?" Irving asked them. "It looks like Earth writing, but I can't read it."

"It's Latin!" Marge exclaimed. "A quote from Dante, I think. The fancy big letters say 'Abandon Hope All Who Enter Here.' The standard for Hell."

"Yeah? Then what's that phrase in small letters below?"

133

"It says to have a nice day," Poquah told him.

They walked up the gangplank and onto the ship. Oddly, there was more of a sense of embarking on an adventure than of putting their fate in the hands of their worst enemies.

"Take a good, close look at some of those stained-glass windows," Irving bent down and whispered to her. "My old granny woulda freaked. Yours, too, I bet."

Marge took another, closer look at them and suddenly saw what he meant. Far from being totally abstract, they showed a number of stylized scenes, not at all the sort you'd see in your local church but in some ways parodies of them, with demonic figures shown as all-knowing and all-encompassing angelic-type figures, and below them all sorts of wonderful excesses were depicted in rather graphic detail. Marge hoped that Irving was really as worldly a sixteen-year-old as he seemed, or else this was going to be one heck of an education. Although some of the less interesting sins were depicted, such as greed and gluttony and sloth and the like, it was certainly the sexual ones that paid the most attention to detail and commanded the most attention of voyeurs.

Marge stared at one and wondered if what was depicted with such obvious relish was really possible. It was a Succubus depicted as doing it in the glass pattern, of course, but except for being on different sides, they were sort of in the same business.

"Could you really *do* that?" Irving asked, somewhat appalled but still fascinated. The effect the scenes would have on him if his spell of celibacy was removed was something Marge was glad she didn't have to deal with right now. Hell, they were turning *her* on, and she was way past sixteen.

"Anything *they* can do, Kauri can do better, kid," she responded with a confidence she didn't really feel. Holy smokes! If this sort of stuff was on the passenger-deck windows, what in the *world* could be decorating the bar?

Somehow, this was one heck of a fancier ship than Charon was usually depicted as having.

A tall, gaunt figure stood at the main doorway inside. It was dressed in a black robe and cowl but clearly was no demon by its shape and movement. A skeletal hand—literally—emerged from each sleeve, and they all got the very distinct impression that the rest of the figure was equally bony.

"Tickets, please," the thing said in a hollow voice that was all business rather than conveying any sort of threat.

Poquah handed the thing their documents, which suddenly erupted in a puff of smoke and flame and were gone.

"All in order. See the purser inside for a cabin assignment and meal information."

Irving shifted his pack, the only luggage they carried other than a small garment bag Poquah used, and muttered, "I wonder what they eat in their dining rooms."

"I believe 'don't ask, don't tell' would be most prudent as a policy there," Poquah responded, and they entered the main ship.

Again, in spite of the decor, the cleanliness and overall gleaming opulence of the craft almost overwhelmed them. Even Irving, who had little sense of social graces, felt decidedly underdressed.

The purser proved to be a more conventional sort of demon but of about average height and with an above-average girth, wearing an official-looking gold-braided dark uniform similar to that found on fancy ships everywhere. Marge thought he looked like Uncle Fester, if he enlisted in the navy.

"Hmmm ... I think they made a mistake on you," the demon muttered, checking a clipboard and sounding jolly enough. "They only booked one cabin, number fourteen, for all three of you, but there are only two beds in there and not much room for more, I'm afraid."

"That is quite all right," Poquah told him. "I am more of the day, and the lady is of the night, while the boy can be either way. It seemed silly to book a second cabin when only two of us at best would be using it."

"Ah, yes! Very good, sir. A penny saved is a penny more we can take you for in the casino. Rather *boring* aboard in the daytime, though, sir, if I might say so. Not much of our clientele likes the sunlight, you know, and we get real hovecraft speed and comfort only at night—daytime is the more mundane and much slower kraken pull. Of course, there are always a few people about. You will dine in the forward restaurant, boat deck. It's the Purgatorio. Open all the time, anything you wish, any cuisine, any race. You will find the cuisine here the finest in the world." He turned and reached over to a huge wooden pegboard, took down a large key on a big polished wood key chain, and handed it to Poquah. "You may keep this inside or turn it in if all are outside the room," the purser added, pointing down a well-lit passageway. "Down amidships, then up the forward stairs to the top. It is quite a nice room."

The Imir bowed, and they turned and walked down the corridor. Irving took the key and looked at it. Even the key was a work of art, not just a key but a sculpture of a familiar form.

"Skeleton key," he noted.

Marge chucked. "Wonder if it'll open any door."

"I don't think we want to check that out," Poquah responded. "There are a number of guests who travel this route I should not like to disturb. Those throngs of the damned outside aren't here; they're crámmed below in the holds. Besides, as with virtually any hotel or inn—and this is basically a floating version of a hotel—the key is primarily a formality. They could get in and out with passkeys any time. Elsewise, how could the rooms be cleaned?"

"You're really reassuring," Marge told him sourly.

He shrugged. "Remember, the one thing Hell depends upon is that it is as good as its word and always honors its guarantees. If it did not, nobody would ever try and beat their system. We are warranted safe on this boat. Period. It is a condition of passage. There are no guarantees if we violate the basic rules of passage, which are in every case pretty much what one would expect from anyone—no vandalism, observing the privacy of others, that sort of thing—but there is also no fine print. You see, they count on this ship to bring their own people to Yuggoth and from there to the gates of Hell itself and to send their own agents back into Husaquahr. They control passage in *both* directions. Why should they risk anything on the boat? It is simply not in their best interest."

A few cabins were open in one area, and they revealed interiors very opulently decorated but with what looked for all the world like polished coffins where the beds should have been. Others seemed to have cages that didn't appear to be able to be opened from the inside. Their own cabin, however, turned out to have a king-sized bed in the center, surrounded by a pentagram on the floor and holders for candles and incense. There was also a washbasin with a small pump that actually could feed cold or hot water depending on which way it was pressed. There was also a fairly standard chamber pot with sealable lid.

"Why the pentagram?" Marge asked, looking it over. "They call demons in the bed or something?"

Irving chuckled. "The demons stay in the cabins on *this* boat! Remember, you can use a pentagram to keep demonic forces inside or to keep them outside. Doesn't matter which. I think this is for folks who just might not trust that they didn't catch all the fine print."

"It is indeed mostly a psychological aid," Poquah agreed, examining it. "However, it might well be prudent to set it up, particularly for the night. Irving, you will have to decide if you want to sleep in or out before it is sealed, and Marge, I'm afraid that once it is sealed, you'll be as unable to cross as anything else. Of course, you can yell if need be."

"Fair enough," she told him. "Still, I kind of wonder what protects me when I roam this ship at night."

"Your wits," the Imir replied. "The same as protects you wandering the night skies of Husaquahr."

"You really don't sound worried."

"I'm not. The fact is, in this one and only this one in-stance, Hell and we are on the same side. Remember that there are more than two universes and that the others are even farther from the template of Earth than this one. The djinn you know; the other, reached through the worst depths of the Sea of Dreams, is that of Hell's nightmares. *That* is the one that now threatens to come here. If it does, it is going to find Hell no more kin than Heaven. I would admit that Leviathan versus Cthulhu would be fascinating, but I am not certain that I would relish being on the same dimensional plane as the contest."

"Huh? You're saying Hell wants *us* to win?"

"No, no. By no means. They want the current threat to us all ended. They would most certainly rather do it them-selves, but so long as we are serving their ends, I do not believe we are in mortal harm from the great principalities and powers of the air. That does not, of course, mean that they wouldn't like to see us come over to their side and point of view and enter into their service or that they wouldn't get rid of us if they could triumph for sure with-out our help. Still, I will lose no sleep on *this* leg of the voyage from worry that some ghoulie or beastie or demonic form is going to get me. I believe we should all simply get as much rest as we can, for I can foresee many long and difficult times ahead." He yawned. "Indeed, I believe I shall nap right now."

"Not me," Marge told him. "I'm in my prime time here. Irving?"

"I want to see the rest of the ship and how it moves," he told her. "No way I'm gonna sleep *now*."

They left Poquah and went back to the hall, then forward and out one of the doors to the outer deck. Things were getting very busy very fast, and they could feel the boat shift against its moorings as people and things were loaded on board. Marge shook her head in wonder. "Do you feel that this is strange somehow?"

"*Those* windows? And coffins in the rooms? Sure," he admitted.

"No, that's not it. You kind of *expect* that. It's that most of this is *not* bizarre. There's no feeling of dread, of monstrous evil, blood and gore, all the rest. This could be any large, new luxurious craft going anywhere on the ocean. There's just something *wrong* about it."

"You mean you think we're being conned or something?" he asked.

"No, no! I mean that this *is* pretty much what it is, that *nobody's* conning us, but it isn't what it *should* be. Demon ships to a horror continent that is the gateway to Hell? *This?*"

"So you think they get people over to their point of view by scaring them to death?" Irving asked her. "Heck, I mean, you heard that demon. They're at war. They see all that evil power stuff, all that blood and gore, as striking at their enemy, but you wouldn't expect *them* to live that way. I bet you Satan's so beautiful, he'd make you cry, too."

"Huh?"

"He was in charge of all the angels, right? And he controls all the organized evil in at least two universes, right? That's *power*. These little guys, these demons or bad angels, they're just ones that got conned or suckered or maybe just talked into going with the revolt. No big deal. But I bet you the big ones, the princes, are something else—and their chief the grandest of all. You figure he's gonna sit back with the best wines and the finest foods and all the stuff anybody can enjoy in spades, right? Everything your preacher ever told you not to do, and no penalties, no aging, no guilt or nothin'. I bet he don't need a ship to be anywhere, but this is the kind you'd build for your people, right? Not the suckers—we saw them all chained up back there. The ones who really run things."

Marge sighed. "Maybe. Still, it just doesn't seem *right* somehow. Not to me."

Was it just her old cultural upbringing, she wondered, or was it the fact that she'd seen the evil those creatures could do and had learned of more? Hitler, Stalin, war, pestilence, disease, suffering—that was the business of those who owned and operated this craft. How terribly depressing to discover that they literally saw it as their business, nothing personal.

Still . . . "If they're so powerful, why do they need us at all?" she asked him. "You're so smart, kid, you answer *that* one. Why can't the big man who can corrupt nations and enslave whole worlds and chuckle over a nice Chianti about it, him and all his princes who run things, take care of this turf war with somebody else muscling in? What could a sixteen-year-old green kid on his first outing and two faerie do that all that power and glory and such can't?"

It was Irving's turn to shake his head. "Sorry, I been thinking about that one myself. Maybe we'll find out if we make it."

The ghostly, roaring sound of lost souls under amplification came from all around them.

"The H.P. Hovecraft Eibon will depart in five minutes. All ashore that is going ashore. All passengers and freight for Red Bluffs, Innsmouth, and points beyond should now be on board."

"Well, we might as well stick here and see how this thing works, anyway," Marge noted. "I still can't figure out why it's called a hovecraft or just how it moves. I don't see any masts, the huge inner tube that seems to surround it doesn't allow for oars, and nothing up front that seems to be used for pulling is broken out."

They waited, hearing the clomping of inhuman feet below them and the shouts of many creatures in many tongues. There were also shapes, human and otherwise, on the docks and at the mooring lines. The gangplank aft and the loading ramp amidships were withdrawn, and they could hear the crew putting up the railings and bulwarks. There was a definite feeling of departure that quite abruptly struck both Irving and Marge in a way they hadn't expected.

"Abandon hope all ye who enter here . . ."

Since coming to this world, they had both traveled to many lands, seen many things of good, evil, and in between, and experienced both magic and nature, but it had all been in Husaquahr. Now, for the first time, both of them were leaving the great northern continent, the largest on the planet, whose heart was the River of Dancing Gods, and heading southward, past the equator, to a place that they didn't know but that was billed as all the bad things of Husaquahr and Earth, with none of the good.

Both felt suddenly very homesick, and Marge again had to suppress the urge to fly up and away, back toward home and familiar lands.

"Eibon *now departing,*" reported a somewhat spooky but far more solid and official-sounding voice. "All passengers remain away from the rails and mooring lines. Let go aft. Let go amidships. Let go forward."

The huge boat drifted free of the dock, with the lines being pulled in from the lowest deck below them and secured. It didn't feel like it was powered by much of anything but rather was simply adrift, its pilot steering with a rudder, using only the outgoing tide to get well away from shore.

"False dawn's starting," Marge noted, pointing. "They won't have much night left."

"Probably not," Irving agreed. "Just enough to get them out to where they can pick up the krakens, I'd guess. Still, he's making pretty good time with just the tide here. At least I *think* it's the tide."

They were well away from shore, and the lights of the H.P. Lines dock seemed extraordinarily distant. Pretty soon they were far enough out to see the whole coast stretching before them for many miles in both directions, and to the rear and the right they could see the resort town and its crowded harbor as a collection of miniature radiances in a gaudily lit gloom.

Somewhere over there Macore was fast asleep, probably surrounded by his crew of nymphs, no longer exposed to the danger of yet one more quest.

There was a sudden bump and lurch of the whole boat,

almost as if it had struck something, and then the sound behind them of massive things rising up, up into the sky and
the breaking of the still air by great downward rushes in a
regular sort of beat.

They were both almost knocked off their feet, and Irving
grabbed the rail, leaned against it, and looked back and up-
ward to see what was going on.

Two great black shapes, each perhaps a quarter the size
of the entire vessel, had risen from apparent resting places
on top of the boat, between the bridge and the aft pilot-
house. Giant, thick, yet amorphous beasts, they now seemed
to loom above the ship and cover it, yet they matched its
position relative to themselves and to each other perfectly.

"What are they?" Marge shouted over the noise of their
beating, great manta rays of the sky.

"I dunno. I think they're some kind of night gaunt, but
I never saw or heard anything that big or powerful before,"
the boy responded. He pointed. "Look! They're attached to
the ship!"

It was true; the two great beasts were linked by lines not
of rope or chain but of the blackest magical forces so that
each carried half the vessel. Now, very slowly but very deliberately, the ship seemed almost to come out of the water,
suspended under the two creatures just above the waves.

There was a sudden, heavy beating now, and the ship began to move forward at a rapidly increasing speed, leaving
the shoreline of Husaquahr behind, moving off with ex-
traordinary haste away from the threatening light of dawn
and toward the still-inviting darkness.

It was clear from the start that they would not beat the
dawn, but they would make a game try of it.

Daytime was definitely *not* the most comfortable time of
passage. Kraken power involved lashing the great sea behe-
moths to lines from the bow and having them pull with
great muscular snakelike motions. That did the job but
caused a fair amount of rocking and definite discomfort
during heavy seas. While the forward motion was enough

to allow them to make time, the comfort zone for the *Eibon* was definitely slated for dusk to dawn.

The dining room was everything the purser had promised, as well. The wines were superb, of legendary vintages, and whatever food you wished for, that mysterious never-seen kitchen could manage not only to come up with but to prepare it precisely the way you wanted it.

There were few eating or wandering the decks by day, even in warm sunshine, and that made Irving in particular more sensitive to the feeling that he was being watched, and not by members of the crew. It wasn't constantly, and it wasn't anything he could pin down, either, but he had the distinct sense of being checked up on constantly by someone or something that was never that far away yet never quite glimpsed save in shadow or out of the corner of the eye. It was always faster than he and cleverer as well, and it was no paranoid delusion. Once he thought he had caught the watcher and almost had, but while there was nobody there when he made the challenge, the doorway was still sliding shut and the inner door was swinging back and forth as if someone had just run through.

Both Marge and Poquah admitted to having the same sensation, although not quite as frequently and certainly with no better luck. "At first I thought it was some fellow passenger who had designs on a neck or thigh," Poquah noted, "but I get no sense of *menace* from this. Imir are very good at this sort of thing—sensing threats. Whoever or whatever it is, while I cannot be certain that it is friendly, it is certainly not our enemy. This suggests someone paid to keep tabs on us or watch our backs. It will be interesting to see what comes of this—or who."

"Great. Just what we need," Marge grumped.

Beyond the luxury of the restaurant and bedrooms there really was little to do on the boat for the average passenger. They did have a nighttime casino, as promised, but it was a rather subdued affair for anybody, let alone Hell, and looked even more impossible to beat than a regular casino. The library tended toward horror novels and collections, many from Earth, together with volumes in many languages of both Earth and Husaquahr on black magic, sorcery, Satanism, and other cheery subjects. Irving did find the complete, bound set of *Tales from the Crypt*, but it provided only a couple of hours diversion at best.

It *was* more comfortable by night, when the giant night gaunts skimmed the ship over the waves regardless of seas or winds and kept things steady and very quick, but Irving in particular found that this was the best time for him to sleep. The constant pulsing and rocking from the two somewhat laboring and slightly out of sync daytime krakens were much easier to get used to than walking about than sleeping in the cabin. That left Marge more to herself at night, which she didn't particularly like but had to accept, and Irving roaming around pretty much on his own during the day. Poquah was never a very convivial sort or great company and tended to use his time reading, studying, and meditating. Once or twice he did try to stalk Irving himself, hoping to catch the elusive shadowing figure in between them, but although he came close, the shadow proved resourceful and the most that could be gleaned was a small black-clad shape whose very race, let alone features, couldn't be determined by short glimpses.

And then there was the girl.

Irving first saw her in the restaurant at the second meal there, eating alone. She was striking in a number of ways, not the least of which was that she appeared dark-skinned and African-featured although quite different from his specific features in many ways. She also was dressed in a light cotton dress that seemed comfortable but hid little and was most remarkable because on Hell's dark ship it was the whitest of whites.

Who was she, this first person of African-type features Irving could remember seeing since leaving Earth? What was she doing here, traveling to Yuggoth on this ship, wearing the plain white that usually signified purity and chastity and all that, and awake by day rather than by night? At first he thought she might be a Succubus; those creatures, after all, did have a tendency to take the form in the beholder's mind of some kind of ideal human. But it was never the same for any two people, and Poquah saw her, too.

"There *is* a Moorish continent, but it is well west of our destination," Poquah noted. "Still, she certainly looks of that continent and place, and most likely the western delta region of that continent. I have no idea why she is here, but I can perhaps make some kind of nasty guess based upon what I see."

"Yes?"

"Note the spell. Not all that different from your own. Chastity, celibacy—she is a virgin. The spell keeps her that way, but it is the power of that unspoiled virginity that shines through and is almost painful in faerie sight. White cotton, virginal, unadorned, and alone. There can be but one possible explanation for this."

"I don't understand," Irving said, frowning.

"She is a gift. Someone made a bargain with a demon back where she came from to provide a firstborn virginal daughter. There is much potential for both good or evil sorcery in such a one. We can safely assume that if she's headed to Yuggoth on the *Eibon*, she is headed for an evil master, a payoff that will almost certainly be a tragedy."

"Huh? What? You don't mean . . . ?"

"I fear so. She is intended as some sort of sacrifice to a power of the underworld. Whoever does it will gain something important, possibly vital protection or even power. The underworld prince will gain a soul that can be used against others like a weapon of iron. There is a whole volume devoted to sacrificial virgins in the Rules, you know."

Irving was shocked. "Hey! We can't let that happen! Particularly to *her*! I mean, it's not *right*!"

The boy seemed so mature and so much an adult that it was a surprise sometimes when the naive kid in him surfaced as it did now. Poquah sighed and said, "Irving, we are on a ship owned by a principality of Hell heading toward, and I repeat, *toward*, the evil continent of Yuggoth.

Aboard are a considerable number of lost souls as well as almost certainly—demons—in sufficient numbers that we could not stand against them if they decided they wanted all of us. To top it all off, we are in the middle of the *ocean*. Just *what* do you think we could do if indeed we had the right, the duty, or the obligation to intervene?"

The boy was somewhat taken aback by the catalog of their weaknesses, but deep down there was a moral sensibility that couldn't walk away from this. Still, he had to think pretty fast.

"I think we *are* supposed to," he replied a bit hesitantly.

"Indeed? Why?"

"Because she's black like me, and I don't ever remember seeing another around here, so the two of us being on this ship this trip has to mean something in the destiny department or something, right?"

"Or it could be sheer coincidence. I suspect there are a hundred million or so of her race about, just not many that get to Husaquahr. And I'm unaware of any monopoly on dealings with Heaven, Hell, or the spirits in between by one race versus another. She is also brown, not black, and you are not only not black, either, you are only half-related to her in any genetic sense. Now, if she'd been a red Indian, I might well have agreed with you on the destiny business—we have some relatives here in a remote land but nothing all that close, and so someone of that type showing up would be *highly* unusual, if not unique. But a girl of one of the Moorish races—don't be absurd. A million times more common than an Imir, for example."

Poquah clearly could not be moved, but Irving wasn't the type to budge on that sort of thing, either. Much of the day he brooded over it, trying to figure out just what to do, what he might be *able* to do, and, if he could come up with something, what was needed to do it.

The first thing, he decided, was to talk to her. Poquah might well be right. Hell, she might even be there of her own free will or to save her family's life or something. He didn't think so. Not only was the racial link much more certain an indication of destiny linked to him than Poquah accepted, but the fact that she was also clearly not much more than his own age cinched it.

And if she *didn't* want to be here, then just to pretend she was never here would be as big a sin as bumping her off. If they refused even to check out somebody who might need help or refused to help somebody who needed it, then maybe they all *deserved* to be going one way to Yuggoth on the *Eibon*.

He was determined to approach her as soon as he had the chance. That, however, was easier said than done; other than at meals, she appeared to be spending most of her time alone in her stateroom, and he didn't even know where that was. Meanwhile, the disapproving Poquah tended to join him for day meals. Marge might understand, but she was for the night, and he'd not seen the girl after dark.

It happened early in the morning of the second day out. He hadn't slept well and had arisen before dawn, breaking and then recasting the stock pentagram of protection around the bed, leaving Poquah out cold. He had slipped out quietly and gone on deck, since he felt far more comfortable in the open air with whomever or whatever he might meet than inside, where unexpected daylight or radiation from the sun through the clouds didn't always reach. The beating of the gaunts and the vast stretches of open ocean made for heavy winds, but it was very hot and they weren't a real problem. In fact, he walked out into a brief predawn shower and found it more refreshing than irritating.

The gaunts were already beginning to slow as light seemed ready to creep above the horizon. He watched as they settled the hovecraft gently into the water, where the telltale rocking and odd pitching of a craft in heavy seas were sudden and unmistakable. Then down they came, gently settling on top, sinking below a rail and possibly down into a recess that would be covered by day. He hadn't had any particular yen to find out for sure about that.

For a short while they just drifted there, bobbling around, the bridge apparently keeping them close to a single position by steering in low, lazy circles wherever ocean current and wave wanted to move them, until, just as dawn broke, the two huge kraken beasts surfaced not far away, looked around with their Creature from the Black Lagoon faces, saw the craft, and oozed over toward it like great porpoises or perhaps a real nightmare of a Loch Ness monster until they were at the bow. Giant webbed hands reached up, took hold of the towing chains, and, with the help of some dark and indistinct crew members below, dragged out the lines until they were well forward of the craft. At that point they began to swim, taking their bearing from the sun, and within a short time were sufficiently in sync to produce the familiar roll of kraken power.

It was still cloudy with light rain, although he could see the sun coming up far off in the distance, showing how localized the shower really was, and he turned from watching the harnessing, or the changing of the power guard as it were, and was startled to see the girl leaning against the rail, looking out at the sea on the other side of the forward deck walk, just below the bridge.

She seemed oblivious to him, to the rain, to much of anything, so he swallowed hard, took a deep breath, and wandered over toward her in what he hoped seemed a casual and natural manner.

She was aware of him, though; as he approached and got very close, she began slowly to edge her way aft and toward an interior hatch.

"I—I'm sorry if I scared you!" he called to her. "I didn't mean any harm!"

She hesitated a moment, and he could see the fear and uncertainty in her eyes but then she bolted into the open doorway and was gone. He resisted the impulse to follow her. He'd made the first move; now it was up to her if she wanted to follow up with him. He was smart enough to realize that any kind of forced persistence would send exactly the wrong message.

He was actually a bit surprised at her action, though; he wasn't used to women not being instantly friendly and attracted to him, even if his own spells kept him from fully understanding why. It was still a matter of ego in a sense, and there was a bit of a nagging letdown that the first girl he'd ever found attractive in any way was somehow immune to the charm all the ones he couldn't care less about found irresistible.

Still, what must she think of anyone with passage on this ship? If she was the prize for some terrible bargain, now being sent to evil as Poquah had surmised, then what did she think he and his faerie companions might be?

She didn't show up for breakfast during the early morning period, so he prepared to go through his exercises, jog a few times around the main deck, and then lounge around in the hot sun on the afterdeck, figuring that he would at least be accessible to anybody during that whole period.

There was seldom anyone on deck—or almost anywhere else on the ship—who was awake and active during this daylight period, with the mornings being particularly deserted. He had that weird feeling of being watched again but no longer even bothered to try to catch whoever or whatever was spying. Let them catch him!

This morning, though, the second time around the deck area, he felt something go in his upper calf and suddenly came up with a really strong muscle spasm that collapsed him onto the deck for a moment in sheer agony. Trying to put some kind of pressure on it while massaging the leg helped a little, and the intensity of the spasm diminished, but he was through running for the time being, that was for sure.

Gingerly, he tried to stand up, using the rail as a support, in one way happy that nobody had seen him go down like that and in another way wishing that there were a few concerned passersby to help him to his feet. *Yow!* He hadn't had a charley horse like that in *ages*!

It wasn't comfortable to walk on, but it was manageable to a degree. The blood flow had been screwed up and there was probably slight bruising from the spasm, but in his experience the only thing that would help now would be a good massage. He made his way carefully to a bench and for the first time saw messages posted on a board just above it. Funny—he hadn't really noticed the board before.

Many were the usual—black masses every night at midnight in the chapel, a promo for a book on the scenic ruins of Arkham available in the gift shop, another flier for pterodactyl tours of Mount Doom, that sort of thing. One item, however, just block printing on a small index card tucked in a corner, caught his eye.

"Massage," it read. "Day or night. Agamemnon Garfia, days, Alestair Crowley IV, nights. Cabin 33, float deck. No appointment necessary, charge to ship's account."

That was fairly far down, on the deck where you boarded, and inside, so it was entirely possible that it was some kind of trap. Still, Poquah had said with some confidence that they wouldn't bother to trap anybody here, not on their way *to* Yuggoth, and certainly nobody had been anything but nice or at worst noncommittal to him since they'd come aboard. Why not? The leg didn't feel much better, and if he got somebody good to work on it now, he might well be jogging again by the next morning.

Aware that he could still be doing something terribly stupid, he nonetheless made his way down to the float deck and sought out cabin thirty-three, an inside cabin down the center hall. It wasn't nearly as pleasant down there as it was topside; you could feel far more of the motion of the ship, and you could also hear the moaning and groaning of the lost souls piled up in cargo below.

Cabin thirty-three looked pretty much like all the others from the outside, but like several others in the center passageway leading aft to the purser's station, it had a small plaque by the door noting that it was not a passenger cabin at all but something more official. Some said "Chief Engineer" or "Medical" or "Clergy"—best to avoid *that* one!—but this one just said "Please Enter." Hesitating yet another moment and wondering if he was being a fool, he took a deep breath, turned the knob, and pulled open the door, almost ready to run for it should the sight that was about to meet his eyes so horrify him that he needed to escape.

But there was no horrible visage, no fangs, no coffins— just a larger than expected area with two roomettes, each with a standard massage table, a bunch of towels, a small dressing room and closet area, and another door. It *was* dark, but the smell was of liniments, not incense, and he'd seen this sort of place at Terindell. If it was a trap, it was a good one.

"Get undressed and lie facedown on the table one to your right," a think, heavily accented man's voice called from somewhere beyond the inner door. "I'll be with you in just a moment."

Well, a loincloth wasn't much in the way of clothes, simple to remove and hang up, and he hadn't used sandals since coming aboard, so it was pretty easy to do as requested and lie flat.

The door opened, and a black-robed figure emerged, its face swathed in a cowl and an unnatural mistiness that made it nearly impossible to see any features. He wasn't a big man, if indeed he was a man, but he came in and stood right there, and two arms that looked surprising strong and muscular for one who appeared so slight emerged from the sleeves, reaching for the liniments. He stepped up on a platform that pulled out from the side of the table to give him the requisite height and position and started to work.

"You are too tense!" the masseur snapped. "Relax! I am not going to eat you or bite you. I am going to make you feel better!" His voice lost its harsh tone. "I know how this ship can spook some folks, but that is a very different category than what we do here. I do exactly what you are here for me to do, so please relax or I cannot do it."

He was so friendly in his tone and so natural that Irving *did* relax, feeling the liniments go on and then feeling the strong hands and surprisingly supple long fingers work on his body.

"*Unh!* You got a knot in that calf worse than a rock!" the little man said. "You are a runner?"

"Yes."

"Well, don't do it for about a day. Let it relax. I will give you a potion that will help heal it in a hurry. Don't sleep on your side, either. You let me at it now, use the balm as needed, and get some good rest, and you will be back running very quickly."

The little man was very good, and Irving found himself relaxing more and more, although attempts to shift and see the masseur's face were totally unsuccessful.

"You are Mister Garfia?"

"I was once. I suppose I still am, yes. You saw my card, then?"

"Yes, up top."

"We tend to stick the cards where those who need us most might notice them," the man told him. "We provide a full range of services that people need on this ship and beyond, but we aren't for everybody. You would be surprised, though, what we can tell just by such contact as this. For example, I can tell you her name."

Irving suddenly stiffened and started to turn, but strong hands forced him back to the proper massage position. *"What?"*

"She is Larae Ngamuku. Her mother was supposed to be a sacrifice to a volcano god, but her father loved her and made a sacrificial bargain. Spare the mother, and upon their sixteenth birthdays, any daughters would be given to the spirit world. Of course, this had the practical effect of giving her daughter to the demon in charge there, and although they tried to remain childless, it didn't work. The demon, a fellow named Zakaputi, wanted his deferred pay. Quite a story, eh?"

"But how do you know all this? Or that she is what I am curious about?"

"I feel it. I get the questions from you, and of course the answers are pretty easy in this case because she's here and we crew all know the stories. It's one of the few joys we get, swapping these stories. You want to hear the rest of it?"

"I—I suppose." *If it's true.*

"Oh, it's true, all right. I know what you're thinking. Anyway, you can almost figure out the rest between the fairy tales you know and the Rules and stuff. They loved their kid; she was beautiful. Came the approaching sixteenth birthday and they tried hard to figure out how *not* to go through with the deal, but where do you hide from a good, honest demon? Particularly when the whole kingdom knows the story and isn't too thrilled with the idea of lava coming through the nation's capital, if you get the idea. So they searched for a top sorcerer to figure a way out and found an old fellow named Lothar who's been running that region for some time with a showy associate. Anyway, Lothar tells 'em the obvious—the one thing Hell values most is a promise. A contract is a contract. You expect Hell to honor its contracts, and it expects you to do the same. Period. They knew what they were saying and doing back then, and they were stuck with it. She would have to be given over. The old boy was clever, though—devilishly clever, if I do say so myself. He worked out a spell that he felt was so secure, it would at least save the girl's life while also preserving the kingdom. A curse, as it were, that was so strong and so complicated and so outrageous that this Zakaputi fellow couldn't get around it. Blew his cork on the volcano, too, but couldn't do much to the capital because she *had* been given over."

"What did this Lothar do?" Irving asked, fascinated.

"Ah, *that* would be telling. Let's just say that she was duly presented but was no longer fit for sacrifice in the volcano. Zakaputi got so mad, he wanted to wipe everything out anyway, but he got stopped. Rules are Rules, and a bargain's a bargain. Best he could manage was to curse the parents to turn into living statues, take Larae, and send her off to Yuggoth in hopes that somebody there would be able to break Lothar's curse. I personally doubt if he ever expects to see her again, but he knows that once she's in Yuggoth and stuck as she is, all sorts of bad things will just kind of naturally happen, anyway. That's the way things are. So she got the geas to come here, to catch the ship, to go to Yuggoth, and present herself somehow in the Court of Chaos at the Dantean Gate. Of course, no time limit was put on her, so she can be there until she's an old crone and not show up. I don't think he really cares that much, you see."

"Then—what he's done is throw her to the mercy of whatever captures or enslaves her. That's not *fair!*"

"Of *course* it's not fair. To her, anyway. To everybody else it's fair. I'll tell you this, though, kid. If you keep thinking about her and looking at her, you'll eventually be attracted to her real bad no matter *what* your own spells are. Your spells will be weakened by Yuggoth, and any spells of Hell will be strengthened. That's why you find her so much more interesting today than before. Don't fall for it! Remember, you guys are headed for the Range of Fire and the Usurpers, *not* the Dantean Gate. You get involved with her, you'll be pulled the wrong way. No way around that. Her geas will screw up your luck. And you'll find you won't ever be able to get what you want from her, either."

"You mean that no matter what, she's stuck? That there's *nothing* I can do to help her? I can't accept that."

"Oh, you can help her, but only at cost to yourself. And if she *doesn't* get to the gate, you can never have any life with her. No happily ever after. Her curse will see to that. Anything nasty enough to screw up a full-blown *demon*, a volcano god, no less, is more than a match for *you.* You've been warned." The strong hands stopped the massage.

He considered the last part. "Is that what this is all about? Did you or somebody give me the cramp just to send me this message?"

There was silence, although he was certain that the other had not gone anywhere and he'd heard no sounds of movement. Suddenly he rolled over and looked around.

The room *was* empty.

He sat up, got down off the table, and went out and retrieved and put on his loincloth. There was no sign of Garfia either in the two rooms or in the anteroom, and when he tried the side door, it was locked tighter than a drum.

So it *had* been a setup! They'd seen him try to contact her this day, figured or known his interest, and given him the cramp where they did just so he'd see the card and come on down.

Keep off the grass. This property is condemned. Bought and paid for.

Well, he didn't believe in bought-and-paid-for people. He never had and never would. If they'd thought to frighten him with this story, they had made a mistake, because all this did was make him more determined to help her somehow. There *had* to be a way even if all the details were true.

Poquah would never agree to anything of this nature even if he heard the story himself. Marge might be a better ally here and maybe somebody who could even do more to help him contact the girl.

No matter what they said, this was personal now.

A SENSE OF THE FAMILIAR

Destiny shall always draw the hapless to the hopeless.
—Rules, Vol. XVII, p. 135(b)

MARGE LISTENED TO THE WHOLE ACCOUNT WITH A MIX-
ture of fascination and skepticism. Unlike Irving, who'd
stuck pretty well to days and had one view of this strange
craft, Marge had slept by day and seen the majority of passengers and crew by night, when they were most powerful
and in their full glory. She had the strong feeling that if the
other two had seen a fraction of what she had seen by
night, they wouldn't sleep much then, either.

She had, however, seen the girl in question briefly, here
and there, either just after dark or in the predawn, and knew
that she at least was neither a fantasy nor some creature of
faerie. That girl in fact had the most incredibly complex set
of spells on her that Marge, who'd seen a lot, could ever
imagine seeing, let alone figuring out. It made Irving's set
of enchantments seem feeble and childlike in comparison;
the girl's twisted mass of varicolored spaghetti strands of
curse and spell was definitely in Ruddygore territory.

She walked over to where Irving said he'd gotten his
cramp and read the bulletin board. The board was still
there—although Marge hadn't really recalled noticing it before, either—but Irving frowned and searched frantically in
the gloom for the small card. There wasn't even a space
where it might have been removed.

"It *was* here! Right there! Somebody's messed these all
up!" he maintained.

"Don't worry about it," Marge told him. "I believe you.
I didn't expect to find it; I've already looked at cabin thirty-
three. Need I say that it has no tables and not even the

156

slightest scent of liniment? It's a storeroom and packed pretty solid at that."

"I *was* there! I *did* have this talk!" he insisted.

She nodded. "I believe you. The basic layout was right— one big and two small rooms—and I don't see any way you could have known about the connecting door without having been there. Never forget that we're dealing not with flesh and blood here but rather with principalities and powers of the air, sorcerers and creatures of very powerful magic. With the pain and this roundabout way of talking to you, they got their point across."

"Were they telling the truth, though? About her, I mean."

Marge shrugged. "I dunno. Maybe. Probably. At least, they told you all the truth they wanted you to know and no more. That's the way these people work. Never do things directly when you can be sneaky, never tell a lie that isn't wrapped in truth, and never tell everything—or *anything*— that you don't think is necessary to serve your ends. Now, the question is their motive in all this."

"Huh? What do you mean?"

"Well, if they just want us to lay off the girl, there are a lot of ways to handle that. Even by their own account, she's theirs and under their complete control. Just lock her in an unassigned cabin for that matter. Put a sleep spell on her until we dock and the three of us are safely away. You see what I mean?"

"Yeah, but I don't see where it goes."

Marge smiled. "Well, then, either they are actually *trying* to lure you to take the girl, or, just as possible, if we had her along, there's a way we *could* help her that they couldn't control."

"Yeah, but why would they want me to help her? That doesn't make sense."

"It does with all those curses and magical chains she bears. Who knows what they do? Who knows what's buried there? If they control her, even without her knowledge or will, she might well be Hell's own agent sent along with us to represent their interests. We'd never take a demon along, but an innocent girl? You see?"

Irving was skeptical. "Maybe, but would they take a chance on somebody like that? I think maybe it's the McGuffin. If we can get hold of it, we can break her curses and maybe even free her parents, right?"

"Who knows? We're only supposed to *get* the thing, remember; we aren't supposed to *use* it. I seem to remember Ruddygore being very firm that this thing's more dangerous to the wisher than the Lamp, and *that* was risky enough, believe me."

"Well, I still think we ought to help her, damn it!" the boy cried. "We can't just leave her when we *might* help."

Marge sighed. "I seem to remember that this is what got Joe going in this same direction. If I didn't know better, I'd say somebody on high has a one-track mind and not much imagination. Okay, I'll see what I can do. There's not a lot of time left, you know. We've already passed the other ship on this line heading back to Husaquahr, which means we're more than halfway there. That'll get us in at worst the day after tomorrow—or, more accurately, the night after tomorrow night, probably an hour after sunset. That doesn't leave us a lot of leeway, and we have to contact her and see if she *wants* to be helped before we can do anything else."

He was shocked. "Of *course* she *wants* to be helped! Why wouldn't she?"

"If she's guilt-ridden for what happened to her parents, or maybe just flipped out by it all and resigned, or maybe not as pure and clean as we thought—there's lots of reasons. She might even just not believe that there is any hope at all and refuse in order to spare us part of her curse."

"And what about Poquah? If we get involved with her, he's gonna throw a fit."

"Let him. He's a warrior and a sorcerer, and his lot is sneaky by instinct. Maybe it's time he put a little of those old skills to work as well as the new. But why bother him until we can speak with her? And if we can't, it's kind of out of our hands."

"We *got* to get to her, then! One of us! We just *got* to!"

Marge sighed. "I'm a sucker for this kind of thing myself, and it always causes problems. Oh, well . . . I just wish they told us what kind of a curse that fellow Lothar came up with that could even screw up a demon."

As it turned out, it *was* Marge who had the next chance at contact with the strange girl, and she was glad it was she and not Irving who did. It was pretty easy to see how the kid could be pretty intimidating, but a faerie, a female, and one of unknown but beautiful appearance did engender more curiosity than threat.

Truth to tell, though, Marge was pretty damned happy to see Irving acting like a normal teenage human being. Maybe there was hope for him yet.

It was just before dawn again, as before, but because he'd stayed up so late with Marge the night before and had been so excited, Irving hadn't arisen when he'd intended, and Marge was on her own.

She suspected that the girl came up every morning before dawn, and she could understand why. This ship with all its dangers was probably least dangerous at this very time, when all the possible mischief from the dark had been done and denizens were going to their rest lest the sun strike them but before the kraken and the ghouls and demons of the day began their less threatening but still intimidating shifts. It had to lift the spirits of somebody as stuck as the girl was just to watch the magnificence of the sun break over the horizon, filling the world with warmth, light, and glory.

Marge flew up and settled down comfortably on a bulkhead just behind and above the girl, who was staring out at the sea, watching the first small streaks appear signaling first false, then true dawn.

"It's the best part of the day, isn't it?" she said casually, conversationally, as if speaking to a friend.

The girl jumped, whirled around, then spotted the Kauri

with her butterfly wings perched sexily above. "Oh! I did not see you!"

"I'm sorry I startled you. I kinda like this myself, to tell the truth. I'm stuck as basically a night creature, and this ship's pretty damned depressing most of the time. I think if I hear that Tiliki Li Revue one more time, I'll blow this thing up."

"You—you're not one of *them*?"

"Not hardly. Or at least not exactly. Faerie is faerie, and mostly we're neutral. We sit around and do our own things and watch you folks do your own things and shake our heads. Some take sides, mostly on the dark side. More immediate power even if you face oblivion when the Final Judgment comes, if and when it ever does. The Kauri take no sides in the affairs of mortals or in the Heaven versus Hell battle, but occasionally individuals like me do. I like to think I'm on the good side, but mostly I'm doin' favors for old friends, like now."

"I—I'm one of *them*. Not that I wish to be or that I had any choice, but sometimes fate does that to people. At the moment my soul is still my own; it is only my body that they own. How long I can keep that is the question I ask myself."

"I got to admit, you have more spells and curses on you than I ever saw before on anybody. Still, you're heading in the right direction, if you can believe it, if you want any crack at getting rid of that shit."

"What?" The girl acted as if she didn't understand the words.

"Yuggoth. I know the reputation, and I think we'll both find it lives up to that, but in all that crud there's something that can make wishes come true, and its power is pretty awesome. My friends and I are after it. That's why we're here."

There had been a glimmer of hope in the girl's face, but at this news, instead of being elated and encouraged, she seemed to deflate into despair once more. "So you're on a treasure hunt," she said simply.

"In a way, yes. But we have some advantages most others don't. For one thing, we aren't after it for ourselves. My companions and I are reasonably satisfied. We're doing it because a good and powerful friend asked us to and because the father of one of us, the boy you might have seen around here, vanished down there trying to help somebody else on the same quest."

"So *that's*— Uh, so now you're all going down there and you'll vanish, too?"

"I hope not. I've been in this spot before and succeeded. You can't believe the things I've seen and done with some of the same companions and in the service of the same sorcerer."

"Which sorcerer is that?"

"He calls himself Ruddygore of Terindell here. He is on the Council and is overall a good man who's kept a lot of evil from taking over this world. Ever heard of him?"

"I have heard the name mentioned once or twice. I know he is powerful and of the north but little else. I have little use for sorcerers. They are too clever for their own good."

"I understand that one saved you from being sacrificed," Marge noted, trying to verify as much of the story as possible.

"That is true, although I do not know where you heard this. It was not a favor. Had he not intervened, then my parents would still be themselves and I would be dead but my soul would be pure and free. In trying to help me, all of them did themselves harm and me most of all, since I am condemned to a life under these sorts of demons and villains."

Marge was actually impressed with the girl's attitude. Maybe there was somebody here worth saving, just as Irving suspected. "You aren't just looking at sunrises, then? You have thought of throwing yourself into the sea?"

The girl returned a sour chuckle. "It is *all* I think about, but it is impossible. For one thing, one cannot fall from this boat. It is—prevented. But even if this were not so, I could not. I am under a geas. It prevents me from even doing myself deliberate harm until it is fulfilled."

Marge understood the dilemma more than most. "But if you *do* fulfill it, you will probably lose your soul."

The girl nodded. "You see that they did me no favor in saving my life. For what? Now they suffer, and I am truly lost."

Marge gave her a thoughtful half smile as the sun broke over the water and said, "Not necessarily. Alone, I can agree with you, but as part of a group you can find some chance of success. It's called joining a Company, and it's very plain in the Rules. If we get what we're after, Ruddygore can use it to reverse even the dictates of Hell. I've seen it done before. Even Hell plays by the Rules here—sort of."

"What makes you think you can succeed where the boy's father failed?"

Marge shrugged. "First, I don't know if he did or if he's just out of sight and stalking it. He's lost from *our* point of view but probably not from his own. Second, because I've been up against dragons and monsters and evil demonic princes and zombies and the rest, and no matter how hopeless it seemed, we won. Third, because it's in Hell's interest for us to win, too. What we're after solves a problem for them as well. I think they'll help more than hinder us in getting it. It's only after that that we'll need to watch our backs."

"What can the likes of you and your companions do that all the legions of Hell cannot?" the girl asked skeptically.

"A very good question," Marge admitted. "I'm the first to tell you that I don't know the answer to it and that it'll be one of the big surprises at the end of this journey to perhaps find that out. One thing at a time. I'm offering you a chance to come with us. No strings attached, no conditions, and only the obligation of being one of the group, and that is helping where and when you can."

"And this Company is you, the elf, and the boy I have seen?" She didn't exactly sound overwhelmed.

Marge had a certain level of sympathy and understanding for somebody in the girl's predicament—she'd gone through an awful lot at that age—but there was a limit to this. "I just made the offer, and that's all. You can either throw in with us and maybe, just maybe, get out of this if you're a good team player and you work with us, or you can leave, follow your compulsive spells into Yuggoth, and go to your inevitable doom. Never say life isn't full of choices but don't start talking down to gift horses, either. You're just a complication on my job; we'd probably have a little easier time without you and particularly without somebody who feels the way you do toward us. My elfin companion—an Imir, by the way, and quite a dangerous breed—wants us to forget you. The boy wants you included. Since I like the boy and I've been in a few tight spots like yours myself, I'm on his side at the moment, but that's subject to change."

She started to move off her perch and actually turned a bit away from the girl. It was no mock move; she was out of patience and felt absolutely no guilt over her attitude. Given a choice between a chance at life, however slim and improbable, and certain doom, it would take a fool to turn it down. You could get killed traveling with fools through dangerous territory.

"Wait! Please—do not go. Not yet."

It was said so softly and so plaintively that Marge froze, turned, and looked back down at the girl. The Kauri was beginning to feel the lethargy of daylight and knew that it wouldn't be long before she'd have to force herself to stay awake and alert, but this was worth the discomfort.

"I am of the night," she told the girl. "I have no more time today, and I do not audition for the role of helper. The boy thinks like a boy: he sees somebody in trouble, and his innate sense of justice says to help. I see somebody in trouble, and my instinct is to offer some help, too. But neither of us, *neither one of us*, will audition to please anyone. His father was a king once, and I never called him anything but by his first name. Consider yourself on probation here, not us. If you are interested, see the boy today or contact me here either just after dusk or just before dawn. I'll discuss this no more this morning. I need only remind you that we put in to Yuggoth tomorrow night, and the powers that draw you one way and us another will rise even greater."

"No, wait! I—" But it was too late; the Kauri had taken off and flown to the other side of the ship and was gone from sight.

From a point at which all had been predetermined except the details, Larae suddenly had no idea just *what* to do. The logic that Marge had seen as so simple wasn't quite so simple from her side, even though it was clearly in front of her. If only the boy wasn't involved . . . !

She didn't like being out after the sun had set, when things might roam this ship and search for sport, nor did she feel comfortable having a conversation with so many chances of it reaching the wrong ears. But tomorrow morning, here, in the period between false and true dawn, when those same creatures did not want to chance being caught out on deck but when both she and the Kauri could speak, *then* she would lay it all out and the final decision on this be taken. There was no other way.

Marge was as good as her word and wasn't all that surprised to see the girl show up that final morning at sea.

It wasn't the same nice weather as before, though. Clouds covered the sea to the horizon on all sides save due north, and there were dark and fuzzy patches all over, often glowing as if they had inner fires burning, showing that this was going to be a rough last day, particularly when the gaunts settled in for the morning and the kraken took over. Already the waves were breaking over the bow and the sea looked fierce; where they were headed, it seemed as if it could only get worse. A fitting approach to a legendary land of dread, though, if Marge did say so herself.

Much more disturbing than the weather, though, was the same scene in faerie sight. On that level, the sky was even more animated, the clouds all purple and black and *alive*, moving about at frantic speeds and seeming to converge on a distant point just to the southwest. Such a sight Marge couldn't remember seeing since the great war that had climaxed her first great adventure here, and even that had had less power than this scene represented.

"It looks like storms," the girl remarked, much subdued from their previous meeting.

"In more ways than one. If you had faerie sight, you might be really chilled. I just wonder if this is normal for these parts or if it, too, is part of this new element. Poquah will know." *I'll have to talk to him anyway, since I haven't really mentioned you, yet,* she thought a bit nervously.

"I—I wish to join you," Larae told the Kauri. "As you pointed out, there is little choice considering the alternative. I still do not see how this will be done, but I am willing to try, although only under conditions I hope you will not find unusual."

"Conditions?" Hadn't she learned yet that she wasn't in much of a position to make terms?

"Yes. Simple ones. I will be one of you, no more. I will do my part or whatever is asked of me in the course of a journey, but that is all. I do not want the boy to expect more or think in terms of some romantic fable."

Marge nodded. "I see. Actually, I doubt if you have to worry much about that. I know he has an unnatural attraction, but he's also got a spell that keeps him honest, even chaste. There's no guarantee that such a spell will hold up where we're going, but he's no threat on that score, I don't think. If he gets out of control in that department, it'll be from ignorance, not malice, and I'm pretty sure you can defend yourself against the likes of that. Black magic, sorcery—that's something else, but we'll have to cross that bridge if and when we come to it. Fair enough?"

"Fair enough," she agreed. "But what did you mean by him having an unnatural attraction?"

"You didn't feel it when you saw him? Hell, even *I* felt it, and I'm not supposed to. That's my kind of power, and consciously done, not something somebody has over me.

Took help of a magical sort to insulate me. You *really* don't feel it?"

"Not a thing."

Marge frowned. "That curse of yours—it doesn't have you lusting after women, does it?"

Larae looked shocked, even appalled. "Of *course* not!"

"Hmmm . . . Well, it was a thought. Um, out of curiosity, you want to tell me what this big-shot sorcerer did that screwed even a demon? If there's anything sitting out there that might cause me trouble later, I want to know it now."

"I—it would not affect any of you in any way. It is strictly upon me and is much too embarrassing for me to really talk about, much less reveal. I swear to you that it will in no way affect you or the others unless the boy really does lack self-control. *That* is the one danger and is why I hesitated before."

"Hmmm . . . So I should warn him, I guess. In fact, that might be enough to dampen whatever might be waking up inside him. Curses are really nasty, and he's seen the results of some of them. You've got me curious, but it's your right and I'll take your word that it's nothing that need concern us insofar as our goal is concerned. Okay. That leaves us with what we do immediately after we get off this tub and what happens then. Just what are you supposed to do?"

"I do not know. I was compelled to come this far, but I feel nothing in terms of a specific action at the moment except that I must somehow get to a strange place that exists only in a mind picture of a great mountain out of which has been carved a massive gatelike structure that can open to let people enter its darkness. I know what it looks like but not where it is, save that it is in Yuggoth somewhere."

"Well, it's called the Dantean Gate, if that's any help. Dante was the first name of a man from long ago who wrote three books claiming to be accounts of his trip as a living person through Hell, Purgatory, and Heaven. It was fiction but, like much fiction of this type, appears to have had its dream roots in a real place here. I think you're see-

ing in your mind where a lot of the poor souls chained below are headed—the gates to Hell."

"The Dantean Gate ... Yes, it sounds right. I *must* go
there and present myself, but I do not *wish* to go there. Is
it by any chance close to where you are headed?"

"I doubt it. If I remember the directions, we're heading
straight toward the middle of the continent, then off to the
south to a creepy volcanic range. The Dantean Gate is in
the jagged mountain range to the far west. Still, you have
nothing save the image? Nobody is with you or supposed
to meet you?"

"No one is with me. I have not been told of any others,
but it would not surprise me if someone *did* meet me at the
other end, at least to get me going. It has happened before
in getting me this far. Their agents know what to do with
me, or at least they can read and aid my geas."

"Hmmm ... And there are folks aboard who know we're
interested in you. Know enough to try and warn us off."
She sighed. "Well, we're gonna be playing in their ballpark,
but we're also obviously somebody they need for some reason. I don't think they're omnipotent, just clever. How
much luggage do you have?"

"Only what I can fit into a moderate backpack. There
was little that I had in the first place, all things considering."

"Uh huh. Okay, look—there's not much that can be done
until we're off the ship tonight. Act normal, do whatever
you would do if we weren't talking, and disembark as per
normal. I'll be shadowing you. You might not see me, but
I'll be there. Believe it. The guys will try and make contact
with our prearranged guide and hopefully get settled for the
night. We're not about to go off into the interior of a place
like Yuggoth without supplies and information as well as
whatever else we can get. We'll try and keep you in close
proximity to us until we are ready to leave. *Then* we'll join
up. In the meantime I should be able to keep some kind of
contact with you, unless we get into full-scale in-person demons or heavy-duty sorcery here, in which case there isn't

much chance in the first place. Understand? Just trust that I can get to you. You'll see."

"You are not exactly invisible," Larae noted. "You stand out in any setting with your beautiful wings."

"Don't worry. I have a few little secrets myself. I don't want to make this structured, because the more we improvise, the harder it is for anyone who wants to stop us to figure out what we're doing and counter it. You will have to trust me on this. We *do* know what we are doing."

She hoped that she was telling the truth on this one. Hell, she still had to tell Poquah about this . . .

Poquah, however, was anything but surprised. "We should not have involved ourselves with her," he maintained. "What do we know about her? Enough to know that Hell does not want us interfering, in which case we make enemies in their own land, or, conversely, they want to unload her on us by this subterfuge, in which case she's their spy. I fail to see the gain in either situation."

"The gain is that we do what is right in a land where that is rare, and we don't lose our timing or concentration regretting what we didn't do or worrying about who we might have helped but didn't," Marge responded.

"Yes, but what earthly *good* is she? Does she handle weapons well? Does she have great magical powers? Has she any influence to help us in strange lands or any foreknowledge we lack? I can tell you right now that she does not."

"Yeah? How do you know?"

"Would you like an item-by-item inventory of her bag? Don't look surprised—the moment Irving laid eyes on her, I knew she'd be trouble. I tell you that she has a brush, a comb, some minor makeup and perfume, miscellaneous toiletries, and three essentially identical white cotton outfits of no use whatever in the bush. She also has a pair of exceptionally well made sandals but appears comfortable barefoot and a few pieces of jewelry of reasonable but not exceptional quality. No weapons, not even a penknife. One needs only look at her hands to see that she's done little manual labor, if any at all, and I seriously doubt if she can boil water. She carries neither anything negotiable nor any identification or official papers, and since her dresses have no pockets and she carries no purse, I assume she has nothing with her. I don't see a single way in which she is or can be made into an asset."

"You're done?"

"I could continue."

"Well, don't bother. The point is, it doesn't make any difference. Irving is going to help her regardless, which means she's a real liability for us unless we go along with him, and she's so damned helpless-appearing, I can't help but feel she's got something up her sleeve we can't figure out. I'm also damned curious about her curse. If she proves a serious problem, we can always ditch her later, but for now she's coming."

Poquah sighed. "Very well. I admit the magical skills evident in her burden of spells is intriguing. It is a totally different concept, a totally different philosophy than I've ever seen expressed in spells before. Almost as if the impossible were here—a different mathematics. Between Master Lothar's skills and what this minor demon laid upon her, it is most fascinating."

"Really? Do you think you could break any of them?"

"Don't be absurd! She is mortal; I am faerie. Perhaps I am the greatest general sorcerer in the history of my people, but there are real limits. It would take a Ruddygore to have a chance at untangling a Lothar, and as for those set upon one by a true demon—next to impossible. It would take mercy from a creature of Heaven to do that, after examining the will and the worthiness of a supplicant. I don't think she quite qualifies. No, it is an academic exercise, purely academic. Just to figure it out would be a triumph."

Deep down Marge had always known that Poquah was something of a softy.

It hadn't been a great day at sea. Thunderstorms had raged all around, the decks had been awash, waves had pounded the craft as even the kraken had trouble pulling it in this kind of surf, and some of the biggest waves had risen almost up to the wheelhouse and seemed to loom like monsters, only to crash and submerge the bow of the vessel, which then wriggled in all planes at once to get free and slowly rise up out of the water to do it all over again. It made walking almost impossible, and anything that wasn't fastened down inside was instantly transformed into something of a missile.

Irving was excited to know that the girl was in with them, although the idea that she'd be just "one of the boys" hadn't really sunk in as such. Still, he was much more concerned with getting out of the rotten weather, at least for now. Although he wasn't as seasick as some of the others he'd passed in the corridors seemed to be, he certainly felt dizzy and a bit queasy. It was impossible to be anything close to human and not have this condition. He worried that the girl might well be sick in her cabin.

There really wasn't much he could do about it, though, or about anything else right now. He certainly wasn't going to, er, *eat*, and besides, it might be a long night. He stayed in bed as much of the day as he could, even though that put him next to the totally zonked Marge, which was something of an unusual experience.

Poquah might or might not have been affected by the storms, but he chose to demonstrate his mental command of himself by ignoring the situation when that was at all possible. He spent some time checking and rechecking his weapons as well as the copy of the map of Yuggoth they had secured from Macore.

The map was certainly authentic in that it had been made by someone with skill who seemed to know the region well. In fact, the level of detail was so impressive, it seemed almost as if it had been taken not from pieced-together ground explorations and by flying creatures going over it sector by sector, as with most maps of this world, but from some great but detailed height. Poquah had seen Earth satellite photos of continental masses and maps made from high-resolution orbital surveys of Earth's regions that were no better than this one, and who could go that high or get that kind of detail here?

It was absurdly easy, though, to use it to plot a route, and the annotations in a fine handwriting showed a very definite approach to and location of the lair of the McGuffin. It would not be a good idea, the Imir decided, to follow this map so closely that they would head straight toward their goal along that route. If the minions of Hell knew of this, they might well decide that their little party was dispensable. Safer to waste probably close to a week to veer over to the seat of the king of this place and go through the motions anyway. Do the expected and save the unexpected for when it was most needed and when your enemies thought they had you cold.

He carefully refolded and stored the map and then went out, his unnatural faerie balance keeping him on the deck as if all were smooth as glass even though the ship was moving in ways even he never knew a ship could move. *Just so long as it does not move straight down,* he thought, not a little nervous in spite of his appearance and demeanor. The Imir were masters of many things, but they had to breathe just as most other life did, and they could not breathe water.

The crew didn't seem to be any happier about the ride than was the Imir, for what that was worth.

"Usually smooth as silk," the watch officer assured him. "It's this new element trying to move in. You've seen it in the skies, I think, too. Drawing all the powers inward, trying to disrupt everything so much, they can blow a hole right through space-time and open a gateway to this world."

"They are concentrating on a specific spot, then?"

"Oh, sure. Somewhere in the southeast, close to Mount Doom. The attraction's pretty severe, too. They're getting a lot of our people under their influence and some of the normal types, too. Some free advice: you stay out of that area. I hear tell that nobody or nothin' can withstand goin' over to them if they get too close. We sent an entire cohort of demons, medium-powered types, good fighters, veterans of the spiritual wars. Not a one came back, but they're still very much around as the guardians of that damned place."

"Really? That *is* interesting, and disturbing," Poquah responded. Now, for the first time, he understood why even Satan and the minions of Hell weren't directly battling these other dimensionly types who were moving into their turf. "Hell" was almost the very definition of evil in this world, as on Earth; there was little of virtue left in its followers, and even apathy fed their cause—fed it perhaps best of all—so what did Hell do when confronted with a new and alien concept of evil?

In a sense, Hell was as biblical as Heaven; they recognized the same rules, the same morality, the same concepts of good and evil. It was essential that they do so, so that when they acted in the other's reality, they did the opposite of what would be expected of one loyal to that side. Torture, murder, pain, debauchery—these were only the "thou shalt nots" of the heavenly side. The *system* remained, which was why the Rules themselves worked.

The ones attempting to come through near Mount Doom, though—*those* were outside the system, outside the Rules, outside *any* rules applicable to this world or even to Earth. Good and evil had a different meaning in their case, although in one way and one way only it was the same: what served *them* and *their* interests defined "good," and what opposed, inhibited, or impeded them was "evil" in their view. In such a situation those loyal to Hell didn't have a prayer, as it were. The fact their very natures were grounded in the concept of *this* world's evil made them gravitate to the power that seemed the strongest yet would have them.

Only those not already of Hell might have any chance at all of withstanding such power long enough to do any good.

Not for the first time, Poquah found himself silently but internally wondering about Ruddygore's judgment. It had always worked out before, but there had always been an underlying sense of the mathematics of magic and the comfort of the Rules guiding him no matter how odd his routes to goals. But now, in *this* quest . . .

A boy who had never even faced *ordinary* evil of the kind that terrified most men and sent the rest gibbering in the moonlight in helpless insanity; a Kauri with the strength of a small child, whose gifts were all for defense; a silent elfin warrior from a race of warrior-assassins who nonetheless had severe limits on his own powers and was more susceptible to the other side than he wanted to admit; and now added to this a girl no older than the boy, without skills, spoiled and defenseless, and on top of that cursed.

This agent they were supposed to meet in Red Bluffs had better be the equivalent of a dozen legions of high-ranking demons, Poquah thought. Otherwise, how could they stand? How could they hope to do anything at all?

The ship shuddered, then seemed to smooth out a bit, and slowly but surely the severity of the motion simply faded away and there was a steady and comfortable feel to it once more.

"What happened?" Poquah asked the ghoul on duty.

The creature shrugged. "It is sundown. The gaunts have risen and kept us steady above the ocean, and we should be coming in toward the harbor in a little while and protection from the elements. We are running late and will certainly not be getting in before four or five more hours, but it should be all right from this point."

Poquah bolted past him, went out onto the deck, and looked out and forward. In the gloom he could clearly see a dark landmass in the distance, and the rain seemed to have slackened off to a steady but routine little disturbance. Away to the south could easily be seen clusters of lights, as if small towns or settlements along the coast were coming into view, and here and there he could see the unmistakable signal of a lighthouse.

When he shifted to faerie sight, the land came in much more clearly, but in an eerie crimson outline and inky black on gray. This was a place of strong and powerful magic, of deepest sorceries and treacherous spells of a kind that made

Husaquahr seem almost benign to look at. Here all the strings of magic were deep yellows and crimsons and dark purples and blacks.

The ancient land of Yuggoth, from which it was said all magic had sprung, and from where the Tree of Knowledge of Good and Evil had come and to where it had returned after being the instrument for betraying Earth's humanity, and from which all the nightmares sprang was there, now, in plain sight, and they were coming in at a fair clip to its dark shores.

A few hours late, perhaps, but they were at last in Yuggoth.

NOT SO UNFAMILIAR A PLACE

The seat of the worst of evil shall have the face of comfort to the unwary.

—Rules, Vol. XIII, p. 162(a)

"SO THAT'S IT, HUH?" IRVING SAID, STARING AHEAD AS they came inside the breakwater and the *Eibon* made ready to land.

Marge nodded, feeling a bit nervous for the first time. "Yeah, that's it."

This harbor really didn't look all that different from the one they'd left, only a bit larger and more the size of a commercial port than that of a traditional recreational area. The town, more like a city almost, spread out in all directions before them and, from the lights and angles, appeared to be built back into some fair-sized hills. Streets and houses seemed to go right up those hillsides, and the population looked unexpectedly dense.

The harbor had a number of exotic-looking craft in port, many of which were very large sailing ships of designs none of them had ever seen before. The single-masted square sailers could be dismissed as local coastal boats; you wouldn't have much to steer with if you got too far off-shore in those things. Others, however, looked enormous, the size of old Spanish galleons in romantic swashbuckler movies, and still others looked like sleek men-of-war with catapults clearly showing and all sorts of unknowable armaments as well. They were in a variety of colors and finishes, many brightly painted, others almost camouflaged by their colors and patterns, but it was clear that they hailed from many lands and were there for a multitude of purposes.

They were mostly human craft, but here and there could

be seen fairy folk as well, again of unknown races and backgrounds, doing work on the craft and at the docksides as well. Many were of the same sort of elflike classes as were the most familiar ones of the north such as the Imir, but they had strange colors, often nearly luminescent yet somehow dark; blues and deep yellows and reds of all sorts abounded here. Now and again could be seen creatures that looked in some ways to be relatives of dwarves, and some crawled up and down the rigging with abandon and seemed almost insectlike.

The effect was less one of coming into a port of evil than one of entering a port in some strange and foreign land, which was exactly what it was. The first ship to come into old Shanghai or Tokyo Bay in the nineteenth century or Bombay must have afforded its passengers and crew a similar sensation.

"Wow!" Irving said, staring at the scene in absolute wonderment. "I didn't expect *this*!"

"It certainly is, er, *different* than I anticipated," Poquah harrumphed, impressed in spite of himself. "These aren't all Yuggoth lands and races represented here, either. I see flags of several continents here, although none at the moment from Husaquahr, the largest and the mother of them all."

"They kind of understate their names here, too," Marge commented, staring. "I sure would call this a fair-sized city, not 'Red Bluffs,' which sounds like a small town in Nebraska." She frowned. "Still, most of the faerie colors signify dark magic, and the few flying types I've seen are bat-winged. We mustn't forget where we are."

"I concur," Poquah responded as they came slowly right into a form-fitting slip at the foot of a very broad street. He changed his tone and lowered his voice. "Now, if you are following the girl, you'd best get on it. You know the name of the hotel where we are booked, so we will meet there when you have something to say."

She nodded. "Don't worry. Fliers can keep track of people a lot easier than ground huggers."

"You watch yourself! There are creatures here that would

eat a Kauri for breakfast or turn her dark. Don't think it can't be done to you!"

"I'll be careful. Don't worry."

She took off, up into the darkness. Irving turned to Poquah and saw in the always impassive elf something he'd never really observed there before—concern. It was very subtle, almost impossible to notice unless, like the boy, you'd been around the Imir for many years, but to Irving it was as startling as Mr. Spock having a crying fit.

"You really *are* worried about her, aren't you?"

"About all of us," the Imir responded. "But yes, I believe she is particularly vulnerable to the temptations of this place. For one thing, she does not believe that she is, and that makes her far more of a target, and secondly, she sees the threats primarily as external, coming from creatures of the night. That better fits the Ancient Ones for all the legends and terror stories. Hell works best from *inside* and with one's own cooperation. You remember her reaction to the Succubi?"

"Yeah, sure. She didn't like them at all."

"They are the same, really. Not enough difference to matter in the composition department. The difference is that the Kauri cleanse souls and the Succubi devour them. Either is capable of doing the other's work. We faerie are living creatures, and all living creatures must eat. Marge has been faced with a clientele of late that is almost too much of a good thing—a forced banquet, as it were. In Husaquahr she could get rid of it before it became too much a part of her. Here—I don't know." He paused for a moment, looking out at the dock. "Ah! The gangplank is out! We may go ashore! It will be good to get some solid land under us again, eh?"

Irving followed Poquah down to the disembarkation point, looking around for any sign of the girl, but he didn't see her at all. He didn't like that, but there wasn't much he could do about it. Either Marge could link up with her and, he hoped, steer her away from harm and toward them, or she couldn't. There just wasn't anything the two of them could do right now.

As a small child back on Earth, or "back in the real world" as Irving still tended to think of it even though this was by far the more familiar one to him by this point, he remembered seeing a picture that they seemed to run every Christmas. He never remembered all the details, but he remembered that this good guy got real down on Christmas Eve and wished he'd never been born, and Heaven granted his wish to show him how important he was. When he'd gone back home, his nice, peaceful white-bread town had become a wide-open strip of bars, gambling joints, and all the other stuff they thought was awful back then before somebody discovered real drugs. It still had looked pretty mean and ugly, particularly to a little kid, compared to what had been there before.

He flashed back instantly to that scene in that picture as he followed Poquah off the boat and walked down into the town in spite of not having thought of it in so many years that the memory's very existence was a surprise. It was, however, *exactly* the effect of walking off the ship and into the town of Red Bluffs.

The whole place was lit up in every kind of gaudy way; wild music and laughter came from dingy-looking joint after joint up the broad main street, and when he could see in the windows, he saw women, mostly in the wildest imaginable underwear and stuff and in weird poses, and occasionally faerie of the same sort. Well, no, not just women—there was a whole set of guys just as wild-looking and posed like, well, Irving wasn't certain just *what* to make of it, but he had the general idea.

There were sidewalk barkers trying to get passersby into the shops and shows with all sorts of loud and boisterous claims and promises, some of which were clearly impossible without sorcery of a most perverse sort. They also offered other kinds of recreational pleasure, from the wildest of drugs to the weirdest of drinks and potions; all this was wide-open and unconcealed. It was like the most outrageous elements of every bar, burlesque, and red-light district in all the world or worlds.

Shops near the places, sandwiched between, or on narrow side streets offered all sorts of roots, potions, drugs, sexual paraphernalia, weapons, you name it, both conventional and magical. There were also promises of all sorts of cures, curses for sale or rent, curses lifted, fortunes told, and so on and so on. Here and there an occasional boisterous fight would burst from inside one of the establishments into the street, and there would be screams of both delight and terror coming from the various upstairs windows.

Irving absolutely loved it.

Poquah sighed and shook his head sadly at the sights and sounds. He had thought it might be ugly and mean, but he'd never thought it would be this base and, well, *tacky*.

"Gee, it's like a grown-up Disneyland with no cops," Irving commented, unable to stop staring at one attraction or distraction after another.

"There are cops, as you call them," the Imir responded in a low and measured tone. "They simply have a somewhat different agenda." He pointed at two dark-cloaked, uniformed figures walking down one of the sidewalks opposite them as if they owned it. Everybody from patrons to barkers got out of their way as they came, too, and they barely deigned to notice anyone else. Their faces showed them as definite minor demons, horns and all, and they were puffing on big fat cigars and talking to each other.

"The name of the game," Poquah instructed the boy, "is power. Period. That is all that it's *ever* really about. Who's got it, who's subject to it. These are the folks who instructed Sodom and Gomorrah on morality and entertainment value and later on instructed the SS, the Gestapo, and a lot of other cheery authority figures. If this seems so wondrous and fun and romantic to you, think about where the ones who perform these services come from and how willing they were to do the jobs until forced into it. Think of your young woman from the boat in the hands of these folks, walking up this street as we are now doing. People, and parts of people, are bought and sold here, and I doubt if permission is required."

"Hey! Boy! You! The Nubian! Ever dream of having all your fantasies come true?"

The speaker was a nasty-looking fellow with a strong family resemblance to a middle linebacker and a brick wall, and he seemed to have a friend or two about as well.

"The boy is under my protection," Poquah said evenly, not stopping. "He is not for the likes of you."

"Yeah? *Somethin' wrong with the likes of me, piss-elf?*"

"Other than the fact that you are a bully and an idiot who is about to find himself dead and at the Dantean Gates if you persist in this, nothing much," Poquah responded.

A big, beefy hand shot out and grabbed Poquah's tunic. The Imir stopped and stared up into the eyes of the huge man, his face as impassive as ever, but the eyes, something in the Imir's eyes . . .

Even the big man caught it, but it was much too late to back out now. "Stop and face me when you're talkin' to me!"

"I was not talking to you. I was responding to your uninvited comments."

Irving's hand went to his short sword, but he didn't draw it; rather, he positioned himself to cover Poquah's back.

It was impossible to imagine the Imir being anything but a grease spot at the hands of the big man, but Irving knew better.

"I *take* what I want, shorty, and I want *him*," the big man snarled.

"Then, sir, you are dead," the Imir responded.

Absolutely no one could agree later about what happened next. There was a sound and flash something like an electrical charge, and then the elf was a blur of motion, going so fast and moving in such an unnatural series of moves that no watching eye, whether human or faerie, could follow them.

The big man's other hand held a dagger, and it was coming up with professional speed. It never even came close.

Almost instantly, amid the flash and blur of Imir motion, something ripped the big man open as if he were an over-ripe melon. Guts and blood spilled from massive and nearly instantly fatal wounds without it being clear how those wounds had been administered and with such speed that the man was dead on his feet yet his expression showed no change at all. Suddenly Poquah was a few steps to one side of him, his back against Irving's, no visible weapon in hand, and the big man's body was only then collapsing into a gruesome heap in the street.

The big man's confederates were easy to spot; they were the ones with the totally frightened and confused expressions among a crowd of mostly admiring glances. Nobody, friend or foe, was inclined to do much more to the Imir and the youth, and they gave way and made a comfortable path up the broad street for the two newcomers to go. There was even a smattering of applause.

Mostly, however, the people and creatures around them totally ignored the fight and the corpse and just went on with their business as if nothing had happened and no remains were there.

There was a sudden shimmering around the body, and the street itself seemed to turn into something alive underneath him, cobblestones growing long, clawed arms and gaping tooth-filled mouths and growling and chomping as they devoured the big corpse amazingly quickly.

Poquah seemed utterly unfazed by what he'd just done or by its aftermath. Instead of being repelled by the sight of the street literally rending and tearing and devouring the body as Irving was—slightly, at least in his stomach—the Imir commented, "Well, at least they have efficient sanitation here. Come. We have a hotel to reach yet."

Irving felt a mixture of confidence in having passed a test and at the same time a less than pleasant sense that this was not going to be a fun time, after all. He thought of the girl and Marge and, for the first time, his father trapped in that bimbo body and wondered how in hell any of them were going to make it across much of a continent like this.

And most of all he wondered about those tearing limbs and gnashing teeth that were even now cleaning up the last of the body and felt less than certain of his own footing and suddenly uncomfortable that he was barefoot.

Larae Ngamuku needed no imagination to realize what walking up that broad street would mean for her and no wish even to try it. This was a case in which some care and caution might be well repaid.

The problem was, getting off the ship, she had no idea where exactly to go. Compelled to come this far, her path eased by the demonic geas that all of Hell could sense, she had nonetheless come without instructions, as it were, and certainly without resources.

"Go to your right at the end of the dock," a woman's voice came to her. "I'll give you instructions to thread you through this mess as you go."

She looked around but saw no one in the throng of people and, well, others coming off the ship, working to unload it, or waiting on the docks. Whoever had made the comment could have been almost anyone of them.

It seemed silly to obey a mysterious voice, but there also wasn't much of a choice in the matter. Not to obey would leave her no better off.

Turning right at the first opportunity as instructed, she saw only an industrial road paved with uneven stones, mostly dark, and sparsely traveled at this time. She felt something odd as she walked and, looking down, saw that strange metal rods were actually embedded in parallel in the street itself. The rods seemed to run the full length of the street as far as she could see, but she couldn't imagine what they were for save perhaps to catch the side of sandals or boots and twist ankles.

Marge, now above the girl, was equally surprised to see them, but she recognized the parallel rods as rails. A railroad? Here? Up until now she'd never seen any evidence of engines in this whole world, only magic, wind, water, and muscle power. This might well bear much closer examination when she had the chance.

Marge didn't like remaining in the air too long. It made her too conspicuous, and she could see that there were as many unpleasant creatures of the night up in the air, perched atop roofs and lofts and just flying around, as there seemed to be on the ground. She was hardly beyond their notice, either, but so far they seemed content simply to accept her as an equal and not interfere. For the moment the real challenge was keeping their attention off the girl below, not to mention the lurkers, mostly human but no less dangerous, in the shadows.

Not that there were a *lot* of lurkers on the ground; it just wasn't profitable to stake out such places when there was little likelihood of anybody coming past. She had an idea that she might well be able to thread the girl through there and, after a complete survey of the route, decided to risk going to the ground and to the side of the scared but game young woman below.

Larae heard Marge come down, silent as she was, turned, and gasped. The person she saw was not at all the one she'd expected. Rather, it was more the one she *needed*; a tall, muscular warrior woman with a bronze sword.

"Relax, it's still me," the strange woman told her. "I have a knack of being able to be seen pretty much as the needs of others require. Unfortunately, it's not real—it's just an illusion. Still, as long as this is handy, others will see me this way as well, and it might keep then backed off. Even the sword's an illusion. In truth, Kauri have *no* real offensive weapons or abilities at all, but the fakeout's usually pretty effective."

"I—I'm not sure I understand, but welcome, anyway. What do we do now?"

"I already scouted the area from the air. Up this small street here—it runs parallel to Broadway over there, but it's all industrial. Some rats and stuff but nothing really nasty. There's actually a somewhat respectable-looking part of town up on the hill to our right. That's where we're headed, since the hotel recommended for my people is in that vicinity."

"I'm not sure I'd trust *any* appearances around here," Larae noted nervously as she started walking with the strange apparition. "As you point out, *you* aren't even *you*. What makes you think this area really *is* safer?"

"It's high and unobstructed. The morning sun's light will strike it first and leave it last. That's no real guarantee, but it tends to signal things to those of us with experience."

The girl shrugged. "I still do not see why there need be any respectable or decent people or areas here."

"Got to be some. For one thing, just as evil is defined by good, good is defined by evil. One without the other becomes the norm. Also, this is a real place. It's not Hell, it's not some fairyland, it's not in some other dimension. It's real, it's here, and most of its people are alive. Folks are born here, grow up here, work here, maybe marry here, have kids, and so on. Being under Hell isn't always so obvious; mostly it's apathy, just accepting conditions and making do without fighting it or sacrificing against it. I have a very strange feeling that there's more that's familiar than unfamiliar here."

But not at night. Two lone women in the dark, by the docks, at night would be a target in any big city, Marge thought. She wasn't as concerned, being a night creature and a flying one as well, but her ward was neither.

It would be interesting to see this place in daylight, in its normal workday mode, though. Evil didn't go to bed at sunup, nor did it flee the light as many of its supernatural minions did, but it did become more subtle. Still, her own power came from the night as well, and it was ironic that she felt so much safer in the darkness.

The vast majority of her tricks worked only on mortal humans; faerie would see right through them and certainly wouldn't be impressed, nor, of course, would demonic creatures, and around here the supernatural was definitely king.

Still, there were more practical considerations to be faced if they got by all those dark shadows and creepy-looking buildings. "It's gonna be quite a climb up that hill," she noted. "Ten to one the hotel's right smack on top, too." And it would be so very easy to just fly straight up there . . .

The Hotel Usher was at number 777 Avenue Nictzin Dyalhis high atop Morgana Hill. It was an imposing structure but not a scary-looking one, rising six stories and going a square block around the hilltop with a panoramic view of the harbor below and a less interesting one of some of the rest of town on the other side. The whole of it was quite solid and ornate, with white stucco gilded with brightly colored abstract designs and gold leaf on the doors, crests, and such.

There was a doorman who looked to Irving like one of the soldiers who'd guarded the wicked witch's castle in *The Wizard of Oz* movie, high-topped hat and fancy coat and all, even in this tropical heat.

"You sure they'll let the likes of us into a place like this?" Irving whispered worriedly. Poquah paid him no attention at all, but Irving felt conspicuous as the doorman nodded to them and opened the big oaken entry door for them to enter the spacious lobby.

If ever an interior did not disappoint, it was the Usher's. It offered a grand vista of polished wood and marble, with sculptures, interior fountains, vines growing up the sides of the walls and columns, and everything in gold and plush draperies, carpeting—the works—all somehow built and arranged so that there was some sort of constant airflow that made it seem cool and comfortable inside, only the humidity betraying the fact that it was not in truth Earth-style air-conditioning.

The clerk at the front desk was dressed in formal livery and looked like another product of central casting. He looked at the pair who stood in front of him, sharp eyes the only thing betraying an otherwise impenetrable countenance, and said, "Yes? May I help you?"

"I believe we are expected," Poquah told him. "Poquah of Terindell, Master Irving de Oro, and party to follow."

"Indeed, sir. Let me see . . . Yes. Party of—three?"

"Four. We have offered our advantages to someone we met on the voyage and who needed some additional aid. One each, faerie and human, male and female. Will this pose a problem?"

"Indeed not, so long as you are willing to accept full financial responsibility for your added member. Um, *ahem*, it is not *usual* for young ladies to be out without an escort in this town at this time of night. It is quite dangerous out there. When might we expect them?"

"Soon, I hope, or we'll have to go hunting for them. Since our luggage is very light, we might as well remain in reception here until they appear. Would that pose a problem?"

"Indeed not. You may sit in the café lounge over there and you will have a full view of the main entrance."

Poquah nodded. "Then that is what we will do. Um, you don't get too many visitors from the northern continent, I assume."

"Very few, I will admit, although it's not unusual to have some occasionally," the clerk responded.

"A few weeks ago a green wood nymph probably accompanied by a six-armed halfling girl came through here. Did they stay here?"

"Not that I am aware of, sir. But then, I am on duty only part of the time and not always at this desk in any event."

The Imir nodded. "Let's go sit down and get something to drink," he suggested to Irving, who liked the idea a good deal.

It was a very pleasant lounge, replete with a piano and plush padded seats and polished marble tables, and it had a fair number of people, mostly dressed quite well, sitting around in it talking or reading or simply relaxing. There didn't seem to be any faerie there other than Poquah, and while some of the faces were distinctively Oriental in cast and others were white or olive, there were no Nubians to be seen, either. They still stood out, but nobody really seemed to notice.

At least nobody was playing the damned piano, Irving thought thankfully.

Irving looked around at the faces and then turned to the Imir. "Where do these folks come from?"

"Some are probably locals, hanging out here because it is a better place than the joints and trouble of the rest of the city. Some are commercial folk both from other areas of this continent and from others with which there is trade, and the rest are here on a variety of missions. I suspect that Baron Boquillas was quite well acquainted with this hotel in his active days, going to and from assignations here. Many classical villains of Husaquahr probably would find this very familiar. I wouldn't even be surprised if some from Earth came through here now and again, but only the very important ones Hell would actually deal with openly and comfortably."

"Earth? You mean they can go from there to here?"

"Hell touches all points of all universes at once," Poquah told him. "So, of course, does Heaven, but there's little of that here. The chief Prince of Hell is incredibly powerful, a demigod of great proportions, remember. It wouldn't be all that difficult. Many who vanish without a trace wind up here. I once heard that Ambrose Bierce was revising *The Devil's Dictionary* here and that Martin Bormann was acting as the secretary to some important writer of political tracts."

"Who? Never heard of 'em."

Poquah sighed. "Never mind. You don't need that kind of an education in *this* life."

Irving coughed a little. "Seems like everybody smokes here, too. Wow! Worse than Ruddygore's cigars!"

"Yes, well, it's still *sophisticated* here, or at least 'cool' or whatever the term is these days. Not just tobacco, either. The one thing about Hell is that it isn't nearly as hypocritical on its own ground as the saintly sorts. Don't worry, you'll be spending more time outside than in on this trip."

A waitress came over and took their order. Irving couldn't help but notice her rather dull eyes and seemingly one-track mind and movements, almost as if she were some kind of automaton.

"Get used to it," Poquah told him. "Slavery, binding spells, all sorts of things are taken for granted here, particularly among the lower classes. This is an upper-class hotel. You will have to accept a lot of unpleasant things you may see here, but it's not as different as you may think. Many people find our system of having the masses of people poor and starving and willing to do almost anything for a pittance no different in the basics from having slaves and spells of servitude here. It just makes it easier for the Husaquahrian upper classes and freedmen to delude themselves into a sense of moral superiority. As I said, there is often less hypocrisy when Hell is in charge than when it is less obviously so. Your impulse to save every stray dog you see is admirable in the abstract but impossible in practice. You must learn that here if you learn nothing else."

Irving didn't like that whole train of thought, but he didn't have to reach very far to change the subject. He couldn't help noticing that they were no longer being ignored.

"Fellow over there at the bar," Irving whispered, gesturing slightly with his head. "He's real interested in us."

"The one in white? Yes, I've noticed him. Rather odd-looking, frankly. Round face, oval body, yet actually thin and slight of build. He carries himself more like a dandy than a fighter or magician, but such men can be deceiving."

The small man seemed suddenly to become aware that he was being conspicuous and, instead of turning away or backing off, headed slowly over toward them, stopping at their table but not sitting down. "Gentlemen," he said in a thin, reedy, nasal voice with a pronounced foreign accent, "I apologize if I am making a mistake, but I am to meet two of your description along with a young lady faerie with bright wings. Do I have the wrong two men, or is something amiss?"

He's got pointy teeth, Irving noted, fascinated. Not like a vampire but more like some kind of animal carnivore. It made him look both comical and menacing when he spoke.

Poquah stared at him. "You are the one who we were to expect to contact us?"

"Yes. I am Joel Thebes. Um—may I sit down?"

"By all means, yes. We are waiting upon the young lady at the moment."

Thebes looked uncertain. "She is out there *alone*? At *night*?"

"She is a nocturnal and quite capable of taking care of herself," Poquah assured him. "We befriended a young woman on the trip over, and she's helping the girl make it here."

"Not the Ngamuku girl!"

"You *know* about her?" Irving asked, startled.

"Of course. That's the trouble! Almost *everybody* knows that story. You might as well draw giant arrows to yourself at all times and say, 'Here we are!' "

Poquah looked over at Irving. "I *told* you!"

Thebes sighed. "Well, it is not a total loss, anyway. Once we leave the capital and His Majesty, we will be headed toward Mount Doom, where even the forces of Hell have diminished abilities or holds. If the King doesn't decide to give her over and lets her go on with you, she might turn from a liability to at least neutral. You are thinking of freeing her from the curse using the black bird, eh?"

"You know a lot about why we are here and what we are after," Irving noted. "I begin to think we're the headlines in the local paper."

"Not really, but you are not much of a secret, either. Most do not know about the black bird, though. They think you are going because your destinies are still being worked out and cannot be resolved until you reach Mount Doom."

"I have heard a lot about this destiny business but cannot see the relationship," Poquah told him. "How is my destiny, and the Kauri's, and the boy's here all wrapped up in this business? We were sent by our friend, our employer, or our guardian, as it were, but in a sense we all volunteered."

"Don't be ridiculous! You mean you do not *know* who is behind the opening of the way to the Ancient Ones? Ruddygore did not explain to you just what all this is about?"

"Enough, I thought. Do you know something we do not but should?"

"I think I might. You see—"

At that moment, however, Larae and Marge entered the lobby of the Hotel Usher.

Irving jumped up in a moment. "The girl's bleeding!" He leapt over the railing and ran to the two women, and Poquah instantly shifted gears and followed.

"What happened?"

"It's not serious," Marge assured them. "Got faked out almost at the last moment by a bastard who had one *hell* of a nasty dog. It's not a werewolf or anything—don't worry. There's no curse in the wound. I just slipped up, that's all."

"How'd you get away?" Irving asked, examining the ugly wound on Larae's left arm, which was still bleeding.

"I'll show you the trick sometime. Let's just say that even big ugly dogs have things they're scared of."

By that time some of the hotel staff had arrived, and Poquah asked a porter, "Is there a hotel physician? The wound should be tended before there is infection. In the meantime, you might also find somebody with first aid or there are going to be very ugly bloodstains on your very plush carpet here."

That seemed to get to them more than the sight of the wounded girl had.

"Dr. Trowbridge may be available tonight," the porter responded. "I'll send someone." Others went into action, bringing a chair for Larae and a quick and temporary bandage and a bottle of whiskey.

Larae coughed, then muttered, "You should have just let it kill me." Then she passed out from shock.

Dr. Trowbridge proved to be a tall, distinguished-looking man with gray hair and muttonchop sideburns and a thick, bushy mustache that appeared to hide a rather kindly face.

He looked like somebody who'd stepped out of a nine-teenth-century romance novel, but he seemed to know his stuff and was surprisingly modern for a world where sorcery ruled.

"She's not badly hurt, just totally disconsolate. Little wonder she passed out; she has no will to live in her at all, I don't think. Bizarre, although, considering the circumstances, somewhat understandable."

"You know who she is, too?" Irving asked.

"Eh? No, nothing but what you told me. I refer to the curse and all that other stuff piled on her. Worst spaghetti I've seen in decades. That's why I treated her primarily with conventional medicine, as it were. Cleaned and treated the wound—it was luckily not that deep, and I think we can get by without stitches—and bandaged it, gave her an antibiotic and a sedative. She's most in need of rest. Two days and she'll be fine for most things, although she'll have soreness in that arm for a week or more, I'd say."

Marge was fascinated by Trowbridge, who seemed out of another time and place and certainly not the sort of person anyone would expect there. "Are you a native to these parts, Doctor?" she asked, curious.

"Oh, my, no! I just find myself here more of the time than I'd like, and since I have pretty well retired now back home, I have set up an arrangement for things like this with local hotels and such, since I have some medicines and skills little known here."

"You're from Earth, aren't you?"

He looked surprised. "Why, yes. There's not even a lot of folks here who know of Earth's existence. I am impressed, madam."

"I'm from Texas myself. The boy here's from Philadelphia. Only the Imir and the girl are locals."

"Well! Amazing! I must say you *have* to be a bit different than you were in Texas. A changeling, I take it."

She nodded. "Where are you from?"

"A small town in New Jersey. I shouldn't even have been here or known of this sort of thing—the whole of this universe does terrible things to the logical mind of a man of science, after all—had it not been for my encountering and befriending a remarkable man who battles the forces of this place and has for many years. It is only with his knowledge that I can make this transition, and then only to this region. I have never understood why they let him come and go, but they do."

"If he battles evil in New Jersey, he's no threat to Hell," Irving muttered, but nobody paid him any mind.

"We are more permanent residents," Marge told him. "In fact, I hadn't known anyone could go both ways between except demons, angels, and a sorcerer named Ruddygore."

"Oh, it's quite common to have this sort of thing, although most who do are rather of a nasty sort. Ran into a Babylonian chap here a while back. Got his whole country into a war with the West, got trounced, got bombed back to the Stone Age, and he's still in power. Amazing. No, what you cannot do is do it without the permission and aid of some powerful supernatural entity, and you can take only knowledge back with you. Lots of problems here at the moment, though. The whole Sea of Dreams is in ferment. No sure thing, you see. That's why we've been stuck here a while."

"What's causing the problem, Doctor?" Poquah put in. "Why is it impossible to cross?"

"Damned *city* popped up in the middle of the thing! Rotated in from yet another universe. With *that* on the one side and the djinn on the other, we're pretty well stuck in this one. So far, though, while summoned, they've been unable to make a landing. Hell can't do a lot—after all, when disloyalty and dishonesty are virtues, how can you not expect everybody to go over to what they perceive is the strongest side? Satan and some of the other big ones could probably take these blighters on one on one, but there's a lot of them and they work on their own level."

"Then why don't they just come and overrun this place?" Marge asked.

He shrugged. "Something about how supernatural deni-

zens can prepare the way but only mortals can summon the
opener. If I were you, though, I wouldn't go anywhere near
that southern region where they're strongest. Hell may *use*
insanity, but it's not only not insane, it is always quite logical. That may be the case with these others as well, but
their logic is alien to us. Think of it as an invasion from another planet. The creatures are so different and come from
such a different environment and history that they bear no
relationship to us at all. They are delighted to find minions
who will rush to their side, attracted by their obvious
power, but they do not feel an obligation to these minions
or even understand the concept."

"How do you stop them, then?" Irving wondered.

"Destroy the beachhead, boy! Don't let 'em make a suc-
cessful first landing! They must need elaborate preparation
or they'd have been here by now. That's what keeps folks
like me sane, you know—mathematics. It is all mathematics
in the end. Magic, science, you name it: it is all mathematics. The silly Rules here—they are a form of mathematical
order. Trouble is, they're often bad math, as insane as the
American income tax code. I was talking about this with another Earthman passing through just the other day. Fellow
named Shea, I believe. Professor of mathematics somewhere. These invaders are bound by mathematics and its
logic in the same way we are all bound to ours, but it is a
different, an *alien* mathematics. Doesn't matter. Doesn't
even matter if we understand it. Doesn't matter if we are
able to understand it."

"I admit I don't understand you now," Marge conceded.

"Oh, my dear, it's quite simple. Think of a string of
numbers, say, one plus one plus one plus one plus one
equals five. Simple equation, is it not?"

"*That* I can follow."

"All right. Remove one of the ones. Five is still the desired result, even the *required* result to accomplish something, but you've come up one short. The same is true of
the action signs. Change a plus to a minus anywhere in the
equation. Same thing. Now, imagine how impossibly com-

plex *their* math must be. How many things have to be in place, no matter how insane it may seem to us, for their result—invasion of this world—to work. Rather bizarre equation, most likely. One hundred virgin sacrifices on rocky ground at midnight plus forty thousand chanting prayers plus who knows what? I'm just making those up as an example, but you can see that no matter how bizarre the components, it is still building a single equation. Change one item—and the more complex the equation, the better for this—and you thwart them. Change it sufficiently and you'll slam the door in their faces."

"You make it sound so easy," Irving noted, knowing it almost certainly wasn't.

"Well, *they* certainly know it as well," the doctor admitted. "One would expect that their agents on *this* side assembling what's required have a certain level of built-in redundancy. The trick, then, is in finding out how many sacrifices they actually *require* rather than the number they have got, you see." He yawned. "Pardon, but I've had a long day, I'm afraid."

"Perfectly all right. You have been a lifesaver, Doctor," Marge assured him. "Please go back to your hotel room or wherever and have a nice rest."

"It's that blasted Frenchman. Had me up all last night examining the catacombs of Boreas." He sighed. "Well, it certainly has kept life interesting. Charmed. Don't worry about your friend—she'll be fine, at least as far as the wounds go. Superficial. I wish I could say the same about the curse, but that's out of my league. Farewell for now!"

And with that he was gone.

"Fascinating," Poquah commented. "One begins to suspect that Yuggoth has other surprises than the ones we anticipated. This suggests a primary weakness in the dimensional walls separating the two universes right along this continent. Perhaps more than two, since there is also a physical entryway to Hell here and in no other place. One suspects that the two great bubbles of our respective universes *almost* touch here. If so, it would be the ideal invasion point from the Sea of Dreams and the easiest to control access into and out of."

Irving frowned. "Well, if *Hell's* close over *one* way and *Earth's* close by on the other, then where's Heaven?"

"On the other side of Earth, of course. I thought that was obvious," the Imir responded. "We are a bit closer to Hell here. Always have been. Not that Earth folk are any more or less likely to go there than our people are, but here you can *walk*."

Marge tiptoed to the door of the bedroom and looked in. Larae was professionally bandaged on her left arm and shoulder and seemed to be asleep from the release of tension, Trowbridge's drugs and shock, or both. She quietly pulled the door shut again, turned, and for the first time saw the strange little man in the white suit. "Who's Peter Lorre?" she asked.

He smiled. "Joel Thebes, madame. At your service. We were speaking—the three of us—when you and your companion made your dramatic entrance. I am sorry we did not have a calm and proper introduction."

She nodded. "Then you're the native guide we were to meet?"

"At your service. Not, however, a native. Not of this place, oh, no! I, too, was born and raised on Earth, in a small town none would have heard of in the Carpathian Mountains near the Romanian-Hungarian border."

She immediately understood. "You're *really* from Transylvania?"

He brightened. "Oh, my, yes! A descendant of the Wallachians who ultimately subdued and dealt with Vlad Dracul. And no, I am not a vampire or a werewolf or anything like that, although over time some changes have taken place within me. They have nothing to do with my birth or ancestry, though, and do not imperil you. They are the price I have paid to still be chasing the bird after so many, many long years."

"And a fat man and a pretty girl are around someplace, no doubt."

He looked quizzical. "Um, there *was* a very large man, a companion, yes, but he is now dead, I believe. At least, I left him in the last stages of a terrible lung disease in Istanbul long ago, and if I know him, he would have made it here by now were he not long dead and assigned to wherever he was to go. As to women, I have encountered many beautiful women over the years but none in a very long time. Why did you make the comment, may I ask?"

"Never mind. You just reminded me of a different plot I once knew." She should have guessed, Marge told herself, or at least reminded herself that much of the fantasy and fancy of Earth were carried over the Sea of Dreams and there crept into the minds of the most creative and receptive. Earth's fiction was this world's fact, including, it appeared, this little fellow. Well, if he was anything close to his fictional counterpart, he was a very dangerous killer, but he was also more of a threat to Irving than to Larae.

Irving yawned. "Seems to me that we'd all be better off in the daylight around here, except maybe Marge. Maybe we should get some sleep while there's still enough night."

Poquah nodded. "I agree. Mister Thebes, can you meet us for a late breakfast, say, eight-thirty or nine? I assume the hotel has some sort of service."

"It does," Thebes responded. "Mostly European-style— sweet rolls, coffee, tea, that sort of thing—but ample. Shall we say nine, then?"

"By all means. We have much to arrange, and our clock is ticking on this," the Imir reminded him.

With that, Thebes left, and they felt free to relax a bit.

"You trust him?" Marge asked the Imir.

"Not much and certainly not in proximity to the McGuffin, but until then his interest lies in sticking with and even helping us. I also believe that his fanatic obsession for obtaining the Grand McGuffin is such that he will be less vulnerable to many of the truly evil influences we may encounter along the way. Perhaps even more insulated than any of the rest of us."

"You really think *that* is a danger?" Irving asked him.

"Perhaps. It is best to remain on guard. That is why the Master sent me along on this trip, I believe. Duty is all-important to the Imir. It outweighs and overrides all other considerations, and I have my duty to perform on this mission. So far, in fact, it has been remarkably easy; now, I fear, it is going to turn much uglier. It isn't just the institutional dangers, it's the random ones such as the man with the dog tonight. Marge, tell me true, do you believe that he knew who either of you were?"

"No. I don't think so. He didn't even seem to be waiting for us. It was almost, well, he was going along and spotted us and decided to sic the dog on us just for the hell of it."

"Indeed, that is just what I mean. Around here much, perhaps a lot, is just for the Hell of it. That is why we must always stick closely together if possible and always be on guard. Trust no one outside our circle unless we have to and all the rest of us can keep watch. The natives here may seem quite ordinary, be friendly, all the rest, but deep down they have no conscience and no sense of responsibility. Assume that everyone you meet is like that fellow with the dog and you will be a lot safer."

"Thanks a lot," Marge said glumly. Still, they were here and going inland. "I think the sooner we're on our way and the less time we spend in towns and cities, the better, though."

"I agree. Irving and I will sleep tonight; you can keep watch. Tomorrow one of us will do the same for you."

"Fair enough," she responded, "but I may have to go out for just a little bit. That trick I pulled tonight to get us out of that jam used up a *lot* of energy. I will need to feed."

"Be careful. It won't take much to overdose in a place like this!" the Imir warned her. "Still, go."

"Um—Marge?" Irving asked hesitantly.

"Yeah, Irv?"

"What *did* you do that got the dog off her?"

"I can't demonstrate. Takes too much out of me. Let's just say that I can do illusions and that most of my illusions are nice and very easy to look at but that there are a few

I can do that are scarier than all hell. When that dog lit into her, I just reacted instinctively, and suddenly the woman next to her turned into an apparent horrible fiend and snapped at the dog. Last I saw, it was running down the alley yelping, dragging its tail. When I looked around for the owner, I found him knocked out against the far wall! How *that* happened I'm not sure. I got the strong impression somebody else was close by in spite of my aerial surveillance, but with Larae hurt, I couldn't take the time to look. I'd *swear*, though, that there was no way the guy with the dog could have been startled and knocked himself out that way, but, well, who knows?"

"Remind me to stick close to you."

"Don't get too confident," she warned him. "Remember, it's only illusion. Fake. The only reality is what you see right now." She sighed. "Okay, I'll just go out the window over here. Close it after me—there are some pretty mean things flying around these parts. I'll get back in. And don't worry so much! We're gonna *do* this thing! Believe it!"

"I try," Irving assured her. But he wished there had been enough time for Joel Thebes to tell them why their destiny was so wrapped up in this. Well, he was going along, so there would be plenty of time for that. There was still so much that seemed to have been deliberately withheld from him. Like that and like what Larae's curse was.

Damn it, it wasn't fair for perfect strangers to know more about him and his cohorts than they did themselves!

He would find out some of it, he promised himself. He'd find out as much as he could in the morning.

BE MINE ON YUGGOTH

There can never be but one partner in a seduction.
                              —Rules, Vol. XXXIII, p. 261(c)

LARAE WAS SORE BUT OTHERWISE IN FAIRLY GOOD SPIRITS
the next morning. "Go on down," she urged them. "I'll be
all right here, and if I feel up to it, I'll try and dress and
join you. *Please.* I'm not very well going to allow you to
help me in here, anyway."

Irving shrugged. "All right, if that's what you really
want." He looked over at the absolutely comatose Marge,
who seemed to be sleeping the sleep of the dead. "She's
not going to wake up for a hurricane, you know."

"That's all right. I didn't expect her to. You would be
surprised at how self-sufficient I have had to learn to be.
Go on, get your business started."

Leaving the girl, he joined Poquah, who had switched his
usual gray robes for a mottled green and brown tunic and
pants and strong boots. They went down to breakfast.

"Is this your normal Imir garb back in your own homeland?" Irving asked him, curious.

"One of them. The style's rather stock, I'm afraid—the
Rules, you know—but the coloration and cut are often quite
distinctive. Um, I assume you noted how completely un-
conscious the Kauri was?"

"Uh, yeah, but she's always out of it in bright daylight."

"Not *that* out of it. She's functional in daylight; she just
would feel the same as you or I would if we hadn't been
to sleep for, say, twenty-four hours. Groggy but workable.
If she slept that hard normally, she'd be totally vulnerable
during the day, when virtually all of her defenses are from
the conscious will rather than being automatic. No, I fear

199

we will have to keep a careful eye on her because she will be the last to notice."

"Notice what?"

"She feeds on other people's misdeeds, regrets, whatever. There's not a lot of conscience in these people, so the kind of psychic energy she's designed to digest must be dug for more deeply and at its root, which is not in the sense of wrongness but rather in the nature of the deed itself and its stain upon the soul. It is quite easy for her, I think, to mistake the stain for what is her natural food."

"I don't follow you at all," the boy admitted, shaking his head.

Poquah sighed and chose his words patiently. "She thinks she is doing the normal, instinctual, and natural thing by cleansing the soul, but instead she is consuming a part of it."

"Huh? What?"

"She is eating part of their evil-stained souls, which, to someone of a faerie nature, is tantamount to cannibalism. You remember the old saying that you are what you eat?"

"Yeah, but . . ."

"If she is not careful, she will turn from being a Kauri to becoming a Succubus, a predator. In a sense, it would be like a mortal becoming a vampire. It would not matter if she liked the state or not; she would not be able to help herself. She would become a killer to live, but under a whole different part of the Rules. *That* is the danger I feared most from the start and the one which Master Ruddygore was also most concerned about. I still hope that her own ruler, who keeps some connection with all those of the tribe, has a way to control this or she wouldn't have allowed Marge to come, but it is by no means sure. In the end we must drive home to her the need to stop before she turns completely. It is more a matter of will than of compulsion, but one must recognize the problem to deal with it."

"Sounds like drugs and booze," Irving commented.

The dining area was nicely laid out, although by that hour of the morning it had been well picked over. Still, there was much to choose from: the pastries reminiscent of the finest of central Europe, along with juices, countless kinds of tea, and several varieties of coffee.

Joel Thebes was there, idly sipping some coffee and looking more deathly and white in the light of day than he had at night. There was a question as to whether he ever changed the white suit or if it was a part of him. It didn't seem dirty, anyway, which implied that he mostly had a lot of identical ill-fitting, rumpled outfits.

After the two Husaquahrians had gotten their own breakfasts and brought them over to the table, Thebes got down to business.

"The black bird has an incredible history both on Earth and here," he noted, sounding enthusiastic to tell it.

Neither of his listeners was like-minded enough to want to hear most of it. "Forget the legends. How'd it get *here?*" Irving asked him.

Thebes looked disappointed but sighed and said, "The Knights of Malta made dozens of exact replicas to fool everyone but decided that it was far too dangerous to leave in anyone's hands on Earth. Thus, in the year 1476 the head of the order took the original and wished it and himself to go to the place whence its original wood had been carved, and that, although he was not aware of it, was in this universe and on Yuggoth, in a small valley to the east of Mount Doom. It is of the stock of the original trees of Eden, you see, which is why it is indestructible and how it gains much of its power. Well, of course, it didn't take very long for the Archbishop to realize where he was and sense all the snakes and such about, but he knew what to do. Using the bird, he created for it a haven there in which none but mortals consecrated of Earth and baptized in his faith would be able to approach and touch, move, or otherwise command the power of the bird. He made a place for it in the valley, and then he walked out of there and faced down the demon hordes attracted to his very presence. It is quite likely he went to his God shortly thereafter."

"So even Hell can't touch it?" Poquah said more than

asked. "Interesting. And not just a mortal but an Earth mortal anointed by the rituals of his particular church is the only one who can touch or use it? Fascinating."

"Baptism," Irving told him. "A priest puts water on your head and blesses you. Some of 'em put your whole body under. This Archbishop dude—he was Roman Catholic, I bet. Almost everybody was back then in Europe.

"Yes, certainly, as was I once," Thebes admitted. "It was Dracul who saved Romania and Wallachia from the Ottoman Turks, after all, until he went too insane and decided everybody was a Turk. That saved the region for the Catholic Church, and so it remains to this day, as far as I know. Unfortunately, nobody knew of this step back on Earth, and so countless people spent centuries and fortunes and lives chasing the replicas all over the world, only to always be thwarted. Of course, not even Hell is absolutely certain that this story, too, is genuine and that the one they cannot touch is not a fake as well. I do not believe it is, though. I have now accounted for most of the fakes through history, and how was such a medieval man as the Archbishop able to get here and enforce these restrictions if it were not? The only question is whether he brought one or two fakes here with him as well. Still, I am convinced it is there."

Poquah considered the legend. "Then this is why Hell needs the likes of us. They can't enter or even see the blasted thing! Not even any of the sorcerers here could, since they were all Husaquahrian-born or are of this world and so lack the requisite baptism. So the question comes, Who is the one who can truly use this treasure if we can reach it?"

"Marge was raised Catholic. I know because she told me," Irving noted. "And so was my dad, after all."

Thebes looked at him with those bulletlike black eyes and frowned slightly. "But I do not think your Marge can be considered mortal at this point, nor, as I understand it, your father, either. And you were a mere small child."

Irving smiled. "But I was old enough, and I was baptized even if we weren't real good churchgoers. Mom was a

Baptist, but I know I had a Catholic baptism. That used to be the joke. At one point she dated this minister who was A.M.E., and he had me baptized there, and at another point I got nearly drowned by the Baptist relatives. They always said if anybody went to Heaven in the family it'd be me, since I got baptized Catholic, A.M.E., and Baptist. Guess all I missed was her takin' up with a Muslim."

"That's it, then," Thebes commented. "You alone on this entire world can retrieve it, or so it would seem. Your father and your winged companion are outside chances but unlikely to qualify. It seems that all our efforts must be to get *you* to the bird."

"What about you?" Irving asked him. "I mean, you said you qualified, I think."

Thebes sighed. "Alas, I do not. You see, I had to sell my soul to get over here. It wasn't worth much, but it was all I had, and it broke any link to God I might have had, however slender. I am not truly mortal anymore myself, either. No, you are certainly it. And that means that you will be a very tempting target to those who would not want you to get anywhere near the thing."

Irving felt suddenly very uncomfortable. "Thanks a lot." He wondered how much truth was in Thebes' story. Certainly the little man was dependent on them to get there, which indicated he couldn't make it on his own, and some of it hung together, but was it *all* the story? What would happen once he or somebody else who could see and remove it took it out of that valley or shrine? Anybody's game again? That was the way a lot of those kinds of wishes worked.

This was going to be pretty damned hairy. If he didn't get it, the bad guys won, and he was going to be targeted by the invaders to stop him. Okay. *That* much he could take. But if he had the thing in his hands, he'd better wish himself out of there and safe—real, real quick—or everybody in creation was gonna be pouncing all over him.

"I am not certain that Joe or Marge couldn't do it under those restrictions," Poquah noted. "If they are absolute and as you stated them, then what is the point of Joe's earlier odyssey with his strange companion? *She* surely is born of Husaquahr and a proper halfling, so what made her step-father believe that she could see and use the McGuffin? A fascinating puzzle, one of many in this affair without an answer. But tell me, since you seem to know everything else around here, have you heard of the nymph and the halfling? Do you know if they still live?"

Thebes looked around cautiously and then lowered his voice. "They got here, yes. The word is that they remained on their ship and got off at Innsmouth instead. Not a wonderful place to do it, but it is a very small fishing town surrounded by a fair amount of old-growth forest. Lots of fogs and mists, too. You don't want to meet the folks who live in the town, and certainly you won't stay for long around them, but if they made it the much shorter distance from the dock to the forest, well, a wood nymph would have some power there. There's some pretty mean fairies in these forests, but a nymph would be in her element. Word is that they made it at least that far and vanished into the interior. They were sighted here and there for a thousand kilometers, but there have been no sightings in the entire Mount Doom region and none anywhere else for quite a while. Odds are something's got 'em. Dead? Alive? Impossible to say."

"That is the first confirmation that they actually made it ashore whole," Poquah told him. "I am grateful just for that. However, I feel it is best if we depart as quickly as possible for the capital. I am anxious to get this over with, and with every delay and particularly every time we are stuck in one predictable spot, we are vulnerable. When can we leave?"

"In two days, certainly," Thebes assured them. "There is a large party going our way leaving at midday two days from now, and we can certainly join it. It will be the easiest on paperwork and the most comfortable. By river sail, canal, and omnibus we might well be able to reach at least there in no more than two or three weeks."

Poquah nodded. "Get it rolling, then."

Irving frowned. He knew better than to tell the likes of Thebes that they had a map that could bypass all that and take them directly there. "Um, excuse me, but why do we still have to go see this king dude, anyway? From the way you talked, I figure you *got* to know where we have to go, so why waste time?"

"But I *don't* know, not exactly," the little man responded. "I can see how it might seem confusing, but that valley is not easily approached, and where inside it the bird might lie is even more of a puzzle. His Majesty knows. It is one of those things passed down from monarch to monarch. Without it we could tromp around in there for weeks and be vulnerable to attack. Besides, with his command, the second half of the journey will be easier. Even the invader can be influenced by him to a degree. No, it is *unthinkable* that we try this without him."

Irving shrugged. "Okay, okay, you're the boss for now. I take your word for it. Killin' two days in this creepy town won't be fun, though."

"Oh, it is not so terrible in the daytime," Thebes assured him. "You just have to watch your step, as in any big city. There is quite a lot to see, actually. Basilisk Park, the Miskatonic University branch library, the Carnival of Souls, the Illuminati Museum, the Phantom of the Opry, lots of things."

Literally lots of things, Irving thought. "No, I think I'll stick close to the hotel. It seems pretty safe. It might be good, though, to visit some shops and pick up a few spare things for the trip. We packed *awfully* light."

"Two blocks over to the right as you exit," Thebes told him. "Quite a lot of shops and specialty stores."

"I can exchange an ingot for some local currency," Poquah told him. "Perhaps, later, if she is up to it, you might wish to take your young lady with you. I do not think that the several white cotton dresses and those sandals will be sufficient."

Things were agreed on, then, and with handshakes all

around—Joel Thebes had a shake like a limp, dead fish—
they agreed to consult and meet regularly for dinner at the
hotel and to prepare to go inland with the expedition in two
days' time.

As Poquah and Irving walked up to the desk, the boy
whispered, "You got *ingots*?"

"Yes, of course. You never know when they are useful.
I carry them in a sorcerer's pouch. Do not worry. We will
not lack for resources."

That was certainly clear when, at the cashier, Poquah
produced a heretofore invisible leather purse of not very
impressive size and reached into it. Although it wasn't
much larger than his hand to the wrist, he pulled out a complete bar of unmistakable processed gold and put it on the
counter, then made the purse vanish. *Good trick,* Irving
thought approvingly.

The money for it *was* considerable, and Poquah peeled
off several large bills and handed them to Irving. "Do not
lose them or have them stolen from you," the Imir warned.
"I am not going to budget for incompetence."

"I'll be careful," Irving assured him. He looked at the
notes, which were all sorts of oddball denominations. Each
one had a demon on its face and a scene from one of the
circles of Hell on the back. "So what does the big prince
get?" he asked Poquah. "A thousand?"

"Of course not. He's on one of the most common bills
here—the three."

Irving fished one out and looked at it. "Looks like pic-
tures of the angels in churches, only bigger and better," he
remarked.

"Well, that's how he started out, anyway, and how he
probably still sees himself. You never know. He may not be
a god, but with that kind of power and those legions, he's
about the closest thing you'll ever see to one."

Larae had not joined them for breakfast but was up and
changed, sort of, when they got back. She was wearing a
shorter dress, which hung on the hips and went to just be-

low the knees, but nothing else. She had a *very* nice figure, Irving noted, just as he had known she would.

"Does this bother you?" she asked them. "I couldn't manage the full dress, and this is quite traditional and casual in my homeland, although I know that not all cultures are comfortable with it. When this sort of temperature is normal all year, we feel there is no reason to hide ourselves in false modesty."

"N—no, it's fine with me," Irving responded. "After all, I just got this loincloth and stuff on. By all means be comfortable. I—I think they are shutting down the breakfast by now, but we might be able to get something if you want it."

"That is all right. I can wait. I have not had much of an appetite of late."

"I thought I'd go shopping, since we'll need to pick up some things, and if you want to come along, it's fine with me."

She smiled. "I'd like that a lot, so long as it remains daylight and we stay out of that dreadful dockside district."

Irving buckled on his short sword and belt. "Well, I'll take along something for the unexpected, but I think this area right around here should be fine."

And indeed it was—for Yuggoth, anyway.

It was something of a shock to be hit with that blanket of heat and humidity as they exited the hotel. While it had been humid all along, the hotel's ventilation system had kept the temperature pretty comfortable. Now, out in the beating tropical sun shining down from a cloudless sky, the full impact hit them.

"Feels very much like my home," she told him. "Very different land, but that sun and temperature are familiar. Do not be surprised if around midday there is a sudden gathering of clouds and a torrent of rain for at least a brief period. It is common in my land."

He felt far less comfortable than she, but, worse, he was soon sweating like a stuck pig and she seemed dry and hardly affected. It was embarrassing.

The row of shops and stores was also easy to spot, and

as they walked along, they saw that in the midst of the expected there was always the Yuggoth touch, with potion stores and shops with all sorts of voodoolike paraphernalia intermixed with clothing and shoe and food and sundry shops, some of which seemed downright conventional but all of which had at least one item that was questionable, from the type of skin on a leather handbag to the small shrunken-head necklaces.

Overall, though, it was kind of a fun day. He really liked being with Larae, and he'd never quite felt this way or this comfortable with any girl before. He was feeling things in his head and in other parts of his anatomy that the spell had long blocked and that were totally new to him for that reason. Clearly, though, the warning about his spells had been right, and the farther he was from their source and the closer to the spirits of Yuggoth and its atmosphere, the less effect the spell would have, possibly even dissolving.

There were some skimpy leather bands that passed for an outfit he wouldn't have minded seeing her in, but she seemed partial to slit skirts, although now of darker and more complex colors and patterns. She bought only a couple of tops, mostly matching the more numerous skirts, for formal occasions, dinner, and perhaps the potentially cool evening they hadn't yet experienced.

For Irving it was easier. He needed some support for and protection of his genitals, of course, but beyond that he felt most comfortable outdoors in heat like this when wearing the least. He did, however, invest in a pair of solid low-top boots. Walking on the hot stone pavement was frying his feet something awful, and it was either that or admit to Larae that he couldn't take it. She liked sandals and also found a comfortable pair of boots for when they would be necessary, but for now she preferred being barefoot and seemed almost oblivious to the fact that the same surface that she was walking on would, Irving was absolutely certain, fry bacon and eggs without any added help.

The most unusual thing overall about the city, though, was that it wasn't all that unusual. This was a city not all

that different from the ones on the great northern continent,
nor did the people or the dangers seem to be nearly as horrible as their billing. Okay, there was that strip of nasty
joints, but you could find neighborhoods perhaps only
slightly milder in the City-States, ignoring, of course, the
self-cleaning sidewalks. And the back-alley dangers and
random violence didn't seem all that different from the
cities of Husaquahr or, in fact, from those of Irving's native
land, either. What was bent here was not much more bent
than the "good" places, even if it was more consistently
bent in the same direction.

In the main, people went to work here, did their jobs,
went home, raised their kids, and tried to mind their own
business.

It was not, of course, a democracy, but neither was any
place in Husaquahr he could think of.

Yuggoth was positively routine so far, and in a sense that
disturbed him. Did it mean that it wasn't so evil, after all,
or that evil places weren't really all that different from
home, whether home was the lands around Terindell or the
more distant land of Philadelphia?

Joel Thebes certainly thought there were more woes
here. "Forms, forms, and more forms," he wailed. "All this
just to go anywhere at all here, as if anyone out there really
cared."

"You mean they won't collect these papers?" Marge
asked him.

"Oh, these forms will be examined over and over again,
and if there is one *teensy* little error, the inspectors will re-
ject them. It is just that everything in them is totally meaningless. The only reason we must have them is that we
must have them. This is not an efficiency system; it is a
full-employment system!"

"That is usually the case with bureaucracies," Poquah
sympathized. "The direct approach is always more efficient."

Irving was puzzled. "Is there a real problem here? I

thought everybody here was being nice to us because they *wanted* us to get in there."

"Oh, it is not a particular problem for *you*," Thebes assured them. "It is including the *girl*, you see. And I get the idea that some various powers that be are none too happy she has hooked up with you."

"Well, it is not as if we planned this," Poquah noted, giving a menacing side glance to Irving and Marge. "However, we can hardly abandon her now. She has become part of the Company. The Rules would not allow such a thing."

"I know, I know," Thebes wailed. "But that is why they make so much trouble. Here in the real world they cannot get around the Rules very much, either. Still, I would be very careful with her. You know that things *can* happen to people in a Company. Bad things."

"The question is, Will we make our transportation arrangements or won't we?" Marge asked him.

"Oh, yes, yes. I think so. They will cause all sorts of horrible things to happen, but in the end it is as the boy said: you are here because they want you here. In the end they will have to let us all go. You should be ready by nine tomorrow morning if you wish breakfast. We will have a short way to travel, and then we will join and board the river launch."

Marge yawned. "Then I'm going to bed. The rest of you will have to do whatever needs to be done."

Larae didn't want to go out, at least not right then. It was almost as if she were afraid that something would happen at the last minute that would separate her from her only companions in the world. Poquah decided to go along with Thebes and hope to help things along and possibly even contact Ruddygore. That left Irving suddenly all alone with no place to go.

He decided to go out, anyway.

The shop was called, quite simply, Spirits, Potions, and Spells, betraying both a simplicity of mind and something of a lack of real imagination. Nonetheless, it looked interesting as a cross between a magic antiques store and an old-fashioned apothecary shop.

The proprietor was a strange little man with big sharp teeth, a round face, and pointed ears, and he was having a bad hair day. He flashed Irving back many years.

He looks like the Count on Sesame Street, he thought, wondering where the image had come from. He hadn't thought of any of that in a very long time.

The little man came straight up to him and held out a small jar filled with some kind of black powder. "This is it," he said quite casually. "This one is, of course, temporary. The permanent one costs considerably more than you have on you."

"Huh? I beg your pardon. You must have mistaken me for somebody else, 'cause I just walked in."

"Yes, you were wondering about love potions, and this ground powder, which dissolves with virtually no telltale taste or odor, is the finest temporary one I know."

"I—I was just idly thinking. You don't read minds or something, do you?"

"Not unless I use various spells, I don't, no. Would you like that?"

"Um, no. I just was trying to figure out how you knew what I was thinking about."

"Oh, that is simple. A very minor spell on the whole establishment. It tells me as you come in why you were interested enough to enter. What kind of a sorcery supply store would I be if it were otherwise?"

Irving was impressed and fascinated. "What about removing any last vestiges of a spell put on yourself?" he asked the little man. "I can't touch it, and it might well interfere."

The proprietor examined him carefully. "You have both a spell and a curse. The curse, in fact, might well make this powder irrelevant if the spell was totally removed, you know."

"A curse? Who would do that to me?"

"I have no idea, but it is a strange one to be placed involuntarily on another. Hmmm ... Let me see. Yes, there, and *there,* and over *here,* and um, uh huh. All right."

"Well, what does it curse me with?"

"Oh, that part's easy. It states that you will exert an enormous attractive influence over women."

"Oh, *that.* I've known about *that* since I discovered girls. Sometimes it's more of a pain than anything else, and it hasn't done me any good at all, even if I knew how to use it."

"Interesting. Well, the spell was obviously overlaid to neutralize the curse. Remove the spell and you will, I believe, discover a number of ways to use it. Interesting. Suppose you could turn it off or on at will. Would *that* be of interest to you? Assuming we remove the rather weak and simple restraining spell."

"Huh? Um, you can do that?"

"Removing the spell is simple enough. I'm surprised you haven't had a go at it with someone else before this. Almost anyone could handle it."

"I have pretty straight guardians."

"Um, yes, I see. Well, as I say, ridding you of it is no problem. Do you still have this guardian problem?"

He thought of Poquah. "Yeah, I'm with somebody who can read these like a book—and fix them."

The little man sighed. "All right, then, what about this? I'll remove the *effect* of the spell while leaving it on. Like wearing a light jacket or wrap; it will still be there, but it will have no effect on you."

"Yeah, that sounds great. But how much?"

"Oh, I wouldn't *think* of charging for something so simple. But the other one—*that* is a different story. Making that one voluntary will require work and a higher power than myself. There are, of course, some interesting additional powers implied by that as well. I know what you have on you. It will take all of it, but I can handle it."

Irving was startled. "What? Now?"

"Unless you wish a more convenient time."

Irving thought about it. There *was* no other convenient

time, of course. They were leaving tomorrow. All the remaining cash on him, though, was a fair amount even after
his purchases. Explaining what had happened to it to
Poquah wouldn't be easy, but it might well be handled. But
the idea of lifting the curse to find out what these odd feelings were like unimpeded and to be able to *act* on them
like any other normal young man his age—*that* was tempting. As for the curse—which he *did* know how he'd gotten,
fooling around with sorcerous attempts of his own to break
the first one a couple of years ago—that wasn't so pressing,
but it *did* seem like a great idea. To be able to turn it on
or off . . .

He thought of Larae, who, unless she had tremendous
self-control, was somehow not affected by it. "You guarantee that all women would be affected by it?"

"Absolutely. Would you like to do it now?"

Oh, hell! "Yeah, I think so."

"You understand that a curse requires a demon to modify
it. Come on back and I'll treat the spell, and then we'll
summon someone appropriate. Um, leave your shoes and
cloth outside. Nothing but you inside, please; we wouldn't
want anything to contaminate the work."

The proprietor took him in the back, where there was a
small, dark room lit with candles and with a small altar in
the center. "No pentagram?" Irving asked him.

"In *Yuggoth*? Whatever *for*? I mean, demons can just as
easily walk in off the street and do. It's only when you're
dealing with the really powerful ones, the ones of a kind
even their fellow demons can't control, that you need any
sort of protection along those lines, and usually in that case
a mere pentagram is inadequate." He fumbled under the
small altar, and then there was a hissing sound under it.
The little man struck something, and a fire caught under the
bowl sitting atop the altar, which he adjusted with some
sort of curved rod control. It seemed for all the world that
he had a gas flame there, and maybe he did.

The proprietor handed Irving a small ceremonial awl.

"I'll need at least two drops of blood," he said, as if that were totally routine.

"I'm not sure I like giving anything of myself to one like you," the boy responded. "No offense, but there's a lot of control in this."

"Oh, relax! I'm bonded! Besides, it will all be consumed. And anyway, the authorities have everybody's hair and nails and skin and whatever. It's routine for coming here."

Irving didn't like that idea one bit. Still, he said, "Okay, okay. Let me jab . . ." He made a small puncture, and the man grabbed his finger and shook it over the bowl. A drop or two splashed down and sizzled. He then added a few small potion-type ingredients and stirred with a whisk, as if he were making an omelet. Soon there was a very small burned ball there, round and surprisingly shiny, which the proprietor picked up with tongs.

"Looks like it's good," the magician told him. "You are welcome to take this with water or wine if you like. I have some over here of either."

Irving looked at it. "You mean *swallow* it like a pill?"

"Exactly so. It will decouple the spell. It is quite cool now, but I would prefer if only you touched it. I want no contamination."

Irving took it, examined it, shook his head, then took the offered water and swallowed it as best he could. It was a little tough getting it down, but with enough water he made it.

He handed the cup back to the proprietor and waited. "I don't feel any different," he said.

"Of course not. And you won't, not right away. It will dissolve and circulate through your body. You'll start feeling it soon enough. In fact, if you've never had these feelings unrestricted before, I would take it easy tonight. Now, for the other. Stand over on that symbol on the floor and relax."

Irving looked down and saw an area where some kind of hex symbol had been drawn on the floor, looking like a stylized bird's head of the sort you'd see in Egyptian hieroglyphics or something. He went over and stood on it and almost jumped off. The spot was uncannily cold on his feet.

"That's natural," the dealer told him. "Now, just stand there and do not move. I will have to go out before this can happen. It's just between the two of you, but he'll know exactly what the problem is and how to fix it."

"He?"

"Mysteroth, a demon of the tribe of Prince Leviathan. I told you not to worry. This is a demon who could just as easily do whatever he willed to you if he met you on a sunny street. This is strictly business. He couldn't care less about you or what you want this for; he's simply doing me a service and will take it out in trade."

Before Irving could say another word, the little man departed, leaving him alone to wonder if he was indeed doing the right thing or something incredibly stupid.

He was just about to call it off—after all, he already had cold feet—when he felt the whole atmosphere of the room change. He knew that feeling; he'd felt it in Ruddygore's study in Terindell. No matter what, he couldn't walk out now. The demon was there.

Mysteroth did not, however, believe in dramatic entrances. Instead, the curtain over the door was pushed back and he walked in rather casually, kind of like a dentist walking into a room to examine your teeth.

He was about six feet tall, thin, and very birdlike, just as his symbol suggested. In fact, he had bird's eyes and a short but curved ibislike bill. His skin, however, showing through his dark robes, was a mottled purple and green and somewhat reptilian.

"Hmmm," the demon said thoughtfully, examining him. "Been kind of limp up to now, eh? You'll enjoy this. Kind of an impressive little curse you had stuck on you, too, but rather juvenile. You're old enough now to really appreciate the power. Okay, I'm going to put you into a kind of stasis. Don't panic; it's no big deal. It'll feel a little weird, maybe tickle. As with all curses, it will hurt for a short bit when I pull it away, but it shouldn't be unbearable and won't be for very long—sort of like pulling a sticky bandage off body hair. Then I'm going to rewire it and put it back. Ready?"

Irving wasn't at all sure about this now, but he could only nod.

Suddenly he felt himself drop away from the floor, and he felt as if he were flying in some dense, liquid atmosphere. He could breathe and he was aware, but he couldn't move, couldn't talk, and was entirely helpless, suspended there in, well, whatever.

It didn't tickle. It *itched*. Itched like all get-out, and he couldn't scratch it. He *knew* better than to trust a demon. But if it itched like hell, then what would the curse removal feel like, really? The anticipation was almost worse than the real thing, which was a very short but severe stabbing pain. Still, it hurt enough that he would have cried out if he could have done so, and he felt tears come to his eyes as the aftereffects of the pain washed over him.

There was sound now, the crackle of strong electricity, and the vision of swirling multicolored bubbles all around, then joining, congealing in the crackling liquidity, then spiraling, creating threads that began to wrap themselves around him. At least it didn't hurt or itch; in fact, *this* tickled.

Suddenly it was over. He was out of it, and aside from a little dizziness and an aftermemory of the sensations his body had undergone, he felt okay, even normal.

The demon was still there.

"Now, let me tell you," Mysteroth said, "to anyone but an expert looking at and for some changes, this looks to be the same curse. Nobody will know what you had done here today. The effects are simple, and I know a lot of men who would sell their souls for this—and you didn't have to do that. The default now is *off*, not on. You must consciously turn it on. It will take a little practice, and you should concentrate if you have specific women in mind, but it will work. In fact, if you concentrate it all on *one* individual, you may find that she loses any will of her own and will do whatever you command. It will work on any female designed to have sex with a human male, so that means many faerie as well."

"You mean somebody could be like a slave?"

"Absolutely. No limits. They would be love slaves, absolutely doing what you commanded even if it meant their own destruction or the destruction of others. You could even do it, then command as your last command that they not remember it at all. Perfectly safe to you and useful for fending off jealous husbands and those who can't keep secrets. It should be a fun toy."

"And the downside?"

"For you? Only if they catch you at it! That is not my problem. Very well, that is all. Put on your clothing when you leave and pay at the front door."

And with that the demon turned and walked out.

Irving felt too excited at the possibilities here to worry much about it. He still would look the same to Poquah, and now he had some control over that nonsense. He wasn't sure if he'd like turning people into love slaves, but then again, who knew?

He wasn't so naive about sorcery, though, that he didn't realize that the curse, no matter how it looked, hadn't merely been modified but removed and that another far stronger and darker one that looked pretty much like it had been left in its place. No matter what the monetary cost here, there was always some other cost, too, when you got that kind of power from a demon. As Mysteroth had said, some men had probably sold their souls for this kind of power.

He looked around for the demon or at least a sign of where the creature had gone but saw none. The little man was waiting for him near the front of the store, though, and examined him carefully.

"Very good," he said approvingly. "I believe this is going to be the sort of transaction which all merchants hope and dream they will do, where everyone profits and everyone is satisfied. That begins with my own charges. Would you like a receipt?"

"Um, no, I don't think so," he told the sorcery salesman. "That's all I need—for Poquah to find that." He thanked the little man and walked out into the sunlight once more.

The proprietor watched him stand there and then walk up the street, and he smiled. *Yes, go ahead. Use the power. It will become almost a drug the more you do. And every time you do, you will become more and more a part of our side.*

If the Kauri and the boy could be so easily converted, the Imir would pose no problem, not outnumbered like that.

At least the demon Mysteroth, in his disguise as the proprietor of the shop, felt certain of it.

He chuckled in fact at what was awaiting the poor kid, who would find that the thing worked *exactly* as promised and that the only one it *wouldn't* work on was the only one the kid really wanted. It was really one of those perfectly delicious little spells, at that.

Walking up the street, Irving spotted a woman coming the other way. She was fairly ordinary-looking and he normally would never have given her a second glance, but now he decided to test out his high-priced power.

He stared at her and willed that she feel the attraction.

It was as if a thunderbolt had struck her. From virtually not noticing him at all except as an obstacle to avoid while walking, she suddenly gasped, smiled the dreamiest of smiles, and could not take her eyes off him.

He felt the power and the control, and it was really strange—he felt it *there*. He felt it in his loins, which were giving off strange sensations and also undergoing involuntary stiffening as he watched.

He was suddenly a little scared and said to her, "Forget it. You did not see me at any time, nor will you ever think of or remember me," and sent that with an additional bolt of mental force.

She seemed to almost shrivel, shook her head in sudden puzzlement, and started to walk on some more, a very concerned, confused look on her face.

His own new sensations weren't so easily controlled, and it worried him. Not that he wanted to do anything with that strange woman, but it also struck him with sudden force that he really didn't know *how* to do it, at least not all the rules and procedures and things a woman would expect. He wanted to be able to do it right, to do it perfectly, if he could.

He needed a teacher.

A COMPLICATION IN THE RULES

Native guides can be neither fully hired nor fully trusted.
                                        —Rules, Vol. XXIII, p. 104(d)

IT HAD BEEN A STRANGE AND DIFFICULT NIGHT FOR
Irving. Dreams of a kind he'd never really known before
came vividly to his head and remained with him when he
awoke. It wasn't merely that they were sexual fantasies,
which he at least had understood before on a more academic level; it was the *nature* of them. They were ugly—
not him at all: domination fantasies, extreme power trips,
scenarios detailing vignettes where he treated women in
ways he'd *never* treat them in real life or even want to, or
so he thought.

And they were turning him on physically, a process that
wasn't nearly as comfortable or pleasurable as he'd imagined but was making him feel like a tense and tightly coiled
spring demanding release as if from some great pain or
agony.

He was getting all at once what almost everybody else
got in stages through adolescence; the brain chemicals and
bodily sensations that by his age would normally be under
some kind of control were all rushing in upon him in a single night. He awoke drenched with sweat, stiff as a board,
and scared to death.

The worst part was, there was a little bit of him thinking—always thinking but in this case following the flow of
sensations in his body—reminding him, as it were, that unlike most men, he actually *did* possess the power to accomplish in real life what his dreams demanded and his
conscience recoiled at doing. How the hell could he turn
this off now that it was on? How could he possibly with-

stand the temptation to use his strange powers to fulfill those fantasies even though he'd hate himself for doing it?

Who could he turn to for help? Not Poquah, certainly. If the Imir knew that he'd squandered so much on *this*, there was no limit on the spells and curses that might come down upon him. But who else was there? Marge? Hell, she looked a lot like the kind of girl his dreams could easily accommodate, and she was built for it. She was a creature of sex; how could she possibly help him control or overcome it?

Larae—no, that would be even worse. It was a good thing for now that they were off later this very morning, or else they might well wind up alone again, and then who knew what would happen? And yet those people were the only ones he knew and could fully trust in all this bizarre land. He'd been naive enough to get himself into this mess, but he wasn't so naive that he believed for a moment that anyone in this city would help him, even the magic shop proprietor, without the payment of even larger sums than he'd paid to get into this fix. That was how bargains with demons worked, didn't they?

Somehow he'd have to deal with it. Somehow he'd have to learn control, at least to a degree. Otherwise he would turn into a monster, a rapist, or something equally suitable to Yuggoth but not to anywhere else or to his soul.

He got up, although it was still before dawn, and walked out onto the small balcony, forgetting he was stark naked. It wouldn't matter, anyway; there was nobody below or directly across at that point in the morning, and he just needed some air, some cool sea breeze, to comfort him and let him get a grip. It wasn't a lot of good, though. This was the tropics, and the weather was strictly hot, hotter, and hottest.

More comfortable in the predawn heat was Marge, who flew now over the city, heading toward the hotel, intent on getting some sleep before she'd have to be roused for the move to the new ship. She wouldn't be in any great shape during daylight, but she could manage by force of will the couple of hours needed for the move if she turned in a bit early.

Marge, too, was disturbed and not sure exactly why. She'd tried to contact the Earth Mother to draw strength and wisdom while in this place, and it hadn't worked, at least not in the way it always had. Oh, she still felt the link, and there was comfort in that, but it seemed distant, far away, and direct mental communication appeared to be impossible, as if she were too distant to make out any of the words. It had been a long time since she'd been cut off from such contact, and it made her uncomfortable, all the more so because she felt stronger and more powerful than she ever had before. In fact, she felt tremendous.

She banked around toward the hotel window and then suddenly realized that Irving was standing naked on the little balcony outside the window. She wondered why he was up but also noted that the kid was *really* a sexy hunk, far more than his father had ever been. Funny, she hadn't really noticed that or thought about it before.

It didn't take much to see what his problem was, either. In faerie sight, one quite literally burned when one had this kind of lust, and this kid was worse than any sixteen-year-old boy she'd ever seen.

Wait a minute! He shouldn't burn like that! He's got a spell . . .

And it was clearly still there, too. Either the kid had burst right through it, so strong were his impulses and drives, or he'd been playing a little magic trick himself. She wondered why Poquah hadn't noticed it but then realized that he wouldn't see it in Irving—those of the nymph family would be the ones with that sort of sight.

She hesitated to disturb the kid, but there were still a number of potential threats able to fly around these parts, and Irving was frankly standing between her and security. She decided to come in via the direct approach to give him time to either duck discreetly back in or at least be prepared for company.

Irving did start when he saw Marge coming in, but not because she was out there. Rather, she didn't look, well, *right* for some reason. All those shimmering reds and stuff

seemed dulled out, and it was almost as if she were somebody or something different. Still, he didn't fear what he
saw and allowed the flying creature to approach until he
was able to see quite clearly that it was Marge.

Or, rather, opaquely. Frankly, there seemed to be *two*
Marges there, one the old one and the other a larger, differently colored variation that seemed somehow darker.

Marge settled down next to him and said, "*You* got it
bad, kid. I can tell. You can't hold *that* in for very long, not
out in a place like this. Not unless you're Superman, anyway."

He sighed. "I know. It was stupid of me to get that spell
taken off, but what can I do?"

"I don't think it was stupid at all. I think it was dumb to
put it on you in the first place. Kids should grow up feeling
normal and learning how to handle things, damn it."

"Yeah, yeah. It was only because I managed to get that
curse on me that women pay any attention. Ruddygore got
upset, worrying that with that kind of power and the studies
I was doing at the time I might go evil right off the bat. He
wanted to prevent that, and I guess he did, until now. But
here I am, and going evil is what everything inside me says
to do."

Marge gave him a sympathetic chuckle. "Evil is sometimes absolute, but it's also sometimes in the mind of the
beholder. Heck, Irving, I'd be glad to give you some relief
except that I also feel like your aunt. Besides, I couldn't do
it tonight, anyway—not anymore tonight."

He looked at her squarely. "I'm not sure I dare do it with
you. Nothing personal and all that, but you're a little scary
since we got here. A lot more than on the boat over."

It was her turn to be startled. "Huh? What do you mean?
I feel great! And *my* kind of creature never looks or is better than when she feels this good."

"Um, Marge, I'm getting double vision just looking at
you. It's like there are two of you standing there. It's why
I didn't quite recognize you until you were actually here.
You're changing, Marge, and maybe getting a little scary."

"What? Huh? I don't *feel* any different. In what way am I changing?"

"Poquah said it to me, but I didn't really believe him. That you'd—feed—on locals with no consciences at all, consuming parts of souls rather than cleaning them."

"Succubi do that! I'm not a Succubus!"

"Not yet, but you're getting there. You notice you're taller? You barely came up to my chest before; now you're maybe shoulder-high. Your colors are growing darker in faerie sight, and your wings are starting to look a little less like an insect than a fairy."

She grew suddenly alarmed. If Irving was telling the truth . . . "What color are my lips, Irv? My lips. Simple question."

"Um, look crimson red to me."

She gave a sigh of relief. "Not deep purple, not black? Then there's still time."

"Yeah? But how will you eat? Aren't you in some kinda trap here, sort of like me?"

"I'll find some way. There has to be one, otherwise the Earth Mother would never have commanded that I come, nor would Ruddygore have let me. Damn! This place corrupts you, and you don't even *notice!*" She sighed. "Irv, hold on. I'll figure something out for you and maybe for me, too. Can you hold out another day and night?"

He shrugged. "I dunno *what* I can do anymore. I never imagined I could feel so—so *driven*, so much like an *animal* or something. I was always in control."

She nodded. "Yeah, I know. Just hold on for a day and a half or so until I can get some of it worked out. Won't mean a damned thing if by the time we get to Mount Doom both you and I are already in Hell's service, will it?"

"I—I guess not. But I almost feel like I am right now."

She managed something of a grin. "Don't worry about *that*. You'll feel like that *many* times. Just make sure it isn't permanent." She paused a moment. "And stay off Laraē unless *she* wants it, you hear? You dragged her in with us; now don't betray that trust!"

"I won't," he assured Marge, but it was an easy promise to make. After he'd returned that afternoon, he hadn't been able to resist testing out this new power on her, at least to an extent. It hadn't worked. She hadn't even seemed to be aware of him trying.

All that, and he couldn't even attract the girl of his dreams! It wasn't fair.

Man! That was *some* curse she had!

The mystery of the rails in the streets of Red Bluffs had been solved the first day they'd arrived; now they were taking advantage of what the locals called the "omnibus" service to move themselves and their gear to the river embarkation station.

Power was by the old traditional method: horses or, in the case of freight, oxen. The only reason it didn't give the whole city a certain, well, air, was that the same underlying alternate reality that had gone after the big man's body back on the broad street a few nights earlier also seemed really to love manure.

"Below is not Hell, but below is where those whom the princes would punish or discipline for offenses against *themselves* are sent," Joel Thebes explained. "It is not a pleasant existence. Just a short while in it is sufficient to turn the strongest will to their bidding and keep it on the path of total obedience. Most everyone who winds up in their clutches spends at least a *little* time there, just as a sample. It is usually enough. I suspect that this experience is where the idea of Hell as a place of eternal punishment came about. Hell is actually quite nice, quite comfortable and regal. It is where the so-called bad angels, whom the Greeks named demons, live and have lived since before Eden. The souls that come to them, which, let us face it, constitute the majority of those from both Earth and here, wind up either rewarded for services rendered while alive or as slaves to those who live there. Most do not consider it fun, but it is no lake of eternal fire. *That* is what is promised for all of them, demons and minions and slaves alike, if the other side wins the final battle."

Irving's eyebrows went up. "You mean there's some doubt about which will win?"

"*They* seem to think so. Otherwise why bother at all? But if these others come over, if *they* displace Hell as the opposition, as it were, then it could be the worst of everything, you see. Better the devil you know than the ancient horrors you don't."

The river launch was a modest affair, resembling the passenger craft that sailed the River of Dancing Gods. There would not, however, be much in the way of privacy aboard or comfort, either, and the trip promised to be quite boring. Too small for diversions or private assignations, too, which suited Irving, at least for now.

It was, however, a fairly elaborate two-masted schooner with emplacements for oars if the need arose. In addition to their own party, it appeared that about a dozen others were traveling upriver, possibly all the way to their own destination.

They were a curious-looking lot. All humans, more or less—at least as much as Joel Thebes was human—but all of them looked, well, somewhat sinister and not *quite* legit. That is, they all looked like characters out of bad soap operas, at least to Irving.

That one there was a tall, dark stranger; one woman was the malevolent housekeeper; another woman, the damsel in distress. One tall fellow looked like a cartoon mortician; another, the crazy doctor or mad scientist.

"They are all machinists for the King," Joel Thebes told them.

"Machinists?" Irving repeated. "What kind of machinists would *those* people be?"

"They're called deus ex machinists, I believe. His Majesty employs a million of 'em. They're obviously returning to work after some rest and relaxation. Stay away from them. They tend to be nothing but trouble and complications."

Even Marge, as dull-witted as she was in daylight, admit-

ted to herself that *these* clichés looked definitely over-
worked.

The captain and crew had red faces and horns on their
heads and sort of looked like human-sized satyrs of a different color, but they also seemed pleasant and capable
enough. To them this was just a job, another routine trip.

"Stow your gear and yourselves forward of the main-
mast," the mate told them, pointing to the bow. "You'll
have to sleep on deck, you know, being such last-minute
add-ons. You can make a tent of insect netting there. It's
not very hard."

Poquah looked it over and sighed and shook his head.
"Looks like very close quarters. Oh, well, it's only for—
how long on the river, Mister Thebes?"

"Against the current, probably five days. After that it'll
be by caravan to the capital. Well, it could be worse. Doing
it overland and on your own, this could take *months.*"

The river didn't seem all that huge even here, deep
though it obviously was, and Irving wondered about where
it led. "Anything dangerous that might threaten us up
ahead?"

"There is *always* something," Thebes responded. "Nasty
jungle animals, voodoo witch doctors, cannibals: things like
that during the jungle part. More nasty creatures across the
mountains, then desert to the capital. Just keep your eyes
and ears open as usual and don't worry so much. This ship
goes back and forth all the time and loses very few passengers."

"Haven't lost one in three return trips," one crewman
commented, overhearing Thebes' assurances. "Past due,
probably. We usually lose a few every other trip."

That was not exactly what any of them wanted to hear.

Still, at precisely noon the small sloop was pushed away
from the dock and began going upriver, first with oars and
a rhythmic tom-tom beat, then, when the sea breeze began
later in the day, with sail.

Irving, out of curiosity, went to check on who the oarsmen might be who could power this boat and almost

wished he hadn't. They were monstrous, misshapen creatures, things of nightmare, having in common only muscles and miserable expressions.

It didn't take long for the city and its lights to fade from view behind them, leaving only a dull glow on the horizon. Ahead was darkness, a living, very noisy darkness of thick trees and vines and more insects than even Hell might come up with on its own.

It wasn't easy, in spite of his lack of sleep the night before, to get to sleep in this insect din and on this uncomfortable deck, but he managed. As least things were so miserable and uncomfortable that he barely had time to think about his other problem.

Neither Poquah nor Larae seemed to have any difficulty. The Imir seemed to be able to tune in or out anything he wished, and the girl appeared to be right at home in this sort of alien environment.

For Marge the night brought less respite, since she was wide awake, anyway. Still, it was damned difficult to figure a way out of this trap, even though there *had* to be one. First of all, didn't the Rules *require* that there be a way out of any predicament? Not that the solution was necessarily a good one—that same rule was why Joe had become a wood nymph in the first place. It had been either that or death.

That precedent worried her. Since the choice *wasn't* life or death here but Kauri or Succubus, *did* that rule apply? She no more wanted to be one of the foul creatures than Joe had wanted to become a nymph, but it wasn't an end road. The big problem would come if and when her conversion was complete. It wasn't any big deal to eat some of *these* souls, but she could never in that case return to Husaquahr or Earth or anywhere else where good men lived. Or could she? The few such creatures she'd seen had positively enjoyed corrupting good men the most. Nor would she ever again know the communion with the Kauri that had become so dear to her.

So how did she keep from becoming one? Other than Irving, there really weren't any sure targets that could be treated Kauri-style, were there? And she didn't really want to have at the boy, even though she knew it was probably inevitable. He was no relation at all, and she barely knew him; still, it seemed somehow almost, well, *incestuous*.

And yet what other possibility was there?

The area inland of the city was a jungle, and like all jungles, while it looked like a deserted green Hell, it was actually teeming with life of all sorts, including animal, human, demonic, and faerie. Be easy to find a nice cannibal in there, she mused, but to find one who first ate you and then felt *guilty* about it, well, that was a different story.

What this whole damned continent needed, for her sake, was a bunch of Jewish and Catholic mamas roaming around heaping on guilt and making even the demons miserable.

She wanted to fly up and oversee the whole region, but there were some bats around, half as big as she was, and other creatures equally threatening: she wasn't about to become anybody's lunch or dinner. Heck, it was worse there than in the city, where the toughest thing had been ducking the gargoyles.

None of these things looked like fruit bats, that was for sure. She sat perched on a mast and watched two of them team up to swoop down and pick up and carry away a screaming something the size of a wild boar.

They swooped around the ship but didn't land on it or seem interested in snatching things from it. Most likely the complex spells that were woven around it helped; the really nasty stuff was repelled to a degree, which was, she supposed, good for business.

None of this solved her problem, either. She was usually the one who helped people and gave advice to others. Who did *she* have to turn to in a situation like this when she really needed help? Even reaching out to the Earth Mother was closed to her; clearly her altered nature had as much to do with that as distance did.

She thought about Irving's copy of the volume of the Rules on Yuggoth. There might well be something in there—if she could read it. Maybe that would have to be the trade-off after all. He would find something that would get her out of her dilemma, and she could figure a way out of his.

Well, his inhibitions would block him for now aboard this craft, and she could go several days without feeding, particularly after her times in the city. The trouble was, when she *did* run low again, she'd be unable to be very discriminating about who or what she was servicing.

Irving would find the passengers on this ship not very conducive to his powers or desires, either. Although those walking clichés seemed human enough, they were a peculiar kind of fairy, a singular kind that seemed to be able to take the basic shapes and attributes a mortal willed them to have but whose interaction was limited primarily to one another. They could be shaped, their behavior influenced or even controlled by mortal thoughts, but they could not actually physically interact on the real-world level with mortals.

The next day brought dull gray skies—when they could be seen at all—and heavy rain in the afternoon that could be endured only for the hour or so that it lasted. The crew didn't seem to think much of it; it happened almost *every* day, they were assured, in this jungle, and whether the full force struck the ship depended on how dense the forest canopy was when it fell, nothing more or less. Otherwise, nearly one hundred percent humidity was the norm.

The river was so narrow and winding that it was next to impossible to figure out where they were or how much distance was covered. Only at night, with absolutely no glows either on the horizon or from stars above, did it seem as if they were traveling not only south but into another, totally isolated world.

It was also boring as all hell, so much so that they were climbing the walls by the third day out. Time dragged, and the other passengers didn't seem to be able even to speak except in stilted dialogue that wouldn't pass muster with the mildest critic. Beyond their surface attributes and simple and repetitive ways, there was quite simply no "there" there.

One of the satyrlike crewmen, seeing their problem, said, "I cannot make it more exciting—unless we are attacked by cannibals, which is a bit *too* exciting—but I can offer the nonfaerie members some diversion. These roots and leaves are very handy for passing the time and will make it seem pleasant."

Poquah looked at the assortment and snorted. "Drugs! Mild hallucinogens mostly, from the looks of them. I wouldn't touch them if I were you!" That last was said to Irving in a tone that was much less advice than warning.

But Poquah spent most of his time in meditation, ignoring rain and anything else, and seemed not at all troubled by the boredom. Irving was much more tempted in spite of spending a fair amount of time scouring the Rules volume for some solution for Marge, but he was also more than a little scared of going for any of it. What if it were addicting? What if it induced some kind of temporary nutso state that might find him waking up somewhere in the river or the jungle in somebody's stew pot? That last was even more to think about; hell, he'd seen just enough native faces peeking out at them from the bushes to know that the natives here sure looked like real primitive white guys, and he wasn't going to wind up in *their* pot!

"Pleasant, not addicting," the crewman swore. "Just feel good. Maybe a little silly but not dangerous."

It was Larae who was most tempted. "What have I got to lose? I'm going out of my mind anyway," she told him. "Still, I wouldn't want to do it alone. My people used a lot of this sort of thing for various cures, and I can see some familiar things. I am sure that it is as the crewman says. Are you afraid of it?"

"No! Of course not! Um, well, I just haven't had a straightout favor from one of these dudes yet that didn't have a catch in it."

"I think it is the only thing that will keep me from going mad and jumping into the river or the jungle today," she told him. "Still, I just would not do it alone. Together, perhaps? Or are you simply too frightened even to take *my* word for it?"

"Poquah—" Irving began to object, but she cut him off.

"He will be in his trance all day, doing very much naturally what we cannot do without help like this. Will you do it?"

He sighed. He didn't want to, didn't trust those drugs one bit, but he sensed that this was some kind of trust test on her part and didn't want to lose her confidence. Damn it! He would *never* have considered this before. It was because *she* wanted it and his new self didn't want to do anything to displease her.

"All right, but just this once," he told her. "I got a bad feeling about this, and I want you to remember that if it goes bad."

She squeezed his hand and actually gave him a peck on the cheek that made him feel like a million and blew away any hesitancy.

So while Joel Thebes dozed, Poquah sat in his trance, and Marge slept, they took some of the root she selected from the crewman and broke it off in half and began to chew it, remaining well toward the rear of the boat and away from the others.

It didn't seem to do anything for a while, just leaving a sickly sweet, almost purely surgary taste in his mouth. Still, he found after a while that he was staring at things and that they didn't look or seem the same anymore. The jungle blurred, the dull colors mixing and marching and becoming an endless palette of living colors swirling all about. In a little while he was vaguely aware that he was thoroughly soaking wet, but it did not bother him, nor did he much feel it or reflect that he hadn't even remembered the rainstorm.

And then there was Larae, who seemed the object of all desire, and pretty soon she was doing something to him that felt really good and he was doing pretty much the same, imitating her, to her, and there was all sorts of stuff that felt good and had no thought behind it at all, and suddenly it was dark and he was sound asleep.

She had already awakened and moved forward to the usual sleeping place when he came out of it at around midnight. He felt pretty mellow, really, but suddenly realized that he was naked and fumbled around, finally finding his loincloth well to the other side of the area, near the far rail. The straps were *broken*! He managed as best he could, but he wasn't at all sure what had happened. Had he done "it" with her and just not remembered, or had he forced it, or what?

Hell, from the looks of this, *she* had forced *him*!

He also had a headache, a stomachache, and aches in places he never even knew had muscles to ache.

Marge floated down to the deck and handed him a fresh loincloth.

"Thanks. I was kinda stuck for a minute."

"No problem," she assured him. "Poquah's mad as hell at you two, though."

"Um, yeah. But if he's really gonna be Daddy, then he's gotta be as responsible as Daddy and watch over and help me, right? He's got no kick. If they're gonna send me to a place like *this* at my age, then they got to figure I'm at least partly on my own."

"Could be. I guess doing your first drugs and such makes you feel all grown-up, huh? Tonight you are a man."

"No, no! It's not like that!"

"You had no idea what you were swallowing. Some of that shit that these guys have is enough to turn you into one of those muscled morons who pull the oars. Larae I blame more than you, and that's probably what will save your hide in the end with Poquah."

"She only offered me the apple. I was the one who took it."

"Yeah, but she knew just what she was feeding the two of you. I could tell. She knew how much to take and how to take it, figuring you wouldn't. She wanted you blotto."

"No, that's not it. I mean, why would she? *She* was the one who wanted it just to pass the time. It's so damned *boring*!"

"Hell and adulthood are usually boring. No, she wanted

you blotto because she's not much older than you are but she's alone, afraid, and completely frustrated. She wanted you, but if you weren't higher than a kite, you'd find out and remember her nasty little secret. Her curse."

"What? I've heard and seen this curse, but I still don't get it. What could be so awful that she'd go in this direction rather than reveal it even to us?"

"The answer to that will tell you whether you are *really* grown-up and can handle things or whether you're just a kid."

"Do *you* know?"

"Yeah. *Now* I do. And I figured out the rest of her story. Pretty obvious once you put the story together with the sorcerer Lothar and figure his options on the problem. The only reason it wasn't immediately obvious was the way he did it, the way I think even the mighty Lothar was *forced* by the conditions of the curse and the opposition of the demon to do it. It had to be a real curse, not a simple transformation. A transformation wouldn't have done the trick. Probably not allowed under some obscure Rule."

"You're not gonna tell me she's a *guy*. I *know* one sex from the other, and that's the kind of stuff you see in plays and movies, not for real."

"Well, we're living in the heart, soul, and origin of every cliché in fiction," she reminded him. "However, in one sense you're right. She was born female, raised female, and *is* female in almost all respects. That was the problem. Lothar couldn't change her into a male at that stage; the demon would never have accepted it, since no matter what he changed her into, she'd still be the firstborn girl. So, somehow, and I have no idea about this, the sorcerer instead created a curse for her that made her unacceptable as a sacrifice. I don't know what poor unfortunate he used, but he *grafted* a male organ onto her. It is mostly isolated from the rest of her system, I think—the testosterone just doesn't get through to her. She's in every way female, but the route to that femininity is blocked. She became damaged goods, neither fish nor fowl, without the purity a sacrifice de-

manded, but so bound to her is this that to remove it would
rip her guts out. It was a minor demon; he just couldn't figure out a way around it. All he could do was vent his fury
and command her to come here, where even curses of that
complexity might be unraveled by smarter and more powerful demons."

He didn't want to hear it. "I don't believe you!" he almost shouted at Marge, even though he really did. "You
mean that under that skirt—"

"You mustn't blame her. She didn't choose it, and in all
but that one area she is very much still a she, which must
be the most frustrating thing in the world. When you're
dealing with that level of world-class sorcerer, even the little things get handled. It's why she tried to avoid you on
the ship over and why she fled when you contacted her.
Only her fear and loneliness led her to take up my offer."

Irving felt sick. "Then we—that is, tonight, we—oh, no!"

At least it explained why he had no power over her, but
it also meant that she'd reversed his erotic dreams. *She*, if
that was still the right term, had seduced *him*.

"Quit feeling sorry for yourself!" Marge snapped. "*She's*
the one with the curse and the problem, not you. And *you*
are the one who took that drug with her by *your* choice,
your lust. That's what I meant about growing up, Irving. In
the end, nobody did anything to you but you. You removed
your limits and your spells; you fantasized and lusted after
her and dragged her into our group. She didn't try and join
us, remember. And you took the drug with her. Now, how
you handle this inside yourself and how you handle yourself in Larae's presence will determine just how grown-up
you really are."

Right now he didn't feel all that grown-up. It wasn't *fair*!
Damn and double damn! He felt *used*. Unclean, sort of.
Bits and pieces of just what they'd done earlier came back
to him in his emotional torment, and he felt like blaming
anybody but himself. Grow up? Hell, *nobody* ever was *that*
grown-up!

Oddly, as he stared out into the pitch darkness of the rain

forest, a thought came to him from out of nowhere: *This is how Dad must have felt.*

Felt wrong, weak, compromised, ashamed, and unwilling to admit the truth or face down his son. Joe hadn't acted very grown-up, either, had he? And the son had cursed and blasted him for running ever since.

Now it was the son who wanted to run, who didn't want to face the way things were with somebody *he'd* sort of assumed responsibility for. But how could he just keep on after knowing? How could he treat Larae the same as before? Or even as just a friend? Even a companion? Particularly now that she'd *used* him.

But hadn't *he* dreamed of using *her*? Wasn't that why he'd taken that drug with her in the first place?

That was *different*!

How?

Only because in his own scenarios he was the user rather than the victim. Damn it, it made him feel like a skunk. *She* had done this to *him*, and here *he* was feeling guilty about it!

But it was so—so *unnatural*!

In a world of fairies, nymphs, gnomes, curses, demons on street corners, and resident sorcerers, what in *hell* was *natural*?

So Dad had gone off to conquer the evil sorcerer and had been changed in the process into a wimp of a bimbo wood nymph. *"Hi, Irving! Guess what? But don't worry, I'll stick around and be your role model, anyway."*

What if he had been the one who was changed? Would he have acted differently than Joe had? Would he have faced his son like that, *forever* like that, and would the son have accepted it? He'd been blaming his father for not doing just that for years, but what would his own reaction have been?

He knew the answer. He knew that what he'd always thought he *would* have done was what he most certainly *should* have done under those circumstances, but it wasn't what he really would have thought or felt or done. *Nobody* grew up *that* quickly. Nobody should have had to.

Marge had no idea what Irving was really thinking or how he'd finally resolve this, if he could, but she did emphatically sense the growing buildup of guilt, shame, and emotional turmoil within him.

Maybe in another night or so he'd at least have worked up sufficient guilt to allow her to solve her immediate problem by helping him solve his.

Poquah rarely smoked a pipe, and when he did, it was only when the most important things were imminent. It was a pleasure he shared with his elfin brethren but one that also never quite fit his self-image and lifestyle. But in the predawn hours he was on deck smoking the pipe and leaning against the rail, looking out at nothing in particular.

Irving wasn't sure who he wanted less to see and talk to, Larac or Poquah, but as much as he wanted just to go overboard and make his way through the jungle to someplace where they'd never heard of him and wouldn't find him, he wasn't really about to do it. He wasn't at all sure he wouldn't have, though, if he'd also shared his father's immortality.

Marge had reported the Imir as furious, but Poquah never showed emotion and was always in perfect control. He was not in fact nearly as angry as he'd been initially and not entirely angry at the boy or the girl, particularly since Marge had briefed him on all that had transpired and all that had been revealed.

"Poquah, I—"

The Imir, barely visible in the predawn grayness, held up his hand. "Growing up is learning, often by committing mistakes," he said softly. "The trick is to grow up and learn from those mistakes without allowing them to destroy you. Have you learned?"

"I—well, sure, I've learned. I'm just not sure if I learned all that I could have or that the lesson is correct. Damn it, Poquah, it's not *fair*!"

"Nothing much in life is certain except its unfairness. Good people die; evil lives to a ripe old age. Crime pays much of the time. Wars ravage schoolyards as thoroughly as battlefields. People tolerate and even create the grossest of dictatorships rather than risk hunger and uncertainty in freedom. Everybody expects a free lunch, but nobody can give such a thing. Someone *always* pays. That's not just something in the Rules, you know. It's the way things work. If we are not constantly tested by fighting through valleys of weeping and crucibles of fire, then nothing we can gain is worthwhile." He paused. "So what will you do now?"

Irving shook his head. "I don't know. I don't know *what* to do."

"She is asleep now. She has slept better tonight than at any time since she joined us. She also does not know that we all now know her secret. It is her great shame. I believe she is terrified that someone will find out."

"Well, I can't *hide* it. I can't *pretend* anymore. I wouldn't know how. That's something more mature people can handle, maybe, but it's just not in me, not yet."

"Then you must be totally honest with her, but that is a grave risk. If she cannot accept us knowing and you knowing in particular, she will react as your father did and will flee at the first opportunity. At least she cannot kill herself. That option is removed by her geas. She is not the owner of her fate and thus has no right to take her life. *That* at least we need not worry about."

"Yeah, but if she runs, out here, in *this* . . ."

The Imir nodded. "There is still a day and a night left. The creatures in there would be sensitized to her curse, but they would feel free to use or abuse her. She wouldn't die at their hands; she'd just wish she could."

"Great! *More* load heaped on me!"

"I wouldn't do it if there were any other way. Understanding, forgiving, sympathizing aren't enough. You must convince her that you *accept* her. That it doesn't *matter*. She has had enough of pity and of punishment, I think. This past night proved that. She seized an initiative and acted upon it, which is very encouraging. It means she's at the point of finally accepting her situation, of living with it as a permanent condition rather than just moping around and hoping she'll die or wake up. If she were to get the idea, particularly at this crucial juncture in our travels, that she could be an equal and not have to hide in shame, then she might actually have the potential to *contribute* to this expedition, which I think may be far shorter ahead than I originally thought."

"Huh? How so?"

"Something darker than anything I have ever experienced or even imagined is afoot here. I can feel its enormity, its oppressive weight and sheer power, the farther in we travel. Odd to think of Yuggoth as having a cancer, but it does, and that cancer is spreading at a rate that says there is no time for caution now. Something draws me as well to its source. Marge, too, I think, and you to a lesser but still important extent. We must settle all the turmoil within our Company, and we must do so now. We will need each other like never before in very short order."

Irving didn't sleep much at all after that, but he let Larae get up and wash and eat and get comfortable. She *did* seem different, both softer and more self-confident and definitely bound to him in some emotional way.

That was going to make this pretty damned tough, and he'd gone over and over how he'd manage it. In a sense, he knew he had her fate in his hands, and that was a heavy burden if he blew it.

Finally, though, he couldn't put if off any longer.

"Larae?"

She smiled at him. "Thank you for last night."

He tried not to show discomfort. "It's all right. I think maybe it's time I told you a little about my own self and other things in more detail than you've heard them so far."

"You don't have to."

"Yes, I do. And I want to start by telling you about my father . . ."

WE'RE OFF TO SEE THE LIZARD

Just say no to drugs or they will do something wrong to you.
—Rules, Vol. XLI, p. 194(c)

There! What did I tell you?
—Reagan, N.

AT THE UPPER LIMITS OF NAVIGATION ON THE RIVER, whose name they never did quite get clearly in their minds—it meandered horribly, and with every bend it seemed to have a new and totally unrelated name—was a small inland town that nobody had named but that was clearly their first destination.

In spite of its remoteness, the town looked oddly familiar to those from Earth, if a bit out of place in this geographic setting, with large Gothic-style Victorian houses peeking out of the ends of the jungle like an enormous collection of haunted houses. The jungle in fact ended within sight of the town and very dramatically; the mountains seemed to be a two-mile-high wall.

Irving stared at the black rock beyond, and his jaw dropped. "Holy smokes! We have to go up *there*?"

"*Over* it," Joel Thebes told him. "It is not all that bad but can be quite uncomfortable."

"Hey, I'm in pretty fair shape, and there's no way I can climb *that*," the boy maintained. "As for the others, I don't think Marge can even *fly* that high, and she's the only other one with a chance."

"You misunderstand," Thebes told him. "We do not *climb*. As usual, we *ride*. You'll see, you'll see."

Larae was still uncomfortable with her secret out, as it were, but she at least accepted the fact that they were not going to cast her out, not even Irving, who had good cause for doing so. She was determined to do what she could for them.

240

"Will we have to stay in this town overnight?" she asked Thebes. "It does not even look *inhabited*."

"Oh, it is inhabited, all right," Thebes assured her. "Just not by folks who are still, well, like the rest of us." Considering that he was including himself in that "us," that meant that those who lived there were probably *very* unpleasant. "However, we should not have to remain here long if all the connections are right."

Poquah surveyed the small dock area as their things were placed there for them and the chameleon faerie, as Marge had begun to think of them, filed off as well, spouting their inane bad dialogue but seemingly oblivious to their surroundings. Either they were totally in character and thus natural actors or they really were pretty dumb.

"Be on your guard," the Imir warned his party. "Irving, keep your sword ready."

The boy looked around. "You see something I don't?"

"No. I just feel the currents. Not all the denizens of this town are still on the side of the established order here. If that is the case, there might well be an attempt to prevent us from going farther."

"Terrific," Irving responded glumly.

Thebes, too, seemed to sense the danger, but when a creature emerged from one of the nearby houses and shambled toward them, he seemed to relax a bit, even though the thing was certainly tension-inducing.

"*That* thing was once a human being?" Larae gasped.

It was the size of an average man but bent, misshapen, twisted in such a way that it seemed both smaller and more massive. It had the look and stench of decomposing flesh and a skull-like face that looked more like an Eygptian mummy than a living being.

Thebes walked out to the thing, which stopped, and they exchanged some sort of conversation too low to be heard by the others. Thebes pointed back to them, the thing nodded, and two dead eyes looked them over carefully.

"I don't trust that little man," Larae whispered. "I don't care if he's one of you or not."

"We don't, either, and he's not ours," Irving whispered back. "He's just sort of hired help to get us through."

"I am not worried about Mister Thebes," Poquah told them. "Not until *after* we reach Mount Doom, anyway. If he could have reached our goal on his own, he would have been there long before now. He is not on our side or either of their sides. He is on his own side, which is a very lonely and dangerous position to be in."

Thebes came back over to them. "We should get moving without delay," he told them. "There appears to be danger here if we stay. Get your things and follow our gimpy guide there through town. No deviations or temptations, please. There is nothing alive—as we know it, anyway—left here."

"You expect an ambush?" Poquah asked him, looking around.

"I don't know. I don't think they're strong enough for that, but with these types you can't tell. When you're already dead and looking like *that*, you don't exactly have a lot to lose, yes?"

The town *smelled* like death; even Marge, who would not normally be alert enough to do much good for anybody, found herself strangely wide awake in that grim place. There were few signs in writing of what it might once have been but some indications that at one time it had been a much larger place and that part of it had been consumed by fire. Just once was there anything that might be helpful in identifying it, but it was only a fragment of an old sign— interestingly, in Latin letters—that read "J-E-R-U." Nothing more.

They were more than conscious of being watched from the houses and dark places as they walked through the town in the gray gloom. Dead eyes, yes, but envious eyes, too, and hungry ones.

The deathly stillness was also unnerving, and when it was broken now and again by the loud cry of a tropical bird, they all jumped and hands went to weapons. Only the "machinists" seemed unconcerned, just blithely walking through as if it were a bright sunny day in Mister Rogers' neighborhood. Not worth a bite, Irving decided, and they knew it. Their very vacuousness was their protection.

They were very close to clearing the town proper now, going through the remnants of burned-out buildings and charred timbers from a onetime small-town business center, when they saw their destination. While much more ordinary in many ways than the town and its denizens, it was no less scary a sight.

"A cable car? Here?" Marge gasped.

And a big one, too, from the looks of it, more than able to carry them all, some freight that was being hauled along on a cart by the crew of the sailing ship, and anything else that might want to go. It was like a giant old-fashioned trolley car without wheels, and it appeared that once out of its berth, it would be suspended by two thick black cables that went up at perhaps a thirty-degree angle toward the mountain wall, quickly losing them in the clouds and mist up there.

"We're gonna take *that* up *there*?" Irving said, both nervous and incredulous.

"What powers it?" Poquah asked, fascinated more than worried.

"You do not want to know," Thebes responded, then proceeded to pretty much tell him anyway. "A *lot* of very naughty souls on some amazing treadmills beneath us."

"I don't like it," Irving told them. "Once we're in that contraption up *there*, we're sitting ducks."

Poquah was ever the pragmatist. "You would perhaps prefer to *climb*? It is one or the other."

Thebes looked around nervously. "Well, I think we better decide very quickly on this. I'm afraid some of the locals want us to stay!"

Swords came out, and they whirled to see horrors emerging from the cellars of the burned-out structures: misshapen humanoid creatures that might once have been people but were now dripping with foulness.

"Holy shit! It's *The Night of the Living Dead*!" Marge

cried, the last bits of lethargy slipping as she launched herself into the air and then straight for the waiting car.

Thebes opened his white coat for the first time and
revealed a virtual smorgasbord of weaponry in nice little holders along the lining. It was no wonder he always
looked like an unmade bed; there were wooden stakes and
mallets, crosses, crescents, Stars of David, silver daggers,
wolfsbane: it was an incredible sight.

"Zombies!" he muttered irritably. "What the hell stops
the zombies?"

"Take it from experience—very little!" Poquah shouted.
"Run for the car, everyone! Irving and I will try to buy you
time."

Irving gave the Imir a quick, nervous glance and gulped.
"We will? Um, yeah, I guess we will."

The things came on pretty fast for zombies, which had a
reputation for being slow and shuffling. One reached very
close to Irving, who was trying to backpedal and not trip
while making as good time as possible. Now he swung the
short sword in a series of broad, professional strokes that
sliced right through decaying yet animated limbs, shearing
them off as if they were made of butter.

That, unfortunately, stopped neither the severed limbs nor
the trunk from coming on. Slashes at the legs with that
sword were out of the question. "I got to get a longer
sword," Irving muttered, then turned and ran so hard for the
open door that he overran both Poquah and Larae. Thebes
seemed to have given up on his quest for a talisman or
weapon and to have got there ahead of them.

Irving made the open door of the cable car, then turned
to hold it as long as possible. He saw Larae running, but
she stumbled and fell, and he started to run back toward her
to help her. Almost immediately he realized that a zombie
was going to beat him to her.

She turned onto her back as the undead creature lunged
at her, but as the zombie tried to pounce on her and rip out
her throat, her legs came up, caught the thing at the hips,
and then, with a powerful somersault roll, sent the zombie

flying while somehow Larae got back on her feet, pulling her skirt down almost below her ass.

Irving saw a half dozen more of the creatures closing in as he reached her. "Don't bother getting pretty now!" he shouted, picking her up and sprinting for the open door, where now only Poquah guarded the entrance.

He jumped in, falling on the wooden floor, Larae spilling out of his grasp to his right. Poquah jumped aboard and pulled the sliding door shut while the approaching menace was still a good ten or fifteen feet from the car. The Imir looked around, saw an official-looking cherubic fellow in a blue uniform and brass buttons standing there beside two wooden levers, and shouted, "If you can get moving now, we might have a chance!"

"Welcome aboard, neighbors," the conductor responded in a cheery voice totally inappropriate to the situation. Marge was reminded of an animatronics figure at Disneyland. "The Borgo and Donner Pass Transit System welcomes you to what we hope will be a pleasant experience. Please have your tickets ready for collection after we start. Otherwise, I'm afraid you will be dumped overboard and fall a few thousand feet to your death, and we wouldn't want *that*, now, would we?"

The zombies had reached the car and were pounding on it furiously. One found a weak spot in the wood and punched through, a grisly arm dripping hunks of flesh emerging and grasped around for something to get hold of.

Larae screamed and pointed, and Poquah severed the limb with his sword. The arm, drawn laboriously by its hand, continued in motion.

"I'm sorry," the conductor said, eyeing the moving arm. "No pets are allowed on the line. I'll have to open the door—"

"The hell you will! Get us *out* of here!" Irving shouted at him, putting the sword almost at the conductor's throat. "We'll make sure it doesn't make the trip!"

"He's one of those stupid character critters!" Marge

shouted. "He isn't gonna break character unless— Hey! Look! They're leavin'!"

Irving and the others looked and saw that she was right. The zombies had suddenly ceased their assault on the cars and were now shambling back in a fair semblance of a line toward the old town. Poquah stuck the severed but still living arm with his sword, impaling it, threw open the door just a bit, and, with a strong motion of the wrist, sent it flying. Closing the door quickly, he turned to the conductor.

"I do not know what manner of creature you are," the Imir said in that cold but very frightening tone he used when he was very angry, "but if you fear iron, you will get some, and if a wooden stake is more to your taste, you will have that, too. Or we can just get moving. It is your choice. And if you are some sort of infernal mechanical device, we will find a way to run it ourselves. It is not as if we can get lost on this."

The conductor's smile never wavered, and he never looked directly at Poquah or showed the slightest sign that he'd heard or understood anything at all that had been said to him, but after a few seconds' pause that seemed much longer, he suddenly announced, "All those with no business aboard should be off. Now leaving. Please take seats or stand holding firmly to a rail."

Almost before Poquah could sheathe his sword, let alone get into one of the remaining wickerlike twin seats bolted to the floor, the conductor reached up, threw the first lever and then the second, then reached up with both hands and pulled them both back down again.

The car shuddered; then, silently, it began to move. The speed was not great, but it was certainly adequate; the ground was soon far behind, and the clouds and dark rock wall seemed to approach with dramatic speed.

Marge looked out at the deepening vista. "Gonna be dark soon and up in the clouds, too. Hell of an opportunity for someone who could fly at that altitude."

"Don't invite trouble," Thebes cautioned her. "It finds us enough as it is." He turned to Poquah, who was sitting there frowning, staring straight ahead. "Are you all right?" he called to the Imir.

"Huh? Yes, quite all right. I was just trying to think . . ."

"Yes? Sorry if I interrupted."

"No, no. It wasn't coming anyway, and when it does not come immediately, then it is best not to dwell on it but let it simmer. It was just that when I opened the door, I could hear *music* of some sort in the distance, back toward the boat. Very strange music but something I have heard before, although not recently. I just cannot place it."

"Didn't hear much of anything myself, but I wasn't listening for it," the little man replied.

"How long does this trip usually take, Thebes?" Marge called to him.

"Oh, two and a half hours, give or take. It is, after all, mechanical energy."

She nodded as they entered the cloud bank. "Then we'll be at the top at about dark."

Just at that moment they emerged again on the other side of the first layer, and she gasped at the sight of a bird the size of a small plane flying by just above them. Its sheer size and proximity bathed them in the vibrations set up by its wings and the rest of its anatomy as amplified by the rock walls, and it did seem also to be making a series of sounds.

"My God! That thing's *huge*!"

Thebes nodded. "Yes, it is a hard rock roc. Don't worry. So long as you remain inside, it won't bother us. The only problem you might have is if we meet one of its brethren, one that feeds on creatures with a high mineral content, particularly iron. They have been known to weaken or knock cold various faerie just by flying nearby unless you are prepared for them."

"Yes," Marge sighed, wondering just how much of a comedian Thebes thought he was or if he was actually serious about this. "I can see that heavy metal roc would take some getting used to."

Larae had straightened her skirt and managed to get herself feeling at least a bit more comfortable, but she was beginning to feel oddly chilled and wondered if her bag had made it.

"I'll go check," Irving said, but discovered that not much had made it on that wasn't already in their hands. Marge had no luggage and carried nothing, nor would she have been strong enough, anyway. Thebes was supposed to take the two small suitcases, but now it was clear that he'd dropped them and just sprinted for the open car door in a panic.

Poquah's small satchel with the money bag and whatever introductions and magical stuff he'd brought along was safe and on board, but there was not much else. Everything they'd bought of a tangible nature had been left behind.

That bothered Larae a lot more than it bothered Irving. "Then *this* is all I have? Not even a *comb* or a *brush*, let alone a change of clothes?" She sighed and looked *very* unhappy.

"Getting kinda chilly up here," he noted uncomfortably, "but other than that, I can stand it, particularly if it's this hot most of the rest of the way. Poquah can buy you the few things you need."

"If we find another place with real people and stores," she retorted, then sat back and sighed. "I don't know. Perhaps I have been all wrong from the start on this, trying so very hard to keep my own sense of self-identity. If it wasn't for *these*," she added, touching a breast, "I'd be better off simply accepting it, cutting my hair very short, and simply deciding to *become* a boy. Then I could stop worrying so much about such things."

Irving looked at her. "I don't know. There's too much about you of who and what you were—and in effect still are—to ignore, even if that one thing *is* there."

"You speak as if it were a trifle, like a mole or a deep voice. All I am saying is that the true curse isn't *that* being there so much as what you say—that I am almost wholly of one sex with the organ of the other. It is strange somehow, but do you know that I actually have been in some ways more comfortable this way?"

"What!"

She nodded. "I do not fear rape, since the rapist will only get an ugly joke on him, yes? I have had no period in almost a year now, with all that implies, and I cannot be made with child. There is a *confidence* in being male that you would not understand; you were born that way. There's certain *freedom*, a sense of independence and power that as a woman I was without."

"Would you rather have been born a guy?"

"Perhaps. I am still undecided on that. Certainly in *my* culture and in the others I have seen so far, the human ones, anyway, it is preferable if one ever wishes to break out and become someone important, do adventurous romantic things, and take chances on life. And of course, had I been born a boy, I would not exactly be sitting here now, would I? The curse was on the firstborn girl."

"Is that what you'd wish for, then?" he asked her, feeling a bit distanced from someone he was growing to like an awful lot no matter what her problems. "To have been born a boy or to become one fully?"

She shrugged. "I do not know. That is the truth. Your prize is within the Rules. It may have powers to destroy worlds, but it might well not have the power to dissolve a demonic contract. We shall see. We will have to get there first."

He nodded. "That was some maneuver you pulled back there with the zombie. Where'd you learn that?"

"All good girls who wish to remain good girls take some sort of self-defense training in my homeland," she told him. "I am not very good with weapons, but at defending myself with my own body I am not at all bad."

The cable car reached the top of the range, and there was a tremendous lurch and a sound as if the whole roof of the car were being marched upon by an invading army. A number of the car's occupants were thrown right out of their seats, and others were badly bounced around.

"Nothing to worry about, folks," the conductor told them. "Just switching through here to be ready for the down side."

That was reassuring, because the sun had set and they were surrounded by total darkness.

Well, not quite total. In fact, for the first time in this land, and in full splendor, the sky was full of stars.

Even Marge found the stars both friendly and familiar. They were essentially the same stars and constellations as on Earth, for this universe was in many ways a mirror image of Earth.

Now they cleared the tops of the peaks, and as they did, they passed the other car going back to where they'd come from. It was surprisingly lit up and seemed to be filled with ordinary-looking people standing and sitting and reading papers and looking tired like commuters on a subway heading home. Marge looked over at the "mechanics" on their car and realized that those others were more of the same. Fresh clichés were replacing tired old ones.

Now they were on their way down, but there were few clouds in sight on this side of the mountains. Instead, there was a vast sea of blackness below, broken only here and there by solitary lights whose origins could not be guessed. From that height it wasn't unlikely that they were seeing eighty or a hundred miles, but if there was any city or town over there, it certainly was hiding itself well.

It didn't appear that much weather of *any* sort made it over the mountain wall; all below, as far as the eye could see, was one vast desert.

Larae's adrenaline and excitement had worn off, and she drifted off to sleep after a while, her head sinking over onto Irving's shoulder. For some reason it bothered him, as if it weren't *right* somehow now that he knew she wasn't all a she, but another part of him was torn by his respect for her. He really liked her in spite of it all, and it wasn't as if her situation were her own fault. With a very light sigh, he lifted his arm and put it around her.

Damn it! I know what I would wish for if I had that

thing, he thought in frustration, and it wasn't a true-blue boyfriend.

It could be worse, he supposed. She could still have kept her old form down there, but with that demon adding *teeth.* Whoa! He had a sick feeling just *thinking* about that one. If he was going to start thinking like that, maybe it was time for *him* to take a nap, too.

Marge looked at them and smiled. They *did* make a great couple, except for that one little detail that *shouldn't* matter but did. She'd been brought up too much one way, and Irving in another. Still, wouldn't *that* be the final nail in Joe's coffin if he saw *this* and knew all the facts!

She went over to Poquah and gestured toward them. "Any hope for her?"

"Difficult to say," he replied. "I do believe she is correct in that her initial situation is tied up in both a bargain *and* a curse. With the Lamp, which was a product of the djinn universe, it would not be a factor, but the McGuffin is within the Rules and was fashioned by artisans of our own space-time continuum. Remove the curse, and the original bargain is back in force and she becomes a sacrifice and property of the demon. You cannot wish away the bargain; that was sealed in blood with Hell on *their* continuum. I am not even certain she can very much change the way she is right now. The moment the wish is made and the original Lothar curse dissolves, Hell will enforce it, even if it is for mere nanoseconds. About the only thing that might be lifted is the geas, since that was *imposed*, not a part of the original bargain, and in *our* continuum."

"So they're stuck?"

"Well, *she* certainly is. Irving is still the same as always and has other options."

"But you can see the attraction."

"Yes, just looking at them, one can see many threads of common destiny linking one to the other. Of course, this isn't a fatal disease, since such threads are broken all the time by divorce, death, infidelities, and even plots, abductions, accidents—well, you know. His nature, fortified by his own views of his father and his father's condition and reactions, though, makes it almost inconceivable that he could find happiness in what would be essentially a homosexual relationship. *She* could, but not Irving. It simply isn't in him."

She nodded. "And it's eating him alive." She sighed. "I guess there's always wishes to change some things, huh?"

"Not for the likes of them," the Imir commented, "unless of course we *can* solve that Hell's bargain conundrum. Master Ruddygore is actually pretty good at that sort of thing, but there are many such that have no answer. I want no one thinking of this as a wish-at-a-time reward system. First of all, we haven't gotten it yet, and second, if we had it, we don't really know how to use it. It is supposed to be rather tricky. I have been given one wish, one statement carefully crafted by Master Ruddygore, and that is the only one allowable."

She looked at him with a knowing smile. *I wonder how you are going to enforce that, considering it's not you but most likely Irving or even Larae who'll set hands on it, if anyone does.*

She got up and went over to a window and looked out. Although it was very dark inside the car, by her own night vision and faerie sight she saw her reflection in the glass, and she didn't like what she saw at all.

She was taller, thicker built, and more of a sexual bombshell than ever. She was also taking on a golden glow, and the reds in her skin were beginning to darken uniformly. She was far more than halfway across the line from Kauri to Succubus; it was almost impossible to see her old self anymore. It was something that should have angered and repelled her as the sight of such creatures always had before, but . . .

It didn't.

She began to wonder if she could even *try* a legitimate tryst with Irving, whether she dared do so. The very idea she still had reservations about *that* provided some encouragement, but it didn't answer the question. Would Irving help her, or would she harm him irreparably?

She stood there, studying that reflection, wondering how she could solve this problem, or, worse, if she really wanted to.

* Shortly before midnight they reached the other station. It wasn't much different from the one they'd left, except it had no zombies, no jungle, no old houses, no ... well, not much of anything, period.

The welcoming committee consisted of one very large, very tall fat guy who spoke and was dressed like something out of the *Arabian Nights* and had that method of speaking where you could virtually see the exclamation marks.

"Welcome! Welcome, effendis! Please accept my humble greetings to you all on getting this far! Come! Come! I am Ali ben Hazzard, your host for this next and final leg of your journey! Please! Come this way! We have tents over here, and sweet teas and fine coffees, and a way to relax and get some sleep!"

They all looked at Thebes. "Is this guy legit?" Marge asked him.

"Oh, yes. He manages the prepaid expeditions to and from here," the little man assured them. "Why do you ask?"

"Well, um, hasn't anybody told him that for a guy named Ali ben something who talks and dresses like that, he's not an Arab or a Persian? That in fact he's a Mongolian, or so it seems?"

"Oh, yes, *that*. He knows. He just hopes you will not notice. I think there probably was an Ali ben Hazzard many, many years and a number of owners ago. He is actually an improvement over the last one I knew here. He was a snake man with a nasty complexion and big reptilian eyes and all the rest. Made it next to impossible to believe anything he said. He kept saying everything with a forked tongue."

Marge let that one pass.

Hazzard's setup, virtually invisible from the air, was actually quite elaborate. Big tents, thick rugs, and silken coverings, all the comforts of a nomadic home.

There was good stuff there, too: not just the teas and coffees promised but wines as well, and sweet rolls and a savory stew that ben Hazzard assured them had nothing more sinister in it than lamb.

"I didn't think there was anybody this straight and up and up on this whole continent," Marge commented to Thebes.

The little man gave his Lorre-like chuckle. "Oh, he is one of those who is more or less the dishonest side of Yuggoth, really. You see, he offers absolutely safe and honest service at an incredibly exorbitant price."

"What's dishonest about that?"

"Why, I would think that it is obvious. What is a criminal enterprise? It is there to supply those things, regardless of cost, that society has deemed illegal or immoral but that the people want anyway. Here, *everybody* cheats, so you pay through the nose for honesty. It is that simple."

Marge shook her head as if to clear it. "Yeah. Simple as calculus. Never mind."

Ali ben Hazzard was a good host, and after they had eaten and drunk their fill, he took them to a large trough where there was actually tepid water for washing off, then showed them their small tent. It was big enough for them all but wasn't exactly built for privacy.

"It is too late to make the journey tonight, so rest!" their effusive host told them. "Tomorrow you will rise, eat, and have a fairly easy day on your own, and then we shall set off after an early dinner while we still have some sun but the shadows begin to cool."

"We're not going to travel tomorrow during the day?" Irving asked.

He chuckled. "You must be joking, young sir. It is about as cold as it gets right about now and will remain this way until about dawn! Within an hour, the temperature will climb several degrees an hour and will not begin to decline

until the sun is very low. At midday this desert is hot
enough to fry brains!"

Thebes nodded to confirm this. "It is probably about
thirty now—ninety-two or so Fahrenheit. Tomorrow, forty-
five, even fifty is not unheard of, and fifty-five is common
farther inland, Is that not so, friend Ali?"

"Indeed it is, effendi! Not for nothing is the Great Rift
often called the Worse Than Death Valley! So sleep!"

And after a while they did. After the discomforts of the
ship's deck and its eternal wetness and hard sacks, the rugs
and silk over sand were a blessed relief.

Marge, of course, did not sleep but wandered outside.
The heat made no difference to her; she felt neither cold
nor warmth in *any* measure, and once you've jumped into
liquid lava a few times, the kinds of temperatures bandied
about for this desert didn't seem all that big a deal.

She was simply trying to decide what to do.

It took a couple of hours, with a late half-moon rising
well in the sky, before events made her decision for her.

Someone stirred, then slipped as silently as possible out
of the tent, probably too troubled to sleep or perhaps just
overtired. Marge was surprised to see that it was Larae.

A thought suddenly struck Marge, and she found it
quickly maturing into an irresistible impulse, and she'd
been faerie too long to resist one of those.

She went up behind Larae as the girl stood not far from
the tent, looking at the moon. Suddenly she heard someone
and turned and saw not Marge but Irving there. Only it
wasn't Irving, not exactly. It was some kind of dream
Irving, some idealized Irving from her own mind and fantasies . . .

Although very real, the cleansing eventually would lead
Larae back to sleep, in which she'd have more peaceful
dreams and awake refreshed, unsure of any true action but
remembering it as a kind of fantasy pleasure.

Larae had certainly been in need of it, and Marge was
quite pleased that she'd been able to control it and limit it
to the old ways. Not long ago she could have gone a week

or more before feeding again from a load of guilt like that, but after this she was still hungry. She might be able to restrain herself, pace things, if Irving didn't present an opportunity, but Marge knew she'd find it next to impossible not to follow through if Irving should walk out of the tent at some point the way Larae had.

It was worse than she'd thought. She was becoming insatiable . . .

Within twenty minutes a disturbed-looking Irving came outside to look at the moon.

The heat of the day fully lived up to its billing, and the current Ali ben Hazzard still lived up to his effusive hospitality, although Poquah found himself paying for all sorts of extras that might well have been considered essentials. Guaranteed wholesome food, for example, was horrendous; no guarantee, well, that was pretty cheap, but you use *those* grungy pots over there. Water? No problem! Oh, you want a *cup*! Well, that's *different*!

Irving and Larae both slept very late and awoke quite close to each other. It was very strange how he felt this morning, the boy thought, but damn it, she seemed somehow ten times more attractive than before—and he'd been attracted to her since his first glimpse of her back on the big boat.

But it was *wrong*, damn it! He couldn't get around that. He couldn't do what he really wanted to do with her, even though somewhere in the back of his mind was a nearly perfect sensation that somehow they'd done exactly that, impossible though it was. They could be friends, but how could they truly be lovers?

Larae felt no such reservations even though she had exactly the same sensations and vague half memories that must have come out of dream but still seemed so real. She would try very hard to break down that conflict within him; it had bothered her only culturally before, and somehow it troubled her not a bit now. Still, if this mad expedition somehow succeeded, she knew that one way or another she'd get her hands on that thing they were seeking long enough for just one wish. One wish she'd thought of that would solve it all.

They had a midday siesta, then a substantial dinner with the sun perhaps ten degrees above the horizon. Finally it was time to move.

Irving looked around. "I don't see much in the way of camels or horses," he noted. "What are we supposed to do? Walk?"

Ali ben Hazzard looked at him with those almond eyes and grinned. "Of course not, effendi! How would we ever get anywhere with mere *camels* in conditions like this?" He removed what seemed to be a panpipe from a pocket in the folds of his robe and blew a series of notes on it.

Three broad Persian-style rugs approached and braked to a stop.

"Ohmigod!" Irving exclaimed.

"Very good models, effendi, among the best!" Ali assured them. "Now, I want each of you to get a bit of practice before we go. I would not want to lose you out there in the middle of nowhere!"

"Flying carpets?" Marge yawned. "Fascinating. No handholds, though, I note. Doesn't bother me, but I'm not too sure about the rest of you."

"Oh, you will need them as well, madam!" ben Hazzard assured her. "I do not think that anyone flies this fast. Your destination is more than a thousand kilometers that way!" he noted, pointing to the south and slightly west. "If all goes well, we will make it, with one brief stop, in about eleven hours. Now, come! It *does* take a bit of practice, you know, and if you fall off and survive, we will lose time. We do not want to be aloft in daylight!"

It appeared that flying carpets weren't quite as easy to handle as in the old tales, that was for sure. For one thing, the speed was quite good, but balance was the key, and that meant lying pretty well flat and making certain that anything you did was balanced by what someone else did.

The first carpet was to have the "mechanics," along with

some freight. After some balance tests, a couple of the vacuous fairies were shifted to ben Hazzard's carpet.

Irving, Larae, Poquah, and Marge were on the second, or middle, carpet, arranged pretty much to balance out the weight. Again, some small boxes and such were placed in the center, along with a supply kit. The general rule was, no matter what you did, you held on to the carpet, and you *never* stood up.

Ben Hazzard himself, along with Thebes and the leftover "mechanics," made up the third and final carpet, along with probably the most freight.

The first carpet seemed to have kegs rather than boxes, and a hopeful Thebes asked what the kegs contained.

"A yellowish dye, effendi! I have an order for it, and it is quite rare! Very difficult to get! You need to go into the dark jungles and find a particular giant insect, a member of the tick family but one which feeds on certain very large plants rather than animals. It is very lazy, and it simply lies on the plant and drains its juices slowly over time. Inside its stomach, the interaction of plant and tick juices can, if the tick is removed and cut open, result in a very good dye! Different plants produce different colors, but those are yellow, one of the rarest colors!"

It was still not quite dark, but Marge, hearing this outrageous explanation, shook her head and wondered just how little inhibition of any sort she had left. It was so very, very tempting . . .

"How do we go to the bathroom?" Irving asked ben Hazzard.

"If you cannot hold it until the break, use the container in the back. Yes! That squared wooden one there! Just remember how fast you are going and always be the last one to the rear of the carpet, eh?"

Irving looked at it and sighed. "Yeah, okay. So I guess it's time now, huh?"

They got on their carpets, lay down, got one more set of cautions from ben Hazzard, and then it was time.

The caravan master played a series of notes on his pipes,

and slowly, ever so slowly, the carpets rose up into the air until they were lined up in the light of the setting sun about thirty feet above the desert in the order ben Hazzard had determined.

"Ready?" the man with the panpipes called. "All right, then! We go! Hold on!"

He played a few notes, and slowly the first carpet, then the second, and finally the third moved out in a direct line toward the south-southwest, accelerating as they did so, the wind picking up and blowing against them as they went faster and faster.

Marge couldn't stand it anymore. Not at all worried and stuck like glue to the front of the carpet, she sat up and pointed.

"Okay, everybody. Follow the mellow tick woad!"

If any of them got it, they didn't give her the satisfaction of a reaction.

CASTLE ROCK

Always be respectful to the King of Horror or you will be eaten alive by lawyer birds.

—Rules, Vol. XIII, xiv, advice in Preface

IT WASN'T DIFFICULT TO SEE CASTLE ROCK, THE HEART, soul, and center of Yuggoth. It rose up out of the vast, basically flat desert floor like a gigantic black monolith, dominating all it surveyed.

Everyone was impressed, and Irving's eyes narrowed. "Hey! Those look like *lights* up there! Earth-type lights!"

Poquah nodded. "I believe you are correct. I never expected to see such a thing here. It is against the Rules."

"Not right there," Irving shouted over to them. "I remember that from the Rules volume before creepy pants dropped it! The reigning monarch of Yuggoth has a dispensation: almost anything he or she wants, as long as it's limited to this area and *only* this area. This is *real* power, the kind even Ruddygore can't do!"

"He doesn't have to," Poquah noted. "He can go to Earth any time he chooses, and he still chooses to live here."

"What happens when we get there?" Larae asked them. "I mean, I thought you already knew where you were going."

"True, but nobody else knows that," Irving explained. "Besides, it'll be easier with the passes and blessings from this character."

"Be respectful to the King if you should get into his presence and remember to remain respectful about him while in his immediate area. Remember, everybody up there works for him and is totally dependent on him for their present and their future. Anyone who can reach this status has enormous power, at least the equal of the continental powers of all the other great Council members, and in addition, just like them, undoubtedly has a somewhat well-deserved ego. You don't get and keep such a position without it. Just let me do most of the talking and keep a low profile otherwise! We have come very far in a very short period of time. It wouldn't do to screw it up now, and I have the very strong impression that this fellow almost doesn't care if Hell or the invaders win. He's apparently so powerful, he can work with either one! He's doing this strictly as a favor."

Marge had the most brilliant night vision, and she stared at the great rock in wonder. It *did* look like a gigantic castle on top, a function not only of buildings there but also of the rocky spires and prominences, but the rock itself was very odd, too, and amazingly regular. In fact, if she didn't know better, she thought, she'd swear that it was a gigantic Earth beer can. It was almost as if she could see the label on it. S-T-R—nope. Couldn't make out any more.

Had to be her imagination, she told herself. That was absurd. Good lord! Was that a *lighthouse* on top? In the middle of the desert they needed a *lighthouse*?

The top did in fact resemble a rocky coastline, except that the drop was sheer and there were buildings all over the place, mostly old and Victorian style, which brought back unpleasant recent memories of a similar if smaller place at the end of the jungle. Fortunately, this was well lit, looked nicely maintained, and had what were clearly mostly real people going to and fro on top. She wondered how they got up there and where they came from.

Well, at least there isn't a gigantic pull tab, she thought with some relief.

The carpets slowed, turned, banked slightly, and began to settle down in a nice pattern on a broad grassy area right in the center of the mountaintop.

There was a welcoming committee of several serious-looking men and one or two women all dressed as if they shopped at L. L. Bean. It was kind of like landing at a heliport except that there weren't any engine noises or down-draft from rotor blades.

A man of about fifty with a graying beard, long-sleeved work shirt, faded jeans, and boots came up to them, a corn-cob pipe puffing in his mouth. "Howdy!" he greeted them in a clipped, straightforward accent that sounded of extreme New England more than of *this* world. "Welcome to Castle Rock! Name's Latimer. I'm the first secretary here. What brings you out here?"

"I am Poquah, an Imir in the service of Ruddygore of Terindell," the elf responded, standing in relief and bowing slightly. "My companions are Marge, a Kauri; Master Irving, Ruddygore's ward; and Larae Ngamuku, who has joined us and, um, proved quite useful. The fellow coming over now from the other carpet is Joel Thebes, who might already be known here."

"Yeah, I know him," Latimer almost spat. He clearly knew him in a way that most people didn't want to be known. "How'd you get hooked up with the likes of *him*?"

"He is in our employ. Native guide, as it were. The rest of why we are here I shall have to discuss with His Majesty if it is at all possible and with the utmost urgency. I believe he has been expecting us."

Latimer nodded. "Could be. I'll have to contact him and see. He's asleep right now, but he should be up in a few hours. In the meantime, why don't you all come with me. We have a nice hotel here, the Overlook, which has spec-tacular views by day and all the amenities."

Poquah looked uncomfortable. "Um, I fear that friend ben Hazzard has managed to deplete our fortunes far more than we anticipated."

"Oh, there's never a charge for *our* guests. Not at the Overlook," Latimer assured them. "However, the rules are quite different here from the whole rest of the world, and we tend to assign some regular staff to newcomers until they can get used to things here."

"If you mean electrical power, we are pretty well famil-iar with it," Poquah assured him. "I have been to Earth many times with Master Ruddygore, who can do it whenever he wishes, as you might know, and the lad was born there and probably remembers enough. Even the Kauri is from Earth; she is a changeling. Of them all, only the lady there is native; so as long as she remains close to us, I see no problems."

"From Earth, eh? So am I, in fact. So are a bunch of folks here. I'm from Portland myself, a long time back."

"I'm from a small town in west Texas nobody ever heard of," Marge told him. "The boy's from Philadelphia."

"You don't say! Small worlds, I suppose. Outside of the Rock here, you usually run into Earth types only after they've been dead a while. Stay away from the folks in the fourth-floor west wing of the hotel, though. They're all from Hollywood, and you ain't seen sleaze until you set down with some of 'em." He looked around. "You see how the machinists work, so I don't have to tell you their limits. Boss wants some maids, he materializes some maids. Right impressive, but that's all they are. You probably won't have much of a problem, but you always got to watch people and things round here. Boss has a stray thought, almost anything can happen."

"Comforting," Irving muttered.

Latimer thought for a moment. "You know, young feller, come to think of it, you ain't the first one through these parts from Philadelphia."

"Huh?"

"Yep. Never got to Castle Rock, of course, but we pretty well know who comes through the land round here. Didn't see her myself, but she was some kinda changeling, too."

Irving felt his stomach knot slightly. "A wood nymph?"

Latimer shrugged. "Could be. Didn't get that much detail. Lost track of her a few weeks ago, though. She went down toward the south. You might have heard we're havin' a bit of a disturbance down them parts lately."

"I've heard," the boy responded. "But we've been looking for hi— her, and you are the first one in quite a while to report that she got this far. She's a relative. It's my hope we can find her."

"Lots of luck if yer headin' down *that* way," Latimer told him. "Me, I'd rather stick with the usual demons, vampires, ghosts, that kind of thing. Even the boss thinks that way, although he's so damn brainy, he still wants to see what in hell comes through. Me, I say leave 'em."

"Us, too," Marge assured him.

Joel Thebes yawned and stretched. "It is amazing how doing nothing for hours and hours can make you more tired than running many miles," he commented. "Come, friends. The hotel is the finest on this world and perhaps the finest anywhere, and its bar is like no other as well. They will tell His Majesty about us when he wakes up. Let us relax and enjoy what may be the only luxury we have left this trip. I have a feeling that once we leave here, it is going to be very rough indeed."

That at least made sense. "Lead on," Marge told him.

After breakfast they got word from the hotel that the King would indeed receive them and that a messenger would come to take them over. The messenger proved to be a small boy with a very pale complexion even in the daylight.

"He's pretty busy right now," said the strange little boy, who said his name was Sammy, at the door of the King's palace, "but I think he'll fit you in. Just follow me. We don't stand on nearly the ceremony here that most folks expect, but you *do* have to have a good stage setting to keep the locals impressed."

He led them to a large tower on the far end of the top of the rock. Around the sinister-looking spire, sitting on black ledges, were huge birds of a kind none of them had ever seen before. Each was the size of a man and had the face and neck of a vulture, yet they all wore dark humanlike suit jackets, top hats, and glasses and clutched battered leather cases in their hands. Every once in a while someone would come to an open window and call, and the nearest of the huge birds would come over, take something from the person at the window, stuff it into the case using its feet, and fly off.

"Lawyer birds," Sammy explained kind of nonchalantly. "We need a *ton* of 'em around here, both goin' after others and defending ourselves. Seems like it never ends. Hey, here we are! Come on in and enjoy the show!" With that he opened a large wooden door, revealing a vast and otherworldly corridor.

The great entrance corridor that took you into the presence of the King of Horror looked like nothing so much as a Grand Guignol version of the Wizard's palace in *The Wizard of Oz* movie. The motifs were blood red and sickly green streaked with blacks and browns, though not emeralds, and the statuary and tableaux along the way were gruesome in the extreme.

At the end was an enormous piece of statuary, a great demonic idol whose ruby-red eyes blazed down on them. It was right in character, reminding Marge of the demonic figure atop the mountain in *Fantasia*, and when it actually *moved*, as if it were a living thing itself, it was pretty damned scary.

"Who disturbs the King?" the creature demanded in a deep, spooky voice that echoed down the broad entrance hall.

"The ones from Husaquahr," Sammy told it, unimpressed and underawed. "About that stuff goin' on down south."

"Oh, yes. Ruddygore's group. Very well; bring them in."

To everyone's surprise, Sammy ran right up to the demonic figure, pushed something in the base, and made a keystone pop out. He then turned it, and there was a noticeable click and a door was framed in the base. It opened, blasting light into the room, and with it also something else.

Marge at least recognized it as sixties rock music. It sounded in fact like Jim Morrison.

Following the boy through, they emerged not in some creepy place but in a rather modern-looking office with a nice computer sitting on a desk and built-in bookshelves all around containing lots and lots of reference works, classic horror novels, science fiction, history, geography, you name it.

A fairly normal looking human man of average size was at the computer, typing away. He didn't stop when they entered, and they stood there quietly as he continued on, until he finally completed whatever he'd been typing and looked up at them.

"Sorry. When you're going good, you can't just stop. You have to finish the thought or you lose it," he explained in a very friendly American-accented voice.

Irving frowned and blinked. "*You* are the King of Horror?" he asked.

"At your service, at least for, oh, for ten or fifteen minutes or so. Best I can spare today. Lots to get done. It's not easy being the foundation for all contemporary horror on Earth, you know. The imitators drive you nuts, then there's the sycophants, all the folks wanting your money or your endorsement for something, and even strangers deciding you're so damned public, they can tramp through your house. It was that damned Amex commercial that started it. Never should have done that one. I've had to hide half the time over here ever since." He seemed lost in his own world, then suddenly remembered his guests. "Sorry. Just what am I supposed to do for you?"

"Uh, Your Majesty, there are eldritch horrors about to emerge from a crack in space-time near Mount Doom," Poquah said as respectfully as possible. "We're supposed to stop them within the Rules."

The King nodded, sat back in his chair, and sighed. He pointed to one wall of the room. "Those Rules drive you nuts sometimes. Worst part is, when you wind up in *this* job, you find that the next volume's all *your* Rules that everybody's stuck with. What a burden! Still, okay, it's probably not eldritch horrors—they're pretty passé. Most likely the Ancient Ones, I'd guess. That mythos never went out of style and keeps inspiring more and more of our best. Inspired *me*, too. That's the only reason they're still around at all, still a threat as an alternate opposition, see. They're useful, they're valuable, and a lot of Earth still really gets into them."

Irving cleared his throat. "Um, excuse me. Do you mean that all these horrors only exist or have great power because Earth still *believes* in them?"

"Oh, no. I doubt if anybody sane on Earth *believes* in 'em. But folks still sit down and read the stories they inspired, that they communicated to the best of the bunch, starting with Chambers and Bierce, and folks still find the stories scary. When you're scared, then for that period you *believe*. See? And that's enough to keep anything or anybody alive in the Sea of Dreams."

Marge should have been between groggy and comatose, but she was wide awake for some reason here. "But I thought it was the reality *here* that influenced the dreams and nightmares over *there*."

"It's both. No communication is ever just one-way, and this is no exception. The difference is that what we take from *here* over *there* is a dream; what we take from *there* over *here* becomes reality. We go back and forth like that. It's what connects us together. The only way to destroy these Ancient Ones is by destroying all vestiges of them in the imaginations and literature of Earth, which is very unlikely. It would be really interesting if they took over here, I have to admit. It would make things easier for people like me back on Earth. Think of the universal dreams and nightmares that would travel *then*!"

"And yet you are willing to aid us in blocking their coming?" Poquah prompted hopefully, not at all pleased at how this was developing.

"Oh, sure. Take me, for example. Everything you see here isn't what's *real*, it's what enough of Earth thinks of as a kind of fantasy. When all is said and done, I kind of like the job. When people like you, they can make things very nice in their imaginations. I'd find them coming through interesting but not enough to risk all this. So you want me to unlock the gates of the Garden Wood for you. That about right?"

"The Garden Wood? Is that what you call the forest near Mount Doom?" Irving asked him.

"Well, yeah, it's what *I* call it, not what everybody else calls it. See, there's one part of it on every continent here. The trees of the ancient Garden, all split up. This is the part with the mean one, the Tree of Knowledge that screwed everything up but gave us all the plots. Pretty tough to build interest or suspense if you can't tell the difference between good and evil. Of course, it also introduced pain, death, all the things that make life exciting. Used to be a great place for snakes, too, but this business has chased them all out. They're mad as hell about it, too. Just what will you do once you're in there?"

"We'll use the McGuffin," Poquah told him. "I have a basic formula provided by Master Ruddygore. It will seal the rift and restore things to a normal equilibrium without doing much else. It is thought that the status quo is the best possible resolution."

"Okay, I'll buy that. You might have some problems, though. Nobody knows where the McGuffin is in there; the hiding place can be seen only by mortals, and no mortals have survived that place that *I* know of. There's also a lot of turncoats and surreptitious followers of the Ancient Ones all through there. That's a lot of power and a lot of danger roaming around the woods while you go hunting for the sucker." A watch alarm began to beep steadily, and the King shut it off. "Look, that's it. I have a lot to do here. I'll make sure that you're authorized, and that's all I can do. You should also speak with Prince Mephistopheles and see if you can figure a quick and dirty way in. Sammy can show you the way."

"Meph——*the* Mephistopheles?" Marge was amazed.

"Sure. The idea of there being *two* of them is too terrible to think about. At least he's used to dealing with humans. Go on down and talk it out. Good luck. I really hope you make it."

He turned and was soon absorbed once more at his computer keyboard, oblivious to their presence. They knew they had been dismissed.

Sammy came in and looked at them. "Follow me," he piped, and they had no choice but to follow.

The contrast between the opulence and comfort level of where they'd been and the spartan, monastic-looking medieval room where they were taken by the boy couldn't have been more marked. There wasn't even electricity in this underground chamber, just oil lamps.

Marge felt quite comfortable in the cold, stony place, but less so mentally as she realized that this was where they were to meet with the prime minister of Hell. She'd met a demon face-to-face before, one far more minor than this august presence, and it had been among the scarier things she'd ever experienced.

They waited, and finally Irving whispered, "How long do we stay here?"

"Learn patience," Poquah cautioned. "Being too impulsive and in too much of a hurry can get us all killed down there."

"A mature sentiment, sir," said a strange, deep, but quite pleasant voice that seemed half cleric and half schoolmaster for some reason. They all turned and saw that Mephistopheles had arrived through the wall.

He was dressed in dark earth-brown robes like a monk, and there was nothing about him to suggest that he was a major supernatural entity or in fact that he was demonic in any way. The face, deep within the hood of the robe, was next to impossible to make out and darkly shadowed, but the hands looked quite human and, interestingly, quite unblemished.

"They will not let you get in, you know," the demon prince commented.

"Then how do we do it?" Poquah asked him.

"It might have been possible to sneak in even a few weeks ago, but now they have pretty well secured the entire region and the three provinces around it. A great many have been impressed to build some sort of structure in the center of the forest. We're not quite certain what it is or why, but there could be thousands of their minions working on it. It is certain that this is where they will come through."

"When?"

"Soon. There is not much time. We thought we had several months, but now that looks far less likely. One . . . entity . . . has already passed through; we don't quite understand how. The entity itself is quite small, certainly not one of *them*, and must have come through primarily by using their linking of power to push himself through, a worrisome and unheard-of effort. They do not tend to like each other very much, although the Ancient Ones are somewhat elemental in nature and thus can work together to split the rewards. There is one for the sea, one for the land, one for air, one for fertility, one for the space between the stars, and so on. The entity has gathered, built, organized, and seems ready to open the way."

"How does the way get open?" Irving asked, genuinely curious.

"*That* we do not really know, but already there are nightly rituals in the structure. You must get in, and you must close the way as quickly and unobtrusively as possible."

"Two others went before us," Marge noted. "They had an exact map with the location of the object that can close the way to the Ancient Ones. Did they not reach the valley or not get in, or was it that neither one could see it?"

"The companion could see it, halfling or not," Mephistopheles replied. "The key is half-human and mortal, and she is almost precisely that. She is also otherwise a total and complete cipher—to us, to them, to herself. They were in fact a complication, and we moved to stop them lest they get the McGuffin and not use it in the way it must be used. We missed. They got into *their* dominion and beyond ours. We know, however, that they did not get it, for the energy disruption would be easily monitored. The Grand McGuffin

remains in its sanctuary. We assume, then, that they are either dead or have suffered an even worse fate at the hands
of our mutual enemy."

Poor Joe, Marge thought, then realized that Joe *couldn't*
die. That meant that falling into the hands of whatever they
were was almost dead certain. She almost would have preferred Joe dead. If they had the same kind of powers, or
greater, that Hell had, then it might well come down to
fighting Joe for the McGuffin—and Joe couldn't die.

"We will marshal our main forces and push through a
hole that you can use to enter," Mephistopheles told them.
"It will be a challenge, but so long as the Rules hold, we
can do this—and so far, the Rules still command. A legion
of Hell will ride before you, clearing a path straight to the
wood, but it cannot enter. Once you are inside the valley,
you will be entirely on your own. Use every power of
magic and intellect that any of you possess; show no mercy,
for they will show you none. Avoid contact with the enemy
if you can—we shall keep the pressure on and thus keep
their attention upon us for as long as we can. If your companions are caught and their lives or worse threatened, you
must be willing to sacrifice them, since all else can be fixed
but once the others come through, what difference will your
friends' lives make?"

Marge sighed. "We really don't have all that much. I
can't see how we can hope to win."

"All the signs, all the Rules, say that you are the *only*
ones who might do it. Also, you will find them more
deadly and repulsive than filled with strange powers. Their
followers devolve; there is emotion and animalism within
them more than sheer intellect, even though it is intellect
that gets them hooked in the first place, a phenomenon with
which I am very familiar myself. Avoid, however, the Dark
Faerie who serve them, for *they* have such power. We do
not believe that there are many of these, and they are at
least subject to the same restrictions and vulnerabilities as
those on your side."

Irving considered that. "Then are there iron weapons

available here? In deference to these two, I've carried only bronze up to now."

"It will be provided to you, but do not be overconfident with your iron. As it would have little effect on me, it may not work on the entity, depending on its true nature. Unlike its masters, when it emerged here, it was not of godlike strength and thus was bent to conform to the Rules. They must have known that and prepared for it, even come with some sort of template for serving their aims. The entity would have been energy alone in the Sea of Dreams but would have solidified here. As what we cannot say, but beware of putting too much faith on any one thing. Your best bet is secrecy, dedication, and the McGuffin."

"Do you know exactly where the McGuffin is?" Poquah asked smoothly.

Mephistopheles was silent for a moment. Finally he said, "No, but you do. You have the map from the thief."

It wasn't an admonishment, merely a demonstration and reminder. They were not dealing with just another faerie creature here; this was a creature of Hell, of nearly godlike powers, as comfortable in his own dominion or here as on Earth. Although this was his traditional way of appearing to men, he must in reality have been something incredibly grand and powerful.

He read their thoughts, also child's play for such a one, and asked, "Do you know the difference between monotheism and polytheism?" Nobody answered, and so he went on.

"Semantics," he answered. "One angel can slay an entire army or pick out only the firstborn of a nation. That which you read in the ancient books of the powers of angels is understated; they would be gods in any other pantheon under a chief god, just like Odin or Jupiter or Zeus."

"Good point, I suppose," Irving responded after a moment, feeling the power radiate from the strange monk but figuring he had little to lose. "But if you're *that* powerful, why don't *you* go in and *we'll* stay back here."

The others gasped at his nerve and impudence, but

Mephistopheles wasn't at all disturbed, or at least didn't sound so. "Quite correct. There are limits. Were there none, we would own you all and not have to work nearly so hard. We need each other. You need us to get you in there past a kind of power you cannot imagine. We need you to go the rest of the way. It is good to notice, however, who allies with whom here. Hell is at the side of human and faerie. You see none of Heaven here. A bit of war or pestilence or disease from us and everyone curses. But if Heaven commands Joshua to kill all the men, women, and children in three cities and burn them to the ground, it's 'praise God!' Our influence here is about the same as on Earth, no more, no less. *Their* influence would be absolute if they were allowed to materialize here. You'll see their minions. You'll see what this world will easily become under them. And Heaven is content to allow it to happen. Keep that in mind."

Nobody wanted to argue theology with Mephistopheles under the best of circumstances and particularly not now. Instead, Marge asked, "So when do we go?"

"The King has given his blessing. My own ruler has sanctioned the plan. The legion even now is being gathered and briefed. Do you wish to go in by day or by night?"

Now it was the military one among them, Poquah, who took over. "Is there an advantage one way or the other?"

"Not really. We're not dealing with minor creatures like vampires and the like here. Some of the greatest accomplishments of Hell were achieved in bright sunshine. Likewise, they tend to a more normal sort of schedule, with heavy work and such during the day and then reduced activity at night, with little advantage one way or the other in overall powers."

"Then we should go in near sunset," the Imir told him. "This will give us sufficient light to establish ourselves and set up a camp and some cover if we have opportunities later."

"So be it. Use today to try and shift yourselves a bit in schedule and prepare. Use tonight for practice. Tomorrow

sleep most of the day and then awaken refreshed and prepared," the demon instructed. "We will insert you at the
gate of the forest tomorrow at one hour before sunset. Meet
me on the battlement here precisely at eighteen hundred tomorrow night. Let us end this matter, resolve this grave cri-
sis, and quickly."

There had been little discussion about what they should
and should not bring. They had traveled light up to now,
and even cooking would be risky once they were inside, so
supplies would be mostly things that were dried or sealed
and could be eaten cold or raw. Although the forest was
fruit-bearing, there was little likelihood that a large work-
force in there would have left much edible.

For Irving they secured a full and well-balanced sword of
a nice iron alloy with a plain but quite solid hilt. He wasn't
a master swordsman, it was true, but this weapon might
well be just as effective handled crudely. Nothing that
might withstand it or ward it off was going to be any less
clumsy when it did.

For Larae they took a sling, since she claimed to be
adept with one, and a spear of light but aerodynamic wood
that ended in a serrated and polished stone tip that had been
dipped in and coated with a paint high in the mineral mag-
netite. It would do the same damage, depending on where
it struck, whether the object was mortal or faerie. Finally,
she selected a sharp dagger that might well be thrown if it
could not be plunged, again with an iron alloy blade.

Poquah could not handle the iron, but his own short
sword, his bow and quiver, and a sharp boomeranglike device he called a jerun satisfied him as much as anything
could. All those familiar with or from Earth agreed that a
nice submachine gun and grenades would be handy, but
they weren't very common in those parts.

Marge took nothing, as always, and Thebes seemed more
trustworthy without a weapon than with one and not all that
much of an asset considering his cowardice in the face of
the zombies. Still, he had begged to go, swearing that one

way or the other he could get in there anyway. Short of
killing him, which would have been easy enough but still
would have bothered the Company, the only way to make
sure he wouldn't blow their entry was to take him along.

They studied the maps, they studied the drawings Thebes
had of a ravenlike bird sculpture that was allegedly what
they sought, and they decided on the weight and duration of
supplies. The valley was only roughly nine miles long by
three wide; they decided that if they couldn't accomplish
what they sought in seven days, then it was unlikely they
would be able to do so at all. The shrine of the McGuffin
was nestled right into Mount Doom along the valley wall,
but it was only about halfway back on the western side of
the valley and a bit up the side. This would bring them past
whatever was being constructed there but, they hoped, well
west of it and clear.

Finally, there was little to do but practice, and wait, and
hope that they would be tired enough to fall asleep by
dawn.

Marge spent the early morning hours walking the area
and flying up to the battlements. She was anxious to get
away, to get in there, to get it all over with, if only because
she was finding it harder and harder to control her behavior
here. There were men all around, awake and asleep, and not
just those damned "mechanic" ciphers and imaginary types
that kept changing all the time. Real mortal men. She felt
a powerful hunger, a craving that two cleansings the night
before hadn't even dented.

She had hoped to stave it off with a couple of the Hollywood types, but she couldn't sense that they *had* any
souls; they were as meaningless to her as the "mechanics."

There was no one there, she was all alone, but something
seemed to be whispering in her mind, feeding her starva-
tionlike sensations.

"Too late," it whispered. *"Too late. You've already gone
over. You are just fighting it. Park your mind and your reservations. Did you not find it possible to be alert in daylight today? Could a Kauri do that? Physically it has*

already happened. Deep down you already know that. You need only to accept it and let your body do what it must do. Unlike the Kauri, it will give you true power, real strength. Can you stand it, anyway? Can you stand another hour, another day, another week like this? Give in while you can still gain and use that energy . . ."

She felt like crying, but the voice was right; it was like heroin to an addict, blood to a vampire. She could not resist it.

Something inside her just snapped, and she remembered very little of the details of the next few hours, only an eventual sense of enormous strength, of well-being, of being satiated at all levels. She awoke and brought herself to a comfortable sitting position and stretched. She felt *different*. Not completely; she remembered who she was and particularly what was to happen later today. There was a certain irony in that; she who had been in a force fighting those of Hell more than once was now being protected, guarded, and aided by those very same forces.

It was daylight, in fact at least midday, yet she felt no tiredness, no sense of coma. She walked into the hotel bathroom and stared at the mirror. There was no reflection there, none at all.

She hadn't expected one and wasn't all that upset. In fact, it was impossible to remember just why she had fought this so desperately. It wasn't as if she were going to endanger Irving or even Larae.

She turned away from the blank mirror and went over to the polished black marble tile on the wall. In this she was reflected, although not terribly clearly. It was certainly good enough, though, to show the royal purple tinged with gold, the sculpted and overly large insectlike wings, the incredibly exaggerated female form that made even a Kauri seem plain. Dark lips, too. Huge Bardot-in-spades sexy lips.

She felt better, sexier, more gorgeous than ever before, and she could also feel within her the pulsing of the energy she had from using, perhaps overusing, those attributes.

Poquah wasn't going to like it a bit, but the old prude

had expected it, anyway, and if the Kauri leader, whom she now could not even remember clearly, and Ruddygore had not wanted or expected this, then it was their job to have told her how to avoid it.

Not that she wanted to avoid it, not now. Unlike most, she felt no compulsions of obedience to anyone, no servility, nothing. She was totally, absolutely, and one hundred percent a free agent, in total control of herself and what she did, subject only to that one restriction that she found bothered her not a bit.

She was a sexual vampire, and she had total power over men to feed her needs. All the power she needed and not a fear in the world . . .

Unless the Ancient Ones came through. If the Ancient Ones prevailed, what kind of future would *any* of them have?

That, too, though, seemed to give her confidence. Those Kauri wimps could barely knock over a leaf, and they had little offense otherwise at all. She, on the other hand, now had some very great power if the opportunity came to use it. She very much hoped it would.

INTO THE WOODS AT MOUNT DOOM

Hell may intervene directly in world affairs rather than by surrogate only to preserve the status quo.
—Rules, Vol. XIII, p. 37(a)

NOBODY EXCEPT MARGE HAD SLEPT VERY WELL DURING the morning, but all had adrenaline pumping at a massive rate by the time they assembled that evening at the battlement, including whatever Poquah's race substituted for it. He of course was still the only one who did not seem to feel undue concern.

Irving had decided on a minimalist approach, with the idea of wearing a single loincloth seeming both impractical and silly, not to mention unclean. Instead, he opted for nothing but a belt with a basic leather scabbard that would handle the sword and keep it from cutting his leg off in a fall, a black leather codpiece, and the leather straps to support them. He would also carry a backpack into the valley, but that would be left wherever they made camp. Everyone was to carry his or her own supplies.

Larae opted for almost exactly the same thing, except that she had her sling, stones in a pouch, and dagger on a slightly wider belt and would carry her javelinlike spear. The sight of the codpiece looked silly on that body, but Irving knew it was damnably necessary and not just part of the outfit.

Poquah wore brown and green britches and a more standard sword belt and scabbard affair, but he looked a lot more basic and a lot more sinister, as he had the times the others had seen the usually silent Imir go into battle.

Joel Thebes wore his crumpled and very dirty white suit and black saddle-style tie shoes.

They all gasped when they saw Marge, and she gave

278

them the sexy smile and a movie star pose. "Really stunning, the new me, huh?"

"Criminal," Poquah sniffed. "I *knew* this would happen! If you touch either of these two, I'll risk iron myself to finish you!"

She smiled sweetly at him and blew him a mock kiss. "You know you couldn't do it. No *man* is *ever* going to be able to do *that* to me. Don't worry, I'm still on the team and we have the same goals. I'm not about to go after Joe's kid. But if you didn't want this to happen, you shoulda provided some way for it *not* to happen, or Ruddygore or the Sisterhood or somebody should have, right? It feels so *right*, so *normal*, I almost think the reason you all didn't was because I was always *supposed* to be one of these and everybody but me knew it. Irving, close your mouth, pull in your tongue, think of your almost lady love here, and remember that in an hour or so we're gonna be shot right into a situation that's likely to kill us all in the next couple of days, anyway. Right?"

Even Larae, whose only interest in girls until then had been as rivals or critical examples, felt the attraction Marge now exuded. The difference was, she now felt herself torn between a desire to complete her transformation to male and a wish to become one of *those*.

At precisely eighteen hundred, about ninety minutes before sunset at that season in that latitude, the figure of a monk appeared among them on the battlement. In spite of bright sunshine, he still looked as if he were in deep shadow.

Mephistopheles looked at Marge, but not as other men had. "I see that you have made the final transition. More than ever now you must trust your instincts. There will probably be good prey in there for a seductress, but use the power wisely. Iron about fifty millimeters below the heart will kill you as surely as it will kill any other of the faerie, and you have no power over women of any type."

She nodded. "I'll be careful. That much hasn't changed. How do we get to Mount Doom, though? Shouldn't we have left before now in order to travel? I mean, it's like another thousand miles, isn't it?"

"Almost, but that is using the methods of the world. Come! All together now! Have hold of what you wish to bring with you, for there will be no chance to do this twice!" The Prince of Hell put his arms out straight to either side and faced the south-southwest. "All face where I face and be prepared. Even now the battle rages, and we shall soon join it. Each of you touch one other close to you, and at least one of you touch my robe. Yes, thank you. Do not fear what you see—it is being done for your own benefit. Be prepared for bizarre and violent sights and sounds and dizzying sensations, but hold fast. You must hit the ground running and be into that wood in the blink of an eye, as soon as you see the opening. Many lives and souls of great bravery and value are being put on the line for you! Do not let them down!" He paused. "Ready? You see? I am in Hell, and Hell is in all places at once. Therefore, since you are with me, we are already there!"

The entire world, even the entire *universe*, suddenly vanished.

They approached the dark at the end of the tunnel before they could think any more about it.

And like *that* they burst through into an insane, chaotic roar of battle on a vast supernatural scale.

All around them, great dark shapes like giants in a twisted shadow play rode even more horrifying steeds that snorted, exuded, and shot fire and brimstone and electrical energies at an equally horrific series of giant apparitions in front of them. The enemy seemed outlined in bright white energy yet was all animal hatred, with slashing fangs and razor-sharp claws not of flesh and blood but of supernatural energy, the true underlying That behind All That.

It was the most awful, terrifying thing any of them had ever seen, made all the more so by their total lack of control over anything, including being able to run or hide or block from their vision the grisly and grotesque war of the evil gods that raged all around them. Instead, they tried to focus forward on a tiny sliver of light, of reality, toward which they slowly moved even as they stood motionless with Mephistopheles.

The pinpoint grew abruptly larger, surrounding and overwhelming them, and they felt the suddenness of wind on their faces and the heat of the early evening and saw a vast impenetrable-looking forest only a few dozen meters in front of them.

They didn't wait for an invitation; although they were all still stunned and reeling from the incomprehensible violence through which they'd come, they each acted out of an instinct for self-preservation and hit the ground running hard for those trees, not stopping until they were well inside the thick grove and hidden by its shadows.

Irving still wasn't thinking; he flattened himself against a tree, breathing hard, the terror in his face impossible to disguise. He wasn't certain where Larae was, but he thought he could hear her gasping for breath not far from him, while over in another corner came the sound of the oily Thebes whimpering.

Poquah had been in that realm before, although never against that sort of enemy or facing that intensity of sheer hatred. He had felt and been unnerved as they had, but his nearly absolute self-control had not wavered. Only the fact that he was breathing almost as hard as the others showed that there was anything more going on inside his head.

Of them all, Marge felt the least affected, and she wasn't sure why. Certainly she'd never seen anything like *that* before, but what had been total horror and confusion for the others had been to her like a great thrill ride; she could still feel the sense of exhilaration from all the energy that had washed over and through her. It felt as if she'd just come off the greatest roller coaster in the world, one with nothing but superhill after superhill. The sense of extreme danger, of the potential for instant death or psychic dismemberment, far from being so terribly frightening, had only increased the thrill. She hadn't had this much fun, felt this great, since . . . since . . .

Hell, she'd *never* felt this great!

She'd been a wimpy Kauri far too long. *This* was *living* again!

She could see and sense that her companions did not share her enthusiasm, and it amused her. *I'm the only real female in this whole bunch, and I've got all the balls,* she thought with some satisfaction.

She walked through the forest, finding each of them in turn and saying in a normal tone not designed to bring unwanted attention but sufficient to be heard by them all, "Come on, come out! We've got to get moving! The dark's not gonna pose a big problem for me, but it sure will for the rest of you. Let's move in and set up some sort of camp here."

Slowly, shakily, they all managed to let go, although Thebes let go and followed only when it was suggested that the alternative was that he *not* come and thus be left there for whoever or whatever came along.

"What—what *was* that?" Larae managed after a while.

"Just what the demon said it was," Poquah responded. "That is total war in the realm of Heaven and Hell and, in this case, a third force as well. Ugly, is it not? Ugly and beautiful at one and the same time."

"I—I could make sense of little of it," she admitted.

He nodded. "None of us could. Our minds aren't capable of processing that sort of information, nor are our brains fast enough and clever enough to interpret what we were seeing. The result was a series of horrific impressions, true, and all of the chaos of battle, but nothing specific. I must admit, though, that it was useful and instructive in judging the enemy here."

"How so?" Irving asked him. "All I got was a lot of hatred and animal lust."

"True. That's what I got, too. The reason this temporary breakthrough worked was that the forces of Hell were employing carefully plotted battle plans. There was intellect, organization, and discipline there, and it was pitted against raw emotional power. No plan, no coordination, no discipline, just all the base passions. The only reason they are formidable is the depth of their power. Intellect can hold against brute force in most cases, but if that is the force level *now*, imagine what it will be like if these demigods truly come through. I believe that's what Hell fears, what it cannot withstand. If just the followers here can muster this kind of power and wrest and tear even this small spot from the Prince of Hell himself, then who or what could withstand their masters?"

There was a sudden low, ominous rumbling that seemed to come from all around, and the very earth shook and the trees began to sway this way and that. The earth shifted beneath them, throwing them all briefly to the ground.

It went on for a few seconds but stopped almost as quickly as it had started. There was, however, still the sound of only slightly more distant rumbling and the occasional whiff of sulfur.

They picked themselves up in the deepening gloom of the forest. "*What* was *that*?" Irving asked as they set off, unnerved once again.

"A minor earthquake, I believe," Poquah told him. "We are walking into a deep valley cutting right into a gigantic and somewhat active volcano, remember, and these forces all around certainly won't help pacify its normal and natural anger."

"There is no danger of it erupting onto us, is there?" Larae asked nervously.

"I don't think so," the Imir replied, "even though that would be very symmetrical and thus in full accord with the

Rules. To do so, though, would mean wiping out this valley and this forest, and I believe that these specific segments, mostly remnants moved here from Earth after the Fall, are pretty well protected. Not, however, from earthquakes and other similar phenomena."

"You sure you're going in the right direction?" Irving asked him nervously. "It's getting pretty dark."

"I'm an Imir. Being in trouble in my natural forest element would be as unthinkable as it would be for, say, a wood nymph. Ah! See?"

It emerged right out of the ground, surrounded and even overgrown by the trees, but it was a large and very round-looking cave.

"Lava tube," Poquah explained. "There *do* appear to have been some limited eruptions in here, after all. Perhaps we can use that somehow."

Irving looked at it nervously. "You mean *lava* comes out of that thing? Forget it! No way I'm goin' in there!"

"It doesn't tend to happen twice. This was formed in the process; it's not a cannon. It appears perfect for us, and convenient. All of us can fit in there, it's not easy to spot, and there aren't a lot of nasty other things living in it."

"I think I'd rather stay outside than be in there," Larae commented, and Irving nodded.

"No telling what is in those trees after dark; you'd have no warning and no chance if something dropped on you," Poquah pointed out. "This might not be as comfortable, but there's rock and dirt all around you. There is no time when you need more protection than now, when we don't know what is here. Later, when we see what we are dealing with, we can adjust."

Marge looked at it. "No way *I* am crawling in *there*," she told him, then chuckled. "I don't think you'd *want* me in such close quarters. Let me see what I can see."

"No! Not yet!" Poquah snapped. "You more than anyone are vulnerable to them, since they are such raw emotion. I cannot afford to have you engulfed by their power and go over to their side while you know all that we know!"

"*You* can't afford . . . ! You can't stop me from doing anything I want to do. None of you can. It's already dark, and you're gonna have to set up by braille as it is, since even faerie sight isn't all that much use in that lava tube. *I* can see very well. You are all ground huggers. I can fly. You might not approve of my personality change, although I'm getting to like it more and more, but I know which side I'm on. *You* better watch that iron they're packing when you're all stuffed in there, Poquah. *You're* in more immediate danger from *them* than from whatever's out there."

There was no reply for a while as Poquah's legendary control was tested to the hilt, but as he was about to say something, there came the sound of huge crowds and rhythmic chanting that seemed to emanate from farther inside the valley. The friction within their company was forgotten for the moment.

"That's from that structure they have been building," Poquah said. "It sounds like thousands of voices all gathered in some ritual."

"I'm getting mighty curious about that structure," Marge told them. "I think I'm going to have a look at it from the air, from a spot where elevation will prevent me from having to get too close. Set up your camp. I'll be back!" And with that, she lifted off into the air and was soon lost beyond the treetops.

Irving gave a low whistle. "She's sure changed. Cold and sexy at the same time, but dangerous-type sexy. The only thing I can see of the old Marge is the Texas accent."

Poquah thought a moment. "I am inclined to move, since who knows what will happen if she's captured, but she is correct. We'd have to work our way through this in total darkness, and for all its sense of ancient power, it is not a true faerie wood." He sighed. "I *warned* Master Ruddygore that this would happen, but he dismissed it. Now we shall all have to hope that it works out."

"What did she mean, none of us could stop her from doing anything?" Irving asked him, an odd thought occurring to him at that moment.

"No matter what we were originally or behaviorally, we are all sexually male," the Imir noted. "With great concentration, skill, and magical protections, we may well be able to stave off the power of a Succubus and not succumb to her, but we could never hope to reverse it. We can defend but not attack. It would take a true woman to do that—beg your pardon, Larae, but you know that does not include you—and even then, she is not defenseless. The primary difference between a Kauri and a Succubus is that one cleans up small messes while the other is an out-and-out predator."

"That's kinda what I thought she meant," the boy replied. But he couldn't help wondering about that curse, that on-again, off-again curse that he had been assured by a true demon, minor or not, would work on all females who could and did cohabit with human males. That certainly would include a Succubus, a far more minor and elemental being under Hell's domain. If *she* could not resist *him* and *he* could not resist *her*, what would happen if they went head to head? He couldn't help but wonder—and hope that he didn't have to find out.

Marge broke above the treetops with effortless ease and looked around at the spectacular setting they had not been able to see on arrival. The menacing presence of Mount Doom loomed over all else, tall enough that it seemed to make its own weather at the top, including dense clouds that interacted with the hot steam and lava in the caldera to produce local thunder and lightning storms around the top of the mammoth structure.

It was in slow eruption from a flank volcano, but the lava stream was headed away from the valley and toward the ocean of the south coast not too far beyond. *This* valley was more on the inland side, which seemed at the moment to have least volcanic activity.

It did, however, have activity of a different kind. Over along the far side of the valley the forest had been cleared away, and a well-built road cut into the heart of the forest, ending at that central structure.

It was a large rectangular affair, well lit by huge lime-light arrays that bathed the central area as if it were daylight. Startled, she realized that the two structures on either side were bench-type seats filled with living creatures and that they were moving in unison, one side and the other, but to different chants and in different rhythms, and that that was where the sounds were coming from.

If she didn't know better, she thought, frowning, she'd swear . . . No, that was ridiculous! She had to know more, and that meant getting close enough to see just what was actually going on down there. The skies were not safe or unguarded; large creatures with bat wings and lizard faces rode night gaunts around and around in lazy patterns, but they were few, far between, and regular, easy to avoid. They were looking for bigger game and more dangerous menaces than she would appear to them in any event, but they seemed pretty calm and almost bored. Clearly they did not expect anything there, not so close to their heart.

Slowly, cautiously, she approached; as she did, the chants from the two sides of the structure came to her in waves, and she was able to some extent to separate them.

> *"Iä! Iä! Cthulhu! Block that kick!"*
> *"Yá! Yá! Yog Sothoth! Hold that line!"*

As Marge watched openmouthed, she saw denizens—*creatures*—lining up on one side of the field clearly defending a goal before an opposing line of even more loathsome things. They quivered, they gibbered, they dripped, and they slimed, but they moved forward against each other for the prize, a prize that was terrified and very much bloodied but alive.

One team seemed very much at a disadvantage; its creatures seemed to have oozed out of the sea and were very much off balance on land, lacking the coordination to battle the other side, whose own monstrosities appeared to be far

more comfortable on land and in the immediate air. Just as
defeat was staring them in the face, however, there was
what could only have been a time out, and when play
resumed, the land-bound side was suddenly faced with a
massive, countless horde of goatlike things chomping and
slobbering their way forward almost in a wall.

"Shub Niggurah! Shub Niggurah!" the Cthulhu crowd
chanted, apparently delighted at the appearance of an ally.

Marge turned away and decided to check out the rest of
the valley while the creatures were preoccupied. How she
was ever going to get the others to believe this, though, was
something she didn't even want to think about.

All this *couldn't* have been about building some stadium
for some stupid, loathsome game, could it? Or did those
names have other meanings? Were those in the stadium not
perhaps merely playing games but goofing off, relaxing after a hard day's work?

Certainly, from more of a distance, she could see and
even *feel* what was too omnipresent to pick out closer in:
the massive cloud of bizarre evil that seemed to be centered
there, to be oozing from that point out to the whole of the
world.

Right from the center of that stadium, almost like one of
those steam vents on the volcano over there.

So the stadium wasn't just a stadium. Or perhaps it was
more than a stadium. At night they goofed off, but by day
they built, and a fissure in space-time opened there in the
middle of the field and stayed open, spewing forth its evil
ectoplasmic ichor.

It wasn't all that clear whether there was any other development anywhere in the valley, though, and all those
creatures, as loathsome and horrible as they were, were recognizable as having once been far more normal-looking and
probably native to here. If there was an entity—something
new, special, and not of this universe—it had yet to show
itself. If it was still in the valley, though, it was hard to figure how it could hide from faerie sight, if only by a sudden
cessation of it.

She tried to remember the map of the valley they'd gotten from Macore. Over *there*, on a line from the stadium and then just a wee bit farther in. Up inside the rocks, that very different grove of trees—*that* was it! She looked back toward where Poquah had made camp and scowled. So cautious and so limited!

She flew just above treetop level in hopes of attracting no attention and went over toward the spot where she was certain the McGuffin lay. It would take a mortal to get it— she understood that—but if she could spot it and scout a decent route, they might be able to do this in nearly record time. It was beginning to look like a real piece of cake in spite of it all.

She recognized *the* tree almost immediately. It was set off from the rest, and it had its own sort of meadow completely surrounding its vast, thick trunk. The local trees even seemed to bend in just slightly toward it as if deferring to its age and rank, and it was certainly old.

It was unlike any other tree in this forest or in fact most other trees anywhere, but she had seen its kin. Not exactly the same, but you could tell the relationship. This tree, even in darkness, exuded multiple metallic bands of color on the faerie level, glimmering beautifully as it displayed the entire spectrum. Closer in, the trunk seemed almost golden, the leaves like copper or bronze, and the fruit, the perfect fruit, like . . .

Little green apples.

Once she'd seen the Tree of Life. Now she was in the presence of the Tree of Knowledge of Good and Evil.

One bite, she thought bitterly. *One lousy crunch and it screwed* everything *up for everybody*. She couldn't help but wonder what would happen to anybody who had a second bite of the fruit. It wouldn't matter. It had stained the souls of all creation and brought death and judgment to humankind. The knowledge of good and evil . . .

It had cursed the faerie, too. Some in the Garden had failed to prevent the disobedience or even had egged it on. So the faerie had been cast out of Heaven as well and condemned to lose to mortal humankind on Earth and be driven here to await the final judgment.

Somewhere within sight of that tree was the Great McGuffin. She looked around, seeing at last a lava extrusion in back of the tree at the edge of the grove, going up and blending into a rise. It looked a bit like a stage and a bit like an altar as well, but it didn't look like the hiding place for anything important.

Still, it *had* to be there, and they were, oh, at worst, under five miles from their final destination.

She suddenly felt a strong pang of real danger, not from above but from below, from the grove! *What? Who?* she wasn't sure, but it was *very* strong and *very* menacing; it was alive, and it was down there.

And something about it was hauntingly familiar.

She was being probed! Something horribly evil down there was checking her out! She decided to get the hell out of *there* immediately and sped off as quickly as possible back toward the camp.

Her new confidence shaken, she regained most of her composure before she got back to the others after she determined that whoever or whatever had discovered her was not following.

Of course not, she thought nervously. *It knows we either have to come to it or give up, and either way it wins.*

Poquah wasn't going to like *this* at all, either.

He didn't, but he seemed more relieved at her return and her report than concerned about it.

"As you say, it suggests an easy task," he agreed. "Why should they trouble themselves with a heavy defense, manhunts, and the rest when they *know* we must come to them? How much of a force do you think they have around there?"

"Impossible to say, but I didn't sense *anybody*. That *one* was more than enough. I don't remember ever feeling that kind of power or that strange and alien a sensation from it, either, but the funny thing is, I *did* find something familiar there. I just can't put my finger on it!" She suddenly stopped, frowned, and looked around. "Where is Joel Thebes?"

"What!" Poquah shot around and surveyed the scene, looking for auras, and he found two where there should have been three. "I *thought* it smelled better here, but I couldn't be certain!"

"He said he was going to take a leak," Irving noted. "That was quite a while ago now, but I guess I just didn't think about it."

Marge surveyed the whole area. "Well, he's gone now. You want me to try and find him? I might be able to put the come-hither on him if he still has anything between his legs."

"No," the Imir replied. "However, it does mean that we can no longer stay here under any circumstances, and that means you must lead. Whether he is a traitor or simply blunders into one of them, he will betray us all. Get us closer to this grotto, and we will see what we might be up against."

"You're not going to try it *tonight*!" She was appalled at the idea. "You haven't experienced that—*thing*—out there."

"Not tonight, no," Poquah agreed. "However, close to dawn is a different story."

"What have you got in mind?" she asked him.

"Think about the situation. This entity obviously knows that we must make a try for the McGuffin. It must also be assumed that it has at least a reasonable idea of who and what we are by this point. The most important thing is that the McGuffin is still there. It hasn't been used, nor is it currently in anyone's hands. That means the entity can't get at it, either. Possibly all those on his side, even the mortals, get so corrupted with this alien plasma that it prevents *them* from picking it up as well. I do not think they will stop us. I am not even certain they will try to capture us, although I could be wrong in that. They want one of us, probably Irving, to pick up the McGuffin. *Then* they will move without giving him time to use it."

"And you're still going for it? *Now?*"

"Yes. The entity must be cursing itself right now. It made a mistake in probing, in betraying its location and its power to you. Now we know it is there. What is the commonsense approach?"

"Lay off. Try and figure a way in. Sneak in, if possible."

"Exactly. It will not, I hope, be quite so prepared for us rushing straight in as quickly as possible. We will gain nothing by putting it off. We need to act. Now, tell me about what you saw at the structure and the entities you heard as exactly as you can while we gather up what we have here and make ready to shift position."

"You aren't gonna *believe* this."

"Perhaps. What were the names?"

"Forgive my pronunciation problems. One sounded like Cath-oo-loo."

"Cthulhu. Ancient master of all the waters. Yes."

"Yog something or other."

"Yog Sothoth. Master of the Air, the Lurker at the Threshold. He will be first through, for he and his followers alone have the key and power to punch through. Any more?"

"Shub somebody."

"Shub Niggurah. The Goat with a Thousand Young. Yes, very consistent. The seed of this one, that pantheon's symbol of fertility, bears careful watching. You won't be just a pleasure nymph under *her*. You will be used to help breed what they require. Remember that!"

"If she's a goat who has all those kids, why does she need me?"

"Regardless of form or attitude, you were never stupid before, so please do not start now. The goat is often associated with fertility, as are the rabbit and the egg, the symbols of Ishtar upon which your own cult originated. Likewise the satyr, the male nymph, Pan, half-human and half-goat and all the time on the make. It is difficult to say what kind of creations she would make of such as you, but you would not be pleased."

"I get the idea. So, as usual, we're all the way here with no hope and everything against us, huh?"

"That about sums it up," he agreed.

"Figure the entity needs the McGuffin to complete his opening, right? That's why it picked here. Something has blocked him, probably something in the Rules, which it's still stuck with until the takeover, right?"

"Yes."

"So somewhere there's a way for us to win. The Rules demand it."

"That is certainly true," the Imir agreed. "However, finding it simply *can't* work *every* time . . ."

THE ENTITY STRIKES BACK

Old enemies are more likely than new enemies to be at the root of plots.

—Rules, Vol. VI, p. 297(a)

THERE WAS MORE ACTIVITY IN THE WOODS THAN THERE appeared to be from the air or from their initial base not far inside.

Proceeding through the dense thicket, they found a honeycomb of well-developed trails, some obviously quite recent. Now and again there were users of those trails as well, causing the four companions to scramble for cover and hold their breaths—and occasionally their noses—until the creatures were long gone by. They included a small corps of the fish-eyed monsters Marge thought of as cousins of the Creature from the Black Lagoon, looking very much out of place there, as well as furry man-sized things with drooling mouths and hideous laughs and cries and others too indescribable and unimaginable to handle.

Clearly many, if not most, had once been human or faerie and had paid a price for crossing over to this third side, a price they were now too insane even to realize they had paid. Perhaps they had seen what no mind could conceive; perhaps it was a rite of initiation. The fact remained, they saw a great many creatures as they went those few miles in, and at no point did they see anything remotely familiar.

Because of their nature and their insanity, however, those creatures did not keep order and discipline well, as predicted. Only one group, in fact, seemed to maintain any semblance of military bearing as it marched past, and those looked like a cross between trolls and minor demons. They did, however, have a good snappy march and could be heard singing as they passed nearby.

> *"Now Sauron had no friend*
> *To help him in the end;*
> *Not even an orc or a slave.*
> *It was dirty Frodo Baggins*
> *What kicked his little wagon*
> *And laid poor Sauron in his grave!"*

"Haven't they got the wrong mythology?" Marge whispered to Poquah.

He shrugged. "Perhaps. Perhaps they changed sides. Perhaps *all* such denizens of the Sea of Dreams think they're going to emerge victorious."

"Not much farther now," she told them. "Just up here. I don't see or hear much in front of us, so maybe they'll only have a token guard on the place."

"Don't bet on it," the Imir responded. "This is the one place they know we *must* come. Irving, you cannot hesitate. You know the words. The moment you have the McGuffin in your hands, you must say them no matter what happens, no matter who pops out, no matter who gets threatened or killed. It is our only hope."

Irving nodded in the darkness, although he was feeling less and less sure of himself on this.

They reached the edge of the meadow, well within sight of their goal, and Marge put a finger to her lips for absolute silence, then pointed.

Even in the darkness it was easy to see the area. The Tree of Knowledge gave off its faerie glow, and all of them had faerie sight; beyond, they could see the outcrop, and Irving saw something more.

"Right there," Irving whispered *very* quietly. "In the hillside in back of the flat rock, there's some kind of recess with something in it. I bet that's it."

Both Marge and Poquah looked and saw absolutely nothing.

"Suppose I just let it get a little light and then I sneak around and get it," Irving suggested in the same low whisper.

"I see it, too," Larae told them. "Why don't I try it from the other side at the same time. One of us might get to it even if the other is caught."

Irving nodded. "Poquah, you cover Larae. You might be able to get a shot in. Marge can cover me. She's sensitized to the place and can warn me."

"We may have a little complication," Marge whispered, pointing first over to one side of the altar and then to the other. There, deep in the shadows, were two creatures, both armed, one a fair bit larger than the other but both indistinct in the limited real light and giving off only very faint auras.

"Is either one—?" the Imir started, but Marge shook her head to tell him no.

"If the entity is here, I can't sense it at the moment, but it won't take it long once they know we've arrived."

"Well, we should be able to take both of them out pretty quietly," Poquah said confidently. "Still, watch carefully for others."

"It's gonna start getting light any time now," Larae noted. "Let's get moving and get in position."

Irving was nervous seeing the Imir and Larae go off and vanish in the woods, but he knew that it was now or never and that there was no other choice. He found Larae's bravery to be incredible, too, and he only wished he felt as confident or even as foolishly courageous. Instead, all he wanted to do was pee in his codpiece, and he made every effort not to as he moved forward with Marge.

He frankly wouldn't have trusted Marge with Larae, particularly in this setting, but something deep down told him that Marge would never, never harm him. It was a feeling he had to go with.

Marge was trying to get some sort of fix on the guards, who seemed well concealed. Neither was male; she got no sense of reaction from either of them.

As they drew closer on their end, to within perhaps five meters of the nearest guard and nine or ten from the McGuffin's cubbyhole in the rock, she had a sinking feeling, one that was confirmed as the sky began to lighten and they could finally get something of a decent normal-light view of the scene in the light of false dawn.

Irving saw what Marge saw and had the same thoughts she'd already considered.

The figure was definitely a wood nymph, or, more accurately, it had begun as one. The face, arms, upper torso were all still clearly the same, but instead of being inside a tree, she *was* a tree, at least in a sense. Instead of two legs extending from the hips, there was a single green stalk the width of both thighs going down deep into the ground. The creature clearly had some serpentlike mobility, but only within about the three-meter range the roots would allow.

She was also pregnant, obesely so, with an enormously distended abdomen.

Irving felt he had to risk a whisper. "That can't possibly be my dad, can it? I mean, you can't get that pregnant in a few weeks, can you?"

"Not normally you can't," she responded, "but we don't know what black magic and Rules apply here. At the moment I'm concerned with the fact that she's got a light but sharp-looking blade in each hand."

"Yeah, well, I guess she's still easier to handle than the one on Larae's side," Irving noted, gesturing.

It wasn't as easy to see the other creature from this angle, but you could see enough to realize that while fundamentally the same as the wood nymph now, it had not begun as a wood nymph but rather as something else.

Poquah, who had a *much* better view from the opposite side, was appalled. The figure, while "planted," had *three* sets of arms, each with a full-blown sword, and three sets of breasts, and she seemed to be almost three times as pregnant as the other. Both the Imir and Larae examined the guardians, and both determined that pregnant or not, if both extended themselves on their stalks to the fullest, they could cover the entire altar area. Short of killing them both, the only way through, using the original plan, would be to somehow lop off all their limbs, and that didn't seem too likely a possibility.

"This is what became of Irving's changed father and the girl he was with, isn't it?" Larae whispered. "The descrip tion is too close."

Poquah nodded. "I am afraid so. And I think that Irving knows it, too. They are enchanted, of course, or cursed, or something similar. That means they won't recognize *us* in all likelihood and will kill us, even Irving, if they can. Not good."

"I wonder if one of us could get up behind them," she said. "I can virtually *see* the bird-thing from here. If I can just come in from the rocks, I might be able to reach down and grab it and still be just out of *their* range."

"A diversion, then. Good. Go. I will give you five minutes to get into position. Then you do it or I at least will die. Give me your spear. You won't need it now."

He saw that she had removed literally everything, and for the first time he could see her as she really was and as she had been cursed. It was quite the most bizarre thing he'd seen of its kind, and, most unusual of all, it didn't look cooked up by magic. If someone from Mars were to see that body and not understand anything about how the human body was constructed or know of the specifics of the sexes, that person might accept it as "normal."

The leather straps and such had cut into her and chafed; for the first time she felt totally free and took a minute or two before starting off to get full circulation back. Then, taking only the sling but no stones for it in one hand, she eased off to the forest wall at the rock face.

Irving was still trying to figure out what to do. He *couldn't* bring himself to kill his father no matter what, but he didn't want his father, under some weird enchantment, to kill *him*, either.

Marge had no solutions for him, but she couldn't figure out the scene as she saw it. "Little Miss Alvi over there was half-human and mortal. She should have been able to get the McGuffin. Why stop her?"

"Maybe they act first and think later," Irving suggested.

"*Some* do, but not here. I—*look*! It's Larae! Up there!"

Irving frowned, then saw the girl's figure slowly emerge and make its way carefully over on very slender finger-thin ledges and handholds toward the back of the McGuffin's shrine.

As she emerged, Poquah stepped out of the forest and into plain view about halfway between the Tree and the altar area and out of reach of either guardian by at least a small amount, or so he hoped.

Up until then neither of the two planted ones had moved so much as a muscle, imitating the trees around them, but now, suddenly, the eyes opened and they began to seem very animated.

Marge reached out to restrain Irving, but it was too late. The boy drew his sword and stepped out of the other side, just opposite Poquah and perhaps just out of range of Joe.

"Dad!" he shouted. "It's me, Irving! If there's any of you left in there, *don't* try and harm me!"

The nymph's face contorted as if in agony, and finally she managed, "Irving? No! Back! I—can—not—stop—my—self. Go! Get—way!"

Irving felt tears of pity come to his eyes and also tears of conviction. "I cannot, *will* not believe that you can harm me!"

"Believe it!" Poquah called to him. "Do you think he can *control* it? Someone else programmed the body! Someone who doesn't give one damn about you!"

Larae had reached a small, crooked bush growing out of the side of the rock and had locked her legs around it. Irving tried not to watch what was going on but knew full well that the bush and its branches wouldn't have supported *his* weight as they did hers, nor was he in the kind of shape to hang and dangle like that.

Had it been directly over the enclosure with the idol, there would have been little trouble at that point, but it was slightly off, forcing her to swing on her legs like a gymnast. She had the base of the sling in her right hand and, using it, was trying to encircle the neck of the birdlike statue on every pass.

"Go!" Joe shouted insistently. "Run! No hope! No hope! Bo—Bo—"

Larae latched onto McGuffin just as Joe began to speak, and, twisting the handle deftly with her wrist, she pulled up and away and it came loose!

Joe and Alvi could not help but hear it when it happened, hitting against the side of the rock a couple of times, and both immediately turned and began slashing.

"Make the wish!" Poquah shouted to her. "In the name of all that's holy, *make the wish now!*"

But Larae didn't speak, not immediately, gathering up the unexpectedly heavy statue in her hands, swinging one more time, then doing a nearly classical dismount off to one side. A sword from Alvi's top hand came so close, there was a tiny scratch and some blood beaded up on her leg, but she had it, and, grinning broadly and knowing she was out of range, she got to her feet and held it up, totally forgetting that now was more dangerous a time than before.

"Larae! Make the wish!" Irving screamed at the top of his lungs, and she suddenly realized her error and started to speak.

A figure leapt out of the trees nearby and brought her crashing to the ground, the statue falling from her grasp and rolling slightly onto the forest floor. The newcomer rushed for it, picked it up, then stood back against a tree, a look of beatific insanity on its face.

"I wish I was the god of this whole world and all living things within it!" Joel Thebes shouted. "Bow down and prostrate yourself before me—*now!*"

For a moment the entire world seemed to pause, then Marge stepped out behind Irving. "I don't feel like bowing down to him," she noted, as much puzzled as relieved. "Do you?"

"Not a bit."

Thebes gaped, his face changing from a look of godlike power to the sort of horror no one should ever have glimpsed. He looked at the statue in his arms, turned it around, studied it as if it were some new species of creature, and finally read off something stamped on the rough-hewn base.

"USA. 1941!" he read in total disbelief. "No! It can't be! USA! 1941! It can't be! It's not only a fake, it's *the* fake!" And with that he screamed with such terror that it echoed throughout the valley and caused even those who could not remember such things to pause and shudder for just a moment.

Irving ran to Thebes, barely paying him any attention, and helped a shaking Larae to her feet. "I am all right," she assured him. "I just feel very stupid."

Thebes sank down, staring vacantly at the black bird idol and the inscription and otherwise not moving at all.

"Don't worry about it," Irving sighed. "We've lost. I don't see how it's possible with everybody assuring us that the McGuffin wasn't gotten, but it was. It's a phony. A fake. Your wish wouldn't have done a damned thing."

A strange, eerie, yet commanding voice, an inhuman voice, said, "I assure you that it is as much a surprise to me as it is to everyone else here. And in this case, at least, as much of a relief. I certainly didn't go through all that I have endured to bow down ultimately to *that!*"

The troll-like soldiers appeared from all points of the forest, swords and bows at the ready. They were not particularly menacing, but they made it very clear that there was no escape. It was also clear that the one thing they feared and no other was the entity who spoke to them all now and who was in every sense their master.

It was a large creature, perhaps three meters high and in perfect proportion for its size. It had a hideous demonic face, blazing red eyes, and dark sickly purple skin that seemed somewhat reptilian. The mouth was permanently twisted into an insane smile that barely disguised the rows of sharp teeth within, and from its head grew two huge, grotesquely curled, and oversized ram's horns. From the waist it was covered with dense purple hair that made it almost seem as if it were wearing bizarre pants, down to thick legs that ended in granite hooves. It was a satyrlike creature but one from a nymph's nightmares. The arms and hands were huge and powerful and ended in razor-sharp claws a good seventy-five millimeters long. But what struck Marge was the genitalia, which were overly large even in proportion to the gigantic body.

"*Where* did *you* come from?" Marge asked him.

"You would not believe," the creature responded. "However, in the immediate term I have been not very far from right here. You have no idea of my power, but you will. Not even I ever dreamed of such power, and it is only the beginning. You may try your wiles on me all you like, Succubus, but you should be aware that I am not like other creatures in this world and I will drain any energy I deem irritating. Don't worry, though. I have plans for you—for *all* of you. That's what all this has been about. I left the McGuffin right there, where it was, and ordered that none be allowed to approach it, since I knew that if anyone did take it, you wouldn't come. And you *had* to come. It isn't perfect justice without you all."

"Justice? What in hell are you?" Marge screamed at him. "Who are *you* to speak of justice?"

The entity shrugged. "Revenge, then. Justice for one is always revenge for another, in any event, is it not?" The sinister eyes went over them all.

"Ah! Poquah! I had so *hoped* you would be along. It would not be complete without you," the creature said. "And *you*, little Irving, all grown up! And Marge—shorn of all that diabetic-inducing happy fairy nonsense and more gorgeous than ever. And a bonus!" He looked at Larae. "My heavens! That *is* a creative job there! I didn't know there was that much creativity left in all of Hell! There certainly wasn't when *I* was dealing with them. Why, such a combination might well be quite amusing. Makes crossdressing seem rather passé, doesn't it? Perhaps we'll make you a true matched set. Give Irving here a groin more like the one Marge has. Like father, like son, eh?"

Irving started to rush the creature and to hell with the consequences, but even as the soldiers brought up their weapons, the entity held up a hand casually and Irving found himself unable to push any farther forward.

The entity looked down and gave the boy a hideous smile. "Well, you're close enough now. I will think on the rest. It will be sufficient, I believe, for now to simply have your own father, such as *she* now is, cut off the one you were born with. Don't worry; you won't bleed to death. I'll see that it's quite clean."

"Who *are* you, you bastard?" Irving cried.

The creature paused, frowned, then gave that strange smile once more. "Oh, I'm sorry! I forgot to reintroduce myself, didn't I? We all seem to change so *much* these days. This used to be such a *static* place! I am Esmilio Boquillas, of course. Who else *could* I be?"

"You can't be the Dark Baron," Marge said at last. "He fell into a lake of lava, stabbed through the heart by a great sword whose destiny was to do just that."

"Precisely. Hurt like hell, too, but only for an instant," the creature replied. "You, however, leave out part of the story. Before *I* fell into that lava lake, surrounding a tree very much like that one over there, Joe here fell in as well. Fell in and was not consumed but instead was transformed. If Holmes survived the falls, why not Moriarty, eh? Even then I had more power in my little *finger* than any of you and more than sufficient power to have preserved my faerie soul."

"Come to think of it, you *do* look like Boquillas' soul would look," Marge agreed.

"I was forced into this form, for, you see, I was trapped, awakening in the Sea of Dreams itself. It took an incredible amount of nonstop salesmanship to talk the entities trapped there into aiding me."

"How *did* you get out, you monster?" Poquah challenged him. "Not even the alternate gods of that place can escape!"

"Not individually, no, but first of all, I was not a god. It's not nearly so much on the overhead, and I do match the mathematics of this world. The trick was to have them influence their vast and mostly hidden followers here—hidden until now—to become aware of me and to bring me through. In a sense, you can say I was *prayed* back into real existence. My soul was incorporeal, my faerie self was in flux, and it flowed into the vessel that they used for their prayers. This is a personification of a statue of a child-servant of Shub Niggurah, the Goat with a Thousand Young. It is quite imposing, is it not? Ah, I can see that you are impressed."

"What is *with* you, Boquillas? It's bad enough you won't stay dead, but you started off as a handsome, charming SOB who at least cared about people, who justified what he did as a rebellion against the system here and for the betterment of most." Marge felt she had nothing to lose, so why not say it all? "Now the only thing that's left is the SOB part."

"I finally learned the truth," Boquillas responded. "That it's all for nothing. That *everything* is, in the end, totally meaningless. That pleasure and power are the only things that matter, and then only because you should have what you will. Think of it! I have beaten all of you! I have beaten Hell itself! There is *nothing* I cannot do or have!"

"You haven't won a damned thing except a little petty revenge," Irving spat at him. "You're *nothing*, Boquillas. You're lower than whale shit, and *that's* on the bottom of the ocean! What *have* you accomplished? Revenge on a bunch of people who beat you at your own game several times when they couldn't have beaten a *competent* sorcerer even once? So you can be a big monster around here until those things you made the deal with show up. Then you're right down there lickin' their boots just like you would be if you'd stuck with Hell. And if you *don't* bring 'em through, Hell and the Council will just quarantine you here and eventually gang up and crush you unless the little creatures you betray around here get you first. You got *nothin'*, Baron! Nothin' that means anything at all! You're *still* a

loser! You'll always *be* one! That's *your* destiny. Trouble-
maker, misery maker, but endgame loser! And somewhere
around there's the real black bird, 'cause there's *got* to be.
Somebody—maybe Ruddygore or Lothar or somebody—is
gonna get hold of it, and then you are *really* toast. There
ain't *no* way of gettin' around it. You got *nothin'*!"

"Perhaps," the Baron responded coldly. "But I have all
of you."

That was a heck of a lot harder to argue with, Irving had
to admit to himself.

"Now, I believe we will start with a bit of fun," Boquillas said almost to himself. "While the rest of you watch, I
shall allow Joseph here to emasculate the son. Then a rather
simple spell, and we can load an entire functioning vagina
into the space thus vacated, using the same creative model
of a curse visited upon the lovely lady here, only, of course,
reversed. Then everyone—friends, companions, father—can
watch as I none too gently rape the new daughter right
here, then let you roam the forest for a while, with an un-
breakable desire only for women, with even the *thought* of
a man repulsive. As you can probably surmise, *my* impreg-
nations *always* take, no matter what the condition of the
mother or the time of the month, and they develop with astonishing speed. You can't go far. The birth pains will be
excruciating, and then we will begin it all again. After that,
we'll see to the lovely Marge here, who is not immune
from the same sort of treatment, perhaps clipping her wings
so she will stay around. And Poquah, I have a whole new
mold for your faerie flesh, one that will keep you handy
and in a cage nearby for years." He sighed. "Now, who am
I leaving out? Ah, yes, the lady here with the wrong organ.
I *could* restore you, I suppose, since that curse is tied to the
authority of Hell, which touches not this wood, but this so
appeals to me. It is so delightfully *perverse*. Hmmm . . ."

Boquillas was obviously having an enormously good
time and was in no hurry at all. Not that they could do anything about it. Still, he was itching to demonstrate his total

power over them and understood that anticipation was often torture of the worst kind.

He suddenly threw out his left hand toward Larae, and bolts of pure energy so strong that they seemed almost solid struck her. Irving cried out but could do nothing.

One by one the layers of spell upon her were neutralized, vaporized, until only Lothar's key spell was left, the one that had made her not a woman. Now, without radically changing her body and by sheer force of will, making up and implementing the complex magical equations in his head as if they were a child's arithmetic, he refashioned her, tweaked her, emphasized every feminine line, move, and curve, exaggerated the form in much the same way Marge's was exaggerated, and then actually enlarged the male genitalia at the same level of exaggeration. The result was obscene, a photo composite of the ultimate woman and one major flaw.

"There! There is your girlfriend, boy, for as long as I choose her to be that way, and that may be until tomorrow or until Armageddon! Behaviorally the dream sex object, crazy about the boys, unable even to be turned on by a woman, yet like that, naked, displayed to the world, and on the make. Let us call it *perfecting* an imaginative concept." He turned back to Irving, whose expression of hatred was unbelievable, and bathed in it.

"All right, boy, it is your turn!" The clawed hand came out again, and Irving felt all the leather vanish, and everything else as well, save the sword blade itself, which clanged to the ground.

"Come, altar boy!" Boquillas chuckled. "Approach now and lie down here on your back next to Daddy. Yes, that's right. Ah!"

Helpless, terrified, and close enough to the creature to smell its bad breath without being able to do a single thing, Irving lay there, naked and stretched out, watching as his father's nymph face and torso turned toward him, sword in hand.

The blade! He couldn't dissolve the blade!

It was iron alloy! *The Rules still applied!* But was there any iron in his father's sword? His father was the only faerie other than dwarves who could touch or handle it. If the double intention *was* to make her a guardian of the McGuffin, as seemed likely, then at least one of the swords *had* to be iron or contain it.

The nymph, the pain and torture showing on her face and tears streaming out of her big eyes, reached out to touch and lift Irving's most private parts so they might be cut off. Under such circumstances it might have been tough to concentrate on something else, on influencing Dad instead, but even vague whiffs of incest didn't deter Irving from sheer necessity.

You love me, Joe. You love me and only me. You would do anything for me. Look at me, Joe. Love me. Love me and protect me from all mutilation and harm. Both of you love me. Both of you. Love and protect . . .

That most eerie of looks came over Joe's face, and clearly there was only one thought there, one overriding set of emotions . . .

Both Joe's and Alvi's swords plunged into Boquillas' midsection.

Alvi's swords had no effect, but the sword in Joe's hands erupted in smoke and flames as it entered the entity's flesh, and Boquillas roared in horrible pain.

For the briefest of moments, as pain removed his concentration and before rage replaced it, they all suddenly felt themselves freed of influence.

"The spear!" Irving screamed, sitting up and jumping down. "The spear and the short sword! Iron! *He's still under the Rules! Iron can kill him!*"

Poquah could do little on that score, nor could Marge, but they both turned and began to work whatever magic they could on the gaping soldiers, who were too stupid and too confused to figure out what to do. This wasn't supposed to happen. You weren't supposed to be able to give a god the hotfoot.

If iron in fact could harm or kill the monster, then they'd

been conned! One by one, without even glancing at each other, they faded quickly back into the woods and vanished.

Boquillas grimaced in pain, but the roaring subsided, and with a mighty effort of will he reached down and grabbed the sword and pulled it out of his groin, leaving a gaping, ugly scar that was still smoking.

At that moment, Larae cried, "Irving!" He turned, and she tossed him the dagger. He whirled and threw it right into the Baron's neck. Boquillas' head snapped back, and he roared again in agony.

Poquah looked around, spotted the spear where they'd left it just at the edge of the forest, and said to hell with it. The spear itself wasn't iron-coated, anyway, just the tip. He picked it up, turned, and sent it flying straight at the writhing monstrosity.

It struck Boquillas in the chest and went in deep. He grabbed at it but, still trying to extract the smoking, flaming dagger, broke it off instead. He was clearly in agony.

He was also, unfortunately, clearly still alive and not mortally wounded, although in tremendous pain.

And they were fresh out of iron.

The Baron managed finally to get at the dagger hilt and extract it from his neck, then toss it so high and so far that for all anybody knew, it went into orbit.

Boquillas still had the spear point in him and it was causing him some real agony, but it wasn't the kind that would finish him, only make him even angrier.

Blue energy shot from his fingers and struck Irving but suddenly flamed off as the spear tip continued to move inside him and cause further damage every time he repositioned his body to send out more spells.

"Hey! Irv! Think you know what you could do with a sword with a *real* steel blade?" called a friendly, familiar, but unexpected voice from just over and behind him. Irving looked up and to his complete astonishment saw Macore standing there holding a *huge* sword, the kind out of King Arthur. "Watch it! It's heavy as all blazes!" the thief called, and threw it down with all his might.

Boquillas whirled at the sound of Macore's voice and thundered, "So! Now we *are* virtually complete! Come, thief! I will give you something to remember me by!"

"Me first!" Macore shouted back, and tossed a bag of something at the creature that struck one of the huge horns and burst, spreading a powder all over him, including his eyes.

Macore grinned. "That's one for the professor!" he said cheerily. "Iron filings'll do it every time!"

Irving picked up the huge sword with both hands and, not stopping to think for a moment, rushed right at the huge creature, slashing as he struck.

Pieces of entity began flying everywhere. The giant pseudo-satyr roared and lashed out, but he was blinded, in agony, and nearly helpless against the slashing and cutting sword whose blade was the smoothest and sharpest Irving had ever seen.

"Hey, Joe! Got another not quite as big or fancy!" Macore called, tossing a smaller version to the still-implanted nymph, who caught it and began using it with gusto.

Macore then sat back on the rock and relaxed, watching the show and giving occasional pointers.

He didn't have to. All life went out of Esmillio Boquillas as soon as Irving brought him down with cuts to the legs and then severed his neck from his shoulders.

LOOSE ENDS

*At Quest's end the details shall be explained for the benefit and ed-
ification of the survivors.*

—Rules, Vol. VIII, p. 404(a)

"Is HE *REALLY* DEAD THIS TIME?" MARGE ASKED MACORE,
turning up her nose at the mass of charred and rotting flesh
and limbs on the altar.

"Oh, I'm pretty sure he is," the thief responded. "Of
course, you never know about the likes of him or the Sea
of Dreams. If enough people start believing in him, he may
be *impossible* to kill completely. On the other hand, what's
the difference? You got to figure that he's stuck in the Sea
of Dreams, and there's gonna be nobody else there but lots
of superpowerful godlike beings all of whom received a
bill of goods by him and then got double-crossed. I think if
he *does* survive in some form, he'll quickly be nostalgic for
the old lake-of-eternal-fire business. Out of our hair for
good, anyway."

Marge kissed him. "But how in the *world* did you manage to turn up here just in the nick of time, and with an
iron-based *sword*?"

He shrugged. "I was late. What can I say? I got hung up,
and everybody started doing things before I figured. Next
time warn me and I won't oversleep."

"That's not what I mean! Why and how are you here in
the *first* place?"

"Oh, I've always been fairly close. I told you I have a lot
of contracts and old debts down here. I came across on the
same ship you did. Had one *hell* of a time staying out of
sight."

"Then that was *you*!" Poquah breathed. "So!"

Macore nodded. "You're getting to be too much a crea-

310

ture of habit, Poquah. I read you like a book then. In fact, I got so confident, I even decided I could risk briefing Junior there so long as he didn't realize it was me. I spotted the girl in my disguise as a minor demon and figured she'd be a hell of a lot better off with you."

"*That* explains it! I thought he was being warned off!" Marge exclaimed.

"I had to give that impression, but I knew no son of Joe's would leave a pretty damsel in distress. Something in the Rules about that, I think. Besides, I *did* want you all to know the situation with her before you made your decision." He drew a deep breath and continued.

"Anyway, after that I was able to stick pretty close for a while, but Ruddygore decided that you were going on the straightforward path and drawing all the attention, see. That let me get *here* direct while you all went off to Castle Rock. Man! That was *some* show punching you all through! Seeing you come in like a rocket from Hell guarded by its legions was the height of absurdity. Damn near split my gut."

"Very funny. We were walking into *this* bastard's trap, and you were laughing," Marge grumped.

"Awwww . . . It's not all *that* bad. I figured he wasn't out to kill you. He coulda done *that* anytime, and he was clearly out for revenge instead. So long as you were alive, we could always fix what was wrong later."

"Fix! What . . .?"

"The McGuffin, of course. I stole it maybe four, five days ago. *Those* two never even knew. Neither did Boquillas. I'll tell you how I did it sometime, if I don't write my memoirs. *Damn!* I'm still good!"

"You stole the McGuffin three days before we *got* here?" Even Irving was appalled. "And we did all this for *nothing*?"

"Not for nothing, certainly. I wish I coulda been here early enough to have seen old Joel's face when he found out I'd switched birds, though." He dropped the smile and got serious. "Look, it's more complicated than you think.

The McGuffin has great power, but it has really strong limits. You can feel that evil vortex yet, can't you? Ruddygore still hasn't completely got it closed. It's kind of nasty, since everything you do with it also has all sorts of other consequences. It has a kind of ruthless logic to it."

"But he'll get it closed, right?"

"Sure he will. And he'll get us out of here, too. He got me back here with the swords and all sorts of stuff." He paused. "Look, we also wanted Boquillas, which is trickier than you might expect. You can't kill with that thing, for one example. So, dealing with the Baron, maybe once and for all, was a priority. Second was Joe and her friend. Without Boquillas out of the way, we couldn't get 'em completely out of the Baron's clutches. I told you, it's complicated, but it'll work out."

"So what do we do until he *does* work it out? We're still surrounded by a nasty enemy throughout this forest, we've got virtually no supplies, and there's little left to protect us. Not to mention that both Joe and his friend there are gonna give us little Boquillases any time now."

Macore shrugged. "I only take orders. But I know we'll be protected if we stick around here, and I have some supplies for a couple of days. Maybe we can just start renewing a few old ties, huh? Ruddygore's not gonna leave us in the lurch. Not now."

A lot of sorcery and spells had flown around in those minutes, particularly the last ones, as they discovered when they all tried to relax and get their bearings during the day and evening that followed. The worst thing in fact was keeping Macore from telling or, worse, *singing* the entire saga of *Gilligan's Island* to them.

Irving found that his power, his spells, seemed to have vanished completely. He was certain that something else had changed about him, even though the others couldn't see anything and he couldn't put his finger on it. There had been an initial blast from Boquillas, and it had certainly done something.

Larae had been changed the most, although again it had only exaggerated what was already there. She really couldn't figure out what she was going to do now. "In effect, I am a halfling, like *her*, now," she noted, pointing to Alvi. "The thing is, I don't really *mind* it, not anymore. I talked to her a little, and she had gotten to that same point, what with playacting for a long time, then getting sick of pretending and just being whatever she was. I am tired of it, too. It is just—God! I am getting turned on, and this time I can *really* feel it! *That* is my tragedy, Irving, in the end. I am in love with you. Very much so. Enough so that I can understand why you cannot feel the same about me."

He sighed. "When I watched you go after that idol, to risk that much, swing out, hanging by your feet, and snag that thing, I—I—I couldn't *begin* to tell you what I felt. Truth is, I *do* love you, but it's got to be what they call star-crossed lovers. I *want* you, but I need Marge—or, rather, what Marge used to be. I don't think she'd be real good for me anymore as she is. If you can get by that, I can get by the rest. Deal?"

"Deal. But I am not going to pretend anymore to be what I am not. Whatever I am, I am."

He sighed. "Well, maybe Ruddygore can straighten it out."

"What about your dad?"

"That's a lot harder for either of us to get by," Irving admitted. "I think I want old Santa Claus around before I deal with it too much."

Marge was catching up on things with Joe.

"They caught us very near this spot," Joe told her. "We'd come through some really mean spots and gotten out of some desperate times, particularly running low on food, water, and anything to buy, but we made it, or so we thought. Did it the hard way, vamping a little, doing a few odd jobs making some sick plants well, that kind of thing. But once here, *boom*! Right into Boquillas, who was so beside himself, it was pitiful. He told me what he was going to do, how he was going to lure you all here, all the stuff.

And then he changed us to what you see, literally half plants, rooted us, and raped us both repeatedly while leaving us on guard with compulsions to stop anybody from trying anything. We completely lost track of everything, I have to tell you. I don't know how long we've been here or anything else." She looked at Marge. "*You* haven't stayed a good girl, either, I see."

"Nope. And I don't know if it's the condition or what, but I don't care. That's the amazing part. I really don't mind. Until this last business I've had more fun like this than I ever had as a Kauri."

"But you seduce and enslave men and eventually consume their souls."

She shrugged. "Well, there's a downside to everything, I guess. The thing is, there's a ton of bums out there who *deserve* it. You *know*. Believe me, you know. Most any native on *this* continent is fair game, and a fair number elsewhere. The difference between me and a born Succubus is that I came from somewhere and something else, and I remember it. I liked the Kauri well enough, but they were so one-dimensional, so goody two-shoes, their lives so regimented and controlled, I was losing myself, my identity. This brought it back. I've got to tell you, I *need* it and if I don't control it, I'll flip out and take it, so that's something I got to watch out for, but so long as I get my priorities and targets straight, I think I can handle this and not hurt anybody who doesn't deserve hurting. The vampire who only sucks blood from the bad guys, that kind of thing. I'm not on automatic like the others, so what happens from this point's on my account."

"I hope you can handle it as easily as you say," Joe told her.

"What about you? What will you do when you get uprooted?"

Joe sighed. "I don't know. I see Irving, and I want to be Conan the Barbarian all over again. Poor kid—he's got worse shit than I ever dreamed. His girlfriend's a guy, and his daddy's a woman. How the hell has he turned out as good as he has?"

Marge nodded. "Sure would make a great *Donahue*."

It was suddenly different. The change was so dramatic that it woke several of them up, yet there wasn't anything obvious that had changed. No great sounds had been shut off, no brilliant flares had illuminated them, no eruptions or fires. But . . . *something*.

"The vortex is gone," Poquah said at last. "They have closed it down and sealed it off."

"Yeah, and look!" Irving said, pointing to the old altar stone. "No remains!"

It was true. Every last chunk of the final stage of Esmilio Boquillas had gone as well.

Still, it was Marge who summed up the situation. "What a strange, strange adventure this has been! And now, at the end of it, evil has triumphed over evil! Ain't *that* one for the Book of Rules!"

A few hours later, emerging from the woods on a great sedan chair borne by four huge stonelike creatures, came Throckmorton P. Ruddygore in full evening dress, top hat, spats, and cane.

"Well, well, well!" he said, brightening at the sight. "So all's well that ends well, eh?"

"Too deep a subject for me, and too many wells," Marge snapped. "Hello, Ruddygore. You surprised at my condition?"

"Oh, my, no! I *assumed* it would happen. Thought it might be useful. Would you like to be changed back?"

"Talk to you later," she told him. "For now, let's hang loose and stay where we are."

His eyebrows didn't go up even at that. "Very well. Ah! Down, boys! Easy, please. Ah! Thank you."

They lowered the chair to ground level, and he emerged, the triumphant victor as usual.

"You don't have the black bird," Irving noted.

"Don't need it," he responded. "I'm wired in, as it were,

at least for a while and at a certain level. Don't worry—the only problems that might result from this are mine if I blow the kind of wish spells it is capable of doing. Right now the real thing is sitting in the middle of the damnedest sports field I have ever seen but very, very safe, I assure you."

"Maybe. Where's Joel Thebes?"

"He lit out this morning," Larae told him.

Irving wasn't reassured by that. "Are you *sure* he can't get to that bird? That's all his life means to him."

"I am not so certain of that," Larae told him. "He went off this morning muttering something about the 'one ring over all, one ring to bind them,' if you know what that means."

"I think I do," the sorcerer told her. "Well, he's already in the right place for something related to it, anyway," he noted. "I just hope he has all his fingers. Now, tell me the truth—what can I do for the two of you?"

"You mean Larae isn't obvious?" Irving asked him.

"Um, yes, I see what you mean. Hmmm . . . Fascinating math on that spell. Makes me dizzy trying to follow it. No, there's not much I can do about *that*. It's worse than a djinn spell! My word! That's precisely what we were so worried about if they got through and why it took so long for an object of our universe to close up an opening to theirs."

"You mean you can't do *anything*?" Irving was suddenly so crushed that he was close to tears.

"Not what you are thinking, no," the sorcerer responded. "The whole thing is so complex that it would probably kill her at best. About the only thing I can do is some of the superficial stuff. Give you, poor girl, a look closer to your original self and ease the restrictions."

"I'd like that if Irving doesn't mind," Larae told him. "This is—impressive—but it just isn't me."

"No, no, I like the original fine," Irving assured her.

"Well, I'll see to that much, and you are certainly welcome at Terindell. There are many resources there, and perhaps one day we can find something your demon covets more than keeping that curse on you. In the meantime I'll help as best I can. Excuse me, now, though. I must see the prodigal."

"Um—Ruddygore?" Irving said hesitantly.

"Yes, Irving?"

"I been thinking —a lot. About a way around this. It's—hard on me. Gives me the willies, but I figure you can fix that. But I decided that if there was no way for Larae to become fully a girl again, then maybe the one thing Boquillas threatened to do really *is* the best thing. Leave me just like *I* am, but down here give me what *she* should have. That way we'd at least be able to do things right."

Ruddygore thought about it. "That is a big decision to make, Irving, and it is *not* one I am inclined to go along with now, with you at sixteen years old and in a certain stage of emotional development. While complex, though, it is *not* something that requires the McGuffin to do—obviously. So I am going to refuse it for now in your own interest—in *both* of your interests, really. If, over time, this proves to be the best or even the only solution and you still want it, then we might look at it again, but I am not inclined to grant it right now. You are close and good friends and companions now. Stay that way. Let us see where it leads."

Irving had taken such a leap with the offer that being turned down was as much letdown as relief. Still, what could he do?

As Ruddygore left them to go over to Joe, who couldn't exactly travel much in her situation, Larae just stared at Irving and tears flowed from her eyes. She wasn't sure that she wanted Irving to do that, either, but the idea that he'd think of *that* and ask for it locked her love in stone.

Ruddygore was much less pleased by the request but decided to talk it out with Joe. First, though, the sorcerer examined the delicate condition of the two half plants.

"Oh, my! Well, we'll certainly ensure that *this* doesn't hatch! Even without it, though, you're pretty well planted, aren't you?"

"You said it." Joe looked over at Irving and Larae. "Can you help them?"

"Not like they and I and certainly you would want it," Ruddygore admitted. "I can't really help her situation without killing her. Do you know he asked for the reverse to be done to him so they could be a true couple?"

Joe was aghast. "And did you say yes?"

"No, I refused. Sixteen-year-olds shouldn't be allowed to castrate themselves on the second date. But if this goes a year or two or more and he wants it even more, it will be difficult not to do it. In the meantime I can ease it a little for him. From almost, oh, right now, he will no longer mind her situation. It will still be there and a barrier, but he will no longer have that hang-up about it, period."

"Oh, boy! There go the grandkids," Joe commented. "Still, I'd love to see his mother's face if she knew about *this*! It would *almost*—not quite but *almost*—be worth it!"

"You never know. I'm not making him prefer boys unless he normally would anyway. All I'm doing is allowing him to accept a situation and live with it comfortably without harm and getting the most from it. He'll still like girls, and if he finally finds one that's all female, well, you never know. If they really are an enduring love match, though, you might still get the grandchildren at some point—only he might not be the father but the mother."

"That's not helping my thoughts about that."

"Well, then, think about something else. What do you want for *you*?"

"I didn't know I had much choice. I'd like to get uprooted, that's for sure."

"That's not a problem. Or, rather, it actually *is* a problem but not one we won't be able to solve. I may have to rotate both of you in planters to Terindell for a few weeks so I can solve some of that tricky math. Maybe run it through the supercomputer over on Earth just to ensure we don't have any traps there. But what then?"

"What are my options?"

"The McGuffin is pretty limited in some areas. I can't

make you mortal again, but within fairiedom, as it were, I can run a whole range of choices, male and female, type after type. There is only one problem with that."

"Yeah?"

"If you are no longer a wood nymph, you will lose your connection to the Tree of Life. You will, in other words, become not exactly mortal but able to be killed for good as we did with our old friend here. And iron will kill."

"Hmmm . . . Makes it kind of tough, doesn't it? But it's no more risk than I used to have. Well, I'm not gonna get unpotted for a while, right? So I got some time to decide."

"That is certainly true. And what of your companion here? I have been unable to identify her father or find out the slightest thing about her."

"Not even where she was born and raised? I thought that would be pretty easy to find."

"Joe, there is no such place. Not in Husaquahr, anyway. And those soldiers who have been after her don't seem to match anything known. I *can* say this after examining her, even from this distance: I don't think she's a halfling at all. I think that everything we see is a disguise, even her memories."

"What! You mean she's hiding out and on the run and she is *already* disguised like that? Who would disguise somebody like *that*? And why would she keep it up, even with us both planted here?"

"Oh, what you see is what you get," Ruddygore assured Joe. "She fully believes in Alvi and in this reality. I'm just saying it's not real. Someone with a very odd way of thinking and a true fear of discovery constructed this whole business to hide whatever's obscured beneath all this. As you say, none of it makes the least bit of sense."

"Her father, or stepfather, or whatever drove her here with the map in hopes that the McGuffin could change her into a normal girl."

"True, and it could, but if it did, whatever is being hidden would be doubly so—and, so hidden, it may never come out."

"But what's the use of hiding something if it can *never* come out?" Joe wondered.

"Interesting concept, isn't it? I can think of several ideas. One is a resource—something valuable, perhaps information, hidden until and unless needed but so dangerous or treacherous that if it is not needed, it is better never to know. That would explain the interest in her from all over. Another is a timed situation—something, whether it's knowledge or a transformation or a situation or whatever, that will lay dormant and unknown until a date and time or certain condition, after which it will emerge regardless of the form. Other related concepts come equally to mind. We'll work on it."

"But for now you don't want to change her," Joe noted.

"No. I'd like to try and see if I can discover what is hidden. The danger is that others now know what she looks like, and she is extremely difficult to miss or mistake. We may be able to deal with that as illusion."

"Wait a minute! Then what you're saying is that except for me and a little attitude adjustment for the kid, *nobody* is asking *anything* from the bird? That we're all gonna wind up pretty much as we are now, give or take a bit?"

"I'm beginning to suspect exactly that," Ruddygore admitted. "However, look on the bright side. We defeated the great evil once again, we kept the alternate evil from coming through, we've put excitement back in both your life and Marge's, rescued—somewhat—a damsel in deep distress and found her a protector, given Irving somebody to go slay dragons with or whatever he winds up doing, and we really leave only one loose end: your friend there. That's not all that bad."

"Maybe not, but it's not one, it's two. When I headed for Macore's, I found myself in a fantasy ghost town of sorts facing a weird creature in disguise who said they knew who I was and would follow my progress. All I can remember is a weird kind of Hopi getup and a fake Irish brogue a mile wide and an inch deep. I never saw him again, but I don't know who or what that was, either."

"Oh, I think I can explain that one. That was Esmilio. More than anything he wanted you, both for primary revenge and as bait for your son and the others. Sure, you were helping the girl, but he couldn't be certain that you would actually commit to Yuggoth for the sake of a halfling girl he, too, knew nothing about. So he simply baited the hook a bit sweeter so that you would be too intrigued not to come. With all this crud flooding the world, it was easy enough to send that vision right to you."

"I hope you're right. I'd hate to think that some little twerp in a mask and blanket and lousy accent was gonna pop up later and tweak my nose again."

"Anything's possible, but I would be very surprised. So, back on track now, anyway, eh?"

"Yeah, I guess."

Ruddygore sighed and looked at the nymph. "Joe, I don't want to influence you in any way, but what I offer is a one-time thing. The McGuffin is not going to be destroyed or sent out of reach—I've learned my lesson on *that*—but it will be put away in a very, very secure place that even I will not be able to reach on my own. Choose right for yourself. Not for what you think may be right for Irving. The boy's sixteen now, and he's already gone without you. He'd have been happy with you just the way you are, I assure you. You can have any choice you wish that we can grant, but make it the right one for yourself."

Joe sighed. "Well, we'll see, won't we?"

"Indeed we will. For, of course, we *have* left a major loose end, and the Rules are very specific on that sort of thing. Volume 17, one of the early ones, page 141, section 32(e).

"A saga is not truly or properly ended if even one major loose end remains unresolved."

"Oh, boy!" Joe sighed. "Here we go again . . ."

ABOUT THE AUTHOR

JACK L. CHALKER was born in Baltimore, Maryland, on December 17, 1944. While still in high school, Chalker began writing for the amateur science-fiction press, and in 1960 he launched the Hugo-nominated amateur magazine *Mirage*. A year later he founded Mirage Press, which grew into a major specialty publisher of nonfiction and reference books on science fiction and fantasy.

His first novel, *A Jungle of Stars*, was published in 1976, and he became a full-time novelist two years later with the major popular success of *Midnight at the Well of Souls*. Chalker is an active conservationist and enjoys traveling, consumer electronics, and computers. He is also a noted speaker on science fiction and fantasy at numerous colleges and universities. He is a passionate lover of steamboats, in particular ferryboats, and has ridden over three hundred ferries in the United States and elsewhere.

Chalker lives with his wife, Eva; sons David and Steven; a Pekingese named Mavra Chang; and Stonewall J. Pussycat, the world's dumbest feline, in the Catoctin Mountain region of Maryland, near Camp David.

ALSO BY JACK L. CHALKER

Published by Del Rey Books.
Available in your local bookstore.

DEL REY ONLINE!

The Del Rey Internet Newsletter...

A monthly electronic publication, posted on the Internet, GEnie, CompuServe, BIX, various BBSs, and the Panix gopher (gopher.panix.com). It features hype-free descriptions of books that are new in the stores, a list of our upcoming books, special announcements, a signing/reading/convention-attendance schedule for Del Rey authors, "In Depth" essays in which professionals in the field (authors, artists, designers, sales people, etc.) talk about their jobs in science fiction, a question-and-answer section, behind-the-scenes looks at sf publishing, and more!

Online editorial presence: Many of the Del Rey editors are online, on the Internet, GEnie, CompuServe, America Online, and Delphi. There is a Del Rey topic on GEnie and a Del Rey folder on America Online.

Our official e-mail address for Del Rey Books is delrey@randomhouse.com

Internet information source!

A lot of Del Rey material is available to the Internet on a gopher server: all back issues and the current issue of the Del Rey Internet Newsletter, a description of the DRIN and summaries of all the issues' contents, sample chapters of upcoming or current books (readable or downloadable for free), submission requirements, mail-order information, and much more. We will be adding more items of all sorts (mostly new DRINs and sample chapters) regularly. The address of the gopher is gopher.panix.com

Why? We at Del Rey realize that the networks are the medium of the future. That's where you'll find us promoting our books, socializing with others in the sf field, and—most importantly—making contact and sharing information with sf readers.

For more information, e-mail delrey@randomhouse.com